THE TEMPLE
OF THE
THREE WHISPERS

BOOK SEVEN:

THE KEEPER'S DOLLHOUSE

BRIAN HARMON

The Temple of the Three Whispers
Book Seven: The Keeper's Dollhouse

ISBN: 978-1-945559-34-1

Don't miss these other great books by Brian Harmon!

The Temple of the Blind series:

The Box (Book I)
Gilbert House (Book II)
The Temple of the Blind (Book III)
Road Beneath The Wood (Book IV)
Secret of the Labyrinth (Book V)
The Judgment of the Sentinels (Book VI)

The Temple of the Three Whispers series:

The Lady of Cedric's Cove (Book I)
Circles in Hermes' Footsteps (Book II)
Misplaced in Mysteria (Book III)
The Denselands (Book IV)
The Impassible Wall (Book V)
The City Beyond Memory (Book VI)
The Keeper's Dollhouse (Book VII)
Priestess of Ruin (Book VIII)
The Temple of the Three Whispers (Book IX)
Whispers in the Murk (Book X)

The Rushed series:

Rushed (Book 1)
Rushed: The Unseen (Book 2)
Rushed: Something Wicked (Book 3)
Rushed: Hedge Lake (Book 4)
Rushed: A Matter of Time (Book 5)
Rushed: All Fun and Games (Book 6)
Rushed: Something Wickeder (Book 7)
Rushed: Evancurt (Book 8)
Rushed: Relic (Book 9)

Hands of the Architects trilogy:

Spirit Ears and Prophet Sight (Book 1)
Pretty Faces and Peculiar Places (Book 2)
Broken Clocks and Amber Threads (Book 3)

For Katie

Chapter 1

Keith was sitting at a table, surrounded by an eerie, unnatural darkness. A single, dim light hung above him but illuminated nothing beyond a few feet of the table's edge. Across from him sat a beautiful woman in a fancy, silvery dress. She had long, black hair and a bright yellow sunflower tattoo adorning one shoulder. She was staring straight at him, smiling a lovely smile, as if patiently waiting for him to take it all in.

"Is this going to be one of the scary dreams?" he asked her. "Or one of the naughty ones?"

Her smile disappeared and she scowled at him instead.

"Not a naughty one," he sighed, rubbing at his temples. "Gotcha." His head hurt, but not nearly as much as it should have. First when he fell into the hounds' den and hit the back of his head, then that monster slamming him against the stone ceiling... And a third time, too, he thought...against the wall...but his memory by then was a bit hazy. When he woke up again, he was going to have one hell of a headache. (Or would it be *three* headaches all at once?)

"I'm Erin," said the woman.

"I'm guessing you already know I'm Keith."

"I do."

He nodded and looked down at himself. His shirt was still wrapped around his bloody arm and he was still missing a shoe. "Am I underdressed?" he asked. "Or are you overdressed?"

"I don't think it matters, really," she replied, an amused smile replacing the scowl. "It's just the two of us here."

There was something vaguely familiar about this woman, he realized. He glimpsed that same dress when he was following the wet footprints leading toward the feuding brothers...the same footprints he found in the obsidian pool's black sand... But he hadn't seen her face until now. She was stunning. She looked like a movie star.

He reached out and drummed his fingers on the tabletop. "Feels different this time," he observed.

"That's because you're much closer to death than you are to life right now."

He frowned at this. "Not gonna lie. That sounds concerning."

"It's not as serious as it sounds," she assured him. "You've taken a pretty serious blow to the head, but it's not enough to kill you."

"I *have* been called hard-headed a time or two."

"You must be," she chuckled. "You're definitely still kicking."

He rubbed at the back of his head, uncomfortable. "That's good. But should I really be sitting here right now?"

"It's fine. Time flows differently in dreams."

"But...that monster back there..."

"It's gone now. No need to worry about that."

"Gone?"

"Gone."

He squinted at her. "*Gone* gone?"

Erin laughed. It was a great laugh. Charming. Pretty. "Very much gone," she assured him. "Nicole's far stronger and more capable than most women."

He rolled his eyes and leaned back in his chair. "Of course she is. She'll make sure I hear all about it, too."

"But she still needs you."

"She doesn't need *anybody*," he countered. "Much less *me*. She's made that abundantly clear."

Erin shook her head. "No. You're *exactly* the one she needs. You always have been. Why else would the Night Goddess keep sending you to her side?"

"Night Goddess?" He frowned again. "You mean that creepy cat lady?"

"Cats are inherently connected to the dream realm. They always have been. And dreams have always acted as a crossroads between the worlds of the living and the dead. A common link. It's what allows you and I to talk like this."

He stared at her. Somehow he understood exactly what she meant. She wasn't like him. They were on opposite sides of the veil. He wasn't sure *how* he knew this, but he did. In fact, even though this was his first time really seeing her, there was something very familiar about her. "Have we spoken before?" he wondered.

"No. But you've probably sensed me in your dreams. I've been nearby throughout most of your journey. We all have our jobs that the Keeper trusted to us."

"Even you," he sighed.

"Even the dead, sometimes, yes."

He looked down at his one bare sock. He didn't look forward to

going back. It wasn't going to be pleasant. It was going to hurt returning to his waking body. But he couldn't put it off much longer. If he
had questions—which he did—then now was the time for them. He
may not get another chance. "Why *me*?" he asked. "Why do *I* have to
have these stupid dreams? I know there are better people than me out
there who could do this stuff."

"No. The Keeper doesn't make mistakes."

"I couldn't even save my own dad!" he snapped. "What's the
point in dreaming about the future when you can't even stop something
like that from happening?"

Erin leaned forward, her gaze strangely piercing. He wasn't sure
why, but he felt very much as if she were staring deep *inside* of him,
studying his very soul. "Your dad's death was an accident. You couldn't
have foreseen that."

"But I saw *other* things happen!"

"You saw what other people already *knew* would happen."

"What?"

She gave him a sympathetic smile. "Your power isn't to see the
future," she explained. "It's to see what occupies the thoughts of the
people around you."

He squinted at her as if she'd started speaking pig Latin for no
apparent reason. "You're saying I can read minds?"

"Yes," she replied. "But not on a conscious level. It's sort of like a
continuous background noise that your brain automatically tunes out.
You don't notice it, but it's there. And your *subconscious* mind is always
listening." She reached out and laid her slender hand on his. "When
your grandmother was sick, your parents knew for a while before they
broke the news to you. You dreamed about it because it was weighing
on their minds. And the more time a person spends thinking about
something, the more vivid the dream."

He stared at her, confused. "That's how it works?"

She nodded. "All sorts of things that people are thinking about
manifest in your dreams, sometimes in cryptic ways, because that's
simply the nature of dreams. Not everything is clear."

"I see…" So he never could have saved his father from that accident specifically *because* it was an accident. It was unexpected. An unfortunate incident that no one could ever have anticipated. It made a certain kind of sense. But he couldn't decide if he felt better about knowing this or worse. A part of him sill felt cheated. What good was psychic
dream powers if tragic accidents still happened?

"You have the ability to read a great deal about the people around you," she went on. "It even affects your mood. When other people are sad, you feel sad. When other people are cheerful, you're in a good mood. When a woman is interested in you, you're likely to find yourself interested in return."

He remembered Amber, and how they always seemed to end up in bed together. He'd always found it a little odd how quickly things escalated from a friendly conversation to breathless passion. He wasn't even all that into her. The sex was good, in all honesty, and he didn't dislike her in any way, but romantically she really wasn't his type. He'd always wanted someone a little more...*permanent*, after all. A relationship rather than casual sex. But if it were true that his emotions were affected by others, then they'd both find themselves aroused at the same time, feeding into each other's urges... It might even explain why she kept coming back to him the way she did. From her perspective, he was probably a perfect partner, always picking up on her every cue, probably always eager for whatever specific little game she was in the mood for... The more he thought about it, the more sense it made.

"The Keeper doesn't make mistakes," Erin said again. "And right now, you have something important to do."

"Nicole," he breathed. Why did it have to be her?

"She's in terrible danger," warned Erin. "Goar Nangup's puppet is finally gone, but his will lingers. He's inside her head now. Something horrible is going to happen to her."

"Something horrible is *always* happening to her!" he groaned. He reached up and buried his face in his hands, frustrated. "She hates me. Why do *I* have to be the one who keeps having to save her ungrateful ass?"

"Because you're the only one who *can* keep her safe," she replied.

"Sure," he grumbled.

"It's true. And you're wrong. About her hating you."

He lowered his hands and rolled his eyes.

She leaned toward him, her beautiful gaze fixed on his. "It's just a little complicated. That's all."

"Sure," he grumbled. *Mental disorders always are*, he thought, but didn't say aloud.

But Erin's gaze narrowed and she pursed her lips at him, as if she heard the words anyway and wasn't amused.

"Okay," he relented. "Fine."

"You'll be waking up soon," she warned him. "The pain is going to come back. But you can't let it make you forget what we talked about here."

But he didn't move. He stared at her, his expression weary. "What aren't you telling me?" he asked.

This seemed to surprise her. She sat up straighter.

But he shook his head. "No... On second thought, don't say it. I get it."

"I had a feeling you would."

He sighed and leaned back in his chair.

"You have to find her," she told him. "You have to protect her. No matter what."

"No matter what," he said, nodding. "If you say so." He suddenly wanted to be done with this conversation. It was making him feel a little sick.

"Don't worry," she said. "Everything according to the Keeper's plan. Even you and me."

He nodded as if he found those words reassuring in any way and then closed his eyes.

The transition was quicker this time. An instant later, it seemed, he opened his eyes and groaned. As he expected, his head was pounding. He felt as if he'd been worked over with a baseball bat. And his face was tacky with blood.

What happened? It was all hazy, but he recalled the thing grabbing him by the neck and lifting him straight up, slamming him against the ceiling. And he vaguely remembered being thrust against the wall before everything went black. He reached up and probed at a gash in his forehead. That was going to leave a mark, he was sure. He was lucky he didn't get his nose smashed in. How close did that monster come to cracking his skull wide open?

He sat up and blinked at his flashlight, his head swimming.

That woman... She said her name was Erin. Even a week ago, he'd probably have dismissed her as nothing more than a mere, random conjuring of his slumbering brain. Metaphors and riddles of the subconscious, signifying nothing. But now he wasn't so sure he'd ever had a dream that wasn't real in some strange way.

Was what she said true, then? Was the monster really gone? And was Nicole really still in trouble?

Wincing at his aching skull, he grabbed the flashlight and started to stand up, but he paused as he remembered his missing shoe. Just the one wasn't going to do him any good. He removed it and tossed it aside. Better to continue in his socks than stumble around lopsided in just the one.

It was only then that he noticed the blood soaked into his sock.

Vaguely, he remembered feeling a pain when that hound yanked his shoe off his foot. He pulled it down, revealing a slash on his ankle underneath. One of those slashing scales, perhaps? Or was that from one of the thing's jagged teeth?

Just what he needed. Another injury to add to his growing collection. But there was nothing he could do about it now. He pulled the sock back up over it and rose to his feet.

He stepped around the corner where the monster ambushed him and followed the sound and the malodor of those razor-armored beasts. Already, he could see a light glowing somewhere out there.

Nicole?

But as he peered around the corner, the only sign of her was her cell phone lying on the floor of the platform, its light aimed pointlessly at the stone ceiling.

His heart sank at the sight. Why would she leave this area without any light? And as he walked toward it, he saw that there were blood splatters everywhere. Something very violent happened here.

(*She's in terrible danger.*)

He peered over the edge, bracing himself for whatever he might see. There were several hounds down there, all of them covered in blood, scuffling over scraps of gory tatters of cloth and meat.

It was hard to tell just who or what that mess might have once been, but he was fairly sure it wasn't Nicole. He could see scraps of the filthy blue jeans and white tee shirt, but no sign of Nicole's lighter colored denim shorts or gray tank top. And to be nauseatingly blunt, nothing about the scene *smelled* remotely fresh. Whatever those things were eating was rancid.

Unless she ended up in another part of this room, beyond where his light would reach, she wasn't here. That was good. Even better, she'd somehow managed to feed Hotdog Zombie to the hounds.

He stepped away from the ledge, not caring at all for being anywhere near those living reciprocating saws, and picked up her phone. She was going to want that back. He turned off the light and slipped it into his pocket.

But where did she go?

(*You have to find her.*)

He continued along the walkway. There was only one exit, unless she doubled back for some reason, and he doubted that was the case. Even *she* wouldn't be so hateful as to simply step over his body and leave him there. And as soon as the passage came into view, he caught sight of something that wasn't there when the two of them entered from that direction.

One of her sneakers was lying on the floor.

He bent and picked it up, his stomach tightening. "What've you gotten yourself into now?" he grumbled. That woman was going to be the death of him before this was over.

Chapter 2

Andrea trudged through the vile muck for what felt like ages. Her muscles ached from the constant exertion and the perpetual stench had left her stomach feeling sour. She lost her second shoe some time ago. Even her socks were gone now, sucked into the reeking quagmire, never to be seen again. The cold, putrid sludge squished between her bare toes with each step. It had oozed into her shorts and under her shirt, invading her panties and bra, that awful slimy-yet-gritty texture seeping into every crease and crevice, violating every part of her body.

And no matter how much she spat, she couldn't seem to get the foul taste out of her mouth.

So gross!

What was the point in this stuff even being here? What purpose did it serve? Was it supposed to, like, test their resolve or something? Because it just seemed to her like a really good way to catch some god-awful infection.

At least last time she could see where Wayne and the others passed through on their first trip through it. Knowing that they made it across ahead of her was comforting. But there was no sign of anyone *ever* having disturbed this gunk before. And she couldn't stop thinking about the slimy, wriggling thing she felt while trying to retrieve that first shoe. What sorts of horrors could live in a place such as this? If something attacked her, she wouldn't be able to get away. Running was impossible. She was moving at a snail's pace just forcing her way through it. She kept expecting to feel that same cold, wormy feeling against her foot with each step and was fairly sure that when it inevitably happened she was going to scream herself to death.

And there was still no end in sight! Was she even going the right way? She couldn't see any of the walls yet, but she was still breaking up the fine crust dried over the surface, so it was at least easy to see where she'd been, helping keep her from walking around in circles. Except, whether she was still going in a straight line or had veered off course over a greater distance than her meager light revealed, she couldn't be sure.

Erin hadn't called out to her again, but that could just be because the impostor was keeping her away. She warned her that would happen.

So many uncertainties… She hated it. It still made no sense to her why the Keeper's stupid rules kept Ada from telling them exactly what they were supposed to do. It almost seemed like he *wanted* them to fail. And yet time after time, she kept slipping through the cracks. She got away from Hotdog and then from Glum. She escaped the creepy hospital and the dead spirit highway and the gouging station. But would it really have made any difference if she'd known what she was doing the whole time? It seemed to her that all the secrecy did was make everything a thousand times scarier!

Ahead of her, those eerie strands of black murk began to converge, forming a visible lump that was slowly flexing and relaxing, like some slumbering predator waiting to ambush its next meal. It wasn't as big as the growling abyss of swirling teeth, but it was larger than those creepy hand things, so she veered left and gave it a wide berth, keeping one eye on it until it was out of sight again behind her.

She kept wondering how this would all appear to her if she were dead right now. What mysterious things couldn't her human brain comprehend about these eerie surroundings? Ada said she was connected to the spirit world, that she'd been seeing things others couldn't her whole life, but she'd never seen tendrils of black fog or wriggling lumps of pure shadow before. She was fairly sure she'd have remembered something as creepy as that.

Here, whispered Erin, her soft voice beckoning her to the right. *This way.*

She turned to follow it, but then paused. Something didn't seem right.

Hurry. Something's coming.

She didn't move. She stood there, submerged to her bellybutton ring in foul mud, frowning. Then she wrinkled her dirty nose. "You're not her."

Definitely *not* that way. She continued pushing straight ahead.

Clever girl, breathed the impostor in Stella's voice.

She wondered where she would've ended up if she'd listened to that voice, but decided it was probably better if she didn't know. Best case scenario, she'd spend countless hours roaming this darkness in circles, unable to find her way out.

"Good job," whispered the real Erin.

But she was lucky. There were differences between the two. When Erin spoke, she actually heard her manifested voice. She was speaking across the silence, as if she were flesh and blood. The impostor, on the other hand, was entirely inside her head. Yet it was surprisingly difficult to tell them apart. They both sounded so real to her own mind. The one *inside* could be as convincing as the one outside. She saw through the lie this time, but she'd have to be careful of that trick in the future. It would probably be easy to deceive her if she were distracted by nearby dangers.

Stupid Impostor Stella... Like she didn't have enough to worry about down here.

Ahead of her, a wall finally emerged from the gloom. She picked up her pace as much as the gripping muck would allow, hopeful that her ghostly companion had guided her to the exit and not more terrifying darkness-infested passageways.

Slowly, her light illuminated more and more of the wall. Bogged down by the sludge, unable to hurry, it seemed to go on forever, until she began to wonder if there was a way out of here at all. It was starting to feel frightfully as if she'd be doomed to spend the rest of her pitifully short life in this festering pit, until she was too tired to remain on her feet. Would she eventually just collapse and sink into the rancid muck?

The idea was unbearable.

But then, at last, a staircase appeared.

She struggled toward it, eager to be out of this putrid filth, but still it seemed to take forever. By the time she crawled out of the mud and onto the clean stone, she was too exhausted to climb the steps. She collapsed onto them instead and groaned.

This was awful. Her legs hurt. She was out of breath. Her heart was pounding from the exertion. And she was *stinky*. She rolled over onto her back and stared up into the darkness looming over her. "This sucks!" she cried out, her voice echoing across the empty chamber.

Somewhere deep inside her head, she heard Stella's too-familiar laughter.

"Keep moving," whispered Erin.

"Yeah, yeah," she grumbled. Bossy ghosts. Bitchy voices in her head. Smelly mud. And now *stairs*. Even the first temple wasn't *this* bad. Stupid Keeper and his stupid doors...

She rose to her feet, weary, and trudged up the stone steps, leaving a trail of filthy footprints behind her. She didn't even feel bad about it. If someone didn't want her leaving tracks, they shouldn't have filled the room with *stinky mud!*

She felt so gross...

There was no chance of saving these clothes now. She was sure of that. She reached up under her shirt and raked away the mud that had crept up her belly. It was all in her bra now, irritating her as she moved.

She fumbled with it for a moment, trying to clean it out, but something was off. With a frustrated grunt, she unfastened it, pulled the straps through her sleeves and yanked it out of her shirt. It looked fine, but like the rest of her clothes, she doubted it would ever come clean again.

She liked that one, too…

She snapped it back and forth, trying to fling off the mud, then put it back on.

"That was the part where someone was supposed to finally show up," she grumbled to herself. Wasn't that how it always happened on television? The moment the girl needs to check her undies was the moment the love interest walked in on her? She was pretty sure she could handle that kind of embarrassment if it meant finally not having to be alone anymore.

Of course *that* would be the one thing that wasn't real.

After what felt like yet *another* eternity, she reached the top of the steps and found another murk-infested corridor waiting for her. It wasn't completely filled, like the passages leading up to the pitfall that dumped her in the gross mud room, at least, but she had no way of knowing how bad it might get before she reached the end of it. Unlike most of those others, this one wasn't straight. It curved softly to the left in her light, then turned sharply to the right, twisting and winding its way through the labyrinth.

Was she in an entirely different part of it now?

But of course, the better question was whether it was going to get even scarier from here on.

She didn't want to keep doing this. She just wanted to go home and take a shower or six. And then she wanted to go to bed and not leave it for at least three days.

But of course that wasn't an option.

She sighed and set off into the murky gloom, disheartened. She was starting to feel like she was never going to see her friends again…

Chapter 3

"Where did she go?" worried Brandy.

Albert wished he had the answer. One moment, Gina was right there with them, leading the way, and then she simply vanished. Had something happened to her? Did she fall into some kind of trap? Did something get inside her head and snatch her away like it did Nicole? He couldn't imagine her running off on her own in this place on purpose, but that was just as much a possibility. They didn't really know her, after all. Nor she them. Maybe they said or did something to frighten her. He didn't know.

Brandy stopped at the next intersection and shined her light both ways. "Gina?" she called. "Please come back." She turned and looked the other way away and said in a much quieter voice. "She doesn't even have a flashlight."

"She doesn't need one," he reminded her.

"I don't care! Why would she want to wander around in the dark?"

It was a good question. *He* certainly wouldn't want to be stranded in the dark. But then again, he didn't know what it was like to have that kind of psychic power. She said it was different from his own. She didn't get feelings about things that made her look closer at them. She just simply *knew* her surroundings. And it wasn't something she was only now beginning to learn to use, like his was. She'd had it all her life.

But this wasn't just some random place. This was a temple. Nothing made sense in a temple. Would she even be able to trust her senses, psychic or otherwise?

"She's better off without one than we would be," he insisted, trying to convince himself as much as her.

"Which is why we all need to stick together! We have to find her. She could be in serious trouble."

"I absolutely agree. I'm not saying I don't want to find her. I'm worried about her, too. But this might be out of our hands, like losing Nicole."

Brandy made a sound that was partly a curse but mostly a whimper. "We can't lose *both* of them."

"I'm just saying, it might not be meant for us to all stick together.

And I feel a little better knowing that Gina can at least move around in the dark."

"I know," she groaned. "But I *hate* it."

"I do, too."

She turned and shined the light back the way they came. "We should go back and try the other way again. She might come back."

He stepped aside and let her by. Whatever made her feel better. But somehow he knew that she wasn't coming back. Something about the way she told them stay put while she made sure of something.

(*Just trust me. And don't turn on your light yet.*)

She told them the exit was directly ahead of them but when Brandy switched on her flashlight, they were already standing safely in the doorway. She made sure they were in a good place before leaving. It seemed to him that she entirely meant to ditch them back there.

But he simply couldn't for the life of him understand *why*.

And then there was what Brandy said about not being able to feel her anymore. What could have happened that would have completely cut her off like that? Had she somehow gone somewhere they couldn't?

A moment later, they passed the doorway to the sorrow room again, both of them shielding their eyes as they passed it, avoiding so much as a fleeting glimpse of the gloomy statues within. But even so, he felt a strange, wrenching tightness in his chest as he passed by it. Was that the raw emotional energy leaking out of that room? Or was it only a psychosomatic response to what he knew that room could do to him? It was impossible to know for certain.

"Gina?" Brandy called again. She shined her light down into the darkness beside them, over the ledge that Gina warned them about. She said nothing, but he could see the way her face tightened as she peered down into those black depths. She was wondering, just as he had, if she could have fallen down there.

Back in the first temple, pits like that were filled with spikes. And he, for one, had seen first-hand how quickly such a deadly trap could silence a person. There could easily be those same, horrible spikes waiting down there. Or there could be nothing more than hard stone. Either one would be an effective killer. But wouldn't she have screamed if she'd fallen? She should've at least made *some* kind of noise, even if it were only a startled gasp.

Unless she jumped... If the gut-wrenching sorrow of that room had gotten into her head, could it have made her do something rash?

No. He refused to even acknowledge such a horrible idea.

Brandy made her way past the dangerous hole and into the passageway beyond, then she abruptly stopped and turned on him. In an instant, she was pressed against him, kissing him.

"Whoa!"

"Shut up and hold still!" she mumbled against his lips.

Oh, right. Sex magic. She wanted to supercharge her psychic abilities and see if it could reveal where Gina had gone. That made sense. But he wasn't expecting it out of the blue like that. She wasn't exactly in the mood. She was visibly worried. And he could feel the tears on her face as she kissed him. It didn't seem likely that she'd be able to make it work.

But she was quite clearly determined to try.

He gripped her waist and pulled her closer, encouraging her. It was tricky, trying to shift gears so drastically, using erotic emotions as a sort of wedge to force back the worry and the lingering sadness. But it shouldn't be impossible. If he could just relax and clear his mind of everything but her...

She grasped the back of his neck with her free hand and pushed her lips harder against his, practically forcing herself on him.

This was his chance, too, he understood. While she searched the surrounding space for Gina, he could try to grasp the surrounding layout of the labyrinth, mapping it, formulating a plan for forging onward, maybe even glimpsing an answer to where Gina might have gone. If he could only push past all those other emotions and focus on his beautiful bride, on how she made him feel when she kissed him like this.

He was confident he could do it...but it wasn't as easy as it usually was.

She couldn't find the right mindset, either. He could tell. She was kissing him harder, forcing her tongue into his mouth, desperate to find that specific feeling, the proper state of mind to trigger the perverted power the dirty shaman claimed was hidden inside her. She was being too impatient. She needed to relax a little. But instead, she grabbed his hand from her waist and shoved it against her crotch, griding it against the fabric of her shorts.

It was strange, standing here in this darkness, trying so hard to find a sexual mindset in the shadow of a room of heartaches while worried sick about their lost friend.

He pulled away from her kiss and whispered, "It's okay. Slow down. Relax. We'll get there."

She nodded and pressed her lips to his again.

He let her have the moment, but he didn't think it was going to work.

Gina was out there in this temple somewhere. He was sure of it. She was fine. And somehow, he felt like she had her reasons for leaving.

They weren't going to find her.

But now wasn't the time to say so. He needed to let Brandy look for her. She needed to make the decision for herself. She had to feel satisfied that she wasn't here anymore before they pushed on or the uncertainty and guilt would weigh too heavily on her.

He understood her, after all. He wouldn't deserve to call himself her husband if he didn't.

Chapter 4

Gina made her way through the dark and lonely passageway, still wiping at her leaking eyes. The strange effects of that emotion room were still with her. It was similar to what she felt on Tristesse Lane, but by no means the same. Both places made her weep uncontrollably, but the emotions were almost *opposite* to each other. Glum's twisted street sapped away all the positive feelings, leaving nothing but her own despair to overwhelm her. The sorrow room, in contrast, simply flooded her with its pervasive sadness until she could feel nothing else. More than that, she could almost detect the distinct energy of that particular emotion being given off by all those statues, just as Brandy and Albert described.

And there was a *lot* of it.

She never doubted Andrea when she described it back on the boat, but she didn't fully get it then. She'd never thought of emotions as having unique energy, but she could almost understand it now that she'd experienced it this way. Sorrow and grief simply *radiated* from the stone in there, not unlike the way fire radiated heat and light. It would have been intriguing if it wasn't so deeply unpleasant. It made her wonder. Was it that human beings produced these types of energy naturally? Or were human emotions merely the brain's way of detecting those energies in the environment? Which came first? Cause or effect?

Either way, she thought she could understand how that creepy sounding shaman could teach Brandy and Albert to utilize such energies and call it magic. If emotional energy was real, then a means of harnessing that power could easily be real, too, meaning there could definitely be people out there who had mastered all kinds of forms of so-called magic.

It was confusing, though, dealing with so many emotions. It was hard to tell exactly where the room's artificial ones ended and her real ones began. Because she was genuinely sad to leave Brandy and Albert behind. She liked them. Like everyone else she'd encountered on this strange journey, they'd been very kind to her. And she knew they were going to worry.

Now that she had some distance between herself and that chamber of grief, however, she couldn't help wondering if those emotions hadn't skewed her judgment a little. She was still quite convinced that this was the path she needed to follow. There was something about these particular passageways that reminded her of both Tristesse Lane and that awful tower back in Cakwetak where the goddess sent her on her first job. Alternately, she could feel more of that emotional magic radiating from the other passageways. It felt to her like those two were meant to go that way. They had separate paths they were meant to follow. She was sure of it. This was why *she* was here and that was why *they* were here. The time had simply come for them to part ways.

But maybe sneaking off wasn't the best way to do it... It was true that they would have tried to stop her...but at least they'd know she left of her own free will. As it stood, they probably thought something terrible happened to her. She felt like she was going to owe them a really big apology when this was all over. If she made it to the end, that was. There were no guarantees in this big, weird universe, after all. Not even from goddesses.

She pushed onward through the impenetrable darkness, trying not to think too much about everyone she'd already let down. Brandy and Albert. Nicole. Andrea and Keith. She just kept losing people. And she was worried about each and every one of them. She hoped they'd all stay safe.

Again, she wiped at her eyes. The emotions from that room were still affecting her. She had to keep reminding herself that she had no one to grieve today. Not yet. As far as she knew, they were all still out there somewhere, perfectly unharmed and much safer than she was. She couldn't afford to think otherwise. She needed to stay focused on the task before her.

This area looked no different from any other passage she passed on her way here. (Or it would, if she could actually see it, she knew.) It was the same size and material as every other passageway. But they *were* different. There was an odd, *shadowy* quality about these particular walls. It was the only way she could think to describe them. Colors and shades should have nothing to do with how she perceived things in absolute darkness and yet somehow these passages seemed *darker*. But if she could see, she was sure they'd look no different to her perfectly human eyes. If not for her unique connection to the unnatural world, she wouldn't know anything had changed.

And she wouldn't know that she wasn't alone.

Something was moving on the other side of these walls. Something that wasn't human. Something that wasn't alive at all. But also something that wasn't dead...

The goddess said these things she could feel were neither physical nor spiritual. She called them "unnatural," and said that her ability to see and hear these things was one of the rarest she'd ever seen in all her inconceivably long life.

Was that supposed to make her feel less or more like a freak? It was strange. The more she discovered about herself, the less she understood.

She reached out in the darkness and ran her fingers along the smooth stone. It was still difficult to see very far. The storm above and the curious properties of the stone were still interfering somehow. She could still sense Brandy and Albert, but they'd already moved far enough away from her that she couldn't quite follow their movements. They'd been reduced to little more than a familiar presence in the broken haze surrounding her. And somewhere farther away, she thought she could feel two others, but she couldn't tell who they were or what they were doing.

The thing on the other side of these walls, however, was different. She could clearly and precisely track its movements as it prowled these empty corridors. And already, she could tell that those movements weren't random. It was keeping pace with her. Whatever it was, it already knew she was here. And it seemed to her that it knew she could sense it.

But it was here and not back where she came from, stalking her friends. That was what was important. She owed a great deal to both Andrea and to Nicole. And Brandy and Albert had been so kind to her. There was no way she could let anything happen to any of them, even if it meant acting as bait to lure this unnatural thing away from them. She wasn't sure she was strong enough to face it on her own, but she had no intention of letting it hurt anyone else, either. She'd do whatever she had to.

Except...what exactly was it she was supposed to be doing? She was here in these tunnels that reeked of the same unnatural energy as Glum and Tane. Was she supposed to find something? Was she supposed to *do* something? Was she supposed to face the prowling thing head-on? Was she meant to survive? Or was she meant to die? Either outcome seemed equally likely. And the goddess never told them anything about what they were supposed to do once they actually reached the City Beyond Memory. So...now what?

She lifted her hand higher, still feeling the cool surface of the stone as she walked. She could feel areas within these walls that were different from just jumbled passageways and intersecting tunnels. There were large open spaces. There were chasms that felt practically bottomless. There was running water. And there were odd little rooms here and there that were full of things she simply couldn't wrap her head around. But none of those were in *these* particular passages. None of those places were *shadowy* like this.

Not yet, anyway. This wasn't just one little area, after all. These "unnatural" corridors stretched on for a long distance. They snaked throughout the rest of the labyrinth, the far end somewhere well out of her psychic range of sight. She'd have to keep going to discover where it led.

And so she walked, following the shadows in the darkness, one hand on the stone, her thoughts fixed on the unknown thing stalking her behind the walls. This was the job the goddess gave her. This was her duty. She had to be brave.

But goddess help her, she was terrified of whatever was waiting for her in these lonely black depths.

Chapter 5

Violet stood alone on the stone street, the warmth of the sun beating down on her bare skin, her face turned up toward the magnificent colors of that vast sky. It was odd. It was the same sky that was always hanging there, day after day, and yet there were times, like right now, when she found herself strangely convinced that the sky wasn't supposed to be all those colors. In fact, it almost seemed that there were colors up there that she didn't know the names of...colors that she'd never seen before...or even imagined...

She understood somehow that times like these were when her consciousness was closest to the surface, when she was most herself. She was only a visitor here, after all. She spent most of her time deeper within, in a dreamy sort of half-aware state where the passage of time lost its meaning. She didn't fully understand *why* she was here...or even where "here" was...but she knew that she'd been here a long, long time. She'd watched this city of stone take shape like the features carved by glaciers, stretched across immeasurable time, both rising up into the colorful sky and plunging deep into the dark depths of the earth. An immensely complex design with but a single purpose that wouldn't be served until a time unfathomable ages from now.

This was their job, their duty to the Keeper of the Cycle, their purpose for existing. But she wasn't like them. She belonged at the *other* end of this city's lonely eternity. She was only a guest in this strange, faceless body.

You've always liked these quiet places, said the other one, her voice soft and gentle, but startling in the way that she always spoke up inside her head like that. She should've been used to it by now, but somehow it never felt natural. It was a queerly *invasive* sort of feeling. Humans weren't meant to communicate like that.

But this body wasn't human.

She would have frowned if she'd had lips. Human... She'd almost forgotten what it felt like to be human.

She looked down at her hands, awareness flooding back to her. Her fingers were so long and thin. That wasn't how they were supposed to look. And besides that, she shouldn't be able to *see* them at all. She had no eyes. The other one had no such features upon the smooth, hairless contours of her head. She couldn't see or speak or hear or eat or even breathe. She simply...*existed*... It made no sense. She couldn't understand what made these people work.

She was but a visitor in this place. A traveler out of time and space, observing this alien world from deep within the other one's body.

You only ever venture out when we're somewhere like this.

It was true. She didn't like being around the others. They frightened her a little, though she wasn't sure exactly why. They'd never behaved in any kind of threatening way toward her or the one she was hiding within. She was quite sure none of them meant her any harm. All they did was work. But there was something so dreadfully unsettling about the work they were doing. She didn't understand why, but it filled her with a sick sort of unease whenever the other one wandered too close to them.

Maybe it had something to do with their creepy habit of crawling on walls and ceilings. They always seemed to be scurrying up and down the stone, looking less like men than creepy, deformed spiders. Even after all this time, seeing them like that, even through this strangely sightless body, was deeply unnerving.

We've been together for a while now, said the other one, distracting her from her thoughts.

That was a considerable understatement. She'd long ago deduced that she couldn't feel the *real* flow of time in this place. Time passed here as it did in dreams, oozing by in great, heavy globs instead of in a smooth and constant flow, jumping forward by years or decades, sometimes *millennia*. Especially the time she spent deeper within the other one. When she withdrew into the dreaminess, it always seemed to slip through her fingers like sand and was lost.

Her face turned toward the towering city wall. She could and couldn't see it at the same time in that strange, alien way that this body worked. It stretched on in every direction, fading into the colors of the sky in the distance. She remembered a time before that was there. And it had taken such a long time to construct. Ages upon ages, she knew, and yet, looking back, it felt like only the blink of an eye...

Nearby, one of the massive worker-things lumbered past, trailing its countless graspers along behind it, a great, bulky, shambling shape that blotted out the sky and reeked of sweat and shit and acrid smoke that belched from its body in great, black clouds. As she always did whenever she witnessed the worker-things, she shrank a little deeper within the other one, cringing with childlike fright. She still didn't know what they were, exactly, or even if they were beasts or machines, but they gave her the same sort of deep unease that she felt from the other sentinels.

I've enjoyed your company, said the other one.

She could say the same. She'd grown accustomed to her constant presence, to the comfort and warmth of this place safe inside her, a sort of swaddling feeling, cozy with a certain motherly tenderness about it.

But you have to go back soon.

This surprised her. Go back? Back *where?* She could scarcely remember the life she lived before finding herself inside the other one. All she remembered about it was that she was afraid of something last time she left. She didn't want to go back to where she was afraid. She'd grown comfortable here in her murky, timeless hideaway deep within this safe and comforting home she'd made.

Twelve are gathered to do the Keeper's bidding, said the other one. Violet didn't know her by any other name. She'd never had a name. None of them had names. They had no need of them. In their incomprehensible psychic existence, their identities were interwoven with their very presence. They were simply aware of each other. There was no such concept as a stranger among them. *Each one has a part to play in the Keeper's ancient design*, she went on. *Even those who won't return home.*

Won't...return...? She felt a dizzying sort of sensation pass through her as she remembered someone telling her that only ten were supposed to survive their bizarre journey.

A kaleidoscope of memories flashed through her mind, all disjointed and jumbled together. Losing Albert and Brandy. A strange carriage speeding through a dark tunnel. A labyrinth of stone. Creepy twins in a dirty junk shop. Gina and her friends falling out of the sky. A stone road cutting through a black forest. And Everett...

But not *really* Everett... Something strange and monstrous *pretending* to be him...

Did her heart suddenly begin pounding? Or did she even *have* a heart in this strange place inside the other one?

What was she doing hiding here when Everett might be in danger? What if he was one of the two who weren't going to make it? And what if it happened only because she wasn't there to protect him?

Patience, soothed the other one. *The passage of time is not constant across ages and universes. This here and now will cease to be long before yours will ever be born. What remains in your time is little more than the fossilized bones of a long-extinct world.*

Violet tried to say that she didn't understand what any of that meant, but she had no voice with which to speak, no vocal cords, no lips, no tongue... But she didn't need to speak the words. They found their way regardless.

You will find when you return that very little time has passed, the other one explained.

This was so bizarre. She continued to peer up at that colorful sky, somehow seeing it without seeing it. Was she really standing in the past? Had she really witnessed the construction of the City Beyond Memory in a time more ancient than she could ever imagine? Just as it was experienced by the mysterious, faceless race that built it?

This body... She stood tall and naked, bathed in the warmth of a sun that never seemed to set, the ground so much farther down than it should have been, all of her parts stretched out like a ruined sweater.

This was what it felt like to be a sentinel.

And yet, she still understood so little of these mysterious beings. How did they exist with no mouths or noses? How did they eat and breathe? Did they have lungs? Digestive tracts? They had sexual organs. Those were always on full display, and as grossly exaggerated as the rest of their bodies. And yet she'd never seen a young sentinel. Nor had she ever seen an *old* one, now that she was thinking about it. Did these beings even age? Did they have any need for reproductive organs? What a strange dichotomy, possessing parts they didn't seem to need while missing others she'd always thought were essential to life.

Before you return, there is one last thing I have to show you.

The other one turned her head toward the towering structure rising high into that multicolored sky at the very heart of the stone city. The motion was jarring, a sudden and claustrophobic reminder that this body wasn't hers, that she was trapped inside it, merely a guest here. She felt herself sinking back down.

Up there...

She'd never been up there before. It wasn't finished, after all. It was still rising, though it was difficult to tell from this distance. Was there something important way up there?

From her other life, she seemed to remember something about a doorway...

Not just yet, the other one said as she found herself swallowed by the empty, murky depths deep inside this sentinel body. *But soon. And then it will be time for you to close the circle.*

The circle... That took her *way* back...all the way to that mysterious cave all those years ago...but even as she grasped at the word, her consciousness faded into the strange, comforting warmth deep within the other one.

Chapter 6

Olivia shined her light back and forth. She was hoping to find one of those walls they could climb over, the ones that kept them out of reach of the hounds. Instead, those rough, natural-looking stone walls had closed in around them and they were now walking through what appeared to be a sort of canyon.

"I don't like this," grumbled Wayne. "Feels like we're getting boxed in."

These words were barely out of his mouth when an outburst of snarling and growling and machine-like clattering and droning erupted from somewhere behind them. Immediately, they picked up their pace.

Twice since they emerged from the other side of the blazing orange field, she'd glimpsed those cute little droopy-eared creatures. One she startled from a thicket of large, bluish-gray leaves roughly the size of patio umbrellas. The other darted across their path a few minutes later, little more than a snow-white blur against the darkness.

There were also now more creepy crawlies scuttling along the rocky ground. Most of these were a kind of big, thorny beetle, about the size of silver dollars. But there were also more of those glittery centipede things and something that looked like a big, slimy worm all coiled up like a snake. (She made Wayne go *way* around that one.) She also caught just a glimpse of something that looked like a go-kart-sized crab scuttling off into the darkness on long, spindly legs. And something with mottled gray and brown fur was crawling across the ground off to the left that she couldn't make out any head, legs or tail on. It just looked like a ball of fur with something wriggling around inside it.

She couldn't imagine what kinds of other things might be in this room that were skittish enough to stay well out of range of their flashlights.

Wayne shined his light up onto the stone wall towering over them. "Look up there," he said, stopping.

She followed his light. There was a weed-covered slope stretching up into a narrow recess in the wall, ending at a neat, vertical surface with a perfect square opening above it.

"That's what we're looking for!" He was already climbing the slope, making his way toward it, practically dragging her. "Come on."

"You sure?" she asked, uncertain.

"It's exactly the sort of thing we saw in the last temple," he reminded her.

And it was. Even though it was incredibly simple, it was perfectly effective. All it took to keep the hounds in place was a low wall. She'd seen them with her own eyes, throwing great, snarling fits, but unable to get over them. She should've been overjoyed to see it. And yet, for some reason, she found herself strangely unconvinced that it would be so easy.

They reached the top of the slope and Wayne shined his light into the passageway above, making sure it was clear. Then he turned and gave her a boost.

She climbed up and over, then remained kneeling there, shining her light deeper into the passage while he hiked his leg over and climbed after her. It looked the same as a million other passages they found. The same size. The same smooth, gray stone. The same immaculate cleanliness.

She didn't feel any particular sensation of imminent danger...but she also didn't feel completely safe. It was curious. And somewhat troubling in its own right.

Behind them, somewhere in the vast darkness of that enormous chamber, she could hear another hound moving around. Climbing up here wasn't a wrong move by any means. They couldn't stay down there. Eventually they were going to run out of luck. And heaven knew they didn't start with very much...

The path before them was already split. They could go straight or they could veer to the left. Wayne shined his light in both directions, pondering the decision. But they were the same as far as he could see. So he turned and raised an eyebrow at her. "Which way d'you think?"

She looked left, then straight. Nothing jumped out at her immediately, so she looked both ways again, slower this time, trying to take in what little she could see, imagining herself walking one way...then the other... When she still felt nothing, she let go of him and took two steps into the left tunnel, stood there a moment, then turned and did the same in the one going forward.

She frowned. "Nothing feels bad, exactly... I don't think either is particularly dangerous. But there's *something* about this one." She pointed straight ahead. "It's a little hard to read. Part of me says we should go this way, but another part of me doesn't want to. I don't get it."

Wayne stared down the passage, contemplating the decision.

"Sorry," she said. "I'm not very helpful."

"You're fantastic," he told her. He turned and kissed the top of her head. "We all have our learning curve."

He was so sweet. But the truth was that her so-called psychic ability was a dud. Half the time she didn't know what it was trying to tell her. And the rest of the time she didn't know which direction it was coming from or even what it was she was supposed to be looking out for.

"I guess we'll try this way," he decided, starting forward. "Just tell me if we need to turn around."

She nodded and looked back the way they came. The idea of returning to that strange, alien landscape definitely didn't feel right. She felt safer up here in this passage, which was something, at least. Maybe they weren't as lost as she'd begun to fear.

They pushed on through the darkness, her thoughts churning. She still felt shaky from her ordeal over that scary abyss. And she was beginning to feel all those little cuts those hound bugs left on her. Especially where that one tangled itself up in her shirt.

Those things were awful. What kind of sociopath would even dream up something like that? The so-called scarecrow man was in serious need of psychiatric care!

Ahead of them, the passage ended. They stepped out into the open and found themselves on a walkway stretching over that bizarre, alien landscape. She could see some of that bright orange grass far off to the right and more of those huge, bluish-gray leaves on the left. But she wasn't interested in the view. She pressed closer to Wayne and away from the ledges.

At least it wasn't another of those ridiculously *narrow* walkways. But still it was unpleasant being up high looking down again without any railings to keep her safe.

Wayne had paused for a moment to take it in, but he gave her a reassuring squeeze and kept moving. "Something like this has no purpose for the things down there," he reasoned. "If the hounds can come or go, then anything down here could do the same. I'm betting nothing down there can climb, jump or fly. That kind of means that pathways like these must be here as a means of escape. And if the sentinels built in a way out, then they probably intended that we'd make our way down here. I mean, it just makes sense, right?"

She didn't know why he was asking her. She didn't know what made sense anymore. And she was too scared to try to puzzle her way through that much hard thinking.

Somewhere out in that darkness, she heard more hounds revving up their scales, sounding more like machines than animals. She hated that sound. She hated this place. She couldn't understand why anyone would ever want to keep creatures like that. What good were guard dogs somewhere that was supposed to be unreachable by anyone who wasn't supposed to be there?

Ahead, the far wall came into view, revealing that the walkway led to another opening. She immediately urged him to pick up his pace, eager to be off this deathtrap of an overpass.

But as soon as she stepped inside this passage, she stopped.

"Something wrong?" asked Wayne.

"I'm not sure…" It was a strange sort of feeling, one part anxious and one part impatient. She crept forward, still clinging to his arm, her eyes peeled. "It feels like something's close," she whispered.

"What kind of something?"

But she didn't know. It wasn't a feeling she could properly describe. It was all jumbled up inside her head, confusing her.

There was no split in the passage. It was only the one. Wayne stepped in front of her and cautiously continued forward. "Stay behind me."

She nodded and let him take the lead while she tried to puzzle through these enigmatic feelings.

"No scratches on the floor," he observed. "So it's not one of *them*."

"No," she agreed. If it was something like that, she didn't think the feeling would be so confusing. She was pretty sure it would just be the usual panic and dread.

Ahead of her, he eased forward, his light pushing back the oppressive darkness, farther and farther.

She followed him for a few steps, but then she stopped. Her heart was beating faster and faster. She could feel something mounting within her, like watching a timer tick down the last few seconds.

Wayne was still moving, searching the path ahead of them, unaware that she'd stopped. She wanted to call out to him, but she found her throat closed tight. Something was about to happen. She could feel it. But what? And from where? She turned all the way around, a scream building up inside her.

Where? She *hated* not being able to tell which direction the danger was coming from!

She turned to face the wall beside her. Something wasn't as it seemed. Something was *hidden*. She couldn't see what was *really* there, but with each passing second, she was more and more convinced that what she was looking at was a lie.

As she stared, the very wall seemed to yawn open like the mouth of some great and ravenous beast.

There was a blinding flash of light.

She had just enough time to scream as a black shape leaped from the gaping darkness and grabbed her.

Chapter 7

Everett had long ago lost any concept of time or direction or self. He'd dared to force open his eyes in the void and was immediately consumed by it, swallowed whole into something both new and old, fascinating and terrifying, an aberration of existence, a fevered delirium of silence and madness. This was an entire universe of utter nothing, a singularity, a black hole of consciousness, hopelessly drawing him in, devouring meaning, identity and self-awareness. And yet, at the same time, he was surrounded by innumerable and incomprehensible things, neither solid nor liquid, neither hot nor cold, neither living nor dead, all of it stretched out around him in a broken vastness of impossible geometry, shifting and melting and bristling and burning all at once. Here, the tangible and the intangible had become transposed, an upside-down and backward existence, populated not with plants and animals, but with half-remembered dreams and forgotten thoughts, lingering regrets and unrequited feelings. Where concepts like love and hate and joy and grief became physical and sprouted and spread like poisonous vines from the viscous depths of drowning shadows, stretching and twisting across the endless, fractured expanse, creating a negation of meaning across pockets of nonexistence.

Everything was black. And yet there were as many shades of black as there were colors in the world he once knew. Shadows writhed upon shadows like wounded serpents. Darkness bloomed from more darkness, blinding and all-consuming, pulsing with a sickly sort of anti-radiance. And yet everything in this lightless hell had *eyes*. He could feel them on him as he sank deeper and deeper into the maddening depths. They bore into his soul, unraveling his thoughts and breaking apart his memories until he could no longer recall what was now and what was past and what was yet to be.

No sounds reached him here, not even the labored rasping of his own, frightened breathing. And yet he found himself bombarded by a deafening, discordant cacophony of *not-sound* that drilled agonizing daggers into some *other* ear that he never knew he had. The very atmosphere quivered with the intensity of it, filling him with a sensation like a thousand angry wasps squirming under his skin. And beneath it all, something more…something that resembled dreadful and malignant whispers…a chorus of lost souls speaking in fragments of truth, slithering through his brain like invading tendrils, seeking the cracks in his sanity to invade and infect with lies and blasphemy and fractured memories that would poison his mind and pervert his soul until he was forever changed into something vile and hideous.

He didn't want to change. He didn't want to be someone else. He'd only just recently learned what it was to be alive. And yet escape from this dreadful darkness seemed unfathomable. It gripped him like the suffocating coils of a giant anaconda, thickening as he sank ever deeper, becoming viscid, even as his own mind and sanity thinned, threatening to drain away forever. It was swallowing his very identity, slowly dissolving his sense of self, turning him into something soulless and unclean.

(*What's your name?*)

A faint spark of consciousness blossomed within the pervasive darkness. That voice… It was so familiar…

He tried to respond, but he couldn't tell if his lips were moving. He couldn't feel his body. He couldn't even hear his own pounding heart. And yet as his name drifted through his thoughts—*Everett*—he felt a wave of self-awareness wash over him, like a breath of fresh air within a buried coffin.

He was Everett.

He was here with friends. Olivia. Wayne. Andrea. Violet. He needed to get back to them. He couldn't be wasting time here in this black emptiness. If he didn't find his way back to the City Beyond Memory, he'd never finish his journey. He'd never find his angel.

But how did he get back from someplace like this? How did he get *anywhere* when he couldn't even be certain he still had a body? He could feel nothing, neither cold nor heat, neither pain nor pleasure, neither up nor down.

And yet, he was slowly becoming aware of something in the distance. A sprawling metropolis of twisting streets, drunkenly leaning spires and hideous, nightmare structures that burst from the ground like malignant tumors, bathed in this non-world's dreadful version of twilight. It was a terrible place, swarming with unthinkable, ever-shifting things overflowing with despair. They were neither people nor beasts, but something other. Phantoms. Thought forms. Manifestations of forgotten nightmares. Shapeless and hollow. Without conscience. Without souls. They wept and moaned, uttering screams and laughter and weighted sighs that cut at his sanity like a razor's edge.

He didn't want to go there. It was a terrible place, hellish and cold and confounding. But he was already moving toward it, caught in a current of flowing shadows, like a deadly riptide dragging him out to sea.

Or perhaps he wasn't moving toward it at all. Perhaps *it* was moving toward *him*…alive and hungry…eager to consume him…

He was terrified of what came next. But the terror he felt filled him with a strange sort of relief. To feel fear was to be human. It meant he hadn't already been devoured by the darkness.

Not yet.

Chapter 8

Nicole was lost. Everything here was darkness and sludge, a vast, noxious wasteland stretching a veritable eternity in every direction. The air was heavy with foul fumes that burned her nose and throat and made her eyes water.

She couldn't remember how she ended up here, or even how long she'd been trudging through this black muck. It felt like ages, *years* even, dragging herself onward, exhausted and naked and alone, every inch of her body covered in filth.

Sometimes, like now, she could walk, her bare feet sinking into the reeking goop that felt less like mud squelching between her toes than a lumpy, gritty slime, struggling to pull herself free with each and every step. Other times, she was forced to practically swim, her weary body struggling to stay afloat, the burning fumes choking her.

It was these times, as she labored just to keep from drowning, that she felt the *other things*. They swam these inky fathoms, churning their way through the toxic sludge, enormous and unimaginable, terrible and unthinkable. They didn't live in this hopeless place, for they were not alive. They were neither physical nor spiritual. Nor were they psychic. Nor magic. They were something else entirely. And they filled her with unspeakable terror whenever she felt one drawing near.

She was utterly exhausted. So many times she'd wanted to give up, to just sink beneath these slow, black waves and let eternal sleep swallow her forever. But she couldn't give up. There was something important she had to do...

...if only she could remember what it was...

The fumes made it so hard to think. Her head was spinning. The featureless black landscape was a blur of darkness, making it impossible to see with any clarity the shape she was slowly trudging toward.

It was a great, looming thing, so tiny on that impossible horizon...so far away... She needed to get there, though she couldn't remember why. It was desperately important that she reach it, and yet the sight of it filled her with a terrible, visceral dread like nothing she'd felt before in all the frights she'd faced on this long, long journey.

Something terrible was waiting for her there.

Yet she had no choice but to keep pushing toward it.

On and on...

But she was so tired. Her body was too weary to go on, too heavy to keep her head above the black waves. She couldn't go any farther.

She was sinking. Deeper and deeper she descended, into an empty nothingness. Darkness enveloped her. Everything was cold and numb. Her thoughts faded and grew distant.

She couldn't even remember why she was here. It had been so long. She'd traveled so far.

Had she failed everyone? Was that why she was here? Was this her punishment for not being able to bring her friends home like she swore she'd do?

She stared up at the dead branches, tears dripping down her face.

She was here again... Had she been here all along? She could feel the cold water of the pond enveloping her feet, the black mud oozing between her bare toes.

She was naked again. She was always naked in the dreams. Was that what this was? Another dream?

But why here? Why the meadow? What was it about this tree that she needed to keep coming to this dreadful place in these awful delusions?

She was so tired...

She just wanted to give up...

But she had to keep pushing forward...on and on into that endless black wasteland...toward the mysterious and terrible shape on that black horizon...

Chapter 9

Brandy didn't want to move on. She wanted to go back and try again. But Albert was right. Even the pervert's sex magic hadn't revealed where Gina had gone. She'd managed to work up enough sexual energy to give her a glimpse of their greater surroundings. She even managed to see that someone was moving in the corridors on a level somewhere above them. But it wasn't Gina. And she didn't think it was Nicole.

That was all she was able to determine before the awareness subsided and she lost them. The mood faded, the sadness came washing back and all that was left was an unpleasant *dirty* sort of feeling. She felt almost humiliated, as if she'd resorted to desperately throwing herself at a stranger like some junkie trying to sell herself for drug money. And for *what*? Gina was nowhere to be found. She was just *gone*.

"We'll find her," Albert assured her.

She didn't respond. She didn't want to talk to him right now. Her feelings were all tangled up. A part of her wanted to turn around and shove him away. She walked ahead of him, her arms crossed so that he couldn't take her hand again, the flashlight shining out from under her elbow.

"She just has something important to do. You'll see."

He didn't know that. He *couldn't*. He was just making shit up to make her feel better. But she didn't *want* to feel better. She was pissed off. She was embarrassed. Her heart was aching. And she was frustrated.

She hated the idea of leaving Gina behind. She felt *awful*. Her stomach was burning with guilt. She kept sniffing back tears.

"It's that room," Albert assured her. "It's feeding on your natural feelings. Magnifying them."

Again, she didn't respond. He was probably right. But she didn't need the sorrow room to make her feel bad about walking away and leaving that sweet girl to whatever might be lurking in these black passages.

"We both know she's capable," he went on. "Probably more so than both of us together. She came all this way. We can trust her to do whatever it is she needs to do."

She kept her mouth pressed tightly shut, holding back the urge to yell at him. That wasn't really her, after all. She loved him. And none of these feelings she was struggling with were his fault. But she just wanted him to shut up for a little while.

An intersection appeared from the gloom ahead of them. "Go left up here," he instructed.

It seemed that her act of desperate sluttery had at least given him a quick glimpse of the labyrinth's layout, allowing him to navigate for a little while.

(Typical that *he'd* get something out of it…)

She turned left as instructed and continued on, her mouth still firmly closed, biting back that urge to yell at him.

She couldn't let these feelings control her. Because this wasn't her. She knew it wasn't. This was Albert. This was her *husband*. She adored him. He was always so good to her, even when she was feeling moody and selfish, even when she'd had a bad day. All these conflicting emotions…it reminded her of when she used to stay up too late studying, cramming for exams, running on coffee and energy drinks and too little food.

This passage was the same size now as it was when they entered it, and yet it was starting to feel like the walls were closing in on her. Claustrophobia was subtly taking hold of her, squeezing her, making it harder to breathe.

He was right. It was the emotion room. But somehow the sadness it was radiating was getting all mixed up and confused with all these other emotions. Her fear of being back here inside a temple. Her regret at having lost another friend in this darkness. That surge of sexual stimulation combined with those feelings of anger toward the perverted shaman and her sense of shame at having to keep doing things *his* way…and then there was the guilt of knowing that she was inwardly directing all this negativity toward the one person she couldn't live without…

She *hated* this.

Worst of all, she knew she wasn't fooling him. He could feel this unwanted aggression she was directing at him. She could tell by the way he didn't try to take her hand or put his arm around her, despite the fact that he'd barely let go of her since they reunited after dealing with the psychic predator. He was staying close to her but being careful not to touch her.

He was so fucking *mindful*… The big, stupid…*adorable* jerk…

She felt another tear streak down her face and angrily wiped it away.

"Take a right next," he said as the next intersection came into view. "Then go straight through the next one."

She sniffled and pushed onward.

"I can't promise where this will lead us. I could only memorize the path so far out. But we'll at least avoid wasting time with dead ends for a little while."

He better not expect her to stop every ten minutes to grope her just to avoid some stupid dead ends...

She reached up and brushed back a loose strand of hair in her face. Her head was starting to hurt. She better not get sick down here.

No, it was probably because she'd been clenching her jaw almost constantly since she pulled her tongue out of his mouth. Fucking emotion rooms...

Again, she sniffled. Again, she wiped away a stray tear.

Albert followed behind her. For the next moment, he fell quiet, letting her work through it all.

He was always so patient with her. So kind. So loving. Did she really deserve someone like him?

Her eyes welled up again. She squeezed them shut and wiped at her face, irritated.

Ahead of them, another passageway branched off to the right. Albert said to go straight, so she walked past it and continued on.

"That's all I can remember," he said once they were past it. "We'll be continuing blind from here on."

She glared back at him, her watery eyes narrowed, daring him to suggest doing it again.

He squinted right back at her. "What's that look for?" he asked her. "Don't expect me put out every time we get lost. I'm not some piece of meat."

This caught her completely off guard. She laughed. But it wasn't a pretty laugh. Not by any stretch of the imagination. It was more of a snort, and a snotty one at that. She clasped her free hand over her face, embarrassed. "Fuck!" she cried. "Ew!"

He stepped in front of her and lifted the tail of his shirt for her to use.

"That's gross! I don't want to get it all over your shirt!"

"As opposed to what? You think someone left a tissue box in the next room? Here. This shirt's already trashed anyway."

He was probably right. There were still stains on his sleeves from the gross goo that came out of those statues' heads back in Mysteria.

Reluctantly, she pressed her face into it, her watery eyes fixed on his.

"Feeling any better?" he asked.

"Little…" she replied.

He leaned forward and kissed her forehead.

She scrunched up her nose and pouted into his soiled shirt. Big, adorable jerk… She loved him so fucking much.

Chapter 10

The shadow-tainted passageways had been leading downward for some time now, deeper and deeper into the depths of the city's black and mysterious underbelly. Gina could no longer feel Albert and Brandy. They'd strayed much too far away by now. In fact, she hadn't felt *anyone* in some time.

There was only the thing stalking her on the other side of these walls.

It was strange. There was something wrong with the layout of the labyrinth around her. She could feel the passages turning and twisting and winding in every direction, and yet no matter how far she went, the thing was always just on the other side of the wall. It seemed to her that it must be passing right through solid stone in order to keep pace with her like that, and yet it remained on its own side, even when *her* passage turned.

She was starting to feel like there was something she was missing. An element of these passages that she was somehow blind to. Something to do with the way the stone clouded her psychic senses, perhaps. Or maybe something about the thing itself.

Even more unsettling, however, was the fact that it was *familiar*. It reminded her far too much of Tristesse Lane and those abominable apartments. And of all the things that used to torment her growing up. The things normal people couldn't see or hear. The *shadowy* things that slipped through cracks and crawled on walls and ceilings. The *nightmare* things that moaned and wailed and howled outside windows and under floorboards. And the *maddening* things that crept through crowded hallways, across busy streets and into bustling school hallways, always seeming to be drawn to her, always *haunting* her.

The things that made everyone treat her like a freak.

Most of all, it reminded her of the first job the goddess gave her. Located in an unassuming, five-story building in Cakwetak, Wisconsin, Vertical Design was a legitimate business, the area's leading graphic design firm, a veritable dream job for an aspiring artist like her. To everyone else, that was all there was to it. But those five unremarkable stories were only the tip of a terrible iceberg. Unseen to the ordinary residents of the city, the true structure was *much* larger. At twenty-five stories, it towered over every other building in the area, yet remained utterly unnoticed by any of the thousands of people who passed right by it every day. Because in addition to being strangely invisible, it had the curious ability to distort the space around it, making it impossible to perceive even the extra time it took to walk or drive around it.

The truth was that Vertical Industries and all its subsidiaries was much more than just a wealthy mega-corporation. It was a front for all sorts of shadowy activities, run by one of the Twelve Teeth of the Great Enemy, an immortal monster posing as a man named Caducius Turms, who literally held the fate of the world's economy in his hands. It was a terrifying fact to know. One that had kept her up at night on more than one occasion since learning the truth of it all.

The thing stalking her on the other side of these walls had something to do with them, she realized. Those twelve monsters. It was the same kind of energy she felt radiating from Tane and Glum. She'd recognize it anywhere. It wasn't limited to the V. I. buildings. She'd felt that unnatural energy in some capacity everywhere she'd ever been. She even glimpsed it back at the wedding. But what would the likes of them be doing in a place like *this*?

From what she understood, the Great Enemy was one of three very ancient and powerful entities that embodied each of the three worlds that together encompassed the whole universe. The natural. The supernatural. The unnatural. A delicate balance upon which all of reality was built. But now two of the Teeth were gone. How did Tane's death and Thrud's disappearance affect that balance? And could one of those remaining ten have somehow followed her here?

But what would they want with *her*? Did it have something to do with Tane's death? She only played a small role in the events that went down in Cakwetak. She wasn't even there when he died. And yet the very idea of one of those ten horrors holding a grudge against her was pervasive, filling her with disquieting dread. After all, she'd heard that, unlike Tane and Glum, Turms was perfectly willing to defy the Keeper and allow the cycle to end...

Could this be him? Had Caduceus Turms been stalking her all this time, just waiting to catch her alone and vulnerable?

Maybe *he* was the mysterious entity the goddess warned them about way back in Cedric's Cove. The one that had been following them the entire time, allowing that Hochog man to keep finding them.

(*It seems to attract unwanted things. And it delights in your misfortune.*)

She said those words to Andrea, not her, and even posited that it had been watching her since her first encounter with the Keeper five years ago. But was it really Andrea it was stalking?

The passage split ahead of her. One path jutted off to the right. The other curved left again. The thing on the other side of the wall shouldn't be able to keep stalking her without passing into view if she kept to the left. And yet somehow it stayed its course, still keeping pace with her, completely unimpeded by the physical layout of the labyrinth, following a path that simply wasn't there.

Even when the passage began sloping downward again and the space around her remained level, the thing descended with her.

Was there a distortion of some sort that made her misjudge its distance or direction? Or was there some other element to this labyrinth that her psychic mind was blind to?

What wasn't she seeing?

She was regretting having to part ways with Brandy and Albert. That bad feeling was getting worse with every step she took. Was she really capable of dealing with such a thing all on her own?

The goddess didn't prepare her for anything like this.

Was it the fear welling up inside her that made her eyes misty again, or the remnants of that dreadful grief room?

She hated this.

Chapter 11

Violet was running.

She wasn't sure *why* she was running. Or *where* she was in such a hurry to go. Or what she might be running *from*. She couldn't even remember when she started or how long she'd been running. It couldn't have been too long, because she wasn't completely exhausted, but she was out of breath, her stomach was tight and her heart was pounding. All she knew for certain was that she couldn't *stop* running. Not yet.

She slashed at the darkness with her flashlight beam, illuminating the stone wall on one side and a dark, plunging abyss on the other. She turned and dared a look behind her, but there was nothing chasing her.

It was slowly coming back to her. That fake Everett. Fleeing across the top of that winding labyrinth. The other one taking the wheel.

(*I'll take you…*)

Take her where? Away from the Everett thing? To wherever the *real* Everett went? Or simply to where she needed to be?

Was this far enough? At last, she stopped running and stood with her light pointed into the darkness from which she came, watching for any sign of movement while she struggled to catch her breath.

Things were getting confusing. There were a lot of memories buzzing around in her head that weren't there before. She remembered losing Andrea and proceeding through the labyrinth with Everett at her side. But she also remembered being back in that sentinel's body, looking up at a sky full of impossible colors in spite of the fact that she had no eyes with which to see. And she remembered finding a curious cave when she was only ten years old and hearing a mysterious voice calling out to her from some kind of tomb…

That was where it all started, she realized. Almost twenty years ago, in that sunny, Missouri forest. It was never just a dream. It happened just as she recalled. And then she'd promptly forgotten all about it. She recalled something coming over her, leaving her confused. And then the entire ordeal seemed to just flush right out of her mind. What was even the point in it? Why give a little girl a message about the future and then immediately make her forget it?

But then again, she supposed, what was a little girl expected to do with such knowledge? Maybe it was precisely because she was so young that she needed to forget it until the time was right. But even so… That mysterious voice basically foretold her meeting Jeremy more than a decade later.

(When the stranger falls from the sky, your journey will begin…)

It said that would be the beginning of her journey. But by the time she remembered being told that, it had already happened. That was *eight years* ago. Was it meant to be something subliminal? Had those words pushed her to search the earth for those other worlds, just so she'd eventually find her way here?

It was starting to feel as if the sentinels weren't merely building a city, but somehow the foundation on which balanced all the events that would come to pass between then and now. It was a difficult thing to imagine. She couldn't fathom planning such details over the course of a single year, much less across the lifecycles of untold *universes.*

But then again, weren't the sentinels only following the orders of that so-called Keeper? Was *he* the one who really planned all this out? She remembered those creepy twins back on January Street referring to themselves as "just one of many cogs" in some kind of "machine."

It was all so damned complicated!

When no Everett monsters rushed out of that darkness at her, she turned her attention forward. Where was she? How far had she fled? Was this the same floor she was on before? And where did the *real* Everett go? She needed to find him before something happened to him.

He'll find his way back to you.

She stared into the gloom for a moment, trying to decide whether that might merely have been a bit of unwarranted optimism or if it could have been the voice of the other one from those bizarre dreams.

"Hello?" she whispered.

There was no answer. Or…she didn't *think* there was an answer. It was hard to tell when the voice you suspected was intruding on your thoughts was the same voice as the one inside your head.

Maybe it was only her imagination.

She reached up with her free hand and brushed the hair from her damp forehead. If the cave was a real memory and not just a dream, did that mean that these visions of the construction of the city were real, too? On one hand, anything seemed possible at this point. And there was a strange sort of lingering closeness to the other one, as if she really did spend an eternity inside that alien mind and body. But forgetting something that happened when she was ten years old wasn't the same as traveling all the way back to a long-dead universe at the beginning of time. That was the stuff of Corey's old comic books.

Wasn't it?

She stood there a moment longer, distracted, contemplating those impossible memories. By now, it wasn't really a question of whether the sentinels were real or whether that was what this place looked like when their world still existed. It was *real.* She was becoming quite sure of that. And the other one showed her those things for a reason.

She pushed the confounding thoughts from her head and focused on the space around her. She shined her light down into the darkness below. She couldn't see anything, but there were things down there when she and Everett first arrived on this floor. *Monstrous* things. Things only he was able to see with his curious connection to the spirit world. And he wasn't here to tell her if they were still down there. All she could do was assume that they were and remain wary.

Then she turned her light upward, into the gloom hanging over her. With no memory of running here, she had no way of knowing for certain that she was even still on the same floor. Maybe the mysterious squatter in her head led her down a flight of stairs while she was imagining being in *her* mind in the past.

Not that it mattered, she supposed. There were frightening and dangerous things everywhere. The Not-Everett was proof enough of that. Where she was didn't matter very much. She needed to stay clear-headed and alert. Just like when exploring new gateways with Corey.

She pushed on in the direction she was running when she regained her awareness. She could think of no logical reason why she'd want to go back the other way. Her eyes and ears peeled for any sign of danger, she walked through the silent darkness, still pondering those strange visions of colorful skies and rising stone towers.

It was strange, remembering things only now. That cave in Missouri. That field of stones in Arkansas. And now these new visions. She was beginning to understand that there was an order to those events, a certain, twisted chronology. For her, it began in that Missouri cave. But that wasn't the other one's first encounter with her. In fact, it felt strangely as if the other one's timeline was somehow backward to her own…although she couldn't fathom exactly how such a thing might work…

Albert and Brandy claimed to have traveled back and forth through time within the strange walls of the Lucianna Mysteria, but that was over the course of a few short days. This was twenty years of her life and possibly the driving factor in this unusual hobby she and Corey shared.

Was she ever really in control of her life? Or had the other one always decided her way for her? It was all so confusing.

Something made a noise in the dark chasm below, startling her from her thoughts and freezing her to the floor.

Was something there? Was it coming this way?

But seconds ticked by and nothing more was heard.

Slowly, quietly, she crept forward. How long would she have to be alone in this place? She hadn't realized how accustomed she'd become to having someone around to help her stay strong in creepy situations like these. But it wasn't as if she had any kind of choice. All she could do was steel her nerves and push onward.

Chapter 12

"I'm so sorry!" squealed Andrea.

"It's okay," sighed Olivia. She was staring down at her shirt, now soiled with a black and reeking outline of Andrea's very unexpected hug.

She was following the dark, winding passage leading out of the mud chamber when she at long last glimpsed another light in this endless darkness. Hopeful that it was one of her friends, she rushed around the corner and saw Olivia standing there, not ten paces away, staring right back at her. She was so excited, so completely *overjoyed*, that she simply rushed out and hugged her, forgetting completely about the fact that she was still covered from head to toe in that foul sludge.

Adding to the confusion was the fact that, although she appeared to be looking directly at her, Olivia couldn't actually see her.

She didn't understand it at first. They kept asking her where she came from and looking at her like she was crazy when she kept pointing back to the murky passage. But they simply couldn't *see* the passage. It was like Erin explained to her about places in the city overlapping between the spirit world and the living world. Only *she*, with her strange ghostly senses, could see those other spaces. It wasn't until she took them both by the hand and led them inside that they understood.

So the fact was that Olivia wasn't looking at her, as she seemed to be, but rather was staring at what she thought was an ordinary wall and trying to understand why her psychic brain was urgently warning her that something was about to startle her. From her perspective, some black, muddy, stinky thing just sort of belched out of solid stone right in front of her eyes and grabbed her.

No wonder she screamed so loud. That must've been terrifying. She felt really bad now.

You'll end up getting them killed, said the impostor.

She rubbed at her dirty forehead, weary. *Shut it!* she thought at it, forcing the words toward the rude entity with such force that she probably made a strange face doing it. She wasn't going to listen to that stupid voice. She refused to believe anything it said. It was a liar.

"Doesn't matter," said Olivia, oblivious of the argument going on inside her head. "I'm just happy you're safe."

"Agreed," said Wayne. He was prodding at the wall where the hidden passage met the space outside, trying to wrap his head around how it worked. "We were worried about you."

"I've been worried about *you* guys, too. Ever since Everett told me you were here."

"Everett?" gasped Olivia so suddenly that she startled *her* a little. She reached out and grabbed her grubby hands. "You've seen him?"

She nodded. "After we got separated from our original groups, we ended up together for a little while."

"Oh thank God!"

"Told you he'd be fine," said Wayne.

"I know you did, but still."

Andrea nodded. "I met him in some kind of crazy ancient factory place. Him and Violet both, which was weird because we all came here in different groups. But then I got separated from them, too." She frowned. "That keeps happening to me."

Probably dead by now.

Go away!

Olivia turned and looked at Wayne. "Corey was looking for someone named Violet. Remember?"

"Corey's okay, too?" asked Andrea.

"You know Corey?" asked Wayne, surprised.

"Corey and Violet are friends with Gina. She's the one who brought me and Nikki here."

All of them gone by now. Guarantee it.

Oh my god, get out of my head!

"Huh," said Olivia.

"Well…" she amended, struggling to keep her composure. "She's the one who took us to *Cedric's Cove*. It was *Keith* who showed up and brought us *here*. To the Denselands. On his boat."

"Yeah, we ran into Keith," said Wayne.

She brightened at this news. "Keith's okay, too?"

"Yeah." Then he frowned. "I mean, probably. He got a little hurt before he met us, but he was managing fine. Then we got separated from him and Corey."

"That happens a lot, doesn't it?" sighed Andrea, wilting.

"It sure seems like it," agreed Olivia. "What happened to you? Are you okay?"

She rolled her eyes. "I don't even know where to start," she sighed.

"Maybe with how you made this magic tunnel appear?" suggested

Wayne.

She turned and looked back the way she came. He thought she *made* it appear? How was she supposed to explain that it was there the whole time but only she could see it? "Um... That might take a little while. It's kind of complicated."

"How complicated?" he pressed.

"It's like...um...a *ghost tunnel*?"

He stared at her for a moment, an utterly befuddled look on his face. "Okay..." he said at last. "Yeah, that's...pretty complicated."

"Told ya so."

He nodded thoughtfully and glanced around at the stone walls. "Maybe we should sit and take a break..."

"I could go for a break," groaned Olivia.

"Yes *please*," sighed Andrea. Her legs were still sore from struggling through all that filthy muck. She leaned against the wall and then slid down, wincing at little at the aching in her calves. And now that she'd lost her shoes, she doubted things would get any less uncomfortable from here on out. "You have to tell me your story, too. Everett said you came here on a *train*?"

"Yeah," chuckled Wayne as he and Olivia seated themselves on the floor of the passage. "Like you said. Complicated."

Clearly it was. She kept looking at the concerning bloodstain on his shirt and all the scratches on their arms and faces. And she hadn't failed to notice that the *back* of his shirt was tattered and bloodied, too. Olivia had a bandage over her right eye and a painful-looking bruise on the back of her hand. They looked like they'd been through hell and back.

"You said it started with someone named Gina? How'd you meet up with her?"

"She was at the wedding."

"The *wedding*?" Olivia looked back at Wayne, her pretty eyes wide.

Andrea nodded. "God, that feels like so long ago..." It felt like *weeks*. And yet to her own recollection, wasn't it only two days ago? Was that right? She managed to get a little sleep in Gina's car before the horsemen attacked them. But then time went all wonky, impossible days passed and the next sunset she saw was as they left Cedric's Cove. Was that all the same day? She slept again on Keith's boat and she had no idea how long ago that was. Hours? Days? *Months*? She wouldn't be surprised by anything at this point.

"Tell us everything," prodded Wayne.

Yeah, tell them how you got everyone killed.

Andrea ignored her. She was done even reacting to the impostor's lies.

"You said she approached you at the wedding?" he urged.

Andrea wrinkled her dirty nose. "Well... Actually first there was Hotdog," she explained, causing Wayne and Olivia to exchange a bewildered look.

Chapter 13

Everything was upside down here. Not the kind of upside down where everything was upended and the ground hung overhead while the sky yawned open below, but the kind of upside down that defied every kind of logic, where nothing about it should exist and yet somehow it stood here anyway, an afront to everything natural and sane.

Everett felt himself drifting through the broken labyrinth of twisted corridors that served as this city's streets like a lost spirit, incorporeal, little more than litter tossed about in the wind. Did he still have a body? Or was this all that was left of him? The uncertainty was maddening. He couldn't dwell on it for long lest he begin to lose himself to the darkness again.

Instead, he focused on the upside-down nightmare through which he floated.

Somehow, he understood that this was the same city he and Violet entered together. Somewhere in this inverted nightmare was the path they traveled. But gone were the pristine passageways and the smooth, gray stone. This was something *putrid*. A feat of architecture borne of hell, itself, an affront to life and to reason. Every surface was like diseased flesh covered in festering lesions, living and dead at the same time, a macabre cityscape of oozing open wounds latticed with morbid scars made of petrified souls of things that never lived. And it was moving! Like some vile and colossal organism crawling through the void as if in search of death's comforting embrace. It sloughed and pulsed with a will of its own, rearranging itself into new and even more dreadful shapes.

He could almost glimpse the structure's cold purpose. No one ever called this place home, not in all the endless ages it had existed. It was only a tool, crafted by unimaginable hands in an age inconceivable. A means to an end, with secrets woven through its fetid veins.

Was this the Keeper's intention from the start? Was this upside-down perversion a part of his unfathomable design? Some necessary evil he'd long kept buried? Or was this something else? A vile infection eating away at the foundation of his work? Whatever the purpose, it was horrid, a fever-dream made flesh, a wound in the very fabric of the city's existence.

But the worst by far was the twisted and fractured tower at the heart of the city, jutting from the fleshy streets like a piercing dagger, both rising and plunging, defying logic, its disjointed, spiraling staircases encircling it like strangling vines. Its very surface pulsated as if with a living heartbeat, and with each contraction of impossible sinews it oozed foul and noxious blood.

He shouldn't be here. Merely witnessing atrocities like these would soon snap his fragile sanity, fraying his mind and plunging him into a terrible, inescapable madness. He needed to leave. Now. And yet he wasn't in control. He might as well be adrift in the cosmos.

(*What's your name?*)

That voice again… Was that merely a fragment of a memory from before he ended up here? Or was someone calling out to him?

What *was* his name? He couldn't quite remember it. It felt like so long since anyone asked him for it. Far longer, it seemed, than he should have been alive…

Ripples of consciousness swept through him, jarring him like waves in a storm.

He remembered Violet… Where did she go? Was she safe?

Everything had changed. Suddenly he was plummeting through a gaping chasm in the putrid flesh that replaced the temple's stone, falling down and up and sideways all at once, a dizzying, nauseating rush of gravity that made his stomach lurch.

It was deeply unpleasant, but at least it seemed to prove that he still *had* a stomach…

He fell. Deeper and deeper into the vile guts of the inverted city.

Was this the end of his strange journey?

Somewhere in the depths of his memory, that voice called out to him again:

(*What's your name?*)

Chapter 14

"Feeling better?" asked Albert.

Brandy nodded. She was again letting him hold her hand. A good sign.

That room got into her head worse than he imagined, which didn't exactly surprise him. It likely preyed on all the emotions she'd been keeping pushed down throughout this journey. Sorrow could be as invasive as fear, after all. And there was plenty of stuff spoiling her happiness right now. She was disappointed that the last day of her honeymoon was ruined. She was embarrassed about being tricked into that fake sex room and subjected to the shaman's perverted lessons. She felt gross about that skeevy party and all those ogling people. And she definitely felt guilty about losing their companions. Violet and Corey. Then Nicole. And now Gina.

Of course it got into her head. It got into his, too. But he was able to fight it off. And it was precisely because of Brandy that it was possible. She was, after all, his sun and moon. He was confident he could do almost anything as long as she was by his side.

"I'm still worried sick about everyone, though."

"I know."

They were moving upward now, making their way higher through the labyrinth. He wondered if they might be under that tower where Gina said they needed to be, but he doubted it. Finding what they came here for this quickly would probably be way too much to ask.

"And I hate that we have to use sex to make our powers work. It's stupid. That's *our* thing. Our *me and you* thing. It's supposed to be beautiful and private and just between us. And that fucking pervert turned it into a *tool*."

"I know," he said. "I never realized what real-life Harry Potters had to use for wands." He mimed waving a wand in front of his crotch. "Expecto erectus!"

Brandy snorted laughter at the unexpected silliness. "Oh my god!" she gasped.

"There's that pretty laugh," he said. "I was missing that."

She scrunched up her face at him. "That wasn't my pretty laugh. That was my snotty, *snorty* laugh. You've got some seriously weird fetishes."

He chuckled. "I guess I do because I'm even in love with all the snotty, snorty versions of you."

"Weirdo," she replied.

Not the response he was hoping for, but she never let go of his hand, he noticed, so still a win.

Ahead of them, the path split three ways. It would probably be a waste of time to even bother thinking too hard about which way to go.

"Seriously, though..." she sighed, squeezing his hand. "Do you think we'll have to do two more of those rooms? Like in the first temple?"

"I don't know. Maybe. Maybe more. We'll find out together."

She crinkled her nose, unhappy. "I don't wanna."

"I know. Me neither."

He veered right at random and pushed on, his thoughts drifting back to that emotion room and how badly it affected her even though she'd kept her eyes closed the entire time. What other invasive feelings might they have to deal with?

Albert tugged her to a stop and instinctively reached around her, shielding her. "Careful."

"Shit!" she hissed, squeezing his hand.

The passage continued on well beyond the reach of his flashlight, but the floor dropped off a few steps ahead of them. He thought for a moment that they'd discovered one of those offset passages that kept the hounds corralled into their own areas, but it was too deep for that. When she crept closer and shined the light downward, there was nothing but darkness.

"What the *fuck*?"

She took the words right out of his mouth. What the fuck, indeed. Like the one waiting at the exit of the sorrow room, it seemed to be a trap designed to thwart anyone exploring blind. But why was it just here in the middle of the labyrinth?

He glanced down at the flashlight in Brandy's hand. It was the only one they had. What if it broke? Or the batteries went dead?

She was already backing away from the ledge, as if something might lash out from those black depths and drag her down into it. And for all he knew, that was a real possibility.

He squeezed her hand, determined not to let go of her, and then turned back.

"What if Gina stumbled across something like that?" she worried. "She doesn't have a light. I mean, I know she's supposed to be able *sense her surroundings* or whatever, but what if she can't for some reason?"

"She knew the last one was there," he reminded her. "She warned us of it before she left. I'm sure these kinds of things are the least of her worries."

"I hope so."

The previous intersection came into view again. He chose right here originally, he recalled, so he took the left passage, the one farthest from this one.

"And Nikki..." she sighed. "She didn't have a flashlight, either. This one was hers."

"I know. But she's a capable girl. We have to trust her."

She groaned but said nothing more about it. And she didn't have to. He knew exactly how she was feeling. He was feeling it, too. He was worried sick about *all* their friends. What were they all going through out there? What dangers were they facing? And how many of them were all alone like Gina and Nicole?

Brandy stopped, her lovely blue eyes staring forward. "Look," she whispered.

He saw it, too. A light glowing softly in a passage up ahead. A flashlight? But it didn't seem to be moving... A terrible thought crossed his betraying mind. A flashlight dropped and motionless. Someone they cared about lying dead in the silence, victim of some bloodthirsty monster.

No. He couldn't think like that. It wouldn't help anything. He needed to keep a clear mind.

There were plenty of reasons a flashlight wouldn't be moving. Someone was taking a break, most likely. Resting their feet. Catching their breath. Puzzling through a particularly confounding part of the labyrinth that was sending them in circles. But the most awful possibilities were the ones that burned brightest in his thoughts. He couldn't seem to help it.

"Keep behind me," he whispered as he crept forward, careful not to make a sound.

He didn't hear any voices. But that didn't mean anything. People sometimes sat in silence when they rested. Or maybe it was someone who was alone, separated from their group.

"This feels weird," whispered Brandy.

He nodded. The light was getting steadily brighter. He kept moving, staying as quiet as possible, careful to not even drag his feet on the stone. He even struggled to keep his breathing in check, half-convinced that something dangerous up there would hear him and pounce.

He crept around the corner. There was a chamber up ahead. The light was coming from in there. He glanced back at Brandy, who nodded and pressed her finger to her lips. Then she switched off her flashlight.

Somewhere in the eternal darkness of these stone walls were supposed to be ten others like them. At least six of those were people they knew. Maybe eight, if he was right about Wayne and Olivia being here somewhere. That meant the odds that they'd encounter a hostile stranger were very small. But it also meant that the odds of losing someone they cared about were far too high.

Was that a noise just now? A rustling? A whisper of a footfall on the stone?

His heart was racing. He couldn't make himself calm down. He was terrified of what he was about to find.

And as he crept closer to the chamber, his heart sank at the sight of what appeared to be blood splashed on the stone wall.

He reached back and halted Brandy, not wanting her to see it, but it was too late. Her eyes were fixed on that crimson splatter. Her face had paled with dread.

"Stay here," he mouthed at her.

She shook her head. She wouldn't.

He didn't want her to go in there. He didn't want to go in there, either. But he didn't have a choice in the matter. He needed to be sure. There were still too many variables. Who was it? What if they weren't dead, but merely injured?

There was a definite noise from within the room this time. A sort of soft dragging sound. A faint thump.

Was the killer still in there? Were they in danger? Or was it someone injured and in need of help? He couldn't leave without making sure.

He steeled his nerves and crept onward. This chamber wasn't like any of the others they'd seen. There were strange, boxy shapes and odd little bulbous things protruding from the walls. There was a large, roughly hourglass-shaped structure in the middle of the room, blocking his view of the far side. The light was coming from behind it.

He leaned forward and saw a hand on the floor.

It looked like a man's hand. Corey? Or maybe Wayne? No, those fingers were more slender than theirs. Keith, perhaps?

Again, he heard a noise. A shuffle. A tap.

A shadow moved on the wall.

Bracing himself for whatever horror he was about to see, he

clenched his fist and crept forward, peering around the column.

A man he'd never seen before was lying on the ground, covered in blood. His lower half had been torn away and was lying beside him. There were great piles of what looked like bloody string strewn everywhere.

And sitting there in the middle of it all, his clothes bloodied, both of his hands literally *inside* the bisected corpse, was Corey.

He looked up, surprised. "Oh. It's you guys." Then he lifted a great, bloody hand in a lazy sort of wave, as if he weren't up to his elbows in gory remains. "Hi."

"*What are you doing?*" shrieked Brandy.

"Helpin'," he replied at once, seemingly having lost his mind.

"Please don't distract him," groaned the dead man. "Or he'll *never* finish."

Chapter 15

Gina could see the thing that was stalking her on the other side of the wall. Not in a literal sense, of course, as everything was pitch black and her eyes were useless. It was more *imagined* than seen, and yet the images in her head were getting clearer and clearer the longer she was down here, the longer she relied on her psychic brain to lead the way. And what she saw inside her head was unsettling and creepy. It was as if the stone in this part of the labyrinth had been replaced with translucent glass, allowing her distorted glimpses as it kept pace on the other side, still defying the physical layout of the temple, seemingly passing through solid stone. It was much bigger than she was, a great, hulking shape that was difficult to grasp in the wavery twists and warps and bubbles through which she perceived it.

Again, the passage she was following twisted to the left. Again, the passage on the *other* side of the wall snaked right. And again, the shadowy monstrosity inconceivably seemed to pass right through the stone in order to stay with her.

But she thought she was beginning to understand what was happening. Those "translucent" walls she imagined were separate from the stone ones. Not unlike the pocket dimensions she'd found herself caught in while she was still traveling with Andrea and Nicole, the two labyrinths were separate, yet occupying the same space. One existed *within* the other. This passage she was in was like a fold between those two realities, a wrinkle, where the two overlapped. She was aware of both at once, but her body was still physically *inside* the stone one while the other thing was in the glass one. And something about this folded space between the two was…well, *crinkled*, she supposed. Direction and distance were warped in such a way that no matter which way she turned in *this* labyrinth, the other one was always *right there*.

That was probably the only thing that had kept it from attacking her this whole time. And it meant that she would probably remain safe as long as she kept to the stone walls and out of those others. Because that thing was somehow connected to the glass labyrinth. It was like the things that lurked in the hidden upper floors of the Cakwetak Tower. Born of the unnatural, the darkness that oozed from the Twelve Teeth. There was a chance that it couldn't leave that place, that it could only follow her on its side of that warped glass, meaning she should be able to remain safely separated from it.

The problem was that she was becoming more and more sure that whatever she was supposed to find down here was waiting somewhere *deep inside* the glass labyrinth.

At some point, she was going to have to step over that threshold. And when she did, it would be waiting for her.

Her blind gaze fixed on the creature as she walked, her eyes useless yet her mind piecing together an image for her regardless. It was right there, staring back at her, watching her every move with a strange, carnal sort of hunger. There was nothing remotely human about it. It was a monstrous lump of writhing flesh and too many body parts. If she had to face the thing she'd be no match for it. And yet she knew instinctively that it was no mere beast. It had intelligence. And there was purpose to its actions. She wasn't going to be able to slip past it. Nor was it going to simply lose interest and wander off. It had *patience*.

What was she going to do?

Was it supposed to be this way? Did the Keeper plan it so? Did the *goddess* know this would happen?

She kept walking, uncertain. Now that she was aware of the glass labyrinth, she was beginning to understand its layout. This seemed to be a main corridor for both of them, a sort of backbone on which the two were built. Both were looped around themselves so that she could probably continue following this path indefinitely, walking on and on in circles until she eventually collapsed from exhaustion. But she could now also sense the locations of the places where the glass labyrinth branched away. Those were the key to crossing into it.

Except of course for the monster. That thing was going to be a major problem.

Was that the whole idea? Was it simply supposed to frighten her away from the glass labyrinth? Because if that was its goal, it was doing a fantastic job. She didn't know how she was supposed to face something like that.

She stopped walking and turned to face it. It was no trivial feat. She had to steel her nerves. Even with that glass wall standing between them, it was utterly terrifying. It felt like she was opening a door between her and it, practically inviting it to attack her. But she already knew that avoiding it wasn't an option. She needed to know how it was going to react when it realized she was aware of it. Would it freak out and go crazy? Would it grow more agitated and begin pacing back and forth like a hungry tiger? Or might it even turn tail and run? That would be nice, but she doubted it. For all she knew, she was wrong about it being contained in the glass labyrinth and this was all it would take for it to leap out and devour her.

But it didn't do any of those things.

It stopped and stared right back at her. It bristled and swelled, as if angered, with distorted, protruding body parts stretching out at odd angles, seeming to twist and boil like some kind of living sludge, yet somehow she knew that it wasn't angry. In fact, she could almost hear it *chuckling*.

It was *amused*.

Good... growled a voice inside her head that sent a shudder of revulsion through her entire body. *I like it when they pretend to be brave.*

She stood facing the thing, her heart pounding, her knees weak. This was definitely no kind of mere beast. This was something far worse. Intelligent. Cruel. Murderous.

Somehow, she managed to turn and keep walking as if it hadn't just scared the living hell out of her, pretending not to hear the sinister laughter that echoed through the glass labyrinth around her.

Chapter 16

Violet's light came to rest on another set of stairs leading ever farther upward. That, in itself, wasn't particularly unexpected. She was sure there were thousands of these scattered throughout this enormous labyrinth. But even before she turned her light on it, she found that she simply *knew* it was there.

She *remembered* it.

Or more precisely, the *other one* remembered it.

She could almost recall standing in this same place as the stones were being laid, warm sunlight still beating down from that impossibly colorful sky before it was plunged into this eternal, all-consuming darkness in an age long, *long* past. With each passing second that she stood here, she remembered more clearly being here before, standing right in this very spot, her consciousness wrapped in that strange, elongated body, looking out across this sprawling, stone labyrinth in spite of the fact that she had no eyes with which to see any of it. It even felt *larger* standing here in her own, much smaller body.

"What's happening to my brain?" she whispered into the darkness to no one.

Full circle, replied the other one from somewhere deep inside her.

That phrase kept passing through her mind. Full circle... Was she really communicating with an actual sentinel from the far-distant past? Across unfathomable distances and impossible ages? Even as she understood that this was all real, she couldn't wrap her head around how it was possible. But then again, there were plenty of things out here in these strange and broken Denselands that she couldn't begin to understand. That twisted forest with its broken physics. The Not-Jeremy that spirited her away from Corey. The Keeper, himself, with his incomprehensible designs. Her head was spinning. She was torn between clinging to logic that no longer applied and abandoning it altogether, plunging herself into the madness of this dark wonderland.

"Okay," she sighed as she shined her light up the steps, "so if we're really talking right now...can you at least tell me where I'm going?"

The other side of the colors.

"Other side of...?" She crinkled her nose at the ascending darkness, confused. "What does *that* mean?" Why did she think those words? Was it really a message from someone else? Or was her brain simply feeding her lies?

For some reason, she remembered the brilliant colors of that queer, alien sky in her dreams, a display of hues so complex that it seemed to contain shades she'd never even seen before.

These thoughts that filled her head… She was quite sure those weren't her own. Because why would she think such things? And if they were her *own* thoughts, wouldn't she know what the hell she was talking about?

Or was that simply how madness worked?

Hurry, breathed the other one. *It's almost time.*

"Time for *what?*"

But the voice in her head fell silent and a strange feeling of loneliness settled over her. The fact that she was by herself in this darkness was suddenly overwhelming. She turned and shined her light around, anxious. Her free hand clutched nervously at her shirt, tugging at the fabric, an old habit from when she was young and uncomfortable and Corey's shirttail wasn't within reach. She didn't think she'd done that in years. She hadn't even *thought about* that old tendency. But then again, she hadn't felt this vulnerable in a long time…

The emptiness of this enormous chamber was almost suffocating. Had something happened? Did she somehow lose the other one?

No. She was still there somewhere. She felt sure of it. But it required a lot more energy for the other one to remain inside her than it did for her when their roles were reversed beneath that multicolored sky. And it took a lot *more* to take the wheel and carry her away from the Not-Everett like that. It was *exhausting*.

Did the other one explain these things to her in one of those dreams? Or was that just something she knew? She couldn't remember. But she knew it to be a fact, regardless. She was no more alone than she'd been since she followed Corey into that cave twenty years ago.

The other one was resting. That was all.

She started up the stairs. There was no point hesitating any longer. For better or worse, this was the way she was meant to go. Delaying it wouldn't change anything. But she looked back once more as she ascended higher into the darkness.

Everett…

What happened to him? Why wasn't he with her when she woke up back there? How did he get replaced by that…*thing* that pretended to be him?

She couldn't stand the thought of just leaving him somewhere in this darkness.

But the other one promised they'd meet again. And he'd already spent his fair share of time alone on this nightmare journey. He was more capable than he appeared. She had no choice but to cling to these meager facts and trust that she'd see him again.

She turned her attention forward, her heart still racing at the unsettling lonesomeness, and hurried onward.

Ever upward... *The other side of the colors*, she thought, recalling the cryptic answer she received when she asked that mysterious voice where they were going. But what did it mean? What colors? The colors that once filled the storm-choked sky above this city? Those were the only colors she could think of. Everything else, from the stone floor to the churning clouds, was painted in shades of gray. If she kept climbing, would the sentinels' towering structure carry her all the way into whatever was beyond that world's *heavens*?

(Before you return, there is one last thing I have to show you. Up there.)

The sight of that towering structure at the center of the city flashed through her memory. Even in that dreamy distant time, long before it was ever finished, she recalled the way it faded into those hazy colors, well beyond what she could see, as if it continued on and on, piercing the thinning atmosphere, reaching all the way to the mysterious cosmos of that long-dead universe.

Was that what the other one meant?

She closed her eyes as she climbed the steps and focused on the image of that tower.

There was more than one image, now that she was concentrating on it. There were thousands. She recalled seeing this city from a great many angles.

This wasn't that tower. She wasn't there yet. This was one of the many surrounding structures. But it was close. She was on a path that would lead her there. She could almost see it in those hazy memories. If she tried, she could see the path laid out before her.

Because she was *there*.

She watched it being built.

Stairways and corridors and bridges spanning terrifying heights, rising ever upward into the sky, so very slowly, *maddeningly* slow, like the creeping march of the glaciers, but glimpsed in sleepy increments across countless ages, like stop-motion effects in movies, often leaping forward hundreds and even thousands of years at a time.

She was there with the sentinels. They showed it to her. They *shared it with her,* so that she would know the way *now.*

She was where she was supposed to be. She only had to keep moving. The other one would keep her safe until she reached her destination. Those were the jobs they were given all those endless ages ago.

Or was that merely what they wanted her to think?

She supposed it didn't matter much. Now that she was all alone, trusting the sentinels was the only choice she had.

She trudged onward, uncertain, afraid, and so dreadfully alone...

Chapter 17

Wayne stepped out of the cramped passage and onto another walkway looking out over the temple's bizarre ecosystem.

"Wow..." whispered Andrea, shining her light down onto a clump of huge, bluish leaves growing up from a field of fiery orange grass. "This place is pretty freaky."

He nodded. It was, indeed. Although he wasn't sure it compared to the things she'd described seeing on her way here. A murderous cultist with jedi mind trick powers? Towering horse legs capable of running a car off the road? A sentient street full of happiness-devouring apartment buildings? Hellish hospitals? A traveling town with a literal goddess for its lone resident? And all that before even setting foot in the Denselands.

She was a complete mess. Not just the reeking black mud that covered every inch of her, but her usually cute hair was a mat of crusted sludge with two stiff tails jutting down behind her shoulders. All that filth made it difficult to tell just how many scrapes and bruises she'd gathered, but he was pretty sure there was a black eye under there. There was a hole in the sleeve of her tee shirt. And then there was the fact that she was barefoot. She'd clearly been through a lot.

He still couldn't believe it when she said she was separated from Everett and Violet by none other than the very same ghost that murdered him back in that stone city. Was that Erin's goal all along? To bring the three of them together? It made a strange sort of sense when he added up all the pieces. Andrea apparently had the ability to communicate with ghosts and see glimpses of the spirit world in some capacity, including ghostly passages that were invisible to everyone else. And he'd actually *been* a ghost four times now. That was a lot they suddenly had in common.

But then again, maybe they weren't the same at all. He wasn't able to see the ghost tunnel. Andrea called it a "murk passage" and said she could identify it by some kind of thick black fog that collected in ribbons that crisscrossed the stone surfaces. (The way she described it reminded him of those dangerous killing vines, which wasn't a pleasant comparison.) But no matter how hard he tried, he couldn't see them with his own eyes, even when she showed him exactly where they were.

She said that Erin told her they weren't what they seemed, what-ever that meant, and that she'd understand it when she was dead. This, of course, made him curious as to whether he'd been able to under-stand any of this madness while *he* was dead. But of course, he could never remember what went on while he was deceased, so it didn't seem to matter one way or the other.

He was so confused. Just what was Erin doing? She delivered the thorn to Olivia at the reception, then *died* to protect both it and her. Then she came to Olivia's rescue in Gutler's Weep as a helpful spirit. Then she fucking *murdered* him. For a minute or two, anyway. And now she was helping Andrea learn to use her own special abilities to navigate ghost tunnels?

He held onto Olivia's hand as they crossed the walkway, his thoughts churning. He could feel her clinging to him, uneasy about being up so high without any railings.

Somewhere out in that surrounding darkness, he could hear more hounds.

"Ugh," groaned Andrea. "I remember *that* sound."

He shined his light out over the strange landscape below them. "Lucky you didn't run into them before now."

"I've been too busy stumbling around in murk," she grumbled. "Which is like *darker than dark*? So I can't see anything, even with my flashlight."

"That sounds terrifying," said Olivia.

"Yes. It was."

"But for all we know," said Wayne, "one of those 'murk tunnels' might be our only way out of here."

"I sure hope not," she replied, sounding exhausted.

The next passage appeared from the gloom ahead of them. A square of black emptiness against the shadowy gray stone.

Below them, three reddish-brown shapes emerged from the dark-ness as Andrea shined her light down. For a second or two, it didn't process what he was looking at. He couldn't hear them, after all. He could hear their claws tearing through the dirt, but those deadly scales weren't moving.

They disappeared from sight as they ran below them, then emerged from the other side and vanished back into the darkness again.

"Were those hounds?" whispered Olivia, her nails biting into him again.

"Silent mode?" guessed Andrea.

"They can't always be making that noise," Wayne reasoned. "It'd be hard to catch prey when it can hear you coming from a mile away." That was why they didn't trust the hound passages, even when they couldn't hear anything. Albert figured that much out on his first trip down there.

"Is that where we were before?" wondered Olivia. "Down there with *them*?"

"I didn't see any disturbed soil," he reasoned. "There's probably an upper and a lower section. It looks a little farther down than it did before."

She nodded, relieved, but the truth was that he wasn't sure about any of that. It might have all been wishful thinking. However, it was hard to imagine that even the Keeper and the sentinels would have risked dumping them that far into hound territory. No matter how he looked at it, it just didn't make sense.

But then again, nothing about any of this made any sense…

Olivia tugged at his arm, urging him to move faster, and he picked up his pace.

"Kind of funny the three of us would wind up together again, isn't it?" said Andrea.

"That's right!" realized Olivia. "Just like that night!"

"Funny," he agreed. For a while there, between escaping Gilbert House for the second time and reuniting with Albert, Brandy and Nicole, it had just been the three of them making their way through the temple and its labyrinths. But he didn't really want to think too much about that night. Things didn't exactly go as well as he would've liked for him, having died and all. And it was still a little awkward remembering how he and Andrea had seen each other naked down there…

The next passage presented three options for continuing on. Olivia let go of him and examined each one carefully. "I don't feel anything scary," she reported after a moment. "But I feel like maybe this way?" She pointed to the left.

"That's just like back on the mountain," Andrea recalled.

"That's my thing, I guess. Some kind of danger-sensing fortune telling or something."

"Better than creepy ghost stuff."

"Maybe." She took hold of Wayne's arm again as they continued onward.

"Does that mean all of us had something?" he wondered as he pushed his way through the darkness with his flashlight. "I mean, we already knew that Albert and Brandy were psychic."

"Not Nikki, I guess," said Andrea. "Gina and Ada both said so."

"Weird," said Olivia.

"I know, right. How's *she* the normie? She's a complete overachiever in, like, *everything*. She's the one who's out jogging before I ever drag out of bed in the mornings. How does she not have the most badass psychic powers of all of us?"

"Main character energy," she agreed.

Wayne found himself distracted by the mention of Ada. Gina's so-called goddess, the one she called the "Great Beholder," who she said sent her to look after Andrea in the first place.

Goddesses and spirit worlds and sentient streets… His head was still reeling from all of that, and yet he, himself, had experienced a mysterious trailer park woman, zombie animals and even a fairy circle.

Gilbert House was seeming less weird with each new thing he learned about.

"Murk," said Andrea, her flashlight fixed on the ceiling ahead of them.

"Where?" asked Olivia, yanking him to a stop so abruptly that he stumbled a little.

He couldn't see anything, but then again he wasn't supposed to, was he? Only Andrea could do that. It was *her* thing. The reason she was here. All he had was a Get Out of Death Free card, and even that wasn't guaranteed. "Yeah, where?" he asked.

Andrea was sliding her light across the ceiling and walls. "Everywhere," she replied.

Chapter 18

(*What's your name?*)

"Everett," he replied, his voice clear and crisp in the heavy silence. His name was Everett.

But as his head cleared, he found that everything had changed yet again.

He was no longer floating in a grotesque, inverted perversion of the City Beyond Memory, adrift in a nothing-verse of shadows and deafening not-sounds, skirting the very edge of madness at the far reaches of eternity. Instead, he was standing in the middle of a forest. But not that vast, black forest outside the city walls. This was somewhere different. The mottled moonlight shining through the canopy above was proof enough of that.

This was a different kind of dark and shadowy. It was mysterious and gloomy, but in that peaceful sort of way that he liked. He'd spent many a moonlit night these past couple years exploring the quiet places the world kept hidden away. It was his favorite time of day, when he felt most free. When he felt the most *alive*.

His mother never let him go out in the moonlight, after all.

But this wasn't like any forest he'd ever seen before, either. These trees were nothing at all like the night trees out in the Wood, but they were strange, all the same. Tall and thin and oddly prickly, as if they were nothing more than bundles of sharp sticks twisted together. Their branches bristled upward and outward like great, stiff brooms stabbing at the star-littered sky. Even their leaves were spindly, like narrow palm fronds bristling with needles. Fat vines with broad, round leaves weaved their way up the frayed trunks and throughout the branches, filling in the gaps while blades of bluish-gray grass the size of playground slides thrust their way up from the ground. It was the densest forest he'd ever seen, making it impossible to pass through except for a narrow, winding path laid out before him, carpeted in a strange, pale moss that sparkled where the moonlight touched it.

It made him think of a jungle, but it was neither hot nor humid. In fact, it was pleasantly cool. He felt surprisingly light on his feet. And everywhere he looked, the colors were so vibrant. It was like a vivid painting brought to life. It even *smelled* different. There was an odd sort of sweetness to the air. With a hint of petrichor. And it felt...well, he wasn't actually sure how to describe it. *Richer*, perhaps? Crisper? This air was much easier to breathe than that heavy, sickly atmosphere outside the impassible wall.

First Gutler's Weep, then the Wood and that train station. The Denselands. That sprawling sandstone city. Then the Red Waste, the stone circle deep in the Eeshee's jungle and the gouging station. The Impassible wall and the City Beyond Memory. That inverted nightmare. And now *this* place...

Was this happening to everyone, or was he the only one getting the extended tour?

He brushed aside a large leaf that was hanging in his way and examined the crooked, mossy path. Was he supposed to go that way? He glanced behind him to discover that it dwindled to nothing within a few paces. Indeed, forward appeared to be the only option. Another case of the mysterious Keeper leading him by the hand.

He started walking, pushing his way through the crowding leaves, wondering what might be waiting for him. Because *something* must be at the end of this path. There was obviously something here he was meant to find. One didn't get dropped in a mystery forest at one end of a blatantly unmistakable path that lead nowhere interesting.

It went on and on, weaving through the lone gap in those countless, frizzy trunks. He pushed through leaves and branches, stepping between blades of grass twice as tall as he was.

He walked and walked and walked. For what felt like hours.

"And what did you eventually find at the end of the path?"

"Nothing at first," he replied. "It started getting darker. I couldn't tell if the moon was going down or if the sky was clouding over or if the woods were just getting too dense to let the light in. I could barely see the glittering moss."

"But you *did* find what was waiting for you."

He nodded. "Yeah. I finally got to the end of it."

"And?" pressed Dr. Gearlet, his bushy, gray eyebrows creeping up behind those glasses that he always seemed to be looking over rather than through.

Everett frowned at himself as he struggled to remember it all. "It's fuzzy."

"Do your best."

He wasn't sure why he was so interested. It was just a silly dream. He might as well be making it all up as he went. But Dr. Gearlet was always interested in stuff like this. Something about the inner workings of his subconsciousness...or something...?

He didn't know much about how the world worked, but he understood that the people responsible for taking him away from his mother following his near-death experience in that cold lake wanted to make sure he hadn't suffered any severe emotional trauma.

Hence the psychologist.

He didn't *feel* traumatized. In fact, he felt positively *free*. Better than he'd ever felt in his life. Being out from under his mother's oppressive shadow was like being born anew, like feeling the sun on his skin for the first time in his life. Everything in the world that used to frighten him was now suddenly new and exciting. He just wanted to go back outside. He wanted to explore the world. But instead he was stuck here, talking about his dreams, of all things.

Everyone kept calling it a formality. As if using that word made it any less pointless. He wasn't *damaged* in that lake. He was *repaired*. He was *healed*. If anything, it was the *old* him who was broken. But he knew by now that there was no point in saying so. It would only drag this whole boring process out that much longer.

"I think the path opened up," he recalled. "I remember it getting brighter again. That sparkly moss was everywhere. Like the whole forest floor was covered in glitter."

"And what was waiting beyond the glitter?"

He sat there a moment, trying to remember. Parts of the dream were so vivid, but like any dream, it was riddled with holes, missing fragments, gaps in his memory. He remembered being tired and wondering how long he'd been walking. He remembered stopping and looking around, wondering where his flashlight had gone. He remembered looking back the way he came and thinking that it looked so much darker there, as if someone were following along and turning out the lights behind him. It was an odd thing to think, he thought, as if anyone could just turn off the moonlight, and yet it was an odd sort of place.

When he looked forward again, he realized there was a flicker of light up ahead. A fire? He pushed forward, eager to see where the curious path was leading him.

"So you found a house?" said Dr. Gearlet.

"I guess so," he replied. "But it wasn't like any house I've ever seen before."

"How so?"

"It wasn't so much a house as a mound of sticks and mud and that glittering moss. The door was..." He screwed up his face as he tried to think of how to describe it. "Sort of like a flap, I guess. Part of it was stiff, but part of it was malleable, like cloth. It folded up in this weird sort of way, twisting and tucking into itself so it was out of the way. I don't even know how I knew how to open it." He paused here and replayed that last sentence in his head to make sure he was still making sense. It felt like a mouthful, but he wasn't sure how else to say it. "But I guess that's how dreams are, huh? Sometimes you just know stuff."

"So you went inside," surmised Dr. Gearlet, urging him to continue.

He nodded. "I figured that was what I was supposed to do."

"And what did you see inside?"

"I remember staring at the lantern hanging from the ceiling. It looked strange. More like an artsy kind of yard ornament than a lantern. One of those kinds that spins when the wind blows, you know?" One of his neighbors growing up used to have those in her yard. He used to like staring out the window and watching them twirl on breezy days. "Except that it was burning inside instead of spinning."

It was such a curious design. He wasn't even sure how it worked. But apparently Dr. Gearlet wasn't interested in it, because he was already pushing forward: "And what did you see in the light of the lantern?"

The house—or whatever this strange mound of mud and moss and sticks might have been—looked bigger on the inside than it did on the outside, which didn't make much sense…but it *was* just a dream, he supposed. "There wasn't any furniture. Just…strange-looking mounds of earth. It had a sort of caveman vibe about it, I guess. There weren't any windows, but there were scraps of stuff stuck to the walls all over the place. I don't know if they were supposed to be part of the structure or some kind of decoration or something."

"Tell me about the opening at the back of the room."

"It was like a tunnel. It was covered in that glittery moss."

"You crawled through it."

He nodded. How long had he been here? Shouldn't the session time be over by now? He didn't remember it ever dragging on like this before.

"What was at the other end of the glittering tunnel, Everett?"

He sat there, frowning down at the floor, trying to recall it. There was *something*… He was sure of it. Something *important*.

There was a reason he was sent there, after all, a reason he was snatched away from Violet and plunged into that nightmarish void and dragged through that inverted city.

He tipped his head to one side, confused. Wait... Was that part of the dream, too? Something didn't feel right.

"Who did you speak with?" pressed Dr. Gearlet.

Who? Was there some*body* waiting for him at the end of the glittering tunnel? Did he have a conversation?

Something flickered in his memory. A shadowy space with tattered things dangling all around him, making it difficult to see. They looked like the same things that were plastered all over the walls in the first room, what he thought were old rags. But they didn't feel like cloth now that he was walking through them. They had a leathery sort of texture that made his skin crawl when they brushed against him.

What was this place? And why was Dr. Gearlet so interested in dredging up this old dream, anyway? What did his dreams have to do with *anything*?

"Who did you speak with at the end of the glittering path, Everett?" Dr. Gearlet asked again. There was something unpleasant about the tone of his voice. That ever-present patience had vanished. He sounded unhappy. "Who was waiting for you there?"

Something hot and sour seemed to be squirming deep in the pit of his stomach. He stared through the dangling tatters of what he was now quite sure was flesh, into the deepest, darkest part of the room. Someone was standing there, a shadowy figure that he was quite convinced wasn't human, a menacing, monstrous shape staring right back at him, waiting for him to come closer.

"What was in those shadows?"

Everett stared at the ominous shape looming behind the streamers of tattered flesh, his heart pounding. Something was very, very wrong. He shouldn't be here. He was going to mess everything up.

"What did you see?" demanded Dr. Gearlet, his voice rising with a sinister glee with each word he spoke. "What frightened you so badly that you never left that place again?"

Chapter 19

Keith picked up the familiar pair of denim shorts and added it to the growing pile under his arm. So far, he'd collected both her shoes, both socks, her tank top, her bra and now her shorts. She was down to just her panties now. He wasn't typically one to complain, but why the hell was she *stripping*?

It wasn't as if it weren't like her…but *here*, of all places?

But then again, he recalled Andrea telling him that they all had to be naked when they went down to the first temple five years ago. Something about the smell of their clothes attracting the hounds or something? He wasn't sure that part made sense, but Andrea wasn't the most thorough storyteller. She tended to get off track. So maybe he was missing a detail or two that might help explain it.

At least she was leaving him a trail to follow. Erin told him that the god inhabiting Hotdog's rotting corpse was now inside her head somehow. She didn't explain it, but it sounded as if *she* were now the puppet. It was possible the moldy old deity was stripping her naked for the sheer fun of it. Or maybe there was some reason he needed her to disrobe.

Or, just maybe, some part of her was consciously doing it, specifically to give him something to follow. Because without the trail of laundry, he wasn't sure how he'd have known which way she went. And it hadn't gone unnoticed that he was only that one pair of panties from losing her trail. *Then* what was he going to do?

(*You have to protect her. No matter what.*)

No matter what… He had a bad feeling about this. And that feeling was growing worse with each step he took. Something unpleasant was looming ahead of him. An ominous weight that he couldn't quite describe.

He remembered the first night he ever spent with her. She was so amazing back then. An absolute dream. So gorgeous. So sexy. So *fun*. The best part was how he kept making her laugh. He'd always loved being able to make the girls laugh. But there was something extra special about *her* laugh. She was more than just an amazing body. Everything about her was positively *enchanting*.

He never told anyone, but she was the only woman he ever dated who actually broke his heart.

Wow... He was pretty sure he had a concussion. Only a head injury could make him think about nonsense like this. He should probably get himself checked out as soon as he got home. Whenever that might be.

He looked down at the clothes tucked under his arm. It was so surreal. Why her? Why *him*? What was it about the two of them that the universe was fighting so hard to shove together?

Ahead of him, the passage he was following split into two. He stopped and considered both directions. Which way should he go? If he chose wrong, he might never find her in this endless darkness.

He stepped into the left passageway and thrust his light as far in as he could reach. Then he did the same with the right. There was another passage branching off from this one, but that was all he could see from here.

Cautiously, he crept farther down the right path, his light sweeping the floor and walls. Then he peered into the next corridor. He was ready to retreat and try the left passage, but something caught his eye just before he gave up, something on the floor of the passage, little more than a shadow in the gloom.

"Panties," he sighed as he hurried forward.

He felt a little bit like a creep picking them up. She was going to accuse him of being a pervert. He just knew it. But he couldn't just leave them there. She was probably going to want them back.

He added them to the pile, then pushed onward. She was butt naked now. There were no more clothes left to lead the way. Unless she was going to start shedding jewelry next, which wouldn't be nearly as easy to spot in this gloom, she was out of breadcrumbs. If she was too far ahead, he simply wouldn't find her.

She came this way. There was no doubt about that. (Unless, he supposed, she tossed them this way and then went a different direction, but why would she do something like that?)

He must be close. She couldn't have *that* great of a lead on him. Could she? How long was he out back there? How much time had he lost?

The passage ahead opened up into a large chamber of some sort. He didn't hear anything, and yet he imagined that he was looking at another chamber of the hounds, and that she was inevitably walking her naked ass straight toward a very violent and bloody death.

But that was a silly thought. What kind of senile old god would puppet her all this way rather than just fling her over the ledge in the room they just left?

No. It wasn't hounds. As he drew closer to the chamber, his light fell on the floor. Coarse, black earth instead of smooth, gray stone.

The meadow...

(*It's a bad place. It gets in your head.*)

No. She wouldn't go in there, would she? She was terrified of the meadow.

He hurried to the end of the corridor and shined his light into the room.

Nicole was there, her lean, naked back glowing against the darkness all around her. He could see every detail of her night tree tattoo, so starkly black against her tanned flesh. She was on her feet, visibly unharmed, but she was standing up to her ankles in a pool of water, staring up at a dead tree looming over her.

(*When two trees in darkness stand, do what must be done.*)

He didn't hesitate. He dropped her clothes onto the passage floor and rushed in after her.

Chapter 20

Nicole didn't remember how she ended up here again, staring up into those eerie, dead branches. She remembered trudging through that endless black wasteland for what felt like ages, trying so desperately to reach that distant shape on the black horizon. But everything started to grow hazy. She became confused. Lost. Had she reached her destination? Was this what was waiting there for her?

Why did she keep going back and forth between that foul black sea and this dreadful room deep in the belly of the Temple of the Blind? What did it mean? What was she supposed to do?

"Nicole!"

She blinked up at those branches, her mind sluggish. That was Keith's voice. Was he here to save her again? He kept doing that. Every time she screwed up and thought it was over, he came for her.

It was nice. Her own dashing prince, swooping in to save the day. But she couldn't understand why. She'd been so terrible to him, even though he was never anything but nice to her. She was so determined to push him away. Why was she such a fuck-up? What was wrong with her? She didn't *deserve* to be saved by him.

The truth was that she didn't hate that he was nice to her. It was sweet. He didn't mean anything by it. She knew that. It was that she hated that she couldn't explain *why* it bothered her. Because he'd never believe in a million years what she and her friends went through in the depths of that temple. How could he? There was literally no proof. It didn't exist anymore. What did they have? A box full of junk? A strange medallion? Some old newspaper articles? A few scars? That stuff wasn't proof. Not really. The only real proof left was Gilbert House and they could never go back there again. They all promised not to tell anyone. There could be legal ramifications. People had died. There were bodies that were never found.

No matter what she did, she could never have what Brandy and Albert had. She could never have what Olivia and Wayne had. She didn't have someone who went through it all with her, who understood why she had nightmares, why she sometimes needed to keep the light on when she slept, why she wasn't a big fan of horror movies anymore.

She didn't have that...

Until she did. Until he turned up in the middle of this crazy journey and saw it all with his own eyes. But it was too late now. She'd been so horrible to him. She took out all her frustrations on him, turned him into all the things that were wrong with the world in her mind.

He hated her. And he had every right to hate her.

"Snap out of it!"

She heard the sound of splashing in the silence. Water rushed past her ankles. A hand grabbed her arm.

"Nicole!"

She blinked, confused. Where was she? What was she thinking about? She was dreaming about the meadow again, wasn't she?

Keith... She left him back in that passageway. He was hurt. She needed to get back to him.

Except he was right here. Was he a part of the dream, too? What was real and what wasn't? It was getting harder and harder to tell the difference. Had she *ever* been able to tell the difference? Had anything *ever* been real?

Keith cursed. He sounded frustrated. Was he angry at her again? He should be. She deserved it.

She felt so dizzy. What happened? She remembered Hotdog Zombie falling into that pit and then...

Wait...

Where was she?

She stared up at those dead branches, her heart filling with dread. Was this *not* a dream? Was she actually here in this room?

Keith scooped her up into his arms, jolting her. She let out a startled gasp as her head finally cleared.

This was no dream. This was the meadow! Terror filled every cell in her body. Why would she be in the *meadow*? What could possess her to come to such a place? The Keeper, himself, told her never to come here!

She wrapped her arms around Keith's neck and clung to him. Was she going to be okay? Had this room done something to her? Where were her clothes? She didn't understand any of this.

No... There was *one* thing she understood. Keith was here. He came for her. He rescued her. Again. For all the shit she'd put him through, he charged into the *meadow* for her. He was carrying her to safety right now, his strong arms gripping her, her naked body pressed against his.

Just like how Albert once carried Brandy out of the fear room...

She'd always been a little jealous...if only of that one magical little moment…

She pressed herself harder against him. It had been so long since she felt his skin like this…

Why was she so stupid?

He carried her out of the meadow and back into the labyrinth, where he knelt down and gently lowered her to the floor. The stone was cold on her bare butt. It made her gasp.

She loosened her grip around his neck but didn't let go. Before he could pull away, she kissed him.

If he was so wrong, why did he feel so very right? What was wrong with her all these months? She held on, not wanting to let go. But finally, she pulled away.

"Why are you so much trouble?" he grunted.

"Because I'm a colossal fuck-up," she replied. She opened her eyes and reached up to kiss him again, but she stopped. Something was wrong. His pale blue eyes shimmered. His face was contorted in pain. "What's…?"

He let go of her and fell backward with an agonized groan.

"Keith?" She sat up and leaned over him, frightened. "What's wrong? What happened?" She looked him over, trying to find where he was hurt. Was it his head? Did Hotdog Zombie give him a concussion? Or was it maybe a broken a rib?

Then she saw his feet. His shoes were gone and his socks were bloody.

"Oh my god!" she hissed. She reached down and pulled one of them off.

There were holes in his foot. Dozens of them, each one about the diameter of a pencil.

"What did this?"

"Something in the ground," he grunted.

The ground? She looked back toward the meadow, the bare black earth. Were there spikes in there? No, that couldn't be it. They were on the sides and tops of his feet as well. It looked more like something had stabbed him.

And as she watched, she realized she could see something moving in there. Something beneath the dirt, something churning, like worms wriggling beneath the surface… "Oh god…" she breathed. "Oh my god…oh my god…"

(*Stay away from the meadow. There is nothing for you there but pain and death.*)

He ran out into that nightmare for her? And then carried her out again? Why would he do that? It made no sense! He should've just left her there! She didn't deserve to be saved by him, much less like *this*!

She removed his other sock and found that his other foot was no better. Were these bite marks? No… There was no pattern to them. Stingers? Had he walked through some kind of monstrous scorpion nest? Whatever they were, they weren't good. He was clearly in a lot of pain.

And she had no first aid supplies. There was no one to call for help. She was all he had.

It didn't make sense. How did *she* get all the way in there without sustaining those same injuries? She glanced down at her own feet, half-expecting to see them punctured as well, but they were fine. They were just muddy.

He cried out. Whatever those injuries were, they were obviously excruciating.

"Oh my god," she gasped again, fresh tears streaming down her face. "Oh my god…oh my god…oh my god…"

Chapter 21

"Why's the dead guy *talking*?" squealed Brandy.

"Ain't dead," replied Corey. He wasn't looking up at her. He'd gone back to rummaging around in the bloody mess he was sitting in.

"His ass needs a separate bus ticket!" she yelled. "*He has to be dead!*"

"Can't kill something that ain't alive," he explained.

"*What?*"

"Please don't make him talk," groaned Austin. "He's slow enough as it is."

"You stay out of this!" she snapped at him, her head spinning. What was happening here? What did he mean this guy wasn't alive? Did it have something to do with all the stuff coming out of him that wasn't supposed to be coming out of a person? Because those weren't guts. The guy appeared to have been stuffed with piles of strings!

And what the hell was this place, anyway? It wasn't like any other chamber she'd encountered, not in this temple and not in the first. It looked like something off the set of a creepy science fiction movie. There were strange, triangular columns stretching the height of the room, all arranged around a sort of hourglass shape in the middle. The walls were covered in odd, blocky protrusions, some rounded and some square and boxy, some covered in small holes, others carved with strange, squiggly patterns. And there were several lengths of what looked like various lengths of stone rods sticking down from the ceiling. It was so strikingly different from the bland, perfectly flat surfaces that dominated the other spaces within the temples that it baffled the mind. It looked for all the world as if even the sentinels themselves had gone mad while carving it.

"Who *is* he?" asked Albert.

"Austin," replied Corey. "Third group. Stone road."

"With Wayne and Olivia?" he deduced.

"Yep." He glanced up at them then. "That reminds me. They were askin' 'bout you two. Worried."

"They are here!" She turned and looked at Albert. "Just like you said!"

He nodded. "They must've come to the same conclusion about

us."

She wasn't sure how to feel about that. On one hand, she knew that Olivia and Wayne had made it this far. But on the other hand, that was two more of her friends she was worried about. The cat lady's dire warning swirled in her head.

Was this Austin guy one of the two she told them would die? Or did he not count since he apparently wasn't really dead?

This was all so confusing.

She eyed Corey with mounting distaste. "How can you just sit there covered in his blood?"

"Easy," said Corey. "Ain't blood."

"What?"

He lifted his hand and rubbed his thumb and middle finger together. "Don't feel like blood. Too oily. Not getting sticky."

"Well it sure *stinks* like blood," grumbled Brandy. The smell was making her feel nauseous.

"It does," he agreed. "Looks like it, too. But it ain't. Doesn't even work the same as blood. More like the hard drive on a computer, but liquid."

"It's like listening to a baboon try to teach Shakespeare," growled Austin. "You might as well describe the intricate workings of a nuclear accelerator with a stick and a rock."

"That's not blood," pondered Albert. "Those aren't organs. And you said he wasn't alive. So what *is* he? Some kind of android? Like in *Star Trek*?"

"That's what I thought, too," replied Corey. "But it ain't that simple."

"What the fuck is simple about an *actual android*?" asked Brandy, frazzled.

"To understand *him*, you gotta understand what this place is."

"The temple?" asked Albert, glancing around at all the strange, stone shapes protruding from the walls and ceiling.

"It's a machine."

"A gross oversimplification," grumbled Austin.

"He's right," Corey agreed. "But it ain't somethin' can be fully explained. Missing pieces. Changed rules."

"Different physics," Albert reasoned.

"Exactly." He reached into Austin's gaping lower half and pulled out a dripping loop of gory strings, making Brandy turn away in disgust. "The stone it's made from's unique. Nothin' else like it 'cross all the worlds that ever were. It exists across all three universes, natural, supernatural and unnatural, all at the same time. And it has the ability to contain and conduct all sorts of energy and data."

"Or in less moronic terminology," sighed Austin, "the stoneworks of the Faceless Ones are constructed from a primordial foundation element. Ageless. Pandimensional. Able to retain the rules of bygone realities."

"Magic rock," agreed Corey, nodding confidently.

"Magic has nothing to do with it."

"Whole place is one massive *vehicle*," he went on, ignoring him.

"Vehicle?" asked Brandy, confused. Just a moment ago, he called it a "machine." She supposed a vehicle *was* a kind of machine, but was he saying this whole temple was some kind of...*car*?

Corey reached into one of the bloody piles and began unraveling one fine string after another, gathering them in his left hand. "Imagine a giant spaceship leaving a dying earth with a destination millions of lightyears away. Its only purpose is to deliver its cargo—us remaining people—to its new home and nothin' else. One direction. One speed. No stops."

"Intergalactic communications towers..." muttered Albert.

She looked up at him, confused. "What?"

"Back on the road...before we were separated..." Then he frowned. "But that wasn't you...was it? That was...?"

She squinted at him. What was he going on about?

But he only shook his head. "Nothing. Forget it. Just...déjà vu, I guess."

"Okay..."

"This place is like that," Corey went on. "Just a great big ship hurtling on its way, doing its one job. Except instead of traveling through space, it's meant to travel through time."

"Now it's a time machine?" asked Brandy, puzzled.

"Stupid analogy," sneered Austin. "But not entirely wrong. You *could* think of it more as a time *capsule*."

"Sure," agreed Corey. "But a really important one. One that can't be disturbed or lost or damaged. One that has to be dug up at exactly the right moment."

"Don't open 'til Christmas," said Albert, nodding. "Hence the fact that it's buried behind an impassible wall in the deepest reaches of the Wood."

"Yep." He finished plucking the fine strings from the gory mess and then wrapped the entire bundle around Austin's middle finger. Brandy saw as she watched this that there were other bundles already tied around his ring and little fingers. Was he organizing them? How did he know which was which? How could he tell the difference? They all looked the same to her.

"Austin's part of the machine," he went on. "Sort of like a bootup disk. Without him, the door can't be opened."

"How does *that* work?" asked Albert.

"His job," explained Corey, "was to enter the main shaft of this terminal and be uploaded." He gestured at a small, shadowy space behind where he was sitting. "That would've required the contacts to be driven forcibly into his body. Sorta like plugging in a modem."

"Fucking ouch..." muttered Brandy.

"But he got surprised by somethin' nasty waiting here for him. Ripped him right in half. So now I gotta hook him up manually."

Albert shook his head. "Okay. But...the first temple didn't have anything like that. We just made our way through it and opened the door."

"Didn't it?" asked Austin.

Brandy glanced over at Albert, confused. "*Did* it?"

"The first doorway didn't demand any sacrifices?" Austin pressed. "No one left behind?" He lifted one gory hand and let it drip dramatically. "No one who left their life's essence *spilled* into the heart of the machine?"

"Wait..." sighed Brandy. "He doesn't mean..."

Albert met her gaze. "Beverly?"

"No..." she breathed. That couldn't be right. Beverly wasn't a part of any of that. She was never supposed to be there. She was literally the *flaw* in the system. A psychic bystander poisoned by the pull of the temple through the monstrous hallways of Gilbert House, driven crazy by a maddening desire to seek something unreachable to her. Without her, Olivia never would have been trapped in Gilbert House and her three companions never would have died in those dark hallways. Lucas Kneede used her obsession with Gilbert House to try sabotaging them all.

Or...was that only the story the Sentinel Queen told them...?

She was so confused.

"Each doorway serves a very specific purpose in the Keeper's greater machine," explained Austin. "But all of them utilize the same basic components. There will always be one of us. And we will always be consumed by the machine."

Brandy couldn't wrap her head around it. Beverly... She'd felt so much guilt all these years, wondering what they should've done differently. But was she always meant to go that way? And for that matter, was she never even human to begin with? Was she all fake blood and strings inside, too?

Albert shook his head and looked at Brandy. "This is... I don't even..." He sighed and then turned his gaze back to Corey. "How do you know all this stuff?"

"Dunno," he replied, sounding positively cheerful. "Just do. Soon as I got close to that huge wall, I just understood things."

"Preprogrammed knowledge, imbedded in hereditary DNA," Austin droned, managing to sound bored. "Essentially a form of controlled and directed reincarnation. He carries in his subconscious memory banks the basic blueprints of the Faceless Ones' master design. They effectively turned the entire human race into a delivery system for the information that would end up buried inside his head."

"Cool," said Corey without pausing what he was doing.

"Although there's no accounting for what kind of intellect might inherit such information," he sighed.

"Don't be rude!" snapped Brandy. Who was this guy? Corey was literally doing his job for him because he got himself chopped in half and this was how he spoke to him?

Albert ignored the rude half-man. "So you just...know how this guy works? And how he's supposed to tie into this room?"

"I know *lots* of things," said Corey. "For example, if I do this..." He reached into the confounding pile of bloody strings and plucked two of them out as if there were any way to tell them apart. Then he twisted one around the other and held them between his thumb and forefinger. Nothing seemed to happen, but Austin's expression soured. He looked irritated. "...then he can only talk in vegetables."

Brandy scrunched up her face at him, confused. "What?"

"Spinach kale green bean rutabaga," growled Austin, sounding angry. "Cabbage corn."

"Oh!" she said, bewildered. "Vegetables..."

"That can't be a real thing," said Albert. "That's some Dreamworks movie nonsense right there."

Corey chuckled.

"Lettuce onion bell pepper!" shouted Austin.

"This is weird," said Albert.

"I'm *so* confused right now," agreed Brandy.

"It's not so different from the human brain, really," explained Corey. "You're always hearing about people who suffered serious head injuries and their personalities suddenly change. A really nice guy suddenly becomes a total asshole. A jerk nobody likes turns kind. There was a guy who woke up from an accident once and could only speak Spanish."

"I heard about that, I think..." said Albert, thoughtful.

"I can patch him into the machine manually," Corey went on. "Like he said, I know how. Born with the knowledge hidden in my brain. But it'll take time. It would've been a lot easier if he didn't let himself get ambushed."

"Carrot turnip," huffed Austin.

"Language, please," said Corey.

"I like him better this way," decided Brandy.

Albert nodded.

"This is one of three terminals that opens the way to the door. The other two are somewhere I couldn't reach if I wanted to. Takes a certain kind of special to even get to them. Special like me, I s'pose. People with special connections to the other two universes. People who just know things."

"Gina," breathed Brandy.

He glanced up, surprised. "You met Gina?"

"Briefly," said Albert.

He nodded, his pudgy features turning down into a thoughtful frown. "Yeah. She's a part of the machine, too. M'sure of it."

"Which is why we were separated," Albert reasoned.

Brandy looked over at him again, surprised. He kept saying she must have some kind of special job she needed to do.

"Prob'ly," agreed Corey. "Everyone has a purpose here."

Her head was reeling. If he was right and only *she* could reach one of these terminals, then it made sense that she would've had to leave them to do it on her own.

And the truth was that she couldn't have stood there and let her walk away. She wouldn't have accepted it. She had to sneak off like she did.

"The real problem," Corey went on, "is that I can't just plug him in and leave him to it. There's too much damage. I'll have to be right here when the door opens."

"Wait..." said Brandy. "But when the first door was opened..."

"...the temple collapsed," finished Albert.

"It's not ideal," he admitted, looking up. "There's a chance I won't make it out in time."

Chapter 22

Gina pressed onward without progress. Her legs had grown tired from walking, yet those steps had carried her no closer to where she was supposed to be than when she first set off on her own. Plus, her foot was aching from where she cut herself on that glass way before she met Brandy and Albert. She wasn't sure how long she could keep this up. She'd become trapped in an inescapable loop, walking in circles, caught between two overlapping passageways, half in a realm of stone and half in one of glass. The stone one was dark and lonely and would never lead anywhere but in endless circles. The glass one loomed close enough to touch, razor-thin and infested with a strange and unnatural aura. It would take her where she needed to be, but also into the waiting teeth and claws of the terrible thing that was stalking her.

This area was different from the other parts of the labyrinth. It was unique, not merely because of the presence of the glass corridors, but because only *she* could have entered it. It called out to her when she drew near, luring her toward it even as the presence of the unnatural thing filled her with fright. Caught in the throes of the grief room's agonizing aching, she'd found herself distracted and vulnerable. Now, as she walked this fine line between worlds of lonesome stone and treacherous glass, she wondered if she'd made a mistake. Was this really where she was meant to go? Or had she allowed herself to fall into a trap? Because now that she was here, she could think of no way out of this conundrum. Her options appeared to be walking in circles until she collapsed or charging headlong at her monstrous stalker. She could choose to die slowly and pitifully or quickly and violently.

She turned her useless eyes toward the glass wall of the other labyrinth, letting her psychic gaze pass over the thing creeping on the other side of it. She still couldn't quite wrap her head around its exact form. Its shape seemed to change from moment to moment, twisting and stretching in bizarre and unnatural ways with each step it took. She couldn't even tell how many legs it was walking on. But it was apparent to her that it wasn't just blindly stalking her from that other passageway. It knew exactly where she was and what she was doing. And right now, it knew that she was paying attention to it. She sensed it bristling at her, making itself bigger, like an angry dog with its dander raised. But it wasn't anything as simple as fluffing up its fur. She didn't think it *had* fur. Or even any skin for that matter. It wasn't a living creature. And it wasn't any kind of spirit. It was something entirely *other*. Something *unnatural*. And that strange, alien body was swelling and shifting as she attempted to observe it, putting on a display of aggression, changing not merely its size but its very *dimensions*.

And it was eager to pick a fight.

Again, she turned her blind gaze forward. She wouldn't fare well in a direct confrontation with it. It was so much bigger than she was. And was it even possible to kill something that was never alive to begin with? How would something like that work?

It thrust itself at the glass separating them. She didn't scream. She didn't even whimper. All those years of ignoring the terrible things that only she could see had steeled her against any such outbursts, the better to blend into a world full of normal people who weren't tormented by such things and therefore wouldn't believe in them. But she couldn't stop herself from cringing. And she sensed that the thing on the other side of the glass was perfectly pleased with that reaction. It swelled with perverse delight.

This thing was nasty. She could feel its unnatural consciousness worming its way into her head, a foul, almost *slimy* sensation rummaging around within her already compromised emotions and sending sickly waves of revulsion and dread coursing through her. It wasn't like the other unnatural things her psychic eye had spied lurking in the nooks and crannies of the world throughout her life. This thing was far more intelligent. It was singularly malicious. And it was entirely focused on *her*, almost as if it had come to this place specifically to find her. She could feel its monstrous attention fixed on her, not merely a random predator stalking whatever prey had happened by, but a horrific bloodhound in pursuit of a very precise quarry.

But why *her*? She wasn't anyone special. The goddess only sent her to look after Andrea, and she'd failed rather spectacularly at that task.

Was that what this was about? Was this her punishment for that failure? Having lost the one person she was sent here to protect, was this how the Temple of the Three Whispers removed unnecessary players from the Keeper's twisted game?

No. That didn't feel right. She wasn't here by chance. She was here because she felt the familiar pull of the unnatural. The passageways spread out just beyond the glass, a space within this space that only *she* could find, invisible to everyone else in the world, with the same, dreadful aura as the dreary, rain-streaked windows of Glimmering Sunrise

Place and the terrifying, unseen floors of the Vertical Design tower in Cakwetak three years ago.

"Those things aren't from the worlds of the living *or* the dead," she recalled the goddess telling her back in Cedric's Cove. "Neither spiritual *nor* psychic. Those are something else entirely. Those are things from the *other* world. The world of the unnatural. The shadows. The undefinable. The world from which the Great Enemy and his Twelve Teeth were born."

The Twelve Teeth… Her thoughts kept circling back to them. Gwilym Glum and Janon Tane. She'd met them both, looked right into their monstrous eyes and cowered at the sight. Unlike Glum, who was in every sense a disgusting monster, Tane had managed to pass for human. He made himself *likeable*, even. A good boss who seemed to truly care for his employees at the graphic design studio where the goddess sent her to work. A perfect disguise.

Her roommates back in Wisconsin even told her that he died protecting them…but was that really something monsters like that were capable of? She couldn't help wondering if it wasn't something *else* he must've been protecting that day.

She supposed it didn't matter. He was dead. That was all there was to it. And the goddess said that another—Alwyn Thrud—had vanished long ago. That still left ten. Any one of them could be responsible for the monstrosity lurking on the other side of this glass. Including the only other one whose name she knew.

Caduceus Turms.

Tane ran the graphic design studio, but the actual business—as well as the building itself—were under the control of Turms. She'd never seen him, but she'd learned that the entirety of the global supercorporation known as Vertical Industries was run by him, somehow allowing him to maintain an invisible stranglehold on the world's economy. He held the power to plunge the world into recession at his slightest whim.

Because that was what the Teeth did. They manipulated the world in some frightful way, like some all-powerful secret society in some inane-sounding conspiracy theory, herding people like cattle by seizing control of the things *they* couldn't control. Money. Emotions. Even the cycle itself.

And they did it all without anyone knowing they even existed.

No one but her.

(That was why I sent you to Vertical Design. You were the only one who could do that job. You were the only one capable of realizing what that place really

was.)

Had Turms finally found her? Did he somehow follow her into this awful place? She'd been warned that Turms wasn't like Glum or Tane. He wouldn't hesitate to kill her. He wasn't afraid of the Keeper or concerned about preserving the cycle. She'd never been able to understand how even one of the Twelve Teeth could allow the cycle to be broken, but she also never presumed to understand the minds of monsters.

She stopped walking.

On the other side of the glass, the monster stopped and watched her.

She stood there, listening to the sounds of her own heartbeat in the ominous silence. It seemed almost to echo in her ears.

It wasn't a Tooth. She knew this without a doubt. It was only a sliver of one, not unlike Glum's barely-there that attacked Nicole. A mere fraction of its monstrous whole. A shadow of a shadow. And while it reeked of that awful, unnatural aura, it wasn't entirely the same as what she felt when she was near the other two. It wasn't even what she felt when she was inside Turms' nightmare of an office tower.

Was this another one? One even nastier than Turms?

She could feel it *grinning* at her on the other side of the glass…

She took a calming breath. She was getting nowhere walking this same endless corridor. She needed to know what this thing was. She needed to know what she was dealing with.

It terrified her to her very soul, but she knew what she needed to do.

She was going to have to face it.

Chapter 23

Atop the stairs awaited an ominous rumbling.

Violet paused a few steps short of the top, shining her light into the corridor waiting there for her. She recognized that sound. It was thunder, from the storm outside. It sounded just like this when she and Everett were approaching that drenched walkway.

She didn't want to deal with that again. Her clothes hadn't fully dried from the first time. Not to mention that Everett wasn't here to protect her from those freaky draft things. How was she supposed to avoid something she couldn't see coming?

She found herself frozen in place at the thought of going back out there alone. But she couldn't just stand here forever. This was the way forward, the way the other one showed her all those impossible ages ago.

Remember this path, she thought, recalling the words spoken to her in that dreamlike haze. *It waits for you where the circle closes.*

She managed to take another step, but her foot felt like lead.

"Get a grip," she muttered to herself. She hated feeling afraid like this. She wasn't some weak little girl.

Except she knew it wasn't about being weak. It was about being *blind.* Everett was able to see things that she couldn't. Without him, she could end up walking straight into something monstrous. If he hadn't been with her, those storm drafts would have... Well, she didn't really know *what* would've happened. But she saw the look on his face after he pushed her out of the way of one of them. All that cheerful enthusiasm had vanished. For a moment, he was wearing the haunted expression of a traumatized war veteran. The very memory of that look on his face sent a chill up her spine. What did he sense back there? What almost happened to her? Would she be dead right now if not for him?

She forced herself to take another step, then another. She didn't want to go back out into that storm, but standing here wasn't an option.

She reached the top of the steps and trudged forward, her flashlight washing across the stone surfaces all around her, eyes peeled for anything dangerous. She hated feeling afraid, but fear had its proper place. And this wasn't simply being afraid of the dark or of being alone or even of some impending horror movie jump scare. This was fear of something *real*.

Albert and Brandy warned her about the dangers of these temples. They were supposed to be filled with strange and deadly traps. Stone spikes sharp enough to impale her before she knew she'd walked into them. Bizarre statues that could send her emotions wild and make her do unthinkable things. And monstrous guard dog things with slashing razors for skin.

But she'd seen nothing like any of that. These stone corridors were exactly as they described them, but they never said anything about storm-ravaged, invisible monster-infested bridges spanning dizzying heights. In fact, didn't they say the other temple was deep underground?

Except…it was also a huge *mountain* engulfed in flames? A portal, like the ones she and Corey had sought out, except on a much grander scale. They described it as a gateway between their world and the Wood, deep underground in one but a towering mountain in another.

It was all so confusing. Andrea mentioned something about a temple in the Wood when she was recounting her story back in All Trails Crossing, but only a vague mention that some weird stuff went down five years ago that was related to what was happening now. She mostly recounted the events that had just taken place, starting with that murderous "hotdog" guy and ending with the three of them falling out of the sky right over their campsite. Most of what she knew about the so-called "Temple of the Blind" was what Albert talked about on the carriage ride through the Wood. And it was fairly clear that he was giving her an abridged version, which was understandable, given that it sounded like a really long story.

But one of the things he'd mentioned was that this wasn't the same temple from their previous experience. He said they broke the first one. The whole place came tumbling down and they barely escaped with their lives. Although she didn't entirely understand *how* they were able to escape something like that. From this point of view, *inside* the place, the very thought of it collapsing was enough to scare the hell out of her. There was literally nowhere to go. If she were lucky, she'd be crushed flat in an instant, dead before she knew what was happening. Worst case scenario, she'd find herself trapped under a literal mountain of broken stone, unable to move, struggling for every breath, languishing for who knew how long until she finally died. Even thinking about it made her claustrophobic.

And if this really was an entirely new temple, then there was no reason to think that it would be the same. *Everything* could be different here. Like those things Everett saw in those deep, dark spaces back there in that inverted labyrinth before they were separated. Those might only exist here.

The path was curving to the left. The rumbling was growing louder. And did she just glimpse a dim flash far ahead of her?

She really didn't want to go back out into that storm. But the other one told her that she was supposed to find her way to the top of the tower at the heart of the city. In that strange memory that surfaced at the bottom of those last stairs, she'd seen the tower as it was being built. It wasn't the same structure she was in right now. That meant she was going to have to cross more bridges to get there, whether she liked it or not.

You'll remember the way when it's time.

She stopped walking, confused. She could almost remember hearing those words spoken inside her head, in answer to her concern that the city was too large and complex for anyone to navigate.

She pushed onward, pondering the weirdness of it all. *Did* she remember a long, curving corridor like this one? One perhaps leading to an exit somewhere high above the city's strange streets? Even if she did, would she be able to know it from a hundred thousand others just like it? There was no way she'd be able to navigate something like this by memory alone. It was asking too much.

And yet, perhaps she was thinking too literally. Maybe it wasn't about memorizing the complex path. Because there *was* something familiar about these gray passageways. It wasn't merely the idea of going back out into that storm that made her uneasy. She found that she simply knew that the only thing waiting at the end of this corridor was the storm. There wouldn't be anywhere else to go.

She continued onward, watching as the passage unraveled before her and those dim flashes of lightning grew steadily brighter and that rumbling grew into a trembling cacophony of roaring wind and crashing thunder.

The path didn't fork. There were no intersections for her to make decisions at. Just as she'd imagined, the curving passage ended at a single opening with the raging storm just beyond.

You'll remember the way when it's time.

And so she did. It was all there, hidden away inside her brain.

Had it been there since that sunny, Missouri forest twenty years ago? Or only five years ago, after she passed out in that Arkansas clearing? Or did she just learn the way a little while ago, when the other one took control and helped her flee the Everett-thing?

Or were those all just doorways from her various presents to the *same* time in the other one's past?

That seemed like an odd thing to think. More like something Corey would come up with. And yet it seemed to make perfect sense to her when the thought occurred to her, so maybe she was on to something there.

A tremendous flash and crash of lightning and thunder struck somewhere just outside the doorway, startling a piercing scream from her.

She *really* didn't want to go back out into that...

But she wasn't going to find Corey or the others by just standing around trying to understand things that were beyond her comprehension.

She shielded her face and stepped out into the storm.

It wasn't another bridge, she found, but an external staircase leading up the outer wall to her left. And like the bridge, it was covered by a stone roof that did very little to keep the rain off her in this howling wind. It instantly drenched her clothes and was running down the steps and over the edge like a small river. She was going to have to be careful not to slip as she splashed her way up them.

She kept to the inside, as far under the roof and away from the dangerous drop as possible, and kept her free hand pressed against the wall while simultaneously aiming the flashlight and shielding her face with the other. Visibility was terrible. It ebbed and waned with the churning wind, opening up to a few hundred yards for just a moment, then shrinking down to just a few feet. It was disorienting. Not to mention uncomfortable. The rain was bitterly cold. It stung her exposed skin, forcing her to keep her eyes closed to tiny slits, further hindering her.

Her teeth were already chattering.

How high would *these* stairs take her, she wondered. A few flights? A hundred? *Miles?*

If Corey were here, he'd trudge up the steps beside her, using his formidable bulk to shield her. He'd always done stuff like that. He was such a gentleman. And thinking back on it, she couldn't help wondering if she'd ever told him how much she appreciated that. She was pretty sure he knew she didn't take him for granted, but had she actually said it? She felt like she owed him a big hug when she finally found him.

Or would that just be weird?

Get down!

She didn't have time to think about it. She threw herself onto the steps and into the rushing water, flattening herself against the stone as much as possible.

Something seemed to wash over the top of her, an extra-icy sensation that sent gooseflesh prickling up her already-chilled body.

A draft? Already?

She tried to peer up the steps ahead of her, but the rain was pounding her face, making it impossible to see. Where was it? Which direction had it gone? How could she avoid something she couldn't see under *ideal* conditions?

I'll lead you.

"What?" she shouted, the storm stealing away her voice almost before the word passed her lips.

But she didn't need her voice. Already, she was tumbling back down into that dreamy darkness, back into that long-gone world under that sky of impossible colors...

Chapter 24

No matter how hard she tried, Olivia couldn't see the murk. As far as she could tell, there weren't any shadowy ribbons of gathering darkness crawling up the walls or creeping hand-like things dangling down from the ceiling. But if Andrea said they were there, she believed her. And she did her best to follow in her footsteps, hoping to avoid any unseen dangers.

Finding Andrea was a tremendous relief. Not only was she able to see with her own eyes that her friend was safe, but she also brought news that Everett had arrived at the impassible city wall with her before being separated again. And if they'd both made it this far, everyone else most likely had as well, just as Austin insisted they had.

(He was still a jerk, though.)

But where *was* everyone else? What were they doing right now?

"It's getting thicker," Andrea reported. "Like the ones that brought me here. If it keeps getting darker, I might not be able to see. Don't let me fall down another hole. Because *that* wasn't fun."

"I'll bet it wasn't," said Olivia.

"Just let us know if it gets too hard to see," said Wayne.

"Thanks."

They pushed onward, following her. Olivia kept watching the way she weaved back and forth, tiptoeing along the stone floor in her dirty bare feet, avoiding things only she could see. It was unnerving, trying to follow her movements, wondering what strange, unseen things she was trodding through. What was hidden in this place? Her psychic warning alarm wasn't going off, meaning there shouldn't be any danger in her immediate future. But what if her psychic warning alarm was as blind to ghostly things as her eyes? And Andrea *did* warn them that she'd seen dangerous things in the murk.

And the murk was only a small part of what the poor girl had been through. She couldn't stop thinking about her story. For her, it all started that night at the reception. She couldn't believe that maniac attacked her right there in the country club's parking lot! She felt utterly terrible that they'd left her all alone. Brandy and Albert had departed for their wedding night. She and Wayne had retired early in anticipation of their long drive to Dunnen the following morning. Only Nicole was left and she'd disappeared, lured away when no one was looking by some kind of monster. What if something terrible had happened? What if either of them had ended up like Erin? Another pretty face on the front page of the morning newspaper? The very thought broke her heart. And if not for that Gina woman, it sounded like that was exactly what would've happened!

And then what would've become of Nicole? Would she have just disappeared without a trace, never to be seen again, none of them ever knowing what happened to her?

Just like those poor souls in Gilbert House... Just like poor Trish...

(*Why did you leave me here to die?*)

She remembered sitting in the Explorer Sunday evening, expecting a long, uneventful ride home, wondering what all those missed calls the night before were about, and the memory gave her a deeply unpleasant shiver.

Now she understood what Sandy meant when she told them their friends were in terrible danger.

Why did they all have to arrive here separately? Why couldn't they have stayed together? Wouldn't that have been safer? Why did everything have to be so complicated?

The passage they were following was sloping upward, carrying them to higher and higher levels. She hoped that meant that they were leaving that awful hound habitat behind for good. She really didn't want to deal with any more of those things for a while. Preferably *ever*.

"How're you doing?" worried Wayne.

"It's still getting thicker," Andrea replied. "But I'm okay. It's not as bad now that I'm not alone anymore."

"It's so *creepy*," said Olivia, a slight shiver racing through her. "I can't believe there are whole passages down here that are just... I mean, what exactly are they? What *is* a ghost tunnel?"

"It's just shadows, really," she explained. "Everything else is the same as every other passage." Her blue eyes drifted to the ceiling, looking at the things she was describing despite the fact that there was clearly nothing but immaculate stone where she was staring. There wasn't so much as a smudge up there. "I mean, really *dark* shadows. Solid black. And kind of three-dimensional, I guess? They look like streamers of really dense, black fog."

"And that's supposed to be something from the spirit world?" pressed Wayne, trying to wrap his head around it.

"But we can't understand that sort of stuff while we're still alive because our brains don't know how to process the information or something."

"Oh…"

Olivia shook her head. "Yeah, just keep calling them shadows." She didn't have the bandwidth to deal with something as complex as that right now.

"I wish I could remember what happened when *I* was dead," lamented Wayne. "Maybe then I could understand it."

"You're not allowed to do that anymore," she told him. "Don't even think about it."

"It's not something I *enjoyed*."

She knew that was true. She saw the desperate way he gasped for air when he awoke both times. It didn't look pleasant. In fact, it looked *painful*. He had the face of someone on the verge of drowning. It clearly wasn't something he wanted to do again and again. But it felt as if it were even more painful for *her*. She didn't think she could stand watching him fall to the ground again, much less sitting there over him, waiting, wondering if he'd come back or if he'd stay gone forever this time. He was the most important person in her life and she was forced to watch him die twice in just these past few hours. She wasn't sure how many times her heart could take something like that.

The passage carried them higher and higher. She could feel the strain in her legs. She was getting winded. She wondered how far up they were going, how many black, scary levels of the labyrinth they were skipping over.

"It was worse where I was before," said Andrea. "There were places back there where I couldn't see my own light in front of my face."

"That's so weird," said Wayne. "It doesn't look any different to us."

"Lucky me," she grumbled.

"You'd think I'd have some kind of concept of it if I've been on that side four times now."

"That's crazy," said Andrea. "You need to be more careful."

"That's right," huffed Olivia.

"I keep telling you I didn't do it on purpose!" Then he frowned. "I mean, yeah, *once*. I did it on purpose *once*. But I didn't hear you coming up with any better ideas!"

"You didn't ask for any," she reminded him.

"I'm not apologizing for saving my fiancée's life," he informed her. "So you can just go on being mad about it."

"I will."

"You guys are cute," said Andrea. "Way better than traveling with Nikki and Keith."

"Yeah, I imagine *that* had to be awkward," said Wayne.

"It was."

Olivia was starting to think she was going to have to stop for a break when, at last, the floor leveled out again.

Ahead of them, the passage curved to the left. Andrea paused here, as if pondering the abrupt change.

"What's up?" asked Wayne.

She pointed to the wall on the right. "This one's darker," she replied.

"What one's darker?"

She looked back at him, confused. Then she looked at the wall again. "Oh… It's another one you can't see."

"Another passage?" asked Olivia. From her perspective, there was only the one. But the way it abruptly curved to the left… Was it actually a fork? With a second passage curving off to the right?

Andrea sighed. "We should probably go this way, then, huh?"

She didn't want to go that way, but the fact was that a hidden passageway was probably hidden for a reason. And given that the entire purpose of a labyrinth was to hide the exit, it kind of made sense that anything hidden in it would be important to check out.

"Let's get it over with," groaned Wayne.

Chapter 25

Everett stared at the thing looming in the shadows, his feet frozen to the floor. That was no person. Something truly atrocious was waiting for him in this place, something out of his worst nightmares, something capable of driving him mad with fear at a mere glance…

It was tall and thin and crooked and oddly broken. It didn't seem like it should fit in the space it was occupying, like a poorly photoshopped image. It should've looked ridiculous, but somehow that same wrongness paralyzed him with fear.

He was in terrible danger, he understood. He kept telling himself that he wasn't afraid to die, but death was the least of his concerns. This was the sort of thing his mother warned him about. This was the demon that would steal his soul away and torture him for all eternity, just as she always said would happen.

This was a place he should never have come. He'd wandered off the path again, let his curiosity lead him astray. Wayne tried to warn him, but he didn't listen. And now it was too late.

Was it only his imagination, or could he actually hear the screams of the suffering damned echoing from somewhere below the splintered floorboards under his feet?

And for some ungodly reason, his pushy old psychologist was making him relive every terrifying moment of it!

"What were you so scared of?" Dr. Gearlet persisted in that increasingly menacing tone.

But that question, in itself, was the answer, he realized.

"I never said that," he whispered.

Dr. Gearlet gave him a deep and puzzled frown, his overgrown eyebrows scrunched together, the wrinkles in his face deepening. "What?"

Everett leaned forward in his seat, meeting those not-quite-right eyes. "I never said I was scared of anything."

He *was* scared, it was true. Something about the ominous figure standing there in the shadows *terrified* him. It was like the feeling he got from those awful waste walkers. Whatever was in front of him was bad news. But he never *said* he was scared. He never said there was someone waiting for him in this place. He never said there was a passage leading back here. And he never said he found a house at the end of the glittery path.

Dr. Gearlet said all those things. Even though he wasn't there. Even though *Everett* hadn't even been there yet. Because that wasn't just some dream he was recalling. It was completely and utterly real. And it wasn't the past. It was all happening right now.

He was being manipulated, his path painted for him as he went. This man was *steering* him, narrating the adventure like the dungeon master in some deeply immersive role-playing game. (You enter the spooky mud house. You look around. You see a creepy tunnel. You crawl inside... Now roll for perception.) Was he really just following along like some kind of dope? Wayne was right. He really was a danger to himself!

Why would he think he was talking to *Dr. Gearlet* again? He hadn't seen that man in years. He'd moved on to working with other kids, some of whom probably actually *needed* a psychologist.

His head cleared of the strange mental fog, he turned his attention to the thing standing in front of him. Somewhere in the back of his mind, he recalled something the puzzle box implanted in his brain. Something about a game of pretend... Something about getting lost in the fantasy... Something about remembering who he was and taking back control... A dire warning about the future, floating around some-where deep in his subconscious, helping him to see the trap he was caught in and find his way out.

(*What did you see in there? What scared you so badly that you never left that place again?*)

Clever. It was trying to trick him into filling in the blanks for it, ensuring that whatever he imagined would be something he, specifical-ly, found truly terrifying. Like the demons his mother terrorized him with in his childhood, telling him that they would inevitably come for him, regardless of how good he was in his life, that all he could hope for was to prolong that hellish fate by never disobeying her. It was a cunning trap. Diabolical, even. It probably would've worked on the old him, but *this* him was driven by his curiosity. And now that he'd real-ized what was happening, his curiosity was killing him.

"What are you, really?" he asked, brushing aside the dangling, leathery tatters and stepping forward.

The thing didn't snarl or growl. It didn't lunge at him. In fact, it took a step backward.

Was he really afraid of this thing? It wasn't so monstrous. It wasn't even that big. Did it shrink since he entered the room?

Was *it* afraid of *him*?

"How did you do that to my mind?" he wondered, taking another step toward the cowering creature. It was his turn to ask the questions, his turn to be the doctor. He was in charge now. And he wanted answers.

He reached out and brushed aside another tatter of dangling flesh. This time, it came apart against his arm, breaking and crumbling at his touch. Not flesh at all, he realized, but fragile sheets of hoary cobwebs, like the filthy crawlspace beneath the floorboards of a long-abandoned building.

Something moved behind him.

No… Not *moved*… *Skittered*.

He turned and looked back into the darkness. Something large and black moved among the shadows, something on far too many legs.

"Spiders…" he muttered. But there was no panic in his voice. Instead, he actually smiled a little. "That's a cool trick."

When he faced forward again, the cobwebs were gone, replaced with a gray fog.

The thing was backing away, melting into the haze.

"This is that void, isn't it?" he realized. Or, more specifically, the space just *beneath* the void. He was still in that maddening other-space that he'd dared to open his eyes to. The upside-down atrocity that felt like it was breaking his mind apart, making him forget himself. Where he found himself floating through that city of nightmare and insanity where existence itself unraveled around him.

It was like that blistering Red Waste, he realized. A flipside of the City Beyond Memory just as that was a flipside of the endless black Wood.

Everything had a flipside, he realized. Just like Gutler's Weep and that twisted world where he broke the black stone and freed Maeve.

He shouldn't have been able to escape that place. He should have gone mad. He should have crumbled and scattered across those strange cosmos, body, mind and soul strewn like sand in the wind. But somehow he didn't. Somehow, he put the pieces of his shattered mind back together and set foot in that strange, prickly forest.

(What's your name?)

That was it. The voice in the void that kept calling out to him, asking him his name.

But who was that? The toothpick man? Maeve? One of those mysterious, masked Eeshee creatures from the stone circle? Or perhaps even the Keeper, himself?

Whoever it was, he owed them. Because by asking him that question, they forced him to remember who he was. They forced him to acknowledge his very existence. It grounded him, allowing him to piece together a world where he remained himself.

Because that was what this was. It was *his* world. And once he understood that, he could do as he pleased here.

"It's about *perspective*, isn't it?" he said as he reached toward the figure vanishing into the fog. The space before him was as big or as small as he decided it was. This was a realm that transposed everything. Reality and imagination were merged in this place. Nothing and everything were simultaneously physical and fantasy.

He watched his arm stretch into the haze, as if he were reaching into a mere dollhouse, and he closed his hand around the terrified thing that cowered there.

Chapter 26

"You're gonna be okay."

"I really don't think saying it every ten seconds," grunted Keith through clenched teeth, "is gonna be enough to make it true."

"Shush," said Nicole. "Everything's going to be fine. We just have to keep moving." She was propping him up on her shoulder, carrying as much weight as she could manage, but it was slow going. He was in a lot of pain, she could tell. She hated making him walk on those wounds, but they couldn't just stay where they were. She wanted them both to be as far from that fucking meadow as possible. She still didn't know why she kept ending up back there. If it lured her back in again, she was quite sure she'd never leave it. Then who would take care of him? And there was simply no other way to move him. She wasn't strong enough to carry him the way he carried her out of that nightmare.

She still couldn't believe he did that for her. Every step must have been pure agony. And yet he crossed that foul black ground and then carried her back! He even brought her clothes and phone! But *why*? She'd given him no reason to do something like that. If anything, she gave him every reason to leave her to die beneath those awful branches. And every other time he came to her rescue, for that matter, all the way back to the barely-there's horrid version of her apartment building. He had every right to leave her there with that thing, but he didn't. He *wouldn't*. And now he was paying for it with every agonizing step.

She had no idea how to help. They had no first aid kit. She couldn't even clean his wounds properly. He was covered in blood but she'd seen no water outside of that mysterious pond in the middle of the meadow, despite the fact that she awoke soaking wet. The best she was able to do was try to dab some of the dirt away with the cleaner parts of his ruined socks.

She tore her stretched-out tank top in half and used it to wrap up his feet, sort of like Olivia did with his shirt and his injured arm, but she wasn't sure how much help it would be. It wasn't much. She'd dressed for a sweltering Missouri summer, after all. Fewer layers, more tan. But it was probably dirtier than the floor they were walking on.

She thought about giving him her socks to wear, too, thinking any little bit of covering might be better than nothing, but her feet were so much smaller than his. She was worried they'd just squeeze his feet and cause him more pain.

"There aren't any germs here," he informed her when she wouldn't stop fussing over him. Wayne had apparently told him that when Olivia treated his arm. Something about nothing being able to die or be born in the Wood. But she wasn't having it. She reminded him that this *wasn't* the Wood. This was a temple. And if hounds could live here, then germs could too.

But he refused to listen. He insisted she put her clothes on and not worry about him. Eventually she *did* get dressed, minus the tank top, of course. What did she care who saw her walking around in her bra? But she wouldn't be told not to worry. She was allowed to worry. She was the reason he was in this mess. She'd worry all she wanted to.

He was such a jerk. He even tried convincing her to leave him there, all macho like, but there wasn't a chance in hell of that. There was no way she was leaving without him. She might never find her way back. He was coming with her and they were going to find help. All of her friends were out there in this labyrinth somewhere. She was bound to find one of them eventually. And when she did, he was going to be right there with her, not alone and suffering in some dark tunnel only a stone's throw from that evil meadow.

And yet she couldn't help looking down at his feet as he limped along. Why wouldn't they stop bleeding? He'd bled through the thin cloth and had been leaving crimson smears on the stone behind them for some time now. She prayed none of those wounds became infected.

He groaned and began to slump on her.

"Whoa!" she gasped, tightening her grip. "Hey! Keep it together!"

"M'sorry…" he muttered, then winced as he took another step.

"You're okay."

"M'okay…" he repeated.

"Snap out of it!"

He blinked and forced himself to stand up straighter. "I hear you," he grunted.

She was trying so hard to be strong, but tears just kept welling up in her eyes. She didn't want to be doing this all by herself. Where was everybody? She needed help!

Ahead of them, the passage forked. She didn't waste time thinking about it. It didn't seem to matter. She chose right and kept pushing onward, deeper and deeper into this endless darkness.

"Why are you doing this?" he suddenly asked.

"What?"

"You're exhausted. You've been through hell. I'm dead weight at this point. Just leave me here and keep going."

"You don't get to tell me what to do."

He clenched his jaw against a fresh wave of pain and grunted, "You can't even stand me."

"You don't know anything about me."

"No. I guess I don't. I never did."

"Can we not do this now?"

"Do what?"

"*This*," she growled. "This *thing*. Where you make me admit what a total fucking bitch I've been. And then I start crying and blubbering about how I never stopped caring about you."

He squinted at her. "Why are *you* delusional? *I'm* the one keeps getting hurt."

"You must be contagious," she decided.

"Must be..." he sighed, his head beginning to slump again.

"Don't go passing out on me!" she snapped.

"M'sorry..."

"Wake up!"

"M'wake... Really..."

She didn't like seeing him this way. He'd always been so strong. It felt like he was slipping away from her. As she'd expected, the pain was even worse than he was letting on. It was more than he could bear. It was a wonder he'd stayed conscious this long.

Another intersection was waiting for them up ahead. Maybe it'd finally be the passage that led them to help. She tightened her grip on him and picked up the pace.

But when she shined his light onto the floor there, she stopped walking.

A trail of bloody smears lay across their path, left by the blood-soaked makeshift bandages on his feet.

Fresh tears sprang to her eyes and she felt sobs welling up in her chest, too great and too overwhelming to keep held inside.

They were walking in circles.

Chapter 27

Brandy shook her head. "No. That's not okay."

"Absolutely not an option," agreed Albert.

"You're right," replied Corey. "It's *not* an option. It's the only way." He let go of the two strings he was holding, then reached up into Austin's gaping torso and withdrew another handful. One by one, he plucked individual strands out and wrapped them around his hand. "I've gone over it a million times in my head. The only way anyone's going home is if I stay here right up to the moment the door opens."

"We've seen what happens when these things come down," Albert reminded him. "You'll be crushed. Buried alive."

"Or incinerated," added Brandy.

"That too," he agreed.

"It's too dangerous."

"No one's leaving here while the doorway stays closed," said Corey. "That's a fact. And the doorway will stay closed until the terminals are activated and the locks are lifted." He didn't raise his voice. He had no need for any forced emotion in his voice. Bravado wasn't necessary. He wasn't afraid. He felt perfectly calm, even cheerful. "That means no one leaves until we've all done our jobs. You have yours. The others have theirs. This is mine."

Brandy shook her head again. She didn't like it, he could tell. And he didn't blame her. She was probably thinking that it wasn't fair. This was *Austin's* job, not *his*. What was even the point of there *being* an Austin, if this was the only way?

It was easy to think like that. He'd be lying if he said it didn't cross his mind. But he also knew that this was simply the way things were. If he didn't do this job, *no one* would go home. And he simply couldn't have something like that on his conscience.

"'Sides," he added, "I only said I had to stay here 'til the door's open. Not that I had to sit here 'til th'whole place comes down on top of me. It just means I'll have to be quick."

"That's a fair point," said Albert. "Last time, the four of us were on top of that mountain when you opened the door."

She made a face at him. "That was *terrifying*. No one should have to go through something like that."

"The Keeper knows what he's doin'," reasoned Corey. "Me bein' here's kinda proof of that, ain't it? Had it all planned out from the start, seems like."

Albert looked down at Austin, a thoughtful frown on his face. "Wait a minute... If this guy's a part of the temple...just how old *is* he?"

"Very," replied Corey.

"I was created in the last stages of the construction of the stoneworks," explained Austin. "I'm as much a part of the machine as parsnips." His facial features twitched and a furious expression passed over his face. "As *this terminal*," he corrected himself as he glared up at him.

Corey couldn't help smirking, but otherwise went on about his business as if nothing had happened.

"So you've just been wandering around since this place was built?" gasped Albert.

"No. I've *existed* since then, but only as an inanimate piece of cargo within the Faceless Ones' stoneworks. I was awakened when the current universe was beginning to fully develop, only a few millennia ago."

"Only..." laughed Brandy. "Right..."

"Crazy, ain't it?" said Corey. "And *I* get to examine him up close and personal."

"Yeah," she grumbled. "A little *too* personal, if you ask me."

"Gotta be done," he replied.

He took the separated loop from around his hand and laid it neatly on the floor next to him, beside several similar bloody coils that he'd separated earlier. Then he reached inside again, feeling his way through the gory tangle of strings piled up under the ribcage.

There didn't seem to be anything inside him *except* these strings. Nothing there resembled organs or even seemed to mimic the function of organs. There was no heart, no liver, no lungs, no stomach. Nothing. Nor did there appear to be any kind of robotics or computer components. There was no fuel source that he could make out. Unlike the temple and its curious stone, he couldn't comprehend how something as complicated as an artificial human being could function like this, operated by nothing more than a bellyful of strings. And they *were* strings. Or at least, they didn't feel like wires. They were soft and pliable, containing no metal as far as he could see. Unless it was too tiny to be seen with the naked eye. But would wire that thin even be capable of carrying a current? It was all so utterly *alien*.

Was it possible he could be dealing with some kind of superadvanced, yet ancient *nanotechnology*? Robotic components so tiny they merely *resembled* strings when arranged in long strands? He lifted one closer to his face and squinted at it. But of course his human eyes could detect nothing more than ordinary string.

Whatever Austin was, he was created a long, *long* time ago, in a world that no longer existed, with technology that was no longer possible. Everything about him should have been completely foreign to him, and yet, somehow, he knew exactly what he needed to do, which strings needed to be connected where. He even somehow understood enough to toy with Austin's programming, which was a fun trick to show Albert and Brandy. And he could do much more than change his vocabulary. He could make him recite data from his memory. He could make his skin tone change colors. He could even make him smack himself in the face if he wanted, which had been tempting more than once since he sat down here.

"This is *stupid*," huffed Brandy. "I thought the Keeper wasn't supposed to need backup plans."

"The Keeper needs no backup plans," explained Austin, "precisely because he has *infinite* backup plans. He's foreseen every possible outcome and prepared accordingly."

"Well he's still a fucking shithead!" she snapped.

Austin tilted his head to one side as if to say, "Perhaps," but his point was made.

She turned and looked at Albert, her eyes pleading with him.

But he had no answers for her. "If he's right, what else can we do?"

"There has to be *something!*"

"I don't see the problem," said Austin. "As you've already been informed, the terminals have to be operational before the Oblivion Doorway can be opened. Either he stays and completes this task or no one makes it out of the stoneworks alive, *including* him. You don't have to be the Keeper to understand what needs to be done."

But Brandy only glared at him. "You just shut it, Half-and-Half. If you hadn't fucked up, he wouldn't be in this mess."

"She's not wrong," agreed Corey.

"This is why I hate talking to people. They're ridiculously unreasonable and pointlessly emotional."

She pointed at the pile of bloody wires in front of him. "Can you switch him back to vegetable mode?"

"Fine," grumbled Austin. "I'll shut up."

"Thank you."

Corey chuckled. He liked these two. They were fun. He'd wager they'd be awesome to take on a portal investigation. It'd be a blast.

"Seriously, though," said Albert. "There has to be a way for us to open the door without you having to risk your life. It doesn't make any sense."

"Don't have t'make sense," he replied. "I only care 'bout doin' my part. S'like he said, if the door don't open, *nobody* leaves here. Ever."

"Still..." bemoaned Brandy.

"Don't worry," stressed Corey. "I know how this place works. I have a map." He lifted his bloody hand and pointed at his head. "Up here. I'll be able to get out. Like, ninety-nine percent sure."

"And what about that last one percent?"

"The one percent never comes up," he said, as if that solved the whole thing.

She took a step toward him, frustrated. "But what if it *does?*"

"Then if either of you see Violet," he replied, looking up and meeting her gaze. "Tell her I'm sorry."

Chapter 28

Gina stood there in the darkness, listening to the sound of her own trembling breathing and the pounding of her pulse in her ears in the eerie silence. She wasn't going to be able to calm herself completely. She wasn't strong enough to push back this kind of fear. She wasn't sure anyone could be. But she didn't have to suppress it all. She only had to make herself move.

She turned and faced the wall again. She opened her eyes and looked directly at the thing standing on the other side of the warped glass.

It was bigger than it seemed when she was watching it from the corner of her eye. And stranger. Distorted by the uneven glass like some kind of funhouse trick, it was little more than a bizarre collection of shadows that didn't seem to all go together, as if someone had stitched it together from a dozen discarded monstrosities. It had at least five mismatched legs of different lengths and thicknesses, each one twisted and bent at odd angles as if broken and jutting off what sometimes appeared to be two separate torsos and sometimes *three*. It had no arms that looked like arms, but instead things that somehow appeared both skeletal and tentacle-like, both sharp and oozing, solid and liquid. And atop it all were a multitude of inhuman-looking heads and even more *mouths*, all of them opening and closing and snapping and drooling, whispering foul things that didn't quite reach her through the wall, but gave that hateful psychic part of her brain a deeply unpleasant sort of itchy sensation.

And the way it was moving... It didn't seem to turn so much as ooze and flow, less like a creature than a living inkblot splashed across the other side of the glass, constantly shifting, morphing, a kaleidoscope of darkness rather than colors, blossoming and twisting and writhing in maddening undulations of unnatural shapes and patterns.

She could make out no eyes, but she knew it was staring back at her. And unlike her, its view was undistorted. It could see her clearly through the warped glass.

That was its domain, after all.

Frightened... she heard it hiss somewhere in the depths of her own mind in a voice that was almost but not quite imagined.

Yes, she was frightened. She wouldn't deny it. She was *terrified*. But if this thing thought a little fear was going to stop her from doing what she came here to do, then it didn't understand anything about her.

"I've been afraid of much worse than you," she whispered back to it.

In a voice that was less than a thought yet bursting with indescribable dread, the terrible thing on the other side of the glass laughed.

She turned her blind gaze on the wall itself, casting her psychic eye left, then right, calculating the layout of the labyrinth around her as her mysterious psychic eye fed the information to her. There was a way to cross over to the other side, but she couldn't quite perceive it yet. It was nothing as simplistic as an opening. She wasn't going to be able to just step through it. There was a trick of some kind. A simple mechanism that reminded her of a revolving door but was at the same time nothing of the sort.

The Temple of the Three Whispers, as Albert had called it, existed in a world far separated from the one she grew up in. How many universes had bloomed into being and then withered away between then and now? How many times had the fundamental rules of existence changed? If magic had once been real, what else could have once been that no longer was? What wonders had been forgotten over the endless ages?

This was one of those lost things. A concept once as simple and commonplace as the wheel, but utterly lost not only to time, but to mind, incomprehensible to anyone alive today.

So exactly how was she supposed to use it?

Alone... uttered the unspeakable abomination she was inconceivably trying to reach. *No one to protect her...* It was impossible to tell which mouth was speaking at any given time. It was as disorienting as it was disturbing. She had to concentrate to keep from being distracted.

A very concept too alien for her brain to comprehend... Was that something she could even do? How did she work her way through a puzzle whose solution involved non-existent concepts? She was a psychic, not a genius. Maybe it was a mistake coming here alone.

No one to grieve over her body...

She ignored the thing's hateful words. It wanted to get inside her head. But again, it was proving that it didn't know anything about her. She'd been ignoring cruel and hateful words all her life.

No one to miss her when she's gone...

Now that was just rude.

She continued walking, following the corridor with her mysterious inner senses, tracing every part of it, mapping it in her head.

The abomination kept pace with her, those bizarre limbs scratching at the wall. Oozing, slimy flesh, like nothing that had ever lived, slid across the glass, leaving strange *smears* that lingered in her psychic eye.

Make you suffer... it threatened in an evil hiss. *Reach inside your writhing body... Tear your insides apart... Break... Rip... Puncture...*

She needed to focus on the wall. Something around here was different in some way. She just had to find it. She had to ignore the monster's hideous words and concentrate.

Just like the other one...

Gina stopped walking, her blood chilled.

That wasn't just something it said to get under her skin. This thing had killed before. *Recently.* She could almost see it. Her horrid, psychic mind was alive with terrible flashes of bloody imagery. A splash of dirty water. A torn dress. Furious bubbles full of terrified, agonized screams. A white glint of broken bone.

A murdered body in a dark lake...

Her thoughts rushed straight to Andrea. They were near the water just before Glum snatched them up again. Was that what happened to her? Was that why she didn't sense her on Tristesse Lane? Had she ended up failing her after all?

No... That didn't feel right.

It was someone different. Someone in a sleek, silvery dress. Someone whose hair was long and black, not red and playful. And something to do with sunflower petals...?

No. Not Andrea. But *someone.* This thing killed her. Violently. Painfully. *Horribly.* And she wasn't the only one.

There was a man... He was walking through the darkness with his nose in a book, alone somewhere in these gray walls. She didn't know who he was. She'd never seen him before. And she never would. She saw blood splashed across the stone. He met a horrible and violent end.

This thing had killed twice already at least. There was no reason to think that it wouldn't be perfectly willing to kill again.

She continued walking, managing somehow to not freeze in fear at this horrible knowledge, but she could feel her legs trembling beneath her. She felt weak.

Afraid...

Yes, she was. She was petrified. But what else could she do? She didn't have the luxury of simply walking away. The goddess clearly sent her here for a reason.

She forced herself to stay focused on the wall, still scanning the surface for anything that might stand out. A crack. A gap. Even a subtle change in the angle or slant.

There had to be a way into the glass labyrinth.

It was why she was here. She was increasingly sure of it with each second she spent in this ghastly darkness.

Then, at last, she found it.

She stopped walking, her gaze fixed on a narrow sliver where the monstrous shape rippled and doubled, like a refraction of light in a cracked mirror, yet without any light to make any such thing possible.

Not light, she realized. But space. *Reality.*

That was the spot.

But…how did she squeeze through such a narrow space? And how did she keep from being murdered like the woman in the silvery dress the moment she stepped through it?

The thing on the other side of the glass seemed to laugh at her.

Come then… it chuckled at her in its multitude of monstrous voices. *Let me play with you…*

Chapter 29

What were these things? Violet couldn't grasp what she was seeing through this sightless, alien body. It was little more than a writhing, squirming darkness spread out before her. And not just one, but hundreds. *Thousands.* They were all around her, whole fields filled with them. And more beyond these walls, in rooms other than this one.

You might call this a nursery. Like always, the other one's voice was less spoken than a thought passing through her bewildered mind. *The infancy of a life cycle. One perfectly engineered to defy the natural tendencies toward evolution and extinction. A perfect balance, capable of lasting as long as will be necessary to meet the Keeper's ultimate design.*

An artificial life cycle? She recalled Albert talking about monsters living in the depths of the first temple. Horrific, alien things right out of Stephen King's worst nightmares, from the way he described them. *Big* things. And she'd wondered how anything could live so long in a place like that, cut off from the rest of the world, with no sunlight or rain.

Was this the answer to that simple question? A biosphere hidden within the countless corridors of the labyrinth?

Should it surprise her that beings capable of building a wall that extended up and down forever would also be able to create an artificial ecosystem that wouldn't ever change?

She found herself looking up into the darkness above. There was no sign of that colorful sky, meaning they were, indeed, inside the stoneworks. And more than that, she somehow understood that they were *deep* inside them, almost all the way down at the very bottom, miles and miles and miles below those unearthly streets onto which no windows or doors would ever open.

There was something dreadful about the idea of being so far down. She felt strangely lost. Imprisoned in this darkness. It was as if the very air were stifling her. And yet she still wasn't sure whether she was able to breathe in the first place in this body with no mouth or nose...

Weren't they way up in one of the towers last time?

No... That wasn't the last time she was here. There *was* no last time. Time in this body didn't work like that.

In the world around her, with its far-too-colorful sky, this was sometime before. *Long* before. But also long *after* she arrived. Much time had passed. The towers and the impassible wall had risen high into the sky. And throughout all that time, these elongated, faceless beings persisted, on and on, undying, unchanging, unyielding in their duty to build this endless city.

But *inside*, deep within the strange consciousness of the other one, there was no before or after. She wasn't sure she could explain it, but here within, there was only now.

How long did she spend in this world? In this ageless body? In this confounding state of mind?

How old was her own consciousness?

The gatehouses are machines of perfect balance, just like the universes they connect. The Three Powers, turning in harmony, like the gears of a clock. Life and nature. Death and spirit. Shadow and void. All equal. And each one held in check by the other two.

Three Powers… Her friends said something about that once…back in Cakwetak. They sounded almost like rival mob families in a dramatic movie, vying for control of some crime-ravaged city, but caught in a stalemate. But the truth, she'd discovered, was far more bizarre. The "Three" referred to three ancient deities. Actual *gods*. Or perhaps *elder gods* was a better description. The oldest and wisest of an entire pantheon, it sounded like, each representing one of three sides of the whole greater universe.

Was that all this was about? Just some ancient, cosmic rivalry? A childish game of equality among self-serving deities?

No. The Three are at odds, it's true. Each views the other two as threats. They are always watching, always cautious, but the balance between them is a vital component of the machine, a necessity for a universe capable of sustaining life.

Had they moved? She sensed she was in a different chamber from where they were before. The things wriggling in the darkness before her had changed. Their movements were more forceful. They seemed more agitated. More *dangerous*.

The things we created in these depths haunt me. Some of them have done terrible things, caused horrible suffering. But the will of the Keeper is absolute. He is the only reason our circle can exist.

Violet felt conflicted. She wasn't sure she trusted this "Keeper" she spoke so highly of. What made *him* qualified to be the sole being in charge of keeping the universes alive? Was there really no better way?

Didn't Albert say something about the Keeper telling lies? What if the sentinels were all wrong? What if the Keeper wasn't the great and wise savior everyone claimed he was, but instead just a cunning little villain who'd managed to deceive even gods?

She let out a startled cry as a wave of ice-cold water enveloped her, followed by a blinding flash and an ear-splitting explosion of thunder.

She was confused for a moment. Where was she? How did she get here? What was happening? But then it came back to her. The storm. The towering spires of the City Beyond Memory. She turned and looked behind her, but the doorway she exited from was gone. The strobing lightning revealed only shadowy steps descending as far into the haze as she could see.

She was suddenly at the top of the stairs. Another doorway was waiting just ahead of her.

The other one had taken the wheel again, probably avoiding all the storm drafts for her since she no longer had Everett to shield her.

There was a slight lull in the storm as the wind shifted, and a great bolt of lightning revealed the vast, sprawling city far below. Dozens of dark angular towers jutted upward into the churning sky all around her, all of them interconnected with those narrow stone bridges.

Her gaze drifted toward a massive structure that blotted out the sky at the center of it all.

The heart of the city.

The tower that held the doorway they were meant to find.

Their ultimate goal.

But it still looked so far away. Was she really going to be able to get there all on her own?

...dangerous to linger here... sighed the other one from somewhere deep within her thoughts, sounding more distant than before. She sounded so *weary*.

"Right," she breathed. She wasn't alone. The other one was here. And she was absolutely correct. She wasn't out of the storm yet. It seemed her mysterious autopilot had exhausted herself before she could carry them all the way to the doorway. If she continued to stand here like a fool, gawking at the scenery, she'd eventually attract another draft. Or else simply be struck by lightning.

...hurry...

"Yeah," she gasped. "Sorry."

Still shielding her face against the blowing rain, she rushed up the last few steps and back into the waiting gloom of the labyrinth.

Chapter 30

Andrea was still trying to wrap her head around everything Olivia and Wayne told her. Everett didn't say much about how he ended up here. Something about a caveman city...or something? Too much was going on. When she first found him, he was trapped in that metal box. And then she had that strange panic attack and saw all those ghosts turning to look at her. Then they were in that dangerously unstable gouging station where they found Violet unconscious. There wasn't really any *time* for storytelling.

But according to Olivia, they found Everett exploring a creepy forest that kept rearranging itself and was filled with zombie animals and fairies, of all things. Until she heard her talk about them, she would've traded fairies for pervert jedi psychopaths in an instant, but now she wasn't so sure. That sounded like a positively horrifying ordeal, like the absolute *worst* babysitting job *imaginable*.

More importantly, it turned out that Olivia's psychic ability she demonstrated five years ago on the burning mountain definitely wasn't a fluke. She could actually see possible futures! "Threads of fate," she called them. That was pretty cool. *So* much cooler than all this scary ghost stuff.

And apparently Wayne was immune to dying? That was a thing, too? He said it wasn't foolproof, that it was only under certain conditions or something, but still it was pretty crazy.

And then there was the fact that they knew *Erin*. Like, both as a ghost *and before she died*? Because she actually died in the lake Brandy and Albert were married by? *That very night*? Seriously? She remembered sitting at that strange, shadowy bar and thinking that she'd seen that sunflower tattoo somewhere before. Did she see it at the reception? Did they walk past each other in the last hours of her life? It gave her a chill to think too much about it. They were *both* attacked that night. What if Ada had sent Gina to rescue Erin instead of her? What if it had been *her* fate to die? The thought was unsettlingly dreadful. It made her feel a little queasy deep down in her belly.

Ahead of her, the murk within this passage was getting thicker and thicker. Pretty soon she wasn't going to be able to see the stone at all. But so far there were fewer of those creepy hand things in here, which was an improvement. Also, she realized she hadn't seen very many of those shadowy little specks floating around in some time. And the voices had gone silent, too. Was this area different from the other places she'd been? Or did it have something to do with Olivia and Wayne being here with her? Did the murk not like when there were too many living people around? She didn't think that felt quite right. Somehow the idea of the murk withdrawing from groups of people felt wrong. She couldn't help thinking that it wouldn't do that, though she wasn't sure why. It wasn't as if she actually understood it.

"So all this shadowy stuff is all over the place?" asked Wayne, curious. "Right now? And we just can't see any of it?"

"Mm-hm. Like, it's hard to wrap my head around the fact that you guys *can't*. It's everywhere. I told you, there were times I couldn't see anything *else*."

"And it's just…shadows?"

"Like really dark ones. Almost *solid*. But not. Like it *looks* like you should be able to reach out and touch it, but you can't. It's sort of just…crawling all over every surface."

"Ew," said Olivia.

"Kind of, yeah."

"But you said there were dangerous things in the shadows, too," he recalled.

"Sometimes it clumps together," she explained, glancing around in case just talking about the foul things might be enough to summon one. "And then it starts to kind of come alive."

"Again," said Olivia, "*ew*."

"Yeah. The smaller ones aren't really dangerous, I don't think, just a little grabby, but the bigger ones are pretty scary. They can move around on their own. I've heard them growl."

This surprised him. "They *growl?*"

Olivia shuddered at the thought.

"They seem aggressive," she warned, deciding not to frighten them by describing the bottomless abyss of spiraling teeth they had inside them. "But I don't think they can see us. They're attracted by sound, I think."

"Got it," said Wayne. "If you say shut up, don't ask any questions."

"That's probably a good strategy, yeah." They were approaching the end of the passage. It intersected another, allowing them to go left or right. She stepped into it and shined her light both ways. "Can you guys see both of these?"

"Two of them," confirmed Wayne.

That was good. For some reason, she didn't like it when she was the only one who could see things. It sort of made her feel like she was going crazy, even if she *did* have the ability to show these places to them. "The murk looks about the same in both. I don't, like, get any feelings about one or the other or anything." She looked over at Olivia, an eyebrow raised.

Olivia made a face at her, a sort of puckered "do I have to?" kind of look, but she let go of Wayne's arm and stepped forward to examine both passages.

Andrea reached out and took her hand. "What do you think?"

"I'm not sure. I definitely don't get any kind of 'imminent doom' feeling from either of them."

"Well that's good."

"But I'm not really getting a clear 'this way' or 'that way' feeling, either."

"Probably doesn't matter then," reasoned Wayne. "Whole thing's a giant maze. Maybe they both go to the same place."

That was a good point, Andrea realized. Worst case scenario, she'd have gotten a terrible feeling about *both* directions.

No... Worst case scenario would be *all three*, including the way they came, leaving nowhere to go and no escape from whatever was approaching. The very thought made her repress a shiver.

But Olivia continued to look back and forth, her pretty face creased.

"What're you feeling?" asked Wayne.

She shook her head. "I'm not sure..." She took a step closer to the left passage. "Not danger, exactly... But *something*..." She looked back at him, uncertain. "I'm not sure."

Andrea shined her light one way, then the other. "Do we just...pick one, then?"

I wouldn't, rang the impostor Stella's voice in her thoughts, making her jump a little. *But you do you.*

"I don't think it'll matter," replied Olivia. "I don't feel anything telling me not to go one way or the other."

Maybe because there isn't a right way. There never was.

"Just pick a direction and let us know if it starts to feel bad," suggested Wayne.

They're so fucked.

Go away! Andrea thought at her.

"You okay?" asked Olivia. "You looked like you had a pain there for a second."

You have no idea, she thought. Aloud, however, she simply said, "I'm fine. Just trying to decide if *I* can feel anything like you can. Since it's a ghost passage and I'm the ghost girl, I guess."

Erin said the thing following her was some kind of terrifying supernatural entity far too strong for her to fight off. Something she called the "Priestess of Ruin." So why the heck was this chick just following her around and whispering demoralizing things into her head? What was the point in that? It made no sense. Why would something so powerful and evil just be toying with her? Was it really the big, bad, evil thing she'd been warned about? Or just some random imp or something? (That was probably a thing. Everything else was a thing.)

"Let's try this one, I guess" decided Andrea, turning right.

Bad idea.

"Just tell me if anything feels off," she said, ignoring the unhelpful voice in her head.

"I'll let you know," promised Olivia.

Stupid fake Stella, putting doubts in her head, making her second-guess herself. She couldn't waste time over simple, meaningless decisions like this. She still had no idea where the rest of her friends were or what kind of trouble they might be in.

She led the way forward, her eyes peeled for groping hand-things and growling clumps of murk.

"How's it look up there?" asked Wayne.

"Dark," she replied. "But I've been in worse."

"Be careful," begged Olivia. "Something still feels off."

She could still see enough of the stone to tell that there weren't any pitfalls in her immediate path, but those black tendrils of intangible shadow were growing thicker, spreading over more of the floor, making her nervous. It wasn't as scary now that she had company, but she still couldn't help thinking about that hole she fell in last time she couldn't see the floor. She *really* didn't want to take another scary ride. Next time she might land somewhere far worse than a stinky mudhole. Next time it could be a pit of spikes like the one that claimed poor Beverly. Or right into the middle of a nest of hungry hounds. Or maybe just this same, hard stone, but at the bottom of a hundred-foot drop.

She shivered a little at all the possibilities her strange mind could come up with. It was lucky she didn't have time to consider all those imaginative options the first time or she might've scared herself to death before she even reached the mud.

"What's wrong?" asked Olivia.

Andrea looked back to see that Wayne had stopped walking and was standing there, frowning.

"Nothing..." he replied. And rather unconvincingly, she thought. He had a pinched sort of expression on his face and his hands were closed into tight fists, as if ready to fight.

Olivia thought so, too, because she kept staring at him.

"It's fine," he assured her. "Just...thought I heard something for a second there."

Andrea and Olivia both tipped their heads and listened, but it was utterly silent.

"Gone now," he said. "Probably my imagination."

"What did it sound like?" prodded Olivia.

But he shook his head. "I'm not sure. It was really faint." He turned and started walking again. "Like I said, my imagination."

Olivia hurried forward and grabbed his arm again, but Andrea stood there a moment longer, listening. Maybe he heard a ghost. Five years ago, she wasn't the only one who heard and glimpsed the supernatural phenomena. Everyone noticed the activity as they climbed the burning mountain. Did that mean that some spirits could choose who to reveal themselves to?

She continued after her friends before they could get too far ahead. The last thing she wanted was to end up alone again.

You're boring me, sighed the impostor.

Well excuse me, *princess*, she thought back at her. For a terrifyingly powerful entity capable of causing so much mischief, she was surprisingly annoying. It felt less like being haunted than babysitting somebody's spoiled brat of a child.

If only she'd grow bored enough to leave her alone and go bother someone else.

Chapter 31

Was this madness? Because it wasn't quite what Everett had imagined madness being like. He'd always thought there'd be more…maniacal laughter, maybe? In cartoons, mad people always seemed to be laughing. But this wasn't exactly funny. It was just *weird*.

He was sitting in a simple, wooden chair in a stark empty room entirely painted bright white, even the ceiling and floor. There was no door, but rather a somewhat cartoonish *drawing* of a door on one wall. The same was true of the window. It was painted-on and two-dimensional, complete with bright yellow curtains, a potted flower and a sprawling, sunny field in the background. There was nothing else on the walls, drawn or otherwise, no light switches, power outlets, heating vents, not even any trim around the floor or ceiling. But above him was a third drawing, this one of a simple ceiling fan and lamp which, of course, gave off no light whatsoever (being that it was only a drawing) and yet this strange space was somehow illuminated anyway. He couldn't even discern which direction the light was coming from. There didn't seem to be any shadows.

The only other thing in the room was a small table, standing directly in front of him, on which sat a simple, rectangular birdcage.

He was leaning forward in the chair, staring at the curious creature inside the cage, his mind a cyclone of unanswerable questions that simultaneously frustrated and delighted him. He wanted to know everything about it *right now*, but he wasn't sure where to even begin trying to understand what he was seeing.

Currently, it looked sort of like a little wooden doll, with spindly arms and legs and a somewhat oversized head, with no facial features, but covered in strange little fin-like things that sort of twitched and rippled in a way that almost mimicked some sort of expression. But a moment ago, it had a more insect-like look, with large, transparent fans spread into a shape that reminded him of butterfly wings. And before that it looked like a tiny child wrapped up in a sort of leafy blanket, peering out at him with oversized black eyes.

A shapeshifter?

He gave his head a slight, pondering shake. No. Nothing so simple. He was looking at it three-dimensionally, like something he might have found in his own world. It was far more complex than that. He needed to turn his thinking on its head if he wanted any chance of understanding it.

Somehow he understood that it wasn't the creature that was changing forms, but rather *his own perception* that was changing. He was trying to wrap his head around exactly what the little thing was. Like everything else in the upside-down void, cause and effect were transposed, making it difficult for him to grasp *any* of it. Nineteen years of living in the "real" world had trained his brain to trust his senses to send him information. Now, that was all backward. His imagination was changing the way he perceived the things in front of him, creating a bizarre contradiction between truth and fantasy. The longer he sat here trying to understand what he was looking at, the less he understood of it, because he wasn't *seeing* it at all.

This wasn't the physical world. It was an upside-down fantasy that he'd become enveloped in. It had more in common with a dream than with the world he knew. And he had no idea how to escape it.

But of course, escaping wasn't what he was concerned with. Not right now. Right now, the door and window were drawn on. He wasn't going anywhere. Maybe in a while this strange, dollhouse world would turn into something else, the same way this strange little creature kept doing.

He leaned back in the chair without taking his eyes off it.

Was it a creature? "Creature" was a word reserved for natural things, wasn't it? Living things? Specifically animals, whether real or mythical? But this was no kind of animal. It wasn't really alive at all. Was it some kind of spirit, like the storm drafts and the potato men? The Eeshee told him there were a great many different kinds of spirits, only a tiny fraction of whom had ever been human, and that he possessed the rare ability to see them. Perhaps this was some kind of…pixie? Or something?

It didn't look like much. The longer he stared at it, the less frightful it seemed. It was cowering inside the cage, looking terrified in spite of its lack of any real expression. He could scarcely imagine what had scared him so much when he first laid eyes on it.

But that was the thing, wasn't it? His eyes had nothing to do with it. Even now, he was beginning to understand, he wasn't really seeing what was in front of him. His mind was simply trying its best to process something his natural senses couldn't detect and that it didn't understand.

As he watched, the thing changed again. It melted into a bristly lump and began glowing a sickly yellowish shade of orange.

"That's not you," he muttered. It was him. *He* was the one causing it to change. He was trying so hard to see what was in front of him that his brain was rearranging the information on a subconscious level, forcibly feeding him incorrectly calculated data.

And if that was how this was all going to work…

He sat up and leaned forward again. "What should I call you?" he wondered.

It was now a transparent blue, with a shape sort of like a stingray.

"If we're going to talk…you'll need to be something a little more…*relatable*…"

Though he hadn't taken his eyes off it this whole time, he couldn't remember when it turned from the yellowish-orange blob to the transparent-blue stingray. It quite simply was something it wasn't before, as if it had always been what it was now. Just like the way it was now— and had always been—a strange little greenish creature with dozens of thin, twig-like legs.

If this *was* what madness was like, he wasn't entirely sure why people thought it was a bad thing to go crazy. It was sort of fun. Trippy. His brain was delighting in all these bizarre new concepts that he'd never considered before.

But he didn't have time to lose his mind. He still had to find his way back to Violet. He needed to make sure she was safe. And he wasn't going to be able to just walk out through that drawn-on door.

Somehow, he found himself convinced that this…*whatever* it was…could help him with that.

"Entity?" he muttered. Was that a better word than "creature"?

Whatever it was, it was intelligent enough to pretend to be his old psychologist and trick him into following its creepy script. It clearly had the ability to communicate. But as soon as he saw through the illusion and captured it, it clammed up. It hadn't spoken another word.

Because it couldn't actually speak, he realized. It was never going to be able to simply form words. Sound was a physical thing. This was all mental. It was all in his head.

If only he could make it take the form of something capable of communicating with him like that again.

He closed his eyes and concentrated for a moment, focusing on the problem in front of him. Perceptions. Upside down and inside out. Cause and effect. All of it backward and twisted around like distorted reflections in a carnival funhouse mirror...or like some mad wonderland waiting just behind the glass.

His eyes still closed, he smiled. "I'll call you Alice."

Chapter 32

"Take it easy," urged Nicole as she helped ease him to the floor for a well-needed rest.

Keith leaned back against the wall and closed his eyes. He had no idea how long they'd been walking. He was so tired. His feet felt like they were on fire. And he was having trouble focusing his eyes.

How did he end up in this mess? What did he do wrong?

The moment he saw Nicole standing on that dock, he should've turned and ran the other way. She was like a dark omen. Nothing but misery followed him whenever he had anything to do with her. No good came from traveling with this woman. A forest the size of a damned *galaxy* and *she* was the one person he found? There was no way it was any kind of accident. It was like some kind of cosmic joke.

It was that pretty ghost woman... Erin... *She* was the one who sent him down this painful path.

(*Nicole's far stronger and more capable than most women. But she still needs you.*)

"Bullshit," he grumbled.

Nicole leaned closer to him. "What? I can barely hear you."

He opened his eyes. She was so close to him. Her breath tickled his face. He could feel the heat radiating off her body. Her chest was slick with sweat. The magnificent swells of her perfect breasts, pushed upward and together by her dirty bra, seemed to hover before his face. He watched a bead of sweat slide down over the sensuous crease of her clavicle and slip down between them.

God, she was beautiful...

"Keith?" she tried again.

"Hurts..." he replied instead.

"I know. Just hang on a little longer. We'll find someone. I know we will."

Why was she talking like that? Did he really look so pitiful that even *she* had to feel sorry for him? What did she care if he was in pain? She hadn't cared in seven lousy months. She didn't want anything to do with him in all that time. She didn't want him tagging along when they left the boat. She literally *told* him out in that hellscape of a forest that she never needed him.

(You're exactly *the one she needs. You always have been. Why else would the Night Goddess keep sending you to her side?)*

Maybe the hot ghost chick got her confused with someone else? Was that it? Because there was no way she could've been talking about Nicole.

And yet he found her standing in that freaky meadow, exactly where she told him they shouldn't go under any circumstances. Just staring up at those dead branches like she was in some kind of trance, waiting for something terrible to happen to her. She clearly wasn't in her right mind. She even *kissed* him as he was carrying her out. That definitely wasn't her.

(She's in terrible danger.)

It wasn't that he wanted anything bad to happen to her. Regardless of their history, he truly wanted her to stay safe. He just didn't understand why *he* had to be the one to save her. Why not that Wayne guy? *He* seemed like the kind to charge into a monster-infested meadow to save a beautiful girl.

But then again, he definitely wouldn't wish this kind of pain on someone like Wayne. Or anyone else for that matter.

He closed his eyes again as another wave of pain crept up his legs and twisted its way through his guts.

Why did it hurt so much? What happened to him back there? What was living in that dirt? And how did *Nicole* escape unscathed? She had to have walked across the same bare earth he did to be standing out in that water when he found her. He saw the mud on her feet while she was putting her clothes back on. Why wasn't *she* attacked?

He was *glad* she wasn't harmed. He never wanted to see her in pain. If only for that fake version of her that he was so blissfully enamored with before she turned on him, he'd never wish any suffering on her, much less pain like *this*. He simply didn't understand it. Was it because he was running to her? Did he just happen to tread across some kind of nest? It didn't make sense.

He just *kept* getting hurt. First his arm. Then that painful gouge in the belly by those living skeletons. And now his feet? It was starting to feel a little like he wasn't welcome here.

But this was nothing compared to those other injuries. The holes in his feet were *agonizing*. It washed over him in dizzying waves, scattering his thoughts, making it impossible to think straight.

Another one came over him now, like a fire spreading up his legs, burning and prickling and stinging.

Then he felt Nicole's warm cheek against his. The sensation was painfully familiar. He felt an odd pang deep in his weary heart. "I'm right here," she assured him. "I'm not going anywhere. We're getting through this together, okay?"

Was that a tear he felt? Was she crying for him?

What kind of backward world had he stumbled into?

And yet…the feel of her skin was like the presence of an old friend he never thought he'd see again.

She reached around him and pressed herself even closer, her hot, damp skin against his. He was too weary to push her away. And strangely, he found that he didn't want to. He missed that old Nicole, after all, the one who made him feel like the luckiest man alive.

"You'll be fine," she promised. "You'll see."

Her voice was firm and clear. Confident. And yet he could feel her tears on his cheek. And somehow, it made his heart ache.

(*You have to find her. You have to protect her. No matter what.*)

Yes. Protect her. Look after her. Keep her safe at all cost. Because somewhere in there was someone incredibly special, someone he couldn't let down. Not even if it killed him.

He opened his eyes again. It was hard to see clearly. Not just because it was dark. His vision was blurry. He felt sort of drunk.

That explained it. Clearly, the pain was making him delusional. Why else would he suddenly care whether Nicole was crying or not. When was the last time she cared about how *he* was feeling?

And yet…somehow he knew better.

"Come on," she urged. "We have to keep moving."

He didn't want to move. He just wanted to close his eyes and go to sleep.

"It won't be much farther," she promised.

Liar, he thought, but didn't have the energy to say. She knew no such thing. How could she? And yet he found himself rising to his feet, regardless. Something about the subtle crack in her voice seemed to compel him.

He didn't want her to cry anymore.

"That's it. It'll be okay. You can lean on me. As much as you need."

Since when? And yet he found himself pushing forward, clinging to her, as if the past seven months had never happened, as if she never told him she didn't need him. The feel of her skin against his was intoxicating. He craved it. He wanted it with all his being.

It was almost worth the pain that drilled into his feet with each step he took.

Chapter 33

Brandy didn't want to leave Corey there. Albert didn't want to leave him either. But if what he said was true, they really had no choice in the matter. They were all here for a reason. They each had a job to do. And if any one of them didn't finish their job, none of them might ever see home again.

That didn't stop them from trying to argue with him, of course. They did their best. But the fact was that he wasn't moving. He'd already made his decision. They couldn't force him to leave that room. Not with persuasion and certainly not with bodily force. And they both knew they couldn't stay there with him.

"We have to trust him," he said as they walked away from the blood-soaked terminal. "He said he knows the way out. And less likely things have happened in temples. We thought we were leaving Wayne behind once, too."

"It's just not right," she grumbled. "He shouldn't have to risk his life like that. *None* of us should."

"I know."

"I mean… He really said, 'Tell Violet'? Seriously? How are we supposed to look her in the eye and tell her we just left him there?"

"We don't know what'll happen," he said again. Everyone kept telling them that this was all the Keeper's will. Surely it wasn't as simple as sacrificing Corey to his insane machine just because someone cut his rude puppet's strings. "But thanks to him, we *do* have a good idea of why we're all split up like we are. Corey's here to fix Austin. Our job probably has something to do with those magic locks Shanzer told us about."

"Fucking *pervert*," she growled. "I fucking *hate* that filthy creep."

"I know." He looked back, but Corey's light was out of sight now.

His thoughts kept circling back to what Austin told them about Beverly. Could that be true? Could she have been like him? Just an artificial person full of strings and blood that wasn't really blood pretending to be real? It didn't make sense. Her disappearance was in the paper. She had a name and a home and a job. She was a nurse. How could she not have been a real person?

(*Tell them the truth.*)

He looked down at the floor in front of him, a thoughtful frown on his face.

(*All of it. None of the Keeper's self-righteous rules. None of his games.*)

Did this have something to do with Kneede's truth? How deep did the Keeper's lies go? How much of this was real? Was *anything* real?

(*Aren't you familiar enough with deceit and lies to figure it out for yourself?*)

(*I don't like being used.*)

What really happened that night? What lie did Kneede find when Brandy threw open the door atop the burning mountain?

(*If we ever cross paths again...*)

Once again, he found himself wondering if perhaps that wasn't the threat he thought it was. Did the Keeper send him away not to separate them from him, but because he didn't want him to finish that sentence?

Ahead of them, the passage split. Left or right. Brandy shined her light one way, then the other, but they looked exactly the same, as did almost every passage she looked down. "Any suggestions from the psychic map?"

"Is that all you see me as?" teased Albert.

"Yep," she replied without cracking a smile. "You got me. All this time."

He looked both ways, then shrugged. "I got nothing."

"Well that was a waste of six years, then, wasn't it?"

He chuckled. "Now you're stuck with me."

She pressed herself against him and rested her head on his shoulder.

"You okay?" he asked.

"I hate this," she groaned. "I feel just *sick* leaving Corey back there."

"You could try going back and dragging him out by his ear, but I'm pretty sure you won't budge him."

This made her laugh a little. But *only* a little. It was a tired laugh. A huff. Practically only a sigh. She was worn out. How long had they been going at this? It felt like hours since they stepped out of that mysterious carriage, but time wasn't the constant he always thought it was. Not in places like these. How long had it really been? Days? Weeks? Would their bodies even be able to tell the difference? And throughout it all, they'd lost track of friends, they'd been attacked mentally and emotionally.

He turned and wrapped his arms around her. "Everything will work out," he promised her. "We just need to focus on getting through this and going home."

"Home…" she purred. She wanted that every bit as much as he did. "I'm gonna take *such* a long bath…"

"Good idea. No promises I won't peek, though."

"Fuck *that*. You're coming with me."

"Oh. Well what're we standing around *here* for then? Let's get this over with."

She gave him another tired laugh, but she didn't move. Instead, she reached up and kissed him. "You promised me it'd be okay, remember?"

"I did," he assured her. "And I meant it."

"I'm holding you to it."

He kissed her again. Long and slow, savoring her. "You do that," he told her when he finally pulled away. Then he kissed her once more.

It was going to be okay. Because it *had* to. He couldn't bear the thought of it *not* being okay.

She rested her head against his shoulder again and remained there for a moment, the labyrinth silent as a tomb around them. Then she pulled away and reached under her glasses to wipe at her eyes. "Let's go."

He nodded. "Let's go this way," he decided, choosing the path on the right. "Corey can take care of himself. I'm sure of it."

Chapter 34

Corey pulled out another handful of bloody strings and began separating them.

Austin watched him as he worked. He felt no pain. The only things he still had control of were his head and neck and one of his arms, which was a major inconvenience, but there was no helping it now. In fact, if anything, being broken in half offered an unexpected sort of break from his otherwise mundane existence. It had, after all, been quite some time since he last experienced anything truly new.

Reading was his way of passing the time while he waited for his to come. He'd grown bored with the same world year after year, decade after decade. It never changed, after all. Not really. It changed its appearance. It changed its names. It changed its clothes. But it was always the same people and the same troubles and the same gripes and grumbles and prejudices.

But every now and then he found someone who surprised him.

"You lied." he said.

Corey raised an eyebrow. He seemed surprised, and it was no wonder. He made it a point not to engage in conversation. He didn't like talking to people. He didn't like *people*. But Corey didn't say anything about any of that. He simply replied, "Yep," and continued working.

"You know there won't be time for you to escape if you stay here. There's no 'one percent' about it."

"Yep," he said again.

"So why lie?"

"What's it matter?"

"It doesn't. But I'm curious."

He began winding strands around his hand again, separating them from the rest of the mess. "They're good people. Good people can't just walk away when you tell 'em you're not gonna make it. It's not in 'em."

"Even when it's the only way for *them* to survive as well?"

"Yep."

Austin fell silent, processing this.

Corey reached inside him again. This time, instead of pulling out coils of string, he felt his way around the inside of what mimicked his ribs. He was making note of those that had broken too short for him to take out.

He was actually quite good at this. He wasn't sure the Faceless Ones' ancient programming would hold up. Human beings were so unpredictable, after all. He'd long suspected that something had gone lopsided in their genetic code. He wasn't sure how else to explain some of the unfathomable nonsense he'd witnessed over those many centuries. It was astounding how many infallible things he'd seen them foul up.

"You're going to die here," he informed him.

"Yep," Corey said again, paying him no mind.

"That doesn't bother you?"

"Death happens. Can't stop it."

"True."

"Besides," he added, "death is a part of the Keeper's machine, too."

It was Austin's turn to raise an eyebrow. "It is."

Death was but a counterpart to life, a part of the complex balance between the three planes of existence. Death and life were the two realms of man and beast, in direct opposition of the unnatural. Just as death and the unnatural were the realms of darkness and shadow, in direct opposition of the light. And just as life and the unnatural were the realms of the tangible, the solid, in direct opposition of death's ethereal nature.

The stoneworks would be a poor tool of the cycle if they didn't encompass all three. It was why the design utilized this stone, the only material known to reliably transcend all three planes.

"Death's just a mystery we all get to look forward to solving when we're done exploring *this* side of things. To tell the truth, I've always kinda looked forward to it."

"You're an odd one," decided Austin.

"Yep," he replied again.

Chapter 35

Gina stared at the distorted outline of the thing with too many mouths that was waiting for her in the mysterious glass labyrinth. This didn't feel like the sort of puzzle she was going to be able to solve. She was beginning to understand that she was a living, three-dimensional human being attempting to pass through a one-dimensional doorway into a space of *unknown* dimensions occupied by an entity neither living nor dead that absolutely wanted to kill her in unimaginably horrible ways.

It was hard to imagine this working out in her favor, to be honest.

And yet, she understood that she had to find a way to cross into the glass labyrinth. It was clear to her that she was sent here for a reason. She was the only one who could even perceive that other space. It had something to do with her awful psychic abilities and her bizarre connection to the Twelve Teeth.

Perhaps the glass labyrinth was like Tristesse Lane. Or like the twisted pocket universe the barely-there dragged poor Nicole into way back in Briar Hills. A universe unto itself, buried somewhere within the very fabric of space. The home turf of yet another of the Great Enemy's monstrous dozen.

But that mysterious inner sense that always seemed to know all the things she shouldn't know yet knew anyway was telling her that the other labyrinth had been here as long as this one. The two were somehow constructed at the same time, purposefully overlapping, creating this bizarre duality. It was as much a part of the Temple of the Three Whispers as the city above and the storm that enveloped it, just another of its many puzzles and trials, left here by the mysterious sentinels specifically for someone like her.

No… Not someone *like* her.

Her. Gina Sarrelli. Because there was no one else like her anywhere in the world. And perhaps there never had been, not in all the innumerable histories mankind had lived through and forgotten.

She was utterly alone in the cosmos.

She focused her gaze on that sliver of refraction running down the wall, her thoughts swirling. Maybe that, in itself, was the key. If she really was a one-of-a-kind person with a completely unique ability, and if that ability made her the only one capable of even *finding* this spot, then didn't that sort of mean that there *must* be a way for her to cross over? What else would be the point in the glass labyrinth even existing?

All a part of the Keeper's grand scheme.

And the Keeper planned for everything...

But what was his plan for *her*? Did he intend nothing more than to sacrifice her to this monster? Was she fated to die just like the woman in the silvery dress? Could that really be her entire purpose here?

The beast with too many heads laughed. The sound of it within her head was hideous and strange. For some reason, it made her feel *itchy*, as if it weren't a voice inside her head at all, but a swarm of bugs crawling all over her skin.

Was it toying with her? Trying to distract her? Hoping to make her do something wrong? It was such a vile thing, full of malice and deceit. Nothing would delight it more than to lure her into a deadly trap.

She needed to find a way to ignore it and focus only on the doorway. She needed to focus her thoughts on *this* side of the wall.

She leaned closer, studying the odd refraction of light and space in the crack. It was difficult to see, but it wasn't a single distortion. The closer she looked, the more she realized that there were multiple layers. There were multiple *spaces*. And even as terrifying as the monster before her appeared, it couldn't occupy all those spaces at once.

That was the key.

She reached out and pressed her hands against the wall. It was a little disorienting, feeling stone while looking at glass. It was easy to forget that her physical body was still standing in that perfect darkness and, in reality, there *was no glass*. It was just the way her brain had chosen to represent the data her inhuman senses were feeding it. The transparency was likely a literal representation of the fact that she could "see through" the walls with her psychic abilities.

Come... purred the awful thing on the other side, its many foul voices filling her head, each one shivering with an inhuman hunger. *Hurry...*

"I really would rather not," she muttered under her breath. There were precious few things she *wouldn't* rather do, in all honesty, even by her own horrific standards. Even that awful tower back in Cakwetak didn't seem so bad compared to this.

What was she even doing here? She should be running back the way she came. There wasn't a single scenario she could imagine that didn't end in blood and pain. Besides, what more could she do? She couldn't make herself fit through a crack like that. It wasn't possible.

Except that wasn't precisely true.

That psychic part of her brain that she hated so much, the one that told her all the things she never wanted to know about the awful world around her, that fed her nightmares throughout her childhood, was still chugging away, processing all of this weirdness. And it was telling her, beyond a shadow of a doubt, that she *could* do it. She was perceiving it as a mere crack in the glass, but it was much more than that. It was a doorway. And she could use it.

Don't keep me waiting…

She shivered as several slimy, vulgar tongues slid across the other side of the glass.

She wanted to turn and run back the way she came, but if she did that, she was certain that her friends would never reach their destinations. Brandy and Albert. Nicole. Andrea. Keith. Violet and Corey. She'd doom them all. Just to save herself from her own dark and violent inevitability. And to what end? Just so she could die somewhere else in this endless darkness? Because they all had their job to do. And no one was leaving until everyone faced whatever was waiting for each of them.

She didn't have a choice. There was only one way forward from here.

She stood there, her gaze fixed on the wall, that unwelcome part of her brain churning away like some stubborn machine, slowly unraveling the mysterious opening before her.

She was looking at this all wrong, she realized. She was visualizing the space in front of her in the same three dimensions she viewed the "real" world in. She needed to change her perspective to match the much larger universe and its alien geometries.

The truth was that there were cracks like this *everywhere*. Faint. Foggy. Sliver-thin. Difficult to notice, even for her. But there was no danger of anyone inadvertently falling into one. Locked into a rigid frame of thought separating reality from fantasy, people simply didn't realize that they had the ability to access such things.

Come to me…

As terrified as she was, she knew she had no choice.

She focused on the crack in the glass…that narrow little sliver that wasn't so narrow or so little at all. Not if you approached it from the right angle. If she understood the proper way to look at it…

She closed her eyes and stepped through the crack.

Chapter 36

Violet gave her shirt one last hard twist and then shook it out. One advantage to being stranded alone in this darkness was that there was no shortage of privacy. There was no reason to walk around dripping wet when she could just strip down and wring everything out. It wasn't a laundry room and a hot shower, but it was better than nothing. She was even able to get a quick pee in while she was at it, which served the dual purpose of relieving the pressure that had been mounting down there for some time and allowing her to adequately express what she really thought of the sentinels and their giant labyrinth.

She pulled her shirt back over her head, cringing a little at the cold touch of the damp fabric against her bare skin, then picked up her flashlight and shined it back the way she came. She could still hear the distant rumble of the thunder from here, but she was far enough inside that she could no longer see even the subtlest flicker of lightning, meaning she should be perfectly safe from those invisible storm drafts.

And it had been a while since she heard any other noises, like the ones that reverberated through the stone as she and Everett were ascending to the upper level of that maze, just before they were separated.

She turned her attention forward and continued walking. Her boots were squeaking now, making it difficult to move silently, but they'd dry soon enough. They were good quality, after all, made to handle the elements. She hadn't spent all those years hunting portals in all manner of terrain and weather without learning a few things about proper footwear.

Ahead of her, the path diverged into three and somehow she realized that she knew to take the passage on the right. She could simply remember it. Somewhere in those bizarre dreams, she recalled the path as it was being built.

No... She didn't just *see* it in those memories. Someone *showed* it to her.

But something like that shouldn't be possible. Even in a world full of portals to other worlds and monsters and gods and distortions of time and space it was too wild to be true. And yet here she was, *experiencing* it.

Ahead of her, just beyond the reach of her flashlight, were more steps leading ever higher through these labyrinthine towers of mysterious gray stone. She knew it like she knew the way between her own bedroom and bathroom.

And sure enough, those very steps appeared from the gloom.

She stopped at the foot of these stairs and shined her light up them. "This is real," she sighed into the silence around her. She'd already acknowledged this fact, and yet she found that she needed to say it aloud. She kept clinging to her doubt not because she couldn't make herself believe it but because the idea was so overwhelmingly frightening. That world she saw in those dream-like visions, with that impossibly colorful sky and those giant moons and those eerie silhouettes, so thin and tall and strange as they went about their endless labors. It was real. And although there was beauty in those rainbow heavens above, there was also something dreadful about its existence. It was, after all, an entire universe solely dedicated to the construction of this one city…

And she was *there*. Throughout it *all*, her consciousness was present, slumbering away within the other one's strange, sentinel body, waking for only moments at a time, again and again, watching the walls slowly rise.

She and the sentinels were the same.

She drew a deep frown at this thought. She was most certainly *not* the same as a sentinel. Those things didn't even make biological sense. And yet she knew it to be a fact. She was one of them. She was with them throughout it all, carried within the other one like an unborn child.

She was a part of that world.

And she was a part of whatever was going on right here and now, for better or for worse…

It was overwhelming to think too much about. These memories were maddeningly bizarre. Everything about them was contradictory. Seeing without eyes. Hearing without ears. Impossible stone walls rising forever into the sky. Time passing but not passing. Being herself but also someone else.

Yet, was any of that any different from explosions that weren't explosions? Jeremys falling out of the sky? Living shadows and walking corpses and Architects Hands? Hotdog Creeps and shadow roads and killer trees and Denselands?

She closed her eyes and took a breath. Years ago, after the events that began with the Tunipet Boom, she and Corey set off to find the hidden truths of the universe. But maybe it was arrogant of her to think that she'd really be capable of understanding those truths. She was no genius. She didn't have the mental capacity to process things like changes in physics between one universe and the next. She didn't understand how any of this stuff worked and she was never going to.

But the other one had tried her best to explain it all to her, she recalled.

(*The gatehouses are machines of perfect balance, just like the universes they connect. The Three Powers turning in harmony like the gears of a clock. Life and nature. Death and spirit. Shadow and void. All equal. And each one held in check by the other two.*)

Balances. Three equal parts. No one could possibly understand all the mysteries of the natural world, much less the spiritual one. And to think that there was another one out there somewhere...something that was neither living nor dead...something completely and utterly *different* from everything she'd ever imagined...

She opened her eyes and began climbing the steps, her thoughts churning like the storm outside.

Was it really a brand-new concept? Or had she seen a glimpse of a world like that before? Years ago...? Back in her hometown...?

Was it possible that the third of the three precariously balanced universes was the one *Jeremy* came from? He was neither a man nor a spirit. He was a crosser. A thing from another world. An *alien*. But he was much more than that, too. He was a complex mask, stitched together from bits and pieces of the human lives he briefly encountered when he fell through some kind of cosmic crack between worlds and landed in downtown Tunipet that warm afternoon. The *real* Jeremy was a dark and shadowy thing that oozed in and out of reality, both physical and intangible at the same time, a thing completely and utterly devoid of humanity. Gravely wounded, it took on a human shape and dived so deeply into its disguise, so desperate to hide itself in this strange new world of sunshine and color and people and emotions, that it forgot it was ever anything else. And in doing so, he became as real as anyone. He was just some poor guy who was lost and alone and frightened.

She and Corey took care of him. They tried to help him make sense of all the missing pieces of his life. And they tried to protect him from the shadowy monstrosity that seemed to be stalking him. They fled their apartment and the city and eventually took up arms and stood their ground at Corey's uncle's place deep in the woods.

Except all wasn't as it seemed. And protecting their friend was never in the cards for them.

Just like in some tragic science fiction tale, the monster that fell to earth that day died and the humans who fought to protect it wept.

But before he died, he told them something wondrous.

(*There are many worlds besides this one. Some of them more significant than you can possibly imagine.*)

She set off in search of the truth all those years ago. And the truth had led her here.

She reached out and dragged her fingers along the smooth surface of the wall beside her. This stone was so much more than it appeared to be. She couldn't possibly understand it all, but the other one told her at some point that it was one of very few true *constants*. It was able to exist in all three universes simultaneously. That meant this *temple* existed simultaneously in all three.

This whole place—whether you called it a temple or a city or a gateway or a stoneworks—was one colossal crossroads. A nexus connecting all three, allowing them to not only meet, but overlap and intertwine.

How much of the cosmic truth that she and Corey had been searching for might be hidden within these very walls?

Above her, the top of the steps came into view in the rising glow of her flashlight, revealing a small room waiting there.

She stepped out into it, shining her light around. It was bigger than the other passageways, but not by much. There didn't appear to be any purpose for it.

She passed through it and into the next corridor, shining her light behind her as she went. It was curious. She probably wouldn't have thought anything about it, except that there hadn't been another space like that anywhere else in all the time she'd been wandering this labyrinth.

But it was already behind her, so what did it matter?

She turned her attention forward again, dismissing it. But somewhere in the far back of her mind, she felt a vague memory tickling her. Something the other one told her once in that hazy dreamlike time. Something about psychic chains...whatever that meant...

Chapter 37

Wayne stopped and tipped his head to one side, listening.

"Again?" whispered Olivia.

He glanced down at her, one eyebrow raised. "You still didn't hear it?"

She shook her head. "Nothing."

"Me neither," added Andrea. "And I've been hearing a lot of weird stuff since I left home, believe me."

She was right, he knew. By all accounts, it didn't make sense. If anyone should be hearing something the others couldn't, shouldn't it be Andrea? Olivia's thing didn't involve hearing things. It was a feeling. And his was only useful if he happened to croak. And yet that was twice now that he'd heard something unusual. Was it only one of the creatures from back in that freaky alien nature preserve back there? Some strange beast's howl or cry that was echoing through the passageways? Sometimes animals utilized pitches outside the range of human hearing. Maybe it was something like that, something that carried a long way but was only just at the very edge of what he was capable of hearing.

Or maybe it was nothing. Maybe he hit his head when he was flushed down that giant *toilet* back there and was suffering auditory hallucinations.

"Could it be Erin?" wondered Olivia. "I mean, we know she's here if she talked to Andrea. So maybe she's trying to talk to *you* now."

"Why would she talk to *me*? I mean, if she had a message for me, wouldn't it be easier to give it to the person whose *whole thing* is talking to ghosts and have her pass it on?"

"It's not my *whole* thing," said Andrea, crinkling her dirty nose. "But that's a good point, I guess…"

"It is, isn't it?" agreed Olivia.

He glanced back again, trying to remember exactly what it sounded like, but it was so faint and so brief that he wasn't able to narrow it down. He wasn't even sure which direction it might have come from. It hadn't been very long since they left that artificial ecosystem behind. And with all these different passages, he doubted it was very far away yet. That still seemed to him the most likely origin for it.

He pushed it from his thoughts and continued walking. They couldn't afford to waste time standing here, listening to a product of his overactive imagination. These passages were dangerous. It was probably only a matter of time before the scarecrow man and his chainsaw-dog-suit found them again.

"Everything I can see looks pretty normal," he observed. "So tell me about what I *can't* see."

"It's been steadily getting darker for a while now," reported Andrea. "It's more murk than stone now."

"Awesome," he grumbled. Maybe he shouldn't have asked…

"It's mostly on the floor here, though, which is a little weird. Usually, it's about the same on all four surfaces."

He looked down at his feet. He could see nothing but smooth, clean stone. And yet he didn't doubt her for a second. In fact, he found himself fighting back a shudder at the idea that he was wading through some kind of black fog that he couldn't see or feel.

According to Andrea, it had something to do with the afterlife. It was from the other side. The spirit world. *The Murk.* And only the dead could see it for what it really was. Only the dead could truly understand what it was to be a part of that other world.

He wished he could remember what happened when *he* was dead. It seemed like sort of a raw deal that he didn't at least come back with something to show for it. But then again, there were probably plenty of things out there that he wouldn't *want* to be able to see…

They continued onward, his flashlight sweeping across the stone floor ahead of him, his eyes peeled for even the faintest wisp of the eerie black fog she described.

After a few minutes, Andrea stopped walking. "That's weird."

"What is?" worried Olivia.

"The murk," she replied. "It's moving."

Wayne and Olivia both took a step backward, startled.

"Not like *moving*," she amended. "Sorry. I didn't mean it like that."

"Oh…" said Wayne. She told them that there were things in the murk that moved around and that some of them had behaved aggressively. His first thought, of course, was that she'd just seen another one of those. And he still didn't know whether the things in the so-called murk could be dangerous to those who couldn't see them.

"I said it was mostly on the floor earlier," she explained. "But it's, like…*shifted*, I guess…to the wall." She pointed to the right up ahead. "Like it's starting to spiral around the passage or something. I haven't seen it do that anywhere else."

"What do you think it means?" asked Olivia, her voice hushed as if the black sludge might be able to hear her.

"No idea," replied Andrea in the same hushed tone. "I wish Erin would talk to me again, but she hasn't said a word since I crawled out of that nasty mudhole."

He noticed that Olivia pursed her lips at the mention of that name. She still wasn't over the fact that Erin shoved him into that killing vine and left her all alone for a while. And he could hardly blame her. If it had been her instead of him—even if she were able to come back the way he did—he wasn't sure he'd ever be able to forgive that woman.

"Is it safe?" she wondered.

"It doesn't look like there's anything in it," Andrea replied. "In fact I haven't seen any of those weird clumpy things since that mud room, either."

Olivia looked up at him, her lovely eyes shimmering with worry. "I don't feel anything. But I don't know if my psychic threads thing can sense ghostly stuff. What if it's a blind spot?"

He fixed his attention forward again. "I guess we just keep going. Take it slow. Retreat at the first sign of trouble."

She tightened her grip on his arm and together they continued onward.

Again, he heard something very faint in the distance, but this time he ignored it. It wasn't doing any good to keep pointing it out. All he was doing was frightening his fiancée. And it had already faded again anyway in the time it would've taken him to look back.

He pushed it from his mind and carried on.

Several minutes passed without any more mystery noises. Maybe they'd finally wandered out of earshot of whatever he was picking up.

"It's getting thicker," said Andrea. "It's harder to tell if something might be moving in it."

Beside him, he felt Olivia shiver at the thought of hidden things waiting to ambush them in that ghostly unseen realm.

"Just do your best," he said. He didn't bother stopping, but he did begin hugging the left wall a little closer, recalling that she said it was clinging to the right one.

Another couple minutes passed in silence. Then Andrea stopped walking. "Do you guys see a passage on the right?"

Wayne frowned. "No." From his point of view there was only one passage, and it was curving left.

"Didn't think so," she sighed. "It's like all the murk is funneling into it. It's *really* dark inside."

He frowned at the thought. "Does that mean we should go that way?"

"Or that we should stay *out* of it?" hoped Olivia.

"I *really* don't want to go in there," replied Andrea. Her blue eyes were fixed on the wall ahead of them, a frightened expression painted across her usually cheerful face.

Wayne looked down at Olivia, an eyebrow raised.

"I can't even *see* it," she replied, sounding annoyed.

"But we know it's there," he countered.

"I know…" She wrinkled her nose at him. "I don't like being the one in charge of finding the dangerous paths."

"I get it," he assured her.

She sighed and fixed her gaze on the passage she could see. She stood there a moment, pondering the choices, visualizing going each way. Then, at last, she turned those lovely eyes up to him again and nodded. "She's right. It feels like the best way."

Andrea groaned. "I was really hoping to be wrong this time…"

"Let's just get it over with, then," said Wayne.

She stepped forward and took Olivia's hand, then led them straight through the wall and into a passage that only seemed to exist the moment they set foot inside it.

"That's still so weird!" whispered Olivia.

And disorienting. For a moment there, he felt as if he were going to fall over.

He expected to find himself standing in a sea of that shadowy murk, but once again, the passage looked just like any other.

Andrea pointed her light at the corner where the ceiling and the left wall met about ten feet ahead of them. "Something's moving up there," she warned, her voice hushed. "I don't think it's big enough to hurt us, but maybe steer wide of it."

"Don't have to tell us twice," he replied, already crowding the right wall behind her.

She kept her light fixed on the empty corner as they crept past it, never taking her eyes off it. It was such a bizarre thing, avoiding literally nothing. It felt like he was a child again, playing make-believe on the playground. And yet, he never doubted for a second that there was something very real in that spot, something he very much didn't want to risk touching. He realized he was even holding his breath, afraid to make so much as a sigh until it was out of sight behind them.

"It's okay now," Andrea assured them, although she was still whispering. She turned her light forward again, sweeping the path ahead of them. "All clear. For now, at least."

"Is it weird that I think that was scarier than if I'd actually been able to see what was there?" asked Olivia in the same whisper.

"Nope," replied Wayne. He was thinking the same thing, in fact. Something about an invisible monster lurking there. He started forward, eager to be on the other side of this passage, but a sound made him pause and shine his light back the way he came before he could stop himself.

The girls followed his lead, both of them wide-eyed and worried.

He was scaring them, he knew. He needed to get his nerves under control. It was only his imagination. Or at most just the sounds of that anything-but-natural nature sanctuary echoing through the corridors. Nothing more. "Sorry," he said, continuing onward again. "Ignore me. I'm just jumpy."

But they didn't believe him. And he didn't blame them. He didn't believe it himself, after all. Because he was increasingly sure that it wasn't his imagination. And it didn't sound like the temple's alien menagerie.

It sounded like a voice calling out to him...

Chapter 38

Everett opened his eyes and looked at Alice. She was precisely as he'd imagined her. A little, well-loved doll in a simple, frilly dress. Her face was frozen porcelain, hand painted, and her long, golden hair was messy from countless brushings. She was only about twelve inches from head to toe, delicate and dainty, her arms and legs limp. Her torso plump with stuffing.

She was familiar, he realized. His mother used to have one just like this on her bedroom shelf when he was growing up, a remnant from her own youth. He must have subconsciously recalled it when it occurred to him to choose a doll for her form.

The birdcage had vanished, along with the table it was sitting on. In its place was a second chair, just like the one he was sitting in. Alice was propped up there, facing him, as if the two of them were having a casual conversation.

He reached out and gently picked her up. He held her in his hand, studying her, fascinated. She was just a doll. Stuffing and cloth and that pretty porcelain face. Nothing more. And yet she was nothing so simple.

"What are you?" he asked, bringing her closer to his face.

But she didn't answer him.

He frowned at the silence. That wasn't supposed to happen. She looked like a doll. She felt like a doll. He could do as he pleased with her like a doll. But Alice wasn't a doll. She was something special. And somehow—probably thanks to that massive information dump the puzzle box loaded into his brain—he knew that she was able to answer his questions.

He peered down at her, taking in all those fine little details. She was so unbelievably real. She even had all the wear and tear of a well-loved doll. It even looked as if some naughty little girl had once taken a pair of scissors to her poor bangs. He didn't know he could imagine something so perfectly. And yet, upon closer inspection, she also looked strangely *pristine*, as if she'd never been touched until just now. "Unreal" was the word that came to mind. As in literally. She wasn't crafted on an assembly line in some musty factory. She wasn't even lovingly handmade in some warm and cozy workshop. She was *born*.

Just now. Right here.

"It's not defiance," he muttered to himself. She wasn't giving him the silent treatment. She wasn't *refusing* to answer him. That wasn't how this worked. He squinted at her a moment longer, pondering it all, then sat up straight in his chair and smiled. "I see. You *can't* answer me."

Right now, *he* was the problem. He asked her what she was, but how was she supposed to answer that when whatever she was *didn't have a name*? It wasn't as if the duck-billed platypus *told* the first explorers to see one that it was called that. She couldn't tell him she was an elf or a brownie or a dryad or some other fantasy creature like the fairies Olivia ran afoul of back in Gutler's Weep. She wasn't from his world. She wasn't something that ever appeared in any folklore. How could she tell him what she was if he was utterly incapable of understanding her reply?

And then there was the fact that, regardless of whatever she might have been when he first arrived here, she was different now. He'd changed her. When he took control of the illusions, he took control of the reality.

She was Alice.

This was going to be a little more complicated than he imagined. He was going to have to think things through.

"Let's try that again," he said, leaning forward and looking closely at her. "Can you help me get back to where I was before I came here? Back to the city where my friends are?"

Alice did nothing. She didn't move. Her porcelain face never changed. She made no sound. She was only a doll, after all. And yet somehow she answered his question.

Her answer was yes.

It was a strange sort of thing, like everything else. He couldn't explain it. He couldn't even *describe* it properly. She didn't speak. Not aloud for him to hear and not psychically, into his mind. She didn't nod. He just simply found that he *knew* her answer was yes. She could help him get back to the City Beyond Memory.

Again, he smiled. "Awesome." They were definitely going to work on that.

But first...

He placed her back onto the chair again. Gently. He didn't think he *needed* to be gentle. She looked delicate and fragile, with that tiny, painted face, yet somehow he knew that he couldn't harm her even if he wanted to. She was considerably more resilient than he was in that form. But he couldn't help it. It felt like he should be gentle with her. It seemed like the right thing to do.

"Are you all alone in this place?" he wondered, glancing around at the cartoonish door and window of this dollhouse prison that was something entirely different when he walked in.

Again, she answered him. There was no doubt in his mind that she did. It seemed like such a subtle thing, but it wasn't. Not by any means. The answer was right there in his head, as if he'd known it all along and only had to ask the question aloud in order to remember it. But that knowledge wasn't there a moment ago. It blossomed into existence like a firework bursting in the night sky, bright and booming and spectacular. It was a lot like what the Eeshee and the puzzle box did to him, but this wasn't the least bit painful. In fact, it was oddly pleasant. It reminded him a little of when Andrea and Violet took his hand or linked arms with him, a tender sort of sensation, almost intimate in a strange sort of way.

But this time the answer was more confounding.

Yes and no. Always alone, yet never alone.

He leaned closer again, studying her, taking in those pretty blue eyes and her painted-on lashes, listening to her mysterious silence, slowly collecting the pieces.

Awareness flooded his mind. Of darkness and cold. Of emptiness. Nothingness.

And of time.

So much time…

She was showing him the void, where he found himself adrift and became lost after those things in the labyrinth snatched him away from Violet. It was the road that led him to the twisted flipside of the city, where reality was turned on its head and those monstrous, drunken spires stretched into a poisoned sky like something out of a Lovecraftian nightmare.

That place was anything but lonely, crawling with unimaginable horrors that crept and seeped and oozed and writhed. But that wasn't where he was now. He'd fallen through the cracks in that broken realm and landed here, where reality was fluid and dreams took conscious shape. A place she'd lain slumbering in timeless nothingness for endless ages. Unfeeling. Unthinking. Undreaming. Until something changed. Until something *new* descended upon her dark and silent sanctuary, plunging her nonexistence into chaos.

His first instinct was to apologize. He didn't mean to come here. It just sort of happened. He was caught in that strange current, unable to fight as he was dragged through that mind-numbing inversion of a reality. He only wanted to find his way back to Violet before she could worry too much about him.

But as she fed him her story in that queer stream of blossoming information, he realized that *he* wasn't what upended her world.

Someone was here before him. Someone with the ability to come and go as they pleased. Someone capable of incredible and terrible things.

He tipped his head to one side, confused by this new information, and asked, "Who is the Priestess of Ruin?"

Chapter 39

Nicole trudged onward, struggling against Keith's increasing weight. He was slowing down, weakening, and it was no wonder. Those awful wounds refused to stop bleeding. Crimson smears on the stone. Sweat dripping down his face. His eyes beginning to look sunken. She was trying so desperately to save him, but was she only killing him faster by dragging him onward?

"How'd you guys find your way through the first one of these, anyway?" wondered Keith.

She glanced over at him, relieved to hear him speak. If he was talking—and asking relevant questions, no less—then he was still with her. There was still hope. "Albert, mostly."

"Albert..." he repeated. "Right..."

"At first, he had his box."

"Remember that..." he breathed. "Andrea talked about it."

"She did, yeah." She needed to keep him talking, keep him engaged. The more he talked, the better. "Albert's a puzzle geek. Loves that kind of stuff. It's how the Sentinel Queen lured him down there."

"Sentinel Queen..."

"Yeah. *She* was freaky as fuck."

"So weird..."

"Totally." She pushed onward, her thoughts swirling. There was no Sentinel Queen this time. No box of clues. No map to follow. Instead, they had Gina and her goddess, Ada. And Keith wasn't even there when they met Ada. She suddenly realized that, to him, everything began with a bunch of weird dreams and that boat ride across that enormous black lake.

"Why didn't *we* get a box?"

"Good fucking question," she grumbled. Although looking back, she recalled that the box only got them as far as the City of the Blind. After they met with the Sentinel Queen, they were sent into the depths of the labyrinth where they were given no instructions whatsoever. Except for that bit about the meadow, she supposed...

"Doesn't seem very fair."

"No shit." She glanced down at his feet, at the blood-soaked tatters of her tank top, at the trail of bloody smears on the stone behind them. "Albert's smart, though," she recalled. "He brought sidewalk chalk. Marked the walls as we went. Kept us from backtracking."

"Clever."

"I know, right? He's pretty cool like that." She stared into the darkness looming ahead of them. "They're here, too," she recalled. "Somewhere…" She wondered what happened to Brandy and Albert. And Gina, of course. The last she recalled, the four of them were standing at the gateway in that impossibly huge wall, getting ready to use the pendant to open the way inside. Then Hotdog came back.

She hoped they were okay.

But of course, if *she* made it into the city, then they must have, too. Right?

It still seemed so surreal that Brandy and Albert just sort of appeared out of thin air back there. She never once considered that they'd been caught up in all this nonsense, too, and were having their own bizarre little adventure.

She chuckled. "Wanna hear something funny?"

"Sure. Could use a good laugh about now."

"Know how you just sort of spontaneously became a boat captain?"

"Uh huh. Weird."

"Right? Well, apparently those two are sex witches now."

He'd barely opened his eyes while talking up to this point, but now he actually looked up at her. "They're *what?*"

She nodded. "Right? You remember how they were. Always showing up late and leaving early because they couldn't stop screwing around? Apparently they can use all that sluttiness to cast *actual fucking magic.*"

"Damn…"

"Right? I saw them do it. They teleported. Right in front of me. It was crazy."

"That's not the version of *Harry Potter* I remember reading."

An unattractive bark of a laugh escaped her before she could rein it in.

"If we find him in here, don't let him point is wand at me, okay?"

This time, she tried to hold it back but couldn't. It came belching forth in a wet sort of snort that would've been a lot more embarrassing if he hadn't heard her laugh like that more than a few times in the past.

"Just saying," he sighed, closing his eyes again.

Nicole felt a pang deep in her heart. This reminded her of all the times they just sat and talked when they were first dating. Especially their pillow talk. She used to lie there, snuggled up against him, chatting. He was so funny. He always knew how to make her laugh.

She hadn't realized how much she missed that.

She hadn't realized a lot of things…

"What's wrong with me?" she groaned.

"What?" he asked wearily. He didn't look up, didn't open his eyes. He appeared to be concentrating hard on fighting back another wave of pain.

"Why am I such a fuckup?"

"Because you know," he muttered, his voice barely audible.

She frowned. "What?"

"Huh?"

"*What* do I know?"

He opened his eyes and squinted at her, confused. "What?"

"You just said…"

"What'd I say?"

She sighed and tightened her grip on him. "Nothing. Never mind." He obviously wasn't thinking clearly. He probably just muttered something about how much his feet were hurting him and she misheard him. Besides, how the hell should *he* know why she was such a fuckup? He'd probably been asking himself that same question ever since they broke up. What was wrong with Nicole? Why was she like this?

That was the million-dollar question, wasn't it?

If only Gina's goddess could've answered that one for her…

She wished Brandy and Albert were here. She could use her friends. And who knew, maybe their weird sex magic would include some sort of cure for Keith's injured feet.

She stopped walking, her eyes widening. Was that possible? Could they do something like that? They told her Albert was carrying around a book of spells their pervy teacher gave him. Maybe one of them could help save Keith!

But as quickly as this feverish ray of hope shined down on her, it faded. What were the odds of being able to find *anyone* in this endless stone maze, much less Brandy and Albert, before it was too late?

No. She couldn't think like that. There was an answer. Everyone kept telling her that the fucking Keeper knew what he was doing, that he had a plan for everything, that nothing happened without him foreseeing it.

Keith stumbled and slumped to the floor. She cried out, surprised, as his weight pulled her down with him.

"Easy!" she cried. "I've got you!"

But he let out a weary groan, his eyes fluttering.

"Don't pass out on me now!"

But he went limp in her arms.

A great, choking sob shook its way up from deep inside her. "Stay with me! Don't you dare leave me!"

But she didn't have the right to tell him what to do.

She didn't have any right at all...

Chapter 40

Albert held tight to Brandy's hand, unwilling to be separated from her. He'd taken the lead but he didn't try to take the flashlight from her. He didn't need her ability to see the so-called "truth in people" to realize that she felt better holding it. Even a little sense of security like this might help keep her courage up. And it wasn't as if he needed it. She was doing a fine job of lighting the way for him, aiming it wherever he was looking.

"Another chamber up ahead," he observed.

She didn't bother responding. She didn't need to. There was always another chamber or another passage or another fright. And he could tell that she was entirely over it all.

Not that he blamed her in the least. He wasn't exactly having the time of his life, either. He was the one who always wanted to go back, to seek the answers they were denied five years ago, who'd lain awake in bed so many late nights, wondering about those deep, dark mysteries they left buried beneath the city. Was he old enough yet to feel as if maybe he wasn't as young as he used to be? Because that was how it was beginning to feel. He yearned for the safe comfort of his own apartment, his warm bed with his beautiful new bride snuggled up at his side…

Maybe he'd finally grown up a little.

Or maybe he was simply admitting that this entire ordeal was terrifying and even the mere *thought* of losing Brandy was a fear that far outweighed his curiosity. He'd never forgive himself if something happened to her in this endless maze of darkness and stone. The very thought made him grip her hand a little tighter.

The chamber waiting for them was small, only about the size of their apartment's living room, and was less a room than a crossroads. It was symmetrical and ten-sided—a decagon, if he remembered the word correctly—with identical passageways leading away in every direction.

"Oh good," grumbled Brandy. "This is exactly the sort of thing we need to get even *more* fucking lost."

She wasn't wrong. There were at least nine wrong turns standing in front of them. And that was assuming there was ever a *right way* to begin with. Mathematically, the odds of stumbling across the exit in a labyrinth of this size was practically zero. They technically shouldn't ever have found their way through the *first* temple. The only explanation for them doing so, as far as he was able to figure out, was that there were *many* paths leading to the tower in the heart of the labyrinth, so that anyone would eventually find their way out if they simply wandered around long enough. But even that didn't feel right. He'd stood at the base of that burning mountain, after all. He'd seen how enormous it was. How did they not spend *weeks* trapped inside that monstrosity?

Except he knew the answer to that question. It was the Keeper. *He* was the one who made it possible. He'd rigged it somehow. Gave them psychic nudges, perhaps. Or some kind of subliminal trail to follow. It was the only thing that really made any sense, the more he thought of it.

And wasn't that exactly what everybody kept telling them? That the Keeper planned all of this? Every detail? Every step? Every second of every minute?

Brandy shined the light into each passage in turn, revealing nothing more than what they'd already seen: ten identical passages leading away into the same, familiar darkness.

He thought about pulling his wife close and kissing her, working himself up, activating his psychic abilities like Shanzer taught them, but he was sure that wouldn't accomplish anything. She was still upset, after all. He didn't think she'd push him away if he insisted that they try it, but her heart wouldn't be in it. Not really. And somehow he didn't feel like it would help anyway. He had a feeling that even if he cast out his psychic net, he wouldn't be able to see a path leading from here.

Instead of searching for a nonexistent solution to an impossible puzzle, he simply led her to the first path on the left and started walking.

"I'm so over this," she groaned.

"I know."

The passage they were following led straight for about a hundred yards then abruptly turned back on itself. They found themselves walking back the way they came, except on the other side of the wall. He didn't recall any of the other passages doing that. Not here in *this* temple, anyway. Most of these were comprised of long stretches of straight corridors that occasionally intersected or branched off. These were more like the twisting and winding passageways that filled the labyrinth beyond the City of the Blind.

His stubbornly logical and analytical brain wanted to try puzzling through the reasons for this abrupt change in his surroundings, wondering if perhaps they'd made a wrong turn and were caught in a time-wasting series of dead ends. Or perhaps they were nearing something significant hidden within these walls that might be important in their journey. But the fact was that this wasn't one of his puzzles or murder mysteries. This was a *labyrinth*. And *real* labyrinths weren't like the fun little pages you found in children's activity books. Real labyrinths weren't meant to be solved. They were meant to contain and confound. They were random and chaotic and irrational. Logic wouldn't have any place in the design. The more he tried to think his way through, the more likely he was to never leave.

An opening appeared in the wall ahead of them, revealing another passage on the other side, running parallel to this one. Aware that they were heading back toward the decagon chamber, he opted for doorway number one and headed back the other way again. They wanted to keep moving away from there. Those ten passages would create a bottleneck that would keep them going in circles as long as they remained close to it. And should they find themselves back in the room, it would be impossible to know which way was which, meaning they could end up retracing their steps without knowing it and wasting precious time.

But it didn't seem to matter. Within minutes, the path became a confounding tangle of winding corridors and intersecting passages. He completely lost track of how many times they turned. He wouldn't be able to find his way back if he wanted to. But of course that didn't matter. Going back would only waste time and leave them no better off than they were an hour ago.

Another opening revealed yet another passage. He stepped through it and looked back and forth while Brandy lit the way for him.

"This way, maybe?" he muttered, setting off in what he hoped was a direction leading to a less crowded section of the labyrinth.

"We're so fucking lost, aren't we?"

"I mean, it's a giant maze, so yeah."

"You're supposed to lie and tell me you know exactly where we are."

"Am I?"

"Yes."

"Oh. Sorry. Then I meant to say this is exactly where we're supposed to be."

"Yeah?"

"Totally. You can tell by the wall." He reached up and knocked on it as he walked. "You hear that? Nothing at all like the walls we were by before."

"Not at all, huh?"

"We'll be out of here in no time."

Brandy shined her light back the other way, nervous about the darkness at their backs. When she shined it forward again, there was something different ahead of them.

He had time to wonder if they might have actually found the way out, but no such luck. A moment later, he found himself standing at the end of the passage, staring down into a gaping chasm in the stone.

A dead end.

And a deadly one, at that. If they'd been wandering around in the dark, they likely would've fallen to their doom.

"Out of here in no time, huh?" grumbled Brandy.

"*You* told me to lie to you."

"I thought you'd be better at it."

"Sorry to disappoint you." He leaned out over the chasm and looked back and forth. He could see the wall on the other side. It looked like the one from the first temple, where stone bridges were stretched across it. But there were no bridges or other passageways in sight.

"Be careful," she fussed, tightening her grip on his hand.

"I am."

They had no choice but to go back the way they came and try a different way, but he was having a hard time not feeling discouraged. Now they were caught between the decagon room and this chasm. He had a feeling it was going to take a while to find their way out of this area.

She tugged him away from the ledge and led the way back.

Wherever the others were, he hoped they were having better luck than he was.

Chapter 41

Gina stood in the strange, empty corridor of the glass labyrinth, her heart pounding, clutching at her chest as she trembled with fear.

She wasn't certain. She knew stepping through that crack could bring her face-to-horrible-faces with the thing that killed the woman in the silvery dress. She'd braced herself for a terrible fright and was still in the grip of it, still unable to believe that she was safe.

But she was alone in the pitch-black passageway.

It was the layers. Those multiple spaces she sensed with her psychic mind, all smashed together, interconnected and tangled. The unnatural space on this side was skewed. It was *crinkled*, just like the strange, endless acres of the Denselands. The monster was beyond even her ability to fully comprehend, but she was quite sure that it wouldn't be able to occupy all of those places at the same time, meaning the odds were far better that she'd end up somewhere other than whatever part of the glass labyrinth it was currently in.

But those odds were never zero. She could just as easily have stepped across and right into its many waiting jaws, which was precisely what she was convinced would happen. She'd never considered herself lucky by any means, after all. And taking that chance was utterly terrifying.

She leaned against the glass wall, weak with relief, and took a shuddering breath. Her poor heart wouldn't slow down. She felt as if she might throw up. She didn't realize until she was already across just how much she believed she was about to meet a violent and gruesome end. She had to keep telling herself she was okay, as if she couldn't quite make herself believe it.

Perhaps the monster's wicked words had wormed their way into her head more than she realized.

And it wasn't over yet. She didn't dare let her guard down. She might not have immediately found herself in the same corridor with that thing, but she and it were on the same side of the looking glass now. It was only a matter of time before it sniffed her out. She had precious little time to figure out what her purpose was in this City Beyond Memory, why the goddess and her Keeper sent her here.

She stood up straight and winced. Now that the initial terror had passed, she felt strangely disheveled. The trip through that crack wasn't as simple as taking a step. It felt as if she'd contorted herself in the process, stretching and bending in ways that left her feeling as if she'd just finished a light workout. Her skirt felt wonky. And she had a wedgie. She reached behind her and tugged at the fabric, sorting herself out.

What an unusual experience. She didn't think she cared much for traveling that way.

But she didn't have time to dwell on the discomforts of passing through dimensional cracks in imaginary glass walls. She turned her attention to the darkness around her. That monster was likely already searching for her.

She cast her psychic eye across the labyrinth, scanning the greater area. It was clearer here on this side. She wasn't sure if it was because the storm wasn't affecting this space or because the curious stone had been replaced with glass. Or perhaps the stone appeared as glass to her on this side specifically because she could see so much more clearly. Because she was quite sure there was no glass. The surface she was leaning against felt like the same smooth stone she felt on the other side. It was only a trick of her mind. An attempt by her mere human brain to comprehend things it was never meant to sense.

The mind was a curious thing, resilient in so many ways, and yet fragile enough to be broken beyond repair. She often thought it was no small miracle that she hadn't long ago lost hers.

The glass labyrinth was enormous. It seemed to stretch on forever in every direction. But that wasn't quite right, she realized. It appeared to go on and on, but it was all tangled up and twisted. She wasn't looking out in a straight line. In reality, it circled back on itself, overlapping and twisting in unusual and confounding ways.

She saw no sign of the monster, but that didn't mean it wasn't near. It could be lurking in the loops and kinks of the knotted space, hidden just out of view.

Something caught her attention. She turned and squinted into the darkness, trying to focus on something moving several passageways over. It was difficult to make out. Her mind perceived it as looking through several of the warped-glass walls, distorting and refracting the non-existent light, leaving little more than twisting and oozing shapes sliding past in the gloom. It wasn't the monster with too many heads. It was smaller. And there appeared to be two of them. Those terrifying "hound" creatures Andrea described to her, perhaps?

No...

She pressed her hands against the "glass" and leaned closer, focusing on the shapes.

Those were *people!*

Had she circled back around to Brandy and Albert? Or was it possible she'd found Andrea and Keith? Or perhaps even Violet and Corey?

For a moment, her heart was pounding with excitement rather than fear, but that quickly melted away, replaced with a brand-new fear. Why would there be people in the glass labyrinth? It was dangerous here! She had to find them before that monster did!

She scanned the layout of the passages between her and them, looking for a path, but there didn't seem to be one. There was, however, a passage that went in that direction, leading into an oddly complex tangle of intersections not far from that spot. She hurried forward, following it, eager to get closer.

She could hear their voices, now that she was listening. A low, barely audible murmuring of soft conversation.

The first left was a dead end. She hurried past it and took the next, then the first right after that. She needed to circle around this way first. Then she could move back toward those other two.

Except...where were they? She stopped and searched the area again. She couldn't see them. They were gone. Did they move away from her? No... That wasn't quite right. The entire layout had somehow changed.

"Crinkles..." she muttered to herself. Time and space crumpled and turned back on itself. It was different than the way the Denselands were crinkled. That was an effect of all those dead universes piled on top of one another. The City Beyond Memory was shielded from those anomalies by the impassible wall. She hadn't felt any of those since she passed through the gate. *These* crinkles were unique to the glass labyrinth's design, seemingly built into it.

"Easy!" echoed a voice from somewhere in the darkness. "I've got you!"

She turned, confused. It sounded like it came from directly behind her, but there was no one around. She was entirely alone in this place.

"Don't pass out on me now!"

Again, she turned, startled. Was that Nicole? Was she here in the glass labyrinth somewhere? And had something happened? She sounded scared.

But no matter where she looked she couldn't see her.

"Stay with me! Don't you dare leave me!"

"Hello?" called Gina. "Is someone there?" But her voice wouldn't carry very far. She didn't have the courage to speak very loudly.

Slowly, she turned her head, listening. She could definitely hear muted voices, but she couldn't tell where they were coming from. Was she on the other side of the wall? She turned and pressed her ear to the glass, but she could only make out a faint muttering, as if people were whispering somewhere nearby.

It wasn't her imagination. She was sure of it. Someone was there somewhere, but she couldn't pinpoint an origin. She cast her psychic senses outward again, trying to narrow in on it.

Above her?

She lifted her face and stared up into the darkness.

There were more corridors up there, but it wasn't like peering up through a glass ceiling to the next level. She found herself staring into a passageway stretching away from her and forking off in multiple directions, as if she were looking straight ahead instead of straight up.

Except…she *wasn't* looking up…

She turned all the way around, confused. The forking corridor that was above her was now in front of her. The entire glass labyrinth seemed somehow to have turned itself ninety degrees.

Or was it *she* who somehow tipped onto her side?

Even for her, this was starting to feel crazy!

"We're so fucking lost, aren't we?"

She twirled around and looked the other way, her useless eyes wide open in the darkness. That was a different voice. But she couldn't see anyone, not so much as a distorted shadow through the warped glass of the wall.

Someone muttered something, too low and too quiet for her to hear.

She made her way down the passage, following those unintelligible mutterings, trying to pinpoint which direction they were coming from.

She peered around a corner. Left or right? She couldn't tell. Maybe this was the wrong way from the start and she should go back the way she came. She turned around, trying to decide.

Someone said something else, but she couldn't make it out. There were at least two voices.

She took a few more steps, straining to hear better.

"You can tell by the wall."

She stopped and pressed her ear to the glass again. Was that Albert? It was fading in and out, as if they were moving around.

Then she heard another voice. Female. Brandy. "Not at all, huh?"

"We'll be out of here in no time."

Where were they? Why couldn't she see them through the glass?

She held her breath and struggled to hear what they were saying, but all she could hear now was a muffled sort of muttering of their voices. She reached out and pressed her hands against the glass. She wanted to call out to them, to let them know she was here, but she didn't quite dare. That monster was still in here somewhere. She couldn't risk giving away her location.

Now she couldn't hear anything. Were they gone? Or had they simply gone quiet?

She turned and pressed closer to the other wall. Were they over here now?

"Be careful," she heard Brandy say.

"I am," Albert replied.

Then nothing. Everything had gone silent again.

She thought she was beginning to understand what was going on. None of those voices were coming from this side of the glass. She was hearing conversations from the other side, from the stone labyrinth.

She crept forward, still listening. There was another intersection ahead of her. She stepped out into it and cast her inner eye in each direction. There was something moving in a nearby corridor, but she knew immediately that it wasn't a person. It was something on four legs. Something dangerous.

But she also sensed that it was separate from the rest of the labyrinth somehow, unable to get between where it was and where her friends were. There was some kind of border keeping them apart. But she also sensed that there were plenty of places where the two areas crossed, providing ample opportunity for bloodshed.

She turned and tried the passage leading the opposite direction. It curved tightly to the left, then dead ended.

She stood there a moment, an unsettled feeling slowly overwhelming her. This place was strangely *slippery*. She couldn't seem to grasp the layout. It was difficult to tell one corridor from the next through the distorted glass. And there was something dreadfully claustrophobic about feeling lost in here.

Was this what it was like for everyone five years ago in that first temple? No one had her ability to sense the space around her. They were wandering blind. How many dead ends did they find themselves up against? How did they keep from losing hope?

But now wasn't the time to dwell on such unhelpful thoughts. She turned around to backtrack, only to freeze as she found herself staring through the warped glass.

Violet was there.

She was just on the other side of the wall, seemingly staring right back at her.

Gina hurried forward and called out to her, thrilled at the idea of having found someone. But something wasn't quite right. How did Violet get so close without her noticing? She should've been able to sense her approaching.

And more importantly, why was she all alone right now? Where was Corey? Didn't Brandy and Albert say that they were together last they saw them?

Had something terrible happened?

As she watched, Violet lifted the shard of blue glass she wore on a chain around her neck and peered through it at her. She remembered her talking about that shard. It was supposed to give her the ability to see hidden things. Was she able to use it to find others in the labyrinth?

For a moment, it seemed like they were looking at each other, but Violet only frowned, puzzled, and then let it drop back to the end of its chain again.

She pressed her hands to the wall between them, making herself as visible as possible against the warped glass.

Violet stood there, her gaze sliding across the space between them, scanning the area. There were multiple passageways in the area she was standing in, each one identical. She was trying to decide which way to go, which was probably what she was doing from the start. It was only wishful thinking that she'd somehow noticed her on this side of the glass.

Again, Gina pounded on it. But she knew it was pointless. No one else could see the glass labyrinth.

Violet crossed her arms over her chest as if cold. And she looked *wet*, now that she was looking. Her hair was stuck to her face.

What had she been through?

Violet chose a direction and walked away.

Gina tried to follow after her. She turned and withdrew into the passage in that direction. The scene shifted behind the warped glass. Everything tilted and warbled. Then she was looking straight down the passage Violet was walking in, watching her disappear into the darkness.

Frustrated, Gina smacked the glass as hard as she could, stinging the palm of her hand in the process.

Violet stopped.

Her heart skipped a beat. Did she hear that?

She turned and looked back. The glass here was even more warped than usual. It was difficult to see her clearly, but she seemed to be looking right at her.

Again, she lifted the glass shard and peered through it.

She pounded her fists on the glass, but Violet couldn't hear her. Did sound not travel between the glass and the stone? No... That didn't feel right. It was more like an illusion. Or a mirage. She was sure she was looking at Violet right now, but she wasn't really on the other side of this wall. She was somewhere else, somewhere far away from here.

Because *everything* in the stone labyrinth was far away from the glass labyrinth. They were two fundamentally different places.

Violet let the shard drop back to her chest and took a step backward.

"Wait..." she gasped. She wanted to shout, to *scream* at her, anything to make her hear, but she didn't dare. She'd already made far too much noise. It wasn't safe.

It wasn't possible to cross between the labyrinths here. There were no cracks. No distortions to peel open. She couldn't reach her. There was nothing she could do.

Violet turned and hurried off in the other direction.

She stood there, feeling helpless, and watched as her light faded back into the darkness. A dreadfully lonely feeling was settling into her. She didn't want to be left alone again...

She never should've left Brandy and Albert. That was a mistake. She thought she was brave enough to do this on her own, but she wasn't. And now it was too late.

Would she ever leave these glass corridors again?

A hard shiver raced up her back as something ran past the wall directly behind her.

She twirled around, barely stifling a scream, and caught just a glimpse of the monstrous shape with too many heads slinking out of view behind the unnatural glass.

It was drawing nearer.

Time was running out.

Chapter 42

Violet stood shivering in the dark, staring at the dead end blocking her path. This wasn't right. Wasn't the other one supposed to remember the way for her?

She turned around and started back toward the last intersection she chose from. She wasn't terribly confident with that one. Maybe she was just cold and tired. And scared, of course. She didn't like being alone in this place. All this darkness was unnerving.

And she was worried about the others, too. Albert said that two of them weren't supposed to make it home, which still sounded like a total shit deal to her. She kept hoping he was wrong, that the "crazy cat lady," as he called her, was lying to them. Because there just wasn't anything remotely fair about that. Why would any of them have to die out here? None of them chose this. It was just sort of dumped on them when they least expected it. Andrea and her friends were at a *wedding* of all things!

The Keeper sounded like a real asshole, if she were being honest.

Ahead of her, the flashlight beam illuminated the previous intersection. She went left before and that was wrong, so she needed to go right this time (which of course was left from this angle).

But as she turned the corner, she found herself pausing and shining her light down the third passage, the one she originally came from.

It wasn't that she saw something. She didn't hear anything, either. It was…something *else*. She couldn't put her finger on it, but something was making the hair on the back of her neck stand up and she didn't care for it at all.

Was there something in here with her?

Was something *following* her?

One of those storm drafts, perhaps? Or the Everett-thing again?

A fresh shiver rushed through her and she turned and hurried onward.

She missed Corey. He always made her feel safe. He always took such good care of her. He was easily the best adopted big brother a girl could ask for. And she definitely hadn't told him so nearly enough, she decided.

She was moving faster now, her pace steady. It might have only been her imagination back there, but she didn't dare risk it. She didn't even care about trying to remember the way the other one showed her. She only wanted to get as far away from that other passageway as possible. That was all that mattered right now.

She could feel her heart pounding in her chest. Was it only nerves? Or was her body reacting to something in the nearby darkness? She wished the other one would talk to her again, but she hadn't spoken since she handed back the controls at the top of those drenched stairs.

"Keep it together," she muttered under her breath. It wasn't going to do any good to let herself get so worked up that she did something stupid in a panic. She needed to keep a clear head.

But a fresh wave of dread washed over her as her light illuminated another crossroad ahead of her. A small room, not much bigger than her bedroom, round, with passages leading away in separate directions. There were four paths to choose from this time, not including the one she was in. It certainly wasn't ideal. What if she chose wrong and wasted time on three more dead ends while something awful was creeping up behind her? Or worse, what if two of these passages were the *same*? What if she ended up circling right back to this very spot but with no idea which way she was facing? She could end up going in circles forever and never even know it.

She could almost see that horrible Everett-thing crawling after her in the darkness, its drooping face revealing hints of the unspeakable terror lurking behind it.

She closed her eyes and pressed her hand against her chest, willing herself to calm down. The more afraid she let herself become, the more likely she was to make a mistake. She needed to relax. She needed to clear her mind.

She took a deep, calming breath and then opened her eyes and let her gaze slide from one passage to the next, taking in every detail.

If everything she'd experienced so far was real and not some bizarre hallucination, then the other one had brought her here before, somewhere in the far-distant past. She strolled through these very walls, watching the stone rise up around them. All she had to do was remember which way they went next.

But *was* this familiar? How would she know it from countless other intersections just like it? Every passageway looked exactly the same!

"Little help?" she whispered.

But the other one didn't respond. There was only a lonesome silence inside her head.

Should she be concerned that she was starting to worry about the fact that the voice inside her head wasn't talking to her? What stage of crazy was that, exactly?

"Okay then," she sighed, focusing on the four passages before her.

She wished she had Corey's high-powered light. If she could see farther into the dark, maybe it would make things easier. After all, not every passage she recalled from her dreamy time with the other one was bathed in permanent darkness. She'd seen a fair amount of these passages while they were still being built.

At the very least, it'd be nice to see dead ends a little sooner. It'd save her a lot of walking.

But even if she had that flashlight on her, the batteries had all gone dead, drained out in that black forest as if something had come along and sucked them all dry.

She reached up and touched the glass shard hanging around her neck. She'd already tried using it a number of times since arriving in the Denselands but hadn't been able to see anything that wasn't there without it. Still, she withdrew it from her shirt and peered through it, just to be sure.

Still nothing.

"Worth a try," she sighed, dropping it back to the end of its chain again.

She still didn't understand what, exactly, the shard was able to show her. It didn't reveal everything. She'd encountered things that were hidden both to her eyes *and* to the shard, meaning that there was some specific thing that it was attuned to, but it wasn't as if it came with a manual. All she knew for sure was that it wasn't doing her much good *here*.

She turned her attention to the four paths laid out before her.

Why didn't any of this look familiar? That was the real question. Had she already messed up? Did she take a wrong turn a while back and get herself inescapably lost? It was a dreadful thought, but wasn't that the most likely scenario from the start? This was a labyrinth. The whole purpose was to make you get lost.

The real question was why would the Keeper want the sentinels to build a labyrinth to guard a doorway he wanted them to open? It didn't make sense.

Her gaze slid from left to right, considering each of the four passages in turn, trying to decide if anything about this situation felt familiar.

The one on the far right, perhaps?

She wouldn't say it was *familiar*... Maybe it was some kind of intuition? A subtle, psychic nudge? Or was she trying too hard and simply imagining things?

She sighed and hugged herself against the constant chill from her damp clothes. If the other one wasn't going to help, then all she could do was guess.

She set off down the rightmost passage, uncertain of where she might be going, but perfectly aware that she had to go *somewhere*.

But she stopped after a few steps, her body seemingly frozen in place.

Again, it wasn't a sound. It wasn't something she glimpsed in the flashlight's glow. It was just *something*.

She turned and looked back into the room behind her, convinced that the unpleasant something she felt before was about to emerge from the passage she just left, stalking her.

But whatever she felt wasn't coming from back the way she came anymore. It seemed to be coming from one of the other passageways.

Had it found a way to circle around her? Or was there more than one? Was she surrounded?

Her heart was pounding faster now. She didn't like this. She wished she could see what was hidden in all those surrounding darknesses.

Again, she lifted the glass shard and peered through it.

She frowned.

What was that?

For just a second there, something seemed to shimmer in the blue tint of the glass, a shape not unlike a person. Except that there was no person over there. There wasn't even a place for a person to be. It wasn't inside one of the passageways, but between two of them. It looked like it was on the other side of the wall...

Her imagination? Just a brief reflection from her flashlight?

Whatever it was, it was already gone. No matter how she looked at it, there was nothing over there but an empty stone wall.

She dropped the shard again and took a step backward. She didn't like this place. It felt strangely unnatural, as if there were more to this space than she could see. And the idea did nothing to ease her pounding heart.

She turned and hurried onward, her light peeling back the darkness ahead of her, revealing more and more of that endless gray stone.

Chapter 43

"What's it look like now?" wondered Wayne.

"I can't see the stone anymore," replied Andrea. "Every surface is completely covered in murk." She looked down at herself. "And it's getting deeper."

"Deeper?" asked Olivia, startled.

Andrea nodded. "It's past my ankles."

Olivia looked down at her own feet, trying to imagine a carpet of black fog swallowing her shoes, making it impossible to see where she was stepping. Andrea said that at times it grew so thick that she couldn't even see her own light in front of her face. The idea was terrifying. She couldn't imagine having to walk through something like that, especially all alone.

Everyone told her that she was so brave after her nightmarish ordeal in Gilbert House and the Wood, but she was never brave. She was scared out of her mind the whole time. She thought she was going to go mad in that darkness. She did nothing but hide and pray and sob in terrified silence. Andrea was the brave one. She just kept moving forward, even when she was all alone, in utter darkness and surrounded by the dead.

"I know I already said this," said Andrea, "but you guys will let me know if there's a big hole in the floor, right? Because I won't see it. And I don't wanna fall into another mud pit."

Olivia reached out and linked arms with her. "We wouldn't dare," she promised. "We've got you."

"Thanks."

"Even though you're really stinky right now."

"Sorry. It's the stupid murk's fault."

"I know it is."

"It's not like we've come across a lot of holes," recalled Wayne. "I think if we see an open pit, we're probably going to comment on it."

"Good."

"You really can't feel it?" asked Olivia. "It's not even, like…*cold* or anything?"

She shook her head. "If I close my eyes, it's like it's not even there."

"Doesn't sound like something you can't touch could be very scary," pondered Wayne. "But just trying to picture it is eerie."

"I know, right?"

Olivia shined her light up and down the walls. They didn't look any different from any of the other walls. There didn't seem to be a way to differentiate between those with murk and those with none. Not without her unique ability to see them. And if she and Wayne had no way whatsoever to detect them, were they real? There was no doubt in her mind that Andrea was telling them the truth about what she saw, so she knew they were real to *her*. But what *was* reality anymore? Could it be different for different people?

Why was everything so confusing?

Wayne looked down at her, his brow creased. "What?"

She looked back at him, confused. "What?" she parroted.

"*Who's* watching?"

She scrunched up her face at him. "*What?*"

"You just said, 'She's watching,' under your breath. Who's watching?"

But she only stared up at him, bewildered. "I didn't say anything."

He stopped walking and stared at her for a moment, confused. Then he looked back at Andrea. "Did *you* say something?"

She shook her head. "Nobody said anything. Not even the murk voices." She wrinkled her nose at the stone around her. "Which is weird because they wouldn't shut up before I met up with you guys."

"Are you okay?" Olivia worried. She couldn't help flashing back to those killing vines and watching him drop to the floor, stone dead. In this weird world they'd found themselves lost in, there was no reason to think that he was just hearing things, and yet she couldn't help but wonder if he'd suffered some kind of brain injury while he wasn't breathing. It was the nurse in her, she supposed, searching for the most logical explanation even though they left logic behind along with her purse and cell phone what felt like ages ago.

Wayne nodded. "I know I heard it," he muttered, shining his flashlight back and forth, apparently searching for some additional companion that they somehow hadn't yet noticed.

"Could it have been Erin again?" she wondered.

"*She* does all those ghostly things," agreed Andrea.

His eyes narrowed as he considered it. "Maybe...?"

He didn't sound certain and she didn't blame him. It didn't really make sense. Erin spoke clearly to her back in the fairy circle. And Andrea said she had an entire conversation with her after she passed through the city gates. If she could communicate that easily with the two of them, why would she whisper something like that to Wayne without any explanation? And what did it mean?

"*Who's* watching?" Wayne asked again.

Olivia turned and faced him, her brown eyes widening as she remembered something. "That last time you died and came back!" she exclaimed. "What was the thing you said about the scarecrow man being gone?"

He looked down at her, his thoughts churning. "He went back to her," he recalled.

"*Her*," she repeated.

He frowned. "I remember saying that, but I don't know what it meant. It was just something from my jumbled-up dead-time thoughts."

Andrea looked up at him, curious. "The Priestess of Ruin?"

"What?" asked Olivia and Wayne at the same time.

"No one told you guys about her? Erin was the one who used that name, but I think Gina's goddess mentioned her before that. She's, like, some kind of ancient god or something. She's trying to mess everything up. I think she's the reason Hotdog and Glum were chasing us. She sent them to sabotage us."

Olivia looked up at Wayne. "Like how *Maeve* said someone sent the Scarecrow Man to take the thorn from me!"

"The 'chaotic energy' she told us about," he recalled, nodding.

(*I sense a chaotic energy hovering over you, interfering.*)

It was an awful thought. Was this so-called "Priestess of Ruin" powerful enough to have meddled in *both* their journeys here? Were they actually dealing with some kind of malevolent *deity*? It sounded like something out of a movie. But then again, even Sandy warned them that someone or something had attempted to sabotage the cycle, even going as far as murdering poor Erin!

And now this…*thing*…had followed them all here? It was inside the city walls with them?

"I'm pretty sure she was in my head talking to me for a while," said Andrea.

"What?" gasped Olivia.

"She's not very nice," she said, wrinkling her nose at the memory.

"You've actually *communicated* with her?" asked Wayne.

"More like…listened to her try to screw with my head. I think she got bored of me ignoring her. She seemed kinda childish, actually."

"Still…" said Olivia. "If she's really that dangerous—" But she didn't have time to ponder this unpleasant thought. At that moment, she was startled by a sudden scream from Andrea.

"What's wrong?" gasped Wayne. He crowded closer, his eyes wide open, ready to defend them from whatever frightened her.

Olivia was still clinging to her arm. She pulled her closer, shining her light back and forth.

Andrea grimaced, her dirty face pinched into a squeamish sort of expression, as if she'd just discovered a spider crawling in her hair. "Sorry!" she gasped. "Something grabbed my leg."

They both looked down at her legs, but there was nothing there.

"Something in the murk," she explained.

"What, like a *ghost?*" asked Wayne.

"Is it still there?" wondered Olivia.

She nodded. "It's like this cold, creepy hand wrapped around me," she explained through clenched teeth. "It's okay. It happened before. They don't hurt me. They just sort of hold on for a minute and then let go on their own. I don't know why. But they're hidden in the murk, so I can't see them until they grab me. It's startling."

"I'll bet!" gasped Olivia. A creepy, ghostly hand grabbing her out of the blue would make *her* scream like that, too. Probably even louder. *And* the poor girl was wandering around in this frightful place *barefoot*. She couldn't imagine wading through some ghostly black fog like that, unable to see where she was placing her feet, her bare toes vulnerable to all kinds of imagined horrors.

Andrea gasped again, then quickly took several steps forward, pulling Olivia along with her. Then she shined her light back at the spot where she was standing. "See?" she sighed. "They just let go for some reason."

She stood staring at the spot on the floor, bewildered. There was nothing there. Not so much as a shadow. And yet, she *knew* Andrea wouldn't simply imagine something like that. From *her* point of view, the stone floor wasn't visible. She was staring into a carpet of thick, black fog. The "hand" that grabbed her was in *that*, hiding there like some otherworldly ambush predator.

And yet those things just...*let go* after a moment? What was the point?

Andrea shuddered. "I *hate* those things!" She turned and shined her light forward again, scanning the passageway with her light, searching for any more ghostly hands.

"What happens if they grab one of *us?*" wondered Wayne. "I mean, *can* they grab us? If only you can sense these things?"

It was a good question. Olivia found herself staring down at the floor around her, suddenly afraid to take a step. She wasn't sure her heart could take the fright of feeling something like that grab her.

"No clue," replied Andrea. "I was wondering that myself. Is it just a coincidence that it grabbed me again? Or, like, do you guys just walk right through them? Like how you can't see the murk?"

"But you said you can *see* the murk, but not feel it," recalled Wayne. "You just walk right through it too, so that sort of makes sense. But if those things can grab you and keep you from moving, then they must be something tangible."

"I don't know. I don't get it. The murk just sort of clumps in places sometimes." She turned her attention forward again. "It keeps getting darker, so maybe we'll find out."

"I'd rather not," squeaked Olivia. She didn't want something invisible and ghastly grabbing her without warning.

Wayne pulled her closer and hugged her. "We're okay," he promised, as if he had any idea of any such thing.

But she continued onward anyway, her heart pounding with terrified anticipation.

Chapter 44

"Who is the Priestess of Ruin?" asked Everett.

Alice's answer came flooding through his mind in a rush of bewildering thoughts that he could neither keep up with nor fully comprehend. He found himself imagining vast spans of time. Rising and falling seas, repeatedly swallowing and regurgitating the land. Mountains clawing their way up into the sky and then withering away like decaying corpses. Heaving landscapes shifting like desert sand dunes beneath skies of ever-changing stars. Great, crawling walls of devastating ice carving bottomless gouges into the earth like the claws of massive beasts. And inevitable cosmic calamities of darkness and terror descending upon the earth. All of it repeating over and over again, endlessly, world after world, universe after universe, eternity after eternity. A maddening cycle of beginnings and endings stretching backward into the depths of a past so distant that no words could describe it, until it faded into a strange and terrible sort of *blackness* in which everything that came before broke apart and faded into nothing, forgotten and lost forever.

And throughout all of those unspeakable ages, generations long forgotten, worlds too numerous to count, there always existed human beings below and gods above.

His head swam with this strange and incredible knowledge. The truth of it was like a mounting pressure inside him, making him feel as if he might soon burst. He knew beyond a doubt that it was the truth. He could clearly see the people of those lost worlds in his mind.

They weren't the same human beings that existed today. They were different in a great many ways, both physically and mentally, adapting and evolving with each new universe they populated. But they *were* human. They were his ancestors, those who came before and then faded away beneath the weight of unbearable time.

And they weren't always the same *gods*, either. They rose and fell like the mountains, monstrous and grand, mysterious and wondrous. But they always existed, in one form or another.

There was never one without the other, the humans and the gods. It was as if they needed each other, a symbiotic existence spanning all of eternity. They were always there.

And throughout everything that ever was, the Keeper walked among both.

As did the Priestess of Ruin.

Chaos and order. Darkness and light. Ever at odds and ever in balance. All that the Keeper built, the Priestess of Ruin would eventually tear down. And all that the Priestess of Ruin tore down, the Keeper would rebuild in the ever-churning gears of his great machine.

Good and evil? Everett pondered. God and devil? Opposing counterparts ever at odds? An eternal struggle stretching across all the untold ages of man's torturously long existence?

No. Nothing so simple, he found himself understanding. Nothing so black and white.

The ways of beings like them would always lie somewhere well beyond the realm of human comprehension. Because they, themselves, were well beyond the realm of human comprehension. Like the puzzle box and the Eeshee. And the dainty little doll sitting here in front of him. He could grasp bits and pieces, even formulate ideas about the concepts in a rudimentary way that could allow him to *sort of* make sense of some of it, but he could never fully understand them. Not without going completely mad, he supposed. And even then he still couldn't understand all of it.

Because he was, after all, only human.

But he didn't need to understand what the Priestess of Ruin was to understand that she was with them inside the City Beyond Memory, inside the Keeper's machine. An unwelcome invader. Like a virus worming its way into a computer, taking over, making changes, *spreading.*

Everett understood now that she was the one responsible for his falling into the void. And she was the one who disturbed Alice's domain and made her deceive him. She was even the one who dragged him away from Violet.

And she'd done far more, he found himself understanding. She'd been sabotaging everyone. She was the reason Andrea and Violet were separated from their friends. She'd summoned ancient and monstrous things to stand in everyone's way, things he couldn't begin to know, regardless of the strange details fluttering through his brain. Horse-like legs stretching into a dark, churning sky. Hopeless prisoners wallowing in unnatural misery in an inescapable and gloomy mockery of their former lives. A shapeshifting deceiver lurking in a busy hotel hallway. Monstrous things writhing beneath a dreadful red sky. She was a phantom saboteur, he realized, lurking in the shadows, laying obstacles in their paths. It was she who trapped Maeve within her fairy circle and let her never-children run wild. It was she who sent the scarecrow man to steal the thorn.

Because she wanted them to fail.

She intended to break the cycle!

Somehow, she'd slipped through the Whisper Gates without being detected, hidden within their very shadows, for all he knew. A ghost in the machine. A bug in the Keeper's system.

But the Keeper was supposed to be capable of anticipating *everything*...wasn't he?

And yet, even as he thought this, Alice filled his head with visions of chaos and violence, madness and despair, countless paths of destruction carved by the sheer will of a true goddess of darkness. The Priestess of Ruin was like a category five storm on a cosmic level. If she set her sights on breaking something, then nothing could stand in her way.

It was a terrifying thing to comprehend. No one could possibly stand against an enemy like that. They were nothing more than insignificant humans standing in the shadow of a literal god of destruction!

He fought back a frightened shiver and focused his attention onto the doll again. "Okay," he said, forcing his voice to remain even, as if this new knowledge didn't scare the hell out of him. "I'm guessing you don't have some clever idea about how to beat her, then."

The answer, of course, was no.

Alice was only Alice. Even when she was whatever she was before, she was no match for a force like that. None of them were. There was no way to resist the will of the Priestess of Ruin. She was an unstoppable force. He and his friends were only human, after all. And she was, quite literally, a god.

Everything was going to end in disaster. Nothing he did here was going to change that. Even this dollhouse world he'd found himself in would soon come crumbling down around him.

He closed his eyes and let his mind empty of all those terrifying images. He took a deep breath and let it out slowly.

Then he opened his eyes and looked down at Alice again. "One thing at a time," he decided. "Let's start by getting out of here."

Chapter 45

Keith blinked up into an inky darkness, confused. Where was he? When did he get here? And where did Nicole go?

She'd better not be getting herself into trouble again.

But it was hard to think clearly. His feet were killing him. He looked down at them. His shoes and socks were gone. He was standing on rough, black earth. And there were *holes* in his skin. He was bleeding. Waves of pain were crawling up his legs.

He turned and looked around. There was no sign of the pond or the tree. Nor was there any sign of the passage he entered through. But there was only one place in this so-called city where he'd seen bare earth like this.

That meadow...

But why would he be back here? And why was it different from before? He couldn't even tell where the light was coming from. It had no visible source.

Because he wasn't really here, he realized. This was another dream.

Even the pain wasn't as overwhelming as it was before. He could stand without trouble, even though his feet looked terrible.

He must've passed out in that passageway with Nicole.

For some reason, the idea of having fallen unconscious made him feel guilty. He wasn't sure why. What did he care if he was inconveniencing her? He couldn't even understand why she was sticking around. Was she really that afraid of being alone in there?

No... That wasn't it and he knew it.

Something had changed. He wasn't sure why. She made her feelings for him perfectly clear again and again. And he didn't exactly hide his own feelings. How many times did he snap right back at her?

(*Can we not do this now?*)

He frowned. That memory just now... The way she was talking back there...

"Why's she so frustrating?" he grumbled to himself.

"Because she loves you."

He turned around, surprised. Erin was standing there, also barefoot on the meadow's black soil, smiling back at him. She was still dressed in that sleek, silvery dress, her sunflower tattoos practically glowing in the gloom.

"Bullshit," he spat.

But that smile never faltered. She stepped closer to him, those beautiful, dark eyes gleaming with delight. "Deny it all you want, but somewhere inside, you know the truth."

(*This* thing. *Where you make me admit what a total fucking bitch I've been.*)

He pushed the memory from his mind and turned to look out into the darkness around him. "What's with this place?" he asked, changing the subject. "I mean, I know this is another dream, but *this*..." he raked his bleeding foot across the bare earth. The fact that the motion didn't send an unbearable wave of agony up his leg was further proof that nothing here was real.

"The meadow," she replied, nodding. "I don't fully understand it. I'm not sure if anyone does. All I can say is that it's a place of astonishing cosmic significance. It exists in multiple locations at once. It's a terrible place. You already know that all too well. But for some reason, it seems to be a crucial part of the Keeper's design."

"I'm really starting to question why everyone keeps listening to this Keeper guy. He's seriously messed up."

Erin laughed. She had such a lovely laugh. Beautiful. Disarming. She reminded him of the *other* Nicole. The wonderful one. The one he thought was gone forever.

(*And then I start crying and blubbering about how I never stopped caring about you.*)

He closed his eyes, weary, and sighed. When he opened them, he was standing at the edge of the pond, looking at the tree standing at the center of it.

What was the deal with the water and the tree? It wasn't even a live tree. I looked long dead.

"There's something about it," said Erin. She was standing next to him, staring at the same dead branches. "But I can't say exactly *what* that something is."

"It feels..." He stared at it, his thoughts churning, trying to find the right word. Then, at last, it came to him: "...*old*." He glanced over at her. "Like, *old* old...if that makes any sense."

She nodded. "I know what you mean. I don't know if it's even really a tree or if it's something else entirely, but I feel like it's been standing there almost forever..."

Almost forever? In this City Beyond Memory at the center of the

Denselands where countless *universes* had lived and died? With so much time piled up in one place, what did "almost forever" even mean?

Before he could contemplate it any further, a fresh wave of pain rolled over him and he groaned.

He was no longer standing in the meadow. In fact, he wasn't standing at all. He was sitting on the floor, his back propped against the wall. Nicole was with him again, her arms wrapped around him, her half-naked body pressed against his. It sounded like she was crying. Her breath was shallow and ragged.

Before he could wrap his head around it all, he was hit with another wave of pain that made the whole world seem to break apart and drift away.

"It's bad," said Erin.

He blinked at her, confused. "Wha...?" He was still sitting on the stone floor, his back still pressed against the wall, his feet stuck out in front of him. But the other wall and the ceiling were gone. Everything stretched out into darkness all around him. Even Nicole was gone. Instead, Erin was kneeling in front of him, her gaze fixed on his.

"It's a miracle you're not already dead."

"Awesome," he groaned. "Very encouraging." He looked away from that haunting gaze. Why was she staring into his eyes like that? It was his *feet* that were hurt.

"Death waits in City Beyond Memory," said a frightfully familiar voice.

A hard shudder raced through him and he turned around, his hands raised to defend himself from the ghastly corpse version of Nicole that spoke those words to him in another dream.

But there was no Nicole there, dead or otherwise. He was standing all alone in one of the city's endless stone passageways, his heart racing.

"Ten will return," said a voice from behind him. "No more. No less."

He turned to find himself staring at a large, black cat with huge yellow eyes that seemed to glow in the gloom of the shadowy passage.

Cats. And that creepy old lady who looked unsettlingly past her expiration date. The one Erin called the "Night Goddess." The one who was responsible for plunging him into this frightening and painful ordeal.

Dreams and cats and dead broads and riddles about Keepers and death and cities beyond memories...

"Something is different than it was before. We feel it...deep in the memories of old dreams…"

"Right," he said, weary of it all. "So you said last time." This wasn't new information. It was all the same mumbo jumbo she (they?) spewed at him last time.

A recap, he guessed? In case he forgot all the weird stuff she said while he was distracted by the agonizing pain of having tromped through some sort of alien scorpion hive because she decided *he* was the only one in the *entire universe* who could save his possessed ex-girlfriend who hated his guts?

(*You look thin.*)

He frowned.

(*It makes me wonder if you've been eating well. That's all.*)

Did she hate him? What was real and what wasn't?

(*I know what a bitch I've been, but I wouldn't want you to not take care of yourself.*)

He reached up and rubbed at his face, frustrated. It was all so confusing! He didn't even know what to think anymore!

(*…how I never stopped caring about you…*)

Why was she such a colossal pain?

(*Because she loves you.*)

He lowered his hands and found that he was sitting on the stone floor again, his back propped against the wall, waves of agony flowing up his feet like lapping tides.

Erin was still kneeling over him, still staring into his eyes.

"Bullshit," he replied again, but there was no energy behind it. The word barely made it past his lips.

She smiled, but it was a sad smile. "I know it hurts, but you can't give up. She still needs you. You have to wake up and fight the venom."

"Venom…?" He blinked down at his feet. They'd turned black. And there were dark bruises creeping up his legs like shadowy groping fingers. His skin looked sickly and translucent, his veins visible just beneath the surface.

Erin leaned over him until her cheek was almost pressed against his and whispered, "Wake up."

But that wasn't Erin. It was Nicole, her warm skin pressed against him.

"Please wake up," she whimpered.

He looked down at her, confused, as the pain washed over him again. Then he looked past her, at his feet. They were still wrapped in Nicole's torn shirt. His ankles did, indeed, appear to be covered in bruises, but not as noticeably as they looked in the dream. And that sickly, translucent quality was entirely in his head.

Still, he didn't look *good*. That cloth was bloody. And the pain wasn't getting any better.

(*I know it hurts, but you can't give up. She still needs you.*)

With a heavy sigh, he reached up and grasped Nicole's arm.

Surprised, she sat up, wiping at her eyes. "There you are!" she gasped, clearly relieved. "For a second I..." But she didn't dare finish the sentence. She bit back the words and sniffled.

"Help me up," he breathed. "We should keep moving."

Chapter 46

"Already?" groaned Brandy as she swept her light back and forth between the statues lined up on either side of the room before them. "We *just* fucking did this!" She hadn't fully shaken off the waterworks from that last one, but here they were again, standing at the end of another warning chamber leading to yet another emotion room.

Albert turned and looked back the way they came, scratching at the back of his head. "I mean, we *have* been walking for a while now... But yeah. It feels kind of soon, doesn't it?"

"No shit it does."

"What's it going to be this time?" he wondered, already starting forward.

"I'm guessing there's no point in going back."

"Different emotions can be more or less effective," he reasoned. "Like in the first temple. Those were all entirely different experiences. Maybe this one will be more like the hate room. That one was easy."

"Because we learned the trick."

"Yes. But knowing the trick didn't help us in the fear room. That one was hard. I thought back then that it was because fear was stronger than hate...but maybe it's like it said in the book. Maybe it's that we're just less sensitive to that kind of emotion."

"Put me in that same room with the pervert for five minutes and see if you still think that." She turned her light onto each sentinel as it emerged from the darkness, one after another, each pair slightly different. He wasn't wrong. The hate room didn't really give them any trouble. She remembered feeling strangely irritated while making her way through it with her poor eyesight, but even when those blurry shades of gray were close enough to take form before her eyes, they didn't really overwhelm her. It was as if they simply reminded her of times when people had pissed her off. And there were a lot of times like that in her life. She'd worked in retail for a lot of years, after all.

In contrast, the fear room felt like it wormed its way in no matter how hard she tried to keep her eyes shut. And the sorrow room was much like that. Except she felt her eyes welling up even before she set foot in there. Was it just that she knew what it was going to do to her? A psychosomatic response in expectation of it? Or did its emotional energy simply ooze beyond the stone walls that contained it?

Was it possible that learning to utilize emotional energy increased its effect? Could the pervert's "training" make these rooms even worse? She wouldn't put it past the slimy bastard.

Albert stopped and looked back, his gaze washing across each pair of sentinels in the line. "What *is* it, though?"

It was a good question. The sentinel pairs never changed very much from one to the next. The progression was gradual, creating an illusion of animation. But there was something different about the ones here. She couldn't quite wrap her head around what they were doing.

It began in their hands. Those long, creepy fingers curling and uncurling. Then something about their posture changed. They seemed to loosen and slump, but at the same time they seemed to tense up. Were they sad again? Were they becoming angry?

"I don't feel anything," observed Albert. He turned and squinted into the darkness ahead. "The last one felt like it was affecting us all the way out here." He tilted his head thoughtfully to one side. "Do we have to understand what the emotion is before we can feel it?"

Brandy aimed her light forward. She knew there was a face hidden in that gloom. The doorway to whatever fresh horrors were waiting for them beyond this warning chamber. She could almost imagine that she could see it there, an eerie outline hidden in the shadows, but that wasn't possible. These rooms had always been the same size, with the same number of statue pairs. And they weren't halfway across it yet. Her light couldn't possibly reach that far. "I don't know, but my heart is beating really fast right now."

He gave her hand a reassuring squeeze. "Yeah. Mine too."

She didn't want to do this again. She still hadn't fully shaken off the lingering sadness of the last one. And she was exhausted. But she continued forward anyway, her light pushing back the darkness, revealing another pair of sentinels frozen in their eternal game of Guess-The-Emotion.

They were stooping over now, their long arms reaching forward, those creepy, curled fingers clutching at the darkness in front of them with a strange sort of desperation that she still couldn't read.

"Dicks are limp," she observed, pointing her light at the nearest statue's crotch.

"Always a good sign."

"No shit." They'd only ever fully freaked out in the sex room, after all. Even when the fear room got to her that first night and made them turn back, it wasn't anything like the total loss of control they experienced in the first one, before they knew they couldn't look at the statues. The first room caught them completely unaware, after all. But even then, they were spared the full blunt of those emotions. The man with no eyes crept in while they were caught in that storm of uncontrolled lust and stole their only working flashlight. Albert had theorized that if he hadn't, they might never have left that chamber. It would've been so easy to end up hurting each other in there. They were, after all, anything but gentle. That was no slow, romantic lovemaking session. It was wild. It was desperate. It was greedy and hard and frantic. It was almost *violent*. And it was *hot as fuck*. She'd be lying if she said otherwise. It still turned her on to think about how intense that first time was. But it was also *terrifying*. It was *dangerous*. In that state of mind, it wouldn't have been hard for one of them to get strangled or suffocated or knocked hard against a jutting stone foot, cracking one of their skulls open. Or maybe they'd simply have gone on and on until their hearts gave out. There was no end to the awful scenarios when it came to thinking about how dangerous those emotion rooms were. Why would the sentinels leave something so incredibly dangerous for them to just stumble into like that?

Bunch of faceless *psychopaths*.

And now here they were again!

Lust. Hatred. Fear. Sorrow. What was next? What awful ordeal were they going to have to suffer through this time?

The sentinels seemed to be slowly coming undone as they walked. They looked almost as if they were spasming. They were hunched over now, still clutching at the air in front of them. The cords on their already freakish necks were standing out. Their heads were tilting forward. They looked...almost in *pain*? "They kind of look sick," she observed. "Maybe they're constipated."

"That'd make for a weird statue room."

"As opposed to a *normal* statue room?"

"Fair point."

She turned and shined her light back the way they came. She didn't like this. She felt uneasy, as if something were watching them. It was getting harder and harder to keep moving forward. And why was her heart racing like this? It felt like it was getting harder to breathe. Was the air getting thinner?

Two by two, the final pairs of statues came into view. They crumpled to the floor and curled themselves up, clawing at their featureless faces. "Why do they look like they're in pain?"

"It's like they're being poisoned or something," agreed Albert.

"That doesn't make sense!"

"I know it doesn't!"

These were *emotion* rooms, not gas chambers. What the hell was going on here? She wanted to turn and flee. To hell with this room. To hell with the Keeper and his shitty plans.

But she pressed on the last few steps, her gaze frozen on the huge shape emerging from the darkness directly in front of them. A man's face, twisted and contorted in an expression of utter *agony*, his eyes bulging, his lips pulled back in a silent scream.

She was shaking her head. "No! I can't!" Her whole body was shaking. She couldn't get control of herself. How were they supposed to pass through a door like that?

Then Albert was kissing her again.

It happened so suddenly that it actually startled her out of her fear for a moment. "Mm-*fck*?" she mumbled against his lips.

He pulled away from her, just a little, and stared into her eyes. "Not pain," he whispered. "Anxiety."

She squinted at him, confused. An anxiety room? Really? Was that necessary?

Chapter 47

Gina turned yet another corner and circled back the other way. The glass labyrinth seemed to go on and on. And it was weirdly folded, far more so than the crinkled existence of those frightful Denselands. Space wasn't just muddled up and scrunched together here. It was thoroughly jumbled and intertangled with itself, unnavigable, unsolvable, like a cosmic Gordian knot. Forward and backward kept trading places with left and right and up and down. There were drastic differences in the layout of the surrounding stone labyrinth every time the fog cleared enough to allow her glimpses, suggesting that she was jumping around in conjunction with that other space with little regard to concepts like distance and direction. And she was fairly sure time was disjointed, too, because she kept having déjà vu.

At least her psychic eye was consistently able to see the layout of her immediate surroundings. It hadn't stopped her from finding dead ends, but it always allowed her to see far enough that she didn't have to walk all the way up onto them before she knew the way was blocked.

Every now and then she heard things in the other labyrinth. Sometimes voices found their way to her.

("There you are! For a second I…")

("Why do they look like they're in pain?")

("I feel like we're getting close to something.")

And other broken bits and pieces of muttered conversations that she couldn't make out, as well as other, more troubling noises. Shuffling footsteps in the dark. Inhuman things prowling undiscovered chambers long shrouded in darkness. Hidden inner workings that defied her understanding.

That loathsome and unwanted inner eye kept telling her that there were deadly traps, mysterious void spaces and unexplainable things that made her head hurt whenever she cast her psychic gaze in their direction.

And then there was *this* labyrinth. There were things on this side, too, things that she instinctively knew she needed to avoid. She couldn't discern what they were, whether they were traps or pitfalls or even whether they were alive and moving. They were strangely evasive. Simply a product of this queer, folded-up space? Or something with intelligence and intention?

And of course there was her most pressing concern: occasionally she could hear something running past her in adjacent corridors, glimpses of an unnatural shadow darting across the other side of the warped glass. She didn't know how long she'd been wandering these glass passages, but she knew that she was running out of time. How long before the thing with too many mouths finally hunted her down?

She stopped walking. Something had changed. The layout had shifted again. But this time, there was something unpleasant in her path. She couldn't quite grasp the shape of it, or even exactly what it was made of. It seemed to be something completely unfamiliar to her, because it presented itself in her mind as an empty hole. A void in that space. And yet it most definitely wasn't the *nothing* it presented itself to be because its presence there filled her with an overwhelming feeling of primal *fear*. Whatever it was, she couldn't go near it. It was too dangerous.

And yet going back wasn't an option. Everything had moved around and a dead end had somehow popped up back there. She turned her attention upward. Like before, the labyrinth seemed to turn with her gaze. Suddenly, the dreadful nothing-thing was below her and the dead end above.

But the path before her wasn't ideal, either. There was something broken about the space ahead. She didn't understand it, but she felt very strongly that if she continued forward, she might fall through a crack and become even more lost than she already was.

She turned and looked behind her instead. As she did, an image flashed before her. A familiar face. Bright red hair. Twinkling jewelry.

Andrea?

She stopped and searched the space around her. She clearly saw Andrea's face as she turned. She looked filthy and disheveled, as if she'd become covered in dirt and grime, but it was definitely her. Was she near? Or had the twisted nature of the glass labyrinth only given her a glimpse of a different space somewhere far away?

She really wished she understood this stuff better. It was so frustrating sometimes.

But just knowing that Andrea was here somewhere was a tremendous relief. She'd feared the worst since Glum separated them all back in that forest. And it felt like someone was with her, too. She sensed that she was speaking with someone.

("There's just something about this room I don't like.")

That was good. Being alone wasn't fun. Not in a place like this.

Something rushed past her in the dark, startling her. She spun around, her heart hammering. Was that behind her? Or above her? It was so hard to be sure. Either way, it was far too close for her liking. She needed to keep moving.

The way forward seemed clear for the moment. She pressed on, picking up her pace.

Already, she could detect another intersection farther ahead. Left or right. Neither contained anything that gave her any particularly bad feelings, so she wouldn't waste time thinking about it. If she didn't stop, maybe she could put some walls between herself and the monstrosity. She needed to stay out of its reach until she figured out where in this glass nightmare she was supposed to be.

There was something she was supposed to do here. She was more convinced of that the longer she wandered these dark corridors. But so far she hadn't found herself drawn toward any single point.

The intersection she sensed came into view of her psychic eye, as if materializing out of the haze of the twisted glass labyrinth. As she approached it, something shadowy and fluid darted across her path, freezing her to the floor. A wave of nauseating terror washed over her, nearly buckling her knees and dropping her to the floor, but somehow she managed to lean on the glass and stay upright.

Not that way.

She turned and fled back the way she came, panting with suffocating fear.

That was too close!

Was there really a job for her to do in this place? Because how could the goddess expect her to succeed with something like that standing in her path? The very *sight* of it felt like a slap to her sanity. It was both real and unreal at the same time, both physical and psychic. Neither living nor dead yet somehow also both at once.

Was she missing something?

She sensed a crack in the glass wall as she hurried around the corner and away from the danger. Glass and stone refracted and overlapped. Was she supposed to stay here until she found what she needed? Or was she supposed to use the twisted layout of the folded space to move to another part of the *stone* labyrinth? Like a network of secret passages and hidden shortcuts?

She didn't know what she was supposed to do, but it was clear that she couldn't stop to examine the cracks here. She needed to keep moving. It wasn't safe. She could almost hear all those mouths muttering their foul threats at her.

On the other side of the glass, the stone labyrinth had changed. Gone were the claustrophobic passageways of smooth stone. The spaces out there were much larger now. Cavernous, with great stone structures dotted throughout the darkness like some subterranean kingdom in a fantasy novel.

Strangely, the transition was both abrupt and subtle. Thinking back over the past few minutes, it felt like she was aware of the shift from one area to another, and yet she was quite sure she didn't notice it until it had already happened. It was almost as if her past were rewriting itself in order to match the present she was experiencing.

Furthermore, while she was focused on the stone labyrinth *outside*, the glass labyrinth *within* had also changed. There were more passageways than there were before, more intersections. And more of those unpleasant-feeling voids.

This whole area felt more dangerous than it did a moment ago.

Did she take a wrong turn? Did she do something wrong? She wished the goddess would talk to her again and let her know whether she was doing anything right, but of course that was impossible. Even a goddesses couldn't reach her here behind the impassible wall. She was truly on her own in this strange new world.

Left. Away from the nearest of those empty spaces. Then right. Then left again. Another one was up ahead this way. She turned right. Went straight. Turned right again.

Then she stopped. That wasn't it. Was she back where she started? It felt like the spaces farther out were moving, circling around her as she made her way in. It was a crazy thing to think, unless you happened to be her, she supposed. She was used to stuff like this. Exceptions to the world's supposedly unbreakable rules. Things that should be impossible but weren't. Things no one else believed were real. But this place was especially unsettling to her, and not merely because of the terrifying, multi-mouthed monster that was stalking her in this glass darkness. There was something about those voids that felt extra dreadful.

What were they? What would happen if she approached one of them?

She turned back. Turned right. Went straight. Turned right again.

No. This wasn't right. This was the same thing from a new angle.

She looked up. The labyrinth turned on its side again. But it was the same this way. Voids blocking the way. Lefts that went right. Rights that went back.

And somewhere in the nearby passageways, the thing with too

many mouths flashed past, reminding her that it was still there, still looking for her.

She couldn't stay in one place for too long. She needed to move.

She turned left. Then right. Then right again. Then *up*. The glass labyrinth turned and twisted with her, rolling around her like a giant hamster ball, letting her move around without letting her free.

"I can smell you," called the eerie voice of the thing with too many mouths. The sound of it sent a wicked chill through her body, making her tremble with dread. "You can't stay ahead of me forever."

Again, she turned her gaze upward. Again, the labyrinth turned with her.

But as she cast her psychic gaze out across those glass corridors, she found herself at a dead end.

"There you are," hissed the monster.

A great, terrified gasp forced its way up her throat and burst from her lips in a strangled sob.

She wasn't ready for this.

Chapter 48

Andrea stopped walking. This was new.

"What's up?" whispered Olivia.

But she wasn't entirely sure how to explain it. The murk seemed to be changing. The deepening fog had begun to recede again, giving her hope that they might be past the mid-point and heading for "brighter" parts of the labyrinth, but instead of continuing to get shallower, it was starting to gather into strange strands, as if some giant, magical hand were stretching and weaving it into thin, black ropes that snaked and twisted their way through the passage, making them impossible to avoid. Instead of trying to describe it, she simply replied, "I feel like we're getting close to something."

"What kind of something?" wondered Wayne.

"A *good* something?" hoped Olivia.

"Just something," she replied as she started forward again. It was weird, but not entirely unlike the previous tunnel where the murk only covered the floor at first, then gradually twisted to one side and up the wall, toward that passage on the right. It was as if it were attracted to something in this passageway. Was there something here that murk gravitated toward? Like plants turning to face the sunlight?

These knotted strands of murk looked more solid than the rest, as if they might be clumped together like the groping hands and the creeping, crawling, toothy things, but she passed through them as if they weren't there, feeling no sensation whatsoever. She could tell that her companions were as completely unaware of them as they were of the rest of the murk.

They pushed on for a while in silence and she watched as their flashlights pushed back the oppressive darkness, slowly revealing the path before them. The murk ropes grew fatter and the fog around them thinned. Little patches of stone were beginning to show through. And she could see that there were thin, thread-like strands stretching between the fog and the ropes, connecting them. Again, she pictured some giant spinning wheel reshaping the darkness ahead of them. At the same time, however, it all looked strangely organic. She found herself instead imagining some colossal worm slowly weaving itself a cocoon out of this eerie darkness, and the thought made her skin crawl.

Olivia let out a shivery gasp and stopped walking, her grip tightening, pulling both her and Wayne closer to her.

"What's wrong?" worried Wayne, shining his light back and forth, looking for danger.

"I don't know," she replied, her voice unusually small and meek. "I just got an awful chill. All the way down me." She looked up at him, her eyes wide. "Like they used to say about a goose walking over your grave?"

"Is it your psychic alarm?" he wondered.

"I don't know. Doesn't feel the same."

She was right about that, Andrea realized. She looked down at the floor. One of those creepy murk hands were wrapped around Olivia's ankle, gripping her.

A chill? Was that what people who couldn't see the things she saw felt when they were touched by the murk? Was that the reason people sometimes got chills out of nowhere?

She wasn't sure what to do. Should she tell her what was happening? Or would it only creep her out? She didn't want to scare her. And in her experience those things had been fairly harmless, but she didn't like keeping secrets from her friends.

As she watched, Olivia took a step forward, pulling her foot free with surprising ease. Did it simply choose that moment to let her go? It didn't seem to hold on as long as they did when they grabbed *her*. Was it because she was aware of them and therefore actively resisting? She wished she knew how this stuff worked.

At any rate, it seemed as though the others were able to detect *something*. It was sort of validating, at least.

She looked back as Olivia urged them onward and watched those creepy, finger-like tendrils reach after them. From this angle, it almost looked as if it were waving goodbye.

Why did it all have to be so creepy?

"You okay?" asked Olivia, turning to see what she was looking at.

"Yeah. Just nervous." She faced forward and focused on the path ahead of them. Something was coming into view. An intersection? No... More like a chamber. The murk ropes reached out into the darkness at every angle. And as they drew closer, their lights seeping into that other space, revealing more and more of it, the sight only grew stranger.

The room was vast. Like the mud chamber, it went on and on, well beyond the reach of their flashlights. And it was filled with great, blocky columns. The clean, gray stone was covered in a creepy latticework of overlapping strands of eerie murk. Those fat, woven ropes crisscrossed in every direction, stretched taut and compacted together, almost glistening. They stuck to every surface they touched, reminding her of some giant, black spiderweb.

And those little darkling specks were back again. They hung in the air like fluttering ash, fading in and out of sight, a few at first, but then more as they ventured farther out.

"I don't think I like it in here very much," she decided.

"What do you see?" asked Wayne, concerned.

"It's more like something I *feel*," she replied. The idea of a giant murk spider lurking somewhere in this darkness was terrifying, but it was only a product of her overactive imagination. It didn't *really* look like a spider's web. Bringing it up would only scare her friends. They'd almost certainly imagine a scene much worse than it really was. Besides, there was more than just what her imagination was feeding her. "There's just something about this room I don't like."

"Should we go back?"

"No," said Olivia before she could answer. "We need to keep going forward."

Andrea glanced over at her, concerned.

"Back feels like a mistake," she explained. "I can't really say more than that. I don't really get it."

"Forward it is, then," decided Wayne, already starting to walk again, gently pulling Olivia along, who in turn tugged Andrea into motion again. "Just keep pointing the way."

"Keep pointing…" whispered the murk from somewhere ahead of them.

"Oh good," she sighed. "The voices are back."

"Voices…" sighed an old man.

"Hears us…" breathed a little girl.

"Those creepy ones you described?" asked Olivia.

"Creepy ones…." Whispered the murk. Like before, these voices *sounded* human. They spoke English. And the sounds varied widely in age and gender and tone, ranging from creepy children to gruff men to haggard old women.

"Yeah, but they're not as creepy as they are *annoying*."

"Annoying…"

"Annoy her…"

"Bothersome…"

"What are they saying?" wondered Wayne.

"Saying…?"

"Speaking…?"

"Talking…?"

"They're just sort of mocking us."

"Mocking…"

"Tease her…"

"Make fun…"

"Rude," said Olivia, offended.

"Rude…" parroted the murk.

"Rude…"

"So rude…"

Ahead of them, the black strands seemed to gather together, thicker and deeper and somehow even *darker*, until a great, churning *pool* of inky black was spread out on the floor directly in their path, about twelve feet across, so dark against the lighter stone that she thought for a second she was looking at a gaping hole.

She tugged Olivia to a stop and gestured forward with her light. "Not through the middle. We should stick close to the walls."

"Close to the walls…" mimicked the murk.

"Go around…"

"To the walls…"

"What's in the middle?" asked Wayne.

"The middle…?"

"What is it…?"

"What's there…?"

"Maybe nothing," she replied truthfully. "But maybe we shouldn't risk it."

"Don't risk…"

"Scared…"

"Coward…"

"Run away…"

They turned and made their way to the left side of the room, circling wide around that great, shadowy…whatever it was on the floor.

Clearly, Olivia and Wayne could see nothing in that space. They would've said something if they did. And she could see that their gazes swept across the room, alert for any signs of danger, and in the process never paused in that spot. Nothing about it seemed to catch their attention. But if there was nothing there, why was the murk so clumped together like that? Was it some kind of portal? Or a nest of some sort? Home to the spider that went with this huge black web, perhaps? (She very much hoped it wasn't that one!) And was it only her imagination, or were the murk voices coming from there?

Fortunately, there was plenty of room to circle around it. In fact, for a moment, it seemed as if there wasn't a wall to follow. The darkness stretched on and on ahead of them, the room proving to be more than fifty feet across, then sixty, then eighty... But finally, the murk-stained wall came into view. And with it appeared another of those black, swirling pools of darkness, this one clinging to the wall twenty feet above them.

Again, she tugged at Olivia's arm, steering them forward now.

What were those things? At first glance, they looked like big holes, but they were more like great *piles* of murk. Were they clumps? Like the groping hands and the crawling, growling things with all the spiraling teeth? Were they alive? Were they *dangerous*? If they walked too close to one would it unravel itself and attack them?

Her ever-unhelpful imagination offered a terrible image of those great, swirling masses of darkness bubbling up, sprouting legs and splitting open to reveal a bottomless pit of deadly teeth.

Something moved in the darkness above them and she turned her light upward to see one of those groping hands dangling down from a strand of glistening murk.

"What is it?" whispered Olivia.

"What's wrong...?" mocked the cackling voice of a woman.

"Scared..." breathed an old man's voice.

Andrea shook her head. Now that she was shining her light upward, she realized that she could see dozens of those creepy hands up there, each one turned toward her, straining to reach her. "Just darkness," she replied.

"Darkness..." mocked the myriad of voices all around her.

"So dark..."

"Black..."

Her heart was thudding in her chest again. She didn't want to be in this room. The longer she was here, the more uneasy she felt.

"Look," said Wayne.

"Over there..." chimed the murk.

"Look at that..."

"See it..."

Andrea ignored the voices and joined her flashlight to his, illuminating a doorway in the wall ahead of them.

Wayne turned and shined his light across the empty room. "Maybe there's one on all four sides."

"All four..."

"All sides..."

"Maybe…"

(That was getting *really* annoying.)

Olivia stopped and considered the doorway. "I don't get any bad vibes from it."

"Vibes…"

"Bad…"

"Danger…"

Andrea nodded. Nothing would please her more than to leave this room. There was something troubling about those black pools of murk. And was it only her imagination, or were those shadowy strands beginning to *pulsate?* "We should take it," she decided.

"Take it…"

"We should…"

"That way…"

"Fine by me," agreed Wayne. "Let's see where it goes."

"Fine…"

"See where it goes…"

"That way…"

"See what's there…"

"I heard what he said!" grumbled Andrea.

"She heard him…"

"Heard what he said…"

"Listens…"

Olivia and Wayne both turned and looked at her, confused.

"Sorry," she muttered, pointing at her head. "Voices."

"Voices…"

"So sorry…"

Olivia opened her mouth to say something but seemed to lose the words before she could form them. Instead, she tightened her grip on her arm and they continued onward in silence.

At least the voices only spoke when one of them did. If they kept quiet, so would the murk. So she clenched her jaw and pushed forward, her eyes peeled for movement.

Speaking of voices, it had been a while since she heard the impostor's voice inside her head. Fake Stella hadn't said a word since announcing that she was bored. It should have been a relief to have her gone, but something about that silence left her feeling more uneasy than anything.

If she wasn't inside her head, tormenting her, then where was she?

What mischief was the Priestess of Ruin up to?

Chapter 49

Violet closed her eyes. She needed to calm down. This was unnerving, but she could handle it. She just needed to stay relaxed and patient.

The ledge she was standing on was only about fifteen inches wide, forcing her to inch sideways to keep from falling into the black depths lying just beyond the toes of her boots.

Still feeling uneasy about the darkness she was leaving behind her, she'd pushed on through the labyrinth, only to find herself staring across this chasm with no way forward. Her choices were to go back the way she came or to see where this narrow ledge would take her. Ordinarily, she would've turned around (because to hell with *that* shit!) but there was something about this odd little path. It felt so peculiarly out of place that she couldn't help feeling as if it might be important. No other part of the labyrinth looked like this, not that she'd seen at least. And since the other one wasn't speaking to her right now, she was forced to decide these things for herself.

If Corey were here, she knew he'd insist on checking it out, despite the fact that his much larger size would've made this even more treacherous for him. She could almost hear him arguing that it wouldn't be there if it didn't go somewhere.

Everett probably would've agreed with him, too.

Besides, her mind kept circling back to those odd feelings she had a ways back, as if something were watching her from the shadows. She *really* didn't want to go back there.

She took a calming breath and continued moving. One step at a time. Her back sliding along the smooth stone. Her hands out to her sides for balance. Her flashlight illuminating the way. Easy does it.

How far did it go? She hoped she didn't end up stuck out here.

But she couldn't think like that. She concentrated on keeping her breathing steady. Deep breaths weren't her friend here. Anything that shifted her center of gravity, even a little, felt magnified and threatened to upset her balance.

Heights had never bothered her. When she was a girl, she loved climbing trees. And when she was a teenager, she used to like sneaking out her upstairs bedroom window and sitting on the roof, overlooking the back yard in the moonlight. It was always so peaceful up there. And the sounds of the night had always been her favorite kind of symphony.

But this was a different kind of feeling altogether. She had no idea what was at the bottom of that abysmal darkness. How far down did it go? And what might be waiting to catch her if she fell?

Her eyes were still closed. It made it easier to focus on breathing and pacing. Slow and steady. One foot then the other. Shallow, steady breaths. No sudden movements. But she opened them to see if the end had come into view yet.

It hadn't. The ledge only stretched on into that same, eerie darkness.

She closed them again and continued onward. Maybe this was a mistake after all. She didn't remember anything like this in those other-worldly dreams about the other one. But it wasn't as if she could remember all of what happened under that impossibly colorful sky.

It was so quiet in here. *Deathly* quiet. Like the inside of a tomb. It seemed to her that it should help with this process, making it easier to concentrate, but it was the opposite. It seemed to magnify the experience. She had to make a conscious effort to ignore the silence.

Again, she wished she didn't have to be alone here. She could really use someone to talk to, to help take her mind off that uneasy silence.

She wondered what Corey was doing right now. Knowing him, he was probably having a blast exploring this place. This was his kind of thing, after all. Practically the culmination of everything they'd been working for all this time. She wasn't entirely sure what they were supposed to do after this. Those little pocket dimensions they kept finding were going to feel pretty tame after witnessing things like the Wood, the Denselands and the City Beyond Memory.

It really felt like nothing was ever going to be the same after this.

Again, she opened her eyes. She didn't like this. Maybe she should turn back. But this time she found that she could see an opening coming into view up ahead. A passageway leading back into the labyrinth.

That was good. But she couldn't let herself get excited. She couldn't afford to rush. Slow and steady. Seeing the goal was meaningless if she screwed around and fell now.

Just a little farther…

The Wood… That was the big one. Eight years ago, a mysterious creature pretending to be a man named Jeremy told her that there were other worlds waiting out there. (*Some of them more significant than you can possibly imagine.*) His words set them down a path to find those worlds.

"The place I'm from is the foundation for all worlds, even this one," she remembered him telling her. "It's a very dark place. A very hopeless place."

Was he talking about the Wood? Had they found where he came from?

No... Somehow, she didn't think so. She wasn't sure why, but she felt like he came from somewhere even farther than all of this.

Her outstretched hand found the corner of the doorway. She was almost there. She felt a mad urge to jump ahead, but she couldn't let herself rush. One wrong move and it would be all over. The only thing worse than falling would be to fall while trying to make that last turn to safety.

She gripped the corner as she sidled closer to it, easing herself around it.

Almost...

There!

She stepped away from the ledge with a great sigh of relief and leaned against the wall. Now that it was over, her heart was pounding. That wasn't fun.

"*So* not doing *that* again..." she muttered to herself as she set off down the new passage, following her flashlight beam back into the unknown.

She really hoped Corey didn't try doing something stupid like that. She'd be so mad at him if he got himself hurt in this place.

Again, she wondered where he was. What was he doing? Was he learning anything?

Back when they were still traveling with Albert and Brandy, he was talking about how the worlds they'd found in their years of traveling were so different from the Wood. He theorized something about those being *inside* their own world while the Wood was *outside*. It was an interesting thought. Maybe that would be their focus moving forward. A new process for mapping the worlds they found.

She wished he was here. It was always so much easier to stay calm and collected when she was listening to him tell her all his thoughts and theories.

But as she walked, she found herself distracted.

Why was it so *noisy*?

She shined her light down at her feet, confused. Every surface had been so smooth and clean so far, but there was something on the floor in here, something that kept crunching under her feet. It sounded less like solid stone than gravel.

She swept her light back and forth, confused.

Why was the floor in here all chewed up?

Somewhere in the darkness ahead of her, she heard a faint, far-away sound she couldn't quite identify, a strange, almost mechanical sort of droning sound…

Chapter 50

Alice didn't have the power to leave this place. Not on her own. Only *he* could do that. The tricky part was going to be figuring out *how* to do it. She could place the information into his head in that strange way she had of communicating with him, but much of it was too weird for him to understand.

This might take a while.

He walked around the empty white room, studying the drawn-on door and window. He thought for a moment that perhaps if he got up and changed his point of view he might see them differently, as if perhaps they were only optical illusions and if he approached from just the right direction he'd be able to simply open one of them and leave. But he supposed that was only wishful thinking. No matter how he observed them, they remained nothing more than drawings on the wall.

They weren't even particularly *good* drawings. They were rather childish.

All things considered, he wasn't a fan of this place. It felt like being trapped in *Elmo's World* or something.

Ironic, he realized, considering that he was the one who made this place.

He examined the cheerful scene in the window for a moment, wondering if there might be a clue hidden there somewhere, but upon finding nothing, he turned his back on it and looked up at the ceiling fan.

Why was there a ceiling fan, but no light switches, ventilation or furnishings? There weren't even any drawings of pictures on the walls. It was a sort of odd detail to include when there was so much missing, he thought. Was it only that his home had ceiling fans and so that was simply a normal detail to him? Or did it mean something? Was it a clue of some sort?

He stepped up onto the chair he was sitting in before and took a closer look, but again, no matter how he looked at it, it was only a drawing.

The only real things in the room were him, Alice and the two chairs. And he wasn't even entirely sure about Alice. She could probably pretty easily be a product of his imagination.

He reached up and brushed his fingers across the drawing. A strange, childish part of him half-expected the blades to start turning when he did that. But again, it was only a drawing.

He was wasting time.

That wasn't just a realization he had. He didn't simply relent and think, *I'm wasting time.* There were no words, no feeling, no hidden message. It was simply a subtle awareness that wasn't there, then was.

It was Alice. *She* was telling him that he was wasting time.

He hopped down off the chair and frowned at her. "Well, I don't know what else you expect me to do. I can't understand most of what you're telling me."

That strange awareness blossomed in his head again, but it was the same mangled data she gave him the first time she told him what to do. It was like being handed a message that was garbled up, out of order and partly written in an indecipherable dead language.

"Yeah, I don't understand most of that. From my perspective, it sounds like you're telling me to turn my feet around and swallow the fishbowl."

He stared at her for a moment, at that pretty little painted face. Her expression never changed. She never moved. She made no sound. To anyone on the outside looking in, he'd appear to be just some weirdo talking to an inanimate toy. And yet she was speaking to him right now.

"What do you mean, that's pretty much it?" He looked down at his feet, puzzled. "I think there's a language barrier getting in the way."

He sat down in the chair again and scratched at his head. This was hard. At this rate, he was going to be stuck here for quite some time. And he was fairly sure that would be extraordinarily bad. He needed to get out of here and find his way back to Violet and the others.

But was he smart enough to figure this out on his own?

"It's not your fault," he assured her. "Maybe I just need to sit and think for a minute." That was probably what Wayne would do. If Wayne were careless enough to get himself into a situation like this, which of course he wasn't.

He leaned forward, propped his elbows on his knees and closed his eyes. This wasn't very unlike the puzzle box, he was sure. He just needed to keep mulling it over until he stumbled across the answer. It had to be there somewhere. The doll told him as much.

Except, at least with the puzzle box he could actually *try* things. What could he do while locked in this weird dollhouse prison with nothing but some silly drawings?

"You're right," he said to the seemingly random thoughts that wafted through his mind, images of seats, stools, sofas and recliners. "There are also chairs. My bad."

Drawings *and chairs*. But nothing else. There didn't even appear to be any air holes in this strange, white prison. Was there even anything on the other side of these walls?

He stared down at the floor between his feet, wondering if there was something he'd missed.

Chairs...

He tipped his head to one side, his gaze fixed on the legs of the chair beneath him.

Why *were* there real chairs when nothing else here was real? When he first found himself in this room, he was sitting in this one and assumed that it was simply there for him to sit in. He wouldn't have been able to sit on a drawing. But why bother with a comfort like a chair when there wasn't so much as a way out?

The second chair, the one Alice was sitting on, wasn't even a chair until he gave her that name and she became a doll. Before that, when she was still cycling through all those strange, alien shapes, she was inside a birdcage on a little table. It changed when *she* changed.

"Huh?" He glanced up at her, distracted. "Oh. Right. It was me... *I* did that." She didn't simply change her shape as she pleased. She didn't possess the power to do that. That was all *him*. This was an important detail. *Crucial*, even. It was the defining guidelines on which everything here was built.

Because this entire place, from that creepy forest trail to the even creepier house and all the way into this empty, cartoonish room, all of it existed entirely within his head. It was like the upside-down city he found himself drifting through. Everything reversed and backward and inverted, including the physical and the mental. His body had been turned inward and his mind outward.

That was why he could see even though there was no light source. Even the light was imaginary.

Such a place could easily have become his prison. It was where most people were most vulnerable, after all. Inside their heads, where all their fears and insecurities were locked up. But he wasn't like most people. He was too curious, too single-mindedly determined to explore the true universe.

As soon as he realized that she wasn't the monster she was pretending to be, his fear became overpowered by his curiosity and their places swapped. *She* became the prisoner. And *he* became the monster, poking and prying at her, twisting her this way and that, trying to understand her.

She became his plaything.

His doll.

And the same was true of this entire room. For whatever reason, *he* was the one who created the stark white walls with the cartoonishly drawn window and door.

He created this place.

Which brought him back to the chair.

It changed. Unlike the drawings. Unlike the clean, white surfaces all around him that remained the same, the chair changed from a table and a cage. It was the *only* thing in the room besides Alice that had changed.

Why?

He stood up and took a step back, looking at the chair. Now that he was really focusing on it, there seemed to be something off. It looked weirdly displaced, as if he were looking at a photograph that wasn't quite right somehow, a subtle, hard-to-see detail that gave away the fact that it had been photoshopped.

"Turn my feet around..." he muttered to himself. "But not 'feet.'" He shook his head, thoughtful. "Legs... *Chair legs.*"

It was an easy mistake, he decided, given the bizarre way in which Alice spoke to him. Things were bound to get jumbled as his mind struggled to interpret this new kind of input. Moving forward, he'd have to be careful not to get too stuck on specific ideas or words.

He picked up the chair and turned it upside down. He wasn't entirely sure what made him think to turn it precisely like that, and yet it was immediately clear that he'd done *something* right. This way, its proportions were completely different. The legs were much taller, the back much shorter, the seat oddly stretched out. It was like those warped pieces of art that only looked real when you changed the angle at which you viewed them. It was barely even recognizable as a chair anymore.

He walked all the way around it, studying it, taking in all of its new dimensions. It was such a trippy thing to see. It didn't entirely make sense. It looked like something Bugs Bunny might do while screwing with Elmer Fudd.

But it wasn't done yet, he realized.

He plucked Alice off her chair and placed her gently on the floor, then turned around and flipped it onto its side. Again, he wasn't sure how he knew which way to turn it. It was just what seemed right in the moment. But again, it seemed to do the job. The two pieces slid together perfectly.

He took a step back, frowning at the new thing that was now sitting in the middle of the room. What happened to the chairs? This new shape looked nothing like them. Try as he might, he couldn't even recognize the shape of a chair anywhere within the strange and twisted dimensions of the thing.

Nor could he figure out what this thing was even supposed to be. Blocky and angular, cage-like in a way that sort of reminded him of the birdcage that was here a little while ago, but incapable of actually containing anything. The gaps between the bars were too big and unevenly spaced.

Was it still even made of wood?

He glanced back at Alice. "I'm still listening," he assured her. "I'm still supposed to swallow the fishbowl, or something, right?"

Except "feet" didn't mean feet, so why would "swallow" mean swallow or "fishbowl" mean fishbowl?

Again, he looked at the crisscrossing bars of the mysterious object in front of him, at the awkward shape that reminded him of the cage Alice was trapped inside before she was Alice. This was a world of inversions. Upside-downs. Inside-outs. Everything was backward here. Not just reversed, but fundamentally turned on its head.

In a world like that, would he know the difference between a fishbowl and a birdcage?

Chuckling a little at the madness of it all, he reached down and picked the doll up off the floor. "We don't swallow anything," he realized. "We have to *be* swallowed. Because the doors in this place are crazy weird."

Cradling her in his arm, he gripped one of the bars that somehow used to be a chair leg and slipped inside the object. A second later, he stumbled out the other side and into another room.

Again, every surface was stark white. He was standing at the top of a grand staircase overlooking a large room.

Except in reality there was no staircase or lower room at all. It was only a drawing on the floor, like the door and the window and the ceiling fan in the previous room. The perspectives were perfect, making him believe for a moment that it was an actual, three-dimensional space spread out below him, but the details remained strangely cartoonish. There was a blue runner leading down the steps and along the floor below, a scribbling of bright blue that was supposed to represent carpeting, he supposed, leading all the way to the far end of the room where a pair of double doors were drawn in what appeared to be a main entrance. There was a window drawn on either side of the door and a dozen more along the side walls, all of them complete with curtains that matched the blue runner. There was a simple railing on either side of the steps that served no purpose whatsoever, given that nothing, not even the steps, themselves, were real. There were also three large, fancy chandeliers drawn on the ceiling, evenly spaced right down the middle, directly above the carpet. But there was nothing else, no furniture, no pictures, no decorations or vents or switches. Every other surface was smooth and flat and blank and white like untouched paper.

"Weird..." he muttered.

He turned and looked behind him, only to find that the curious not-chair doorway he entered through was gone. Instead, there stood another stark-white wall with a familiar drawn door. The same door from the room before, only mirrored. He was on the other side of it, almost as if he'd somehow managed to step through it in spite of the fact that it was only a drawing.

"I see now," he said, looking down at Alice. He understood what this place was. His brain had subconsciously spelled it out for him.

Right-side-up or upside-down, it was all the same. The City Beyond Memory, the endless, sprawling labyrinth, every stone street and passage within that impassible wall. Like a vast, complex gameboard on which to move around all his pieces. Mazes and monsters and traps and trials. They were mere toys to him, at the mercy of his every whim, playing whatever role he decided they should play, living out any story he decided to tell, with no regard for what his playthings might want.

This was the Keeper's Dollhouse.

Chapter 51

Nicole cursed as the flashlight illuminated yet another dead end. It was getting harder and harder to hold back her tears. This was so *frustrating*. They didn't have time for this bullshit right now!

But panicking wouldn't help anything. She forced herself to stay calm and turned around. "This way," she urged.

Keith didn't respond. He was getting worse. He was barely staying on his feet. And his breathing was becoming more labored and rasping. She felt as if she were torturing him, but they couldn't afford to stop. They needed to find help.

As if she believed there was any help to be found in this Godforsaken labyrinth. The best they could hope for was to run across one of the others lost in here. And what were any of *them* likely to be able to do? Olivia was a trained nurse, but she wasn't a miracle worker. She wouldn't know what to do. And it wasn't like she'd have access to a drug store. His best bet was probably Brandy and Albert's sex magic book, and she didn't even know if that ridiculous shit even worked that way.

But what else could she do? She refused to just sit down and wait for him to die. And yet, it was getting harder and harder to hold onto any kind of hope. She was following the trail of bloody smears he left behind on their way into this dead-end passage. The very sight was painful.

Her chest hitched. The pressure inside her kept building up. How much longer before the sobs came rushing up? And if that dam broke, she wasn't sure she'd *ever* stop bawling.

It wasn't fair. She needed more time. She needed to *fix* it all. Before it was too late.

The path forked up ahead. They came from the left the first time, so she steered him to the right, away from that awful trail of blood. "Please be the right way," she pleaded under her breath, knowing damned well that there might not even *be* a right way.

What if they had to cross one of those hound passages to get out of here? There was no way he'd be able to climb over one of those walls in his condition. And she wasn't strong enough to lift him over it. Or what if they found another flooded chamber like the ones they had to swim across in the temple five years ago? Or one of those shrinking passageways they'd had to crawl through on their hands and knees? And what if they emerged from this labyrinth only to find themselves at the foot of another burning mountain?

These places weren't exactly handicap accessible.

No matter how she looked at it, she couldn't find anything to be optimistic about. Realistically, she couldn't help thinking that she was fucked no matter what she did.

It really felt like she was being punished.

Keith stumbled and slumped to his knees.

"Easy!" she gasped, clinging to him with all her strength, trying to keep him from hitting his head on the stone. "Don't hurt yourself!"

Her heart was racing. What was happening? Did he just need a rest or had he reached his limit? She didn't know what to do!

He was slumped in the middle of the passage, his head hanging. She hooked her elbows under his arms and lifted him up a little. It wasn't the most graceful of maneuvers. She made an awful grunting sound that to her own ears was absurdly pig-like. And she sort of shoved her sweaty breasts into his face in the process. But she managed to scoot him up against the wall so that he could at least rest sitting up.

She knelt down in front of him, placed the flashlight on the floor and grasped his face in her hands, looking him over. He was pale. He felt feverish. And he was sweating badly. His hair was stuck to his face. "Hey! Stay with me!"

"Sorry…" he muttered.

She shook her head. "There's nothi—" Her voice caught in her throat as one of those bottled-up sobs forced its way up. She coughed and blinked hard at the tears that welled up in her eyes and tried again: "There's nothing to be sorry for."

"Jus' need a minute…"

"That's fine. We can rest. It's a good idea."

She picked up the flashlight and shined it at his feet. The remains of her gray tank top were stained nearly black with blood. Why hadn't they stopped bleeding yet? Was it because she was making him walk on them? Was that a mistake? Was she only making it worse?

But they couldn't just stay where they were. They needed to get as far as possible from that awful meadow. Even more than that, they needed to find help.

She leaned over him, holding the light closer. The skin around his ankles were discolored. Was that just bruising? Or was that a sign of infection? She didn't know anything about this stuff!

"Sorry…" he muttered again.

She turned and grasped his chin in her free hand, lifting his face toward her. "None of that," she whispered. Then she kissed him.

"You're being weird," he informed her.

"Yeah…" She pressed her forehead against his and squeezed her eyes closed. She was so tired. Not just physically, but emotionally. Mentally. She just wanted to lie down with him and sleep for a while. But of course she didn't dare. What dangers might come for them while they were vulnerable? And what if she awoke in that meadow again?

No, that definitely wasn't an option. But she could rest, at least. She wrapped her arms around him and buried her face against his shoulder.

"Why're you such a pain?" he groaned.

She laughed a little at this. "I don't know," she replied, her voice cracking. "I'm just a fuckup."

"You're *something*…that's for sure…"

"I'm so sorry."

"I just need a minute," he said again.

"It was my fault. All of it."

"Then we can go again."

"I was stupid."

"A short rest…"

"I don't expect you to forgive me," she said, sniffling. "Not ever. But I *am* sorry."

He grunted at a fresh wave of pain and turned his head.

"I'm here," she assured him, gripping him a little tighter. "I'm not going anywhere. I promise. Not again. Not *ever*."

But of course, why would he believe her? What reason had she given him to think she was anything more than the heartless bitch who shouted at him for being nice to her and then left him to mourn the loss of his mother all alone? Why would he think for even a second that she wouldn't walk out again at the next opportunity?

She sure as hell wouldn't believe her if she were him.

"Need a minute…" he grunted again.

She held onto him. She didn't know what else to do *except* hold on. She didn't know how to make it better. She didn't know how to save him from this pain. She couldn't fix him. She couldn't find the way out. She couldn't guess at what the future might bring.

All she could do was hold on.

Chapter 52

Again, Albert kissed her. "You have to calm down," he whispered.

"Calm *yourself* down," she countered, leaning away from him.

He looked over at the door, at the literal face of an epic panic attack. This was dangerous. Anxiety could be extremely overwhelming. And it had a nasty habit of building on itself. They needed to be careful how they proceeded. "I imagine it'll be a lot like the fear room. Like aiming punches at an existing wound. Everything since that damned *sex museum* has been giving us anxiety. There's no way it won't seep in, no matter how careful we are."

"*How the fuck are we supposed to deal with something like that?*"

"The book," he reminded her. He pulled it from his pocket and held it up. "One emotion to override another."

She pursed her lips at him, unamused. "You want to get in my pants *now?*"

"I want to get in your *head.*"

She blinked, her expression shifting in an instant to surprised confusion. "What?"

"If this is right," he explained, "then we should be able to use *good* emotions to cancel out the bad ones. It means if we can stay focused on each other instead of the statues—"

"Anxiety and horny don't exactly go together," she interrupted.

"If we just *do what we've been doing this whole time.* I'm betting this is exactly why the Keeper sent Shanzer to teach us about sex magic in the first place. We've literally been practicing for this the whole time."

She rolled those pretty blue eyes. Then she pouted.

He hated to see her pout like that. All he wanted was to tell her she didn't have to do it, that they'd find another way. But he knew that wasn't an option. Shanzer told them that the emotion rooms in the first temple were essentially magical locks that opened the way forward and that they never would have been able to continue if they hadn't succumbed to the sex room's overwhelming power. If he was telling the truth, then there was a good chance that they were going to have to pass through these rooms in order to unlock the way out of this one.

He stared at the doorway, at that intense face, at the *emotion* that poured from it. It was making his heart pound, filling him with dread. Shanzer told them that the emotions portrayed by the statues inside these rooms weren't artificial. "Those were real men and women, captured at the precise moment of absolute sexual peak," he said when describing the sex room. "They aren't merely a visual representation. They actually *contain* the memory they're based on." And the fear room was the same way. The people carved into that stone were real people, experiencing indescribable terror, most of them in the very moment of their deaths. But there were statues of monstrous things in there, too. The things *doing* the killing. The things *causing* the fear.

(*It saturates every atom of the stone they're crafted from. It radiates from it.*)

Even without Shanzer's explanation of how emotional energy could be utilized, he thought he understood how these rooms worked. The Temple of the Blind taught them how to pass through them unscathed. It was why he began calling it that. Blindness was the key. What they couldn't *see* couldn't hurt them. Not when it came to the statues, anyway. They had to be wary of those spikes, of course. And apparently deadly pitfalls, if that last room was any indication. But as long as they couldn't see the details of those awful statues, they wouldn't be overwhelmed by their invasive emotions.

But it wasn't perfect. The fear room leaked in through the blurriness, slowly overwhelming them anyway. And trying to backtrack through the sex room once they knew what was inside had proved impossible. It was as if their subconscious minds had memorized all those details in order to piece them together again. They lost control again while trying to leave. But when they came back a year later and let Nicole lead the way, using Brandy's glasses to hamper her own eyesight, they made it. As long as they kept their eyes completely closed, they could still do it.

But that last room was able to infect them with its overpowering sadness even though they walked through it in perfect darkness. In fact, it began working on them before they even knew what the emotion was going to be! And this one was doing the same. The moment they stepped into this warning chamber, his heart began racing and he felt a stifling dread beginning to close around him. He thought at the moment that he was merely anxious about facing another emotion room, but that anxiety *was* the room.

Why were the rooms here so much more difficult? Were they stronger than the three in the last temple? Or did it have something to do with Shanzer teaching them emotional magic?

"I feel like I can't breathe," sighed Brandy.

He could feel that, too. There was a *weight* to the atmosphere here, not so unlike the constant, unpleasant pressure outside in the Denselands. Like a sweltering humid day, but without the heat or the dampness.

She was staring at that awful face, her expression twisted with unease. She was tugging nervously at a lock of her hair. "I won't be able to. I'll lose it. I know I will. I'll fall apart and we'll never get out of this fucking place."

He pulled her close to him, embracing her, comforting her. "I'll do it," he promised.

"You can't either," she groaned, her voice muffled against his chest.

"I can," he insisted, kissing her forehead. "I've got you with me. I can do anything if it means keeping you safe."

"You're so full of shit," she told him.

"You just keep your eyes closed and think happy thoughts."

"You mean *horny* thoughts."

"No, I mean *happy* ones. It doesn't have to be dirty. We've learned at least that much by now. If the dirty thoughts help, then go for it, but make sure they're happy. Because that's who we are. We're not anxious. We're not afraid of some stupid statues. As long as we're together, we're *happy*. And *that's* what's real. Not any of this other shit."

"You're such a dork sometimes..."

"I know."

She sighed, then lifted her face and kissed him. "You'd better be right about this."

He reached up and took off her glasses. He'd seen her countless times without them. She didn't wear them to bed, after all. Or in the shower. But the cute little way she squinted at him whenever she took them off never seemed to get old. She was so pretty! It still stirred his heart every time he looked into those gorgeous blue eyes. "I am," he insisted as he put the glasses on his own face.

"You look ridiculous in my glasses," she informed him.

"I look great," he replied. "You're just blind as a bat."

"You look like a kid getting ready to go trick-or-treating as Harry Potter."

"I said 'happy thoughts,'" he reminded her. "Not mean ones."

The glasses distorted everything, but her face was close enough to his that he could still see that adorable smirk on her face.

"But whatever makes you happy," he decided, turning his gaze toward the screaming door.

It was little more than a great gray blur, but the flashlight against the stone was enough of a contrast that he could still make out the black opening within the mouth. He reminded himself that he'd have to be careful. He didn't want to knock his head against the guy's teeth or trip over his tongue. It only *looked* like soft flesh, after all.

Brandy slipped her arms around him and pressed her face against his back. "Be careful," she pleaded. "Don't overdo it."

"Sure."

"I mean it," she grumbled. "If you fake die on me again like you did in the fear room, I will *so* make you regret it."

"Yes ma'am," he replied.

Chapter 53

One by one, Corey wrapped the bloody strings around the stone spikes. It was a painfully slow process. There were hundreds of spikes in this shaft, each and every one a very specific component in the ancient machinery. It was like a hyper-complex circuit board. One small mistake and the whole system could short out. Or worse.

It shouldn't have been possible. There were *thousands* of strings coiled up inside Austin's mangled body, each one indistinguishable from all the others, yet possessing its own specific purpose. Even if he understood the technology, there was no way to tell one from another. And yet somehow he simply knew where everything went.

Just like he knew how to make the spikes extend like this. He wasn't sure he could do it again because he wasn't entirely sure how he did it the first time. He just reached into the stone like he did before and made them pop out of the wall. He wasn't even sure where they came from. There was no sign of them before they extended. Where were they hiding?

This entire structure utilized properties he couldn't possibly comprehend with the rigid framework of thought the "real world" taught him not to stray beyond, and yet his hands were working almost on their own, completing tasks that his brain was telling him shouldn't be possible.

It was the same as the first time, he realized. A forgotten memory of a dark cave in a sundrenched forest many years ago. A set of stone steps. A circle of gray stones. It had slowly been creeping back to him for some time, but he couldn't decide if it was a real memory or something that appeared when he interacted with the control panels outside the impassible wall. It felt real. He remembered Violet being there with him. But how could he have forgotten something like that?

He wished Violet was here so he could ask her if she had any memories of a mysterious cave. But wishing wasn't going to get anything done. He kept his hands moving, still marveling at how they seemed to know exactly what to do, like muscle memory, as if he'd been doing it all his life.

"Preprogrammed knowledge, imbedded in hereditary DNA," was how Austin explained it to Albert and Brandy. Something about reincarnation and subconscious memory... It didn't matter. The fact was that he knew what he was doing, even though no one in world after world after world of forgotten histories should be able to understand something like this.

Because he was meant to be here.

This was his job. His *duty*, he might even say. It was *who he was.* Every moment of his life had been leading up to this one monumental task. It was why he'd always been so fascinated with the supernatural, with conspiracies, with UFOs and aliens and Mandella effects and alternate timelines and all the other things that Violet was always telling him were bullshit. It was because he *knew*. Somewhere, deep inside, he *knew* that there was something more to the world than what everyone could see.

Because it was embedded in his very genetic code.

The same was true, he now realized, of his fascination with technology. His devices. The internet. It would be difficult to put it into words, precisely, but somewhere on an extremely fundamental level, navigating this tangled mess of bloody strings wasn't so unlike navigating the deep web where he'd found so many fascinating myths and legends to delve into.

He just simply knew which strands were worth following.

"Is this as fast as you can work?" grumbled Austin.

"Yep," he replied without slowing down. He wasn't in the habit of letting other people bother him. It had never been worth his time.

"I should've been uploaded into the stoneworks hours ago."

"Shoulda," he agreed. But the fact was that he simply wasn't. He looked over his shoulder at the artificial man, an eyebrow raised. "If you're so smart, how'd you end up divorced from your ass?"

"That wasn't my fault," he huffed, offended. "Something beat me here. An intruder in the stoneworks."

"Intruder," muttered Corey.

"Yes. An intruder."

"Seems like that shouldn't've happened..."

"It shouldn't have."

"Thought you said that Keeper guy didn't make mistakes, though," said Corey without looking up from his work. "Weren't you going on about that back at the gate? When you were bein' rude to everybody?"

"Like I told that woman who wandered through here before, the Keeper doesn't make mistakes because he's prepared for every possible contingency. It doesn't matter whether this task is completed by me or by you because the end result is the same: the job is done."

"Is it?"

"Is it what?"

"The same," replied Corey. "Your life and mine. Are they equivalent? You're not even human. You never were."

"The result remains precisely the same. Only the cost changes. The cost can be variable and often is."

"Hm…"

He went on working, wrapping the bloody strings around their matching spikes. It wasn't simply *which* spike. The depth mattered, too. The precise distance from the tip. The order. These details were as important as which string went where.

Austin wasn't wrong. It was a painfully slow process. He'd been at it for hours already and was nowhere near done. It would have been so much faster for him to simply impale himself on these spines and be done with it.

It didn't go unnoticed by him, either, that the manner in which Austin was attacked was not merely brutal, but singularly responsible for making this task so much more difficult. If it had simply stabbed him through the heart or tore out his throat or even ripped off his head, he probably could still have been uploaded as originally intended. But the monster ripped him in half, making an absolute mess of the strings, even snapping a great many of them.

He didn't think that was by chance.

"Tell me 'bout the intruder," he said without looking back. "What was it?"

"It was a saboteur. An entity from the universe's unnatural side that likely sneaked through one of the gates at the moment they were opened. Maybe even the one *we* used. I recall that there *were* several concealed presences gathering around while you and your friends were arguing with me about how to proceed."

"Unnatural…" pondered Corey, ignoring the fact that he was blatantly blaming everyone else for the fact that he was no longer tall enough to get on the big kid rides at the county fair.

"Yes. It was particularly reeking of the energy and aura specific to the Great Enemy."

He paused and looked back at this. "Great Enemy…"

"Yes. A high-ranking manifestation. Very powerful. Very dangerous."

"You're talkin' 'bout one of the Twelve Teeth, then?" He remembered his friends in Wisconsin talking about them. Gina's roommates,

Seph and Piper. All of that business with the Hands…and some ancient prick named Janon Tane… Tane was dead now, but there were eleven more out there. And they were bad news.

"It wasn't one of the Twelve," explained Austin. "If one of them had ambushed me here, I very much doubt there would have been anything left of me to salvage. But this was something close to them. Third generation, I'd wager. A direct manifestation of one of them."

That wasn't good. He thought about Violet. She was here somewhere, he was sure of it, wandering this labyrinth like everyone else, probably blindly marching toward whatever duty the Keeper entrusted to her. He thought of Gina. Andrea and Nicole. Wayne and Olivia and Keith. Albert and Brandy. So many good people. And so much *danger*.

"Most of the Twelve wouldn't want to sabotage the cycle, though," reasoned Austin. "It doesn't benefit them in any way. And I doubt that *any* of them would actually allow it to end. Their literal existence is due to the Bargain of the Three. They'd have no reason to exist without it."

The Twelve Teeth. The cycle. The Bargain of the Three. Seph and Piper spoke of all these things. And he and Violet had no reason to doubt a word of it. They were there for some of the story, after all. He even got the chance to save them from a bunch of zombies. But still, there was something surreal about finding his way back to these phrases.

"So what *would* one of the twelve be after by infiltrating the stoneworks and disabling me? Can you think of a good reason for it?"

Of course he could. That was the point. The question was yet another jab at his lowly human intellect. "A delay, obviously," he replied as he went back to work. "Slow you down. Maybe make sure no one finishes what they're doing before it does whatever it's really here to do."

"Hm," was all Austin had to say to that.

Maybe he *would* make the stuck-up robot smack himself a few times. Just for good measure.

But later. He needed to get this done first.

"What'd it look like?" he wondered.

"Darkness, mostly. Like all unnatural things it lacks body and soul. An ever-shifting mass of substance and miasma. A displaced mess of reaching limbs and snapping jaws."

"Sounds crazy. But what if someone else out there runs into it?"

"Depends on why it's here," replied Austin. "But I expect it would be bad. Facing it head-on would be a death sentence. It's of the shadow races, both physical and ethereal at the same time. A human being couldn't fight off something like that."

Corey nodded. That was what he was afraid of.

He hoped everyone remained safe out there.

Chapter 54

Gina wasn't ready to face the thing with too many mouths. She needed more time. She needed more *space*. But there was nowhere to go. All the passages here were dead ends.

She turned her gaze upward, simultaneously turning the labyrinth on its side again. But now she was trapped between two voids that shouldn't have been there. She hadn't moved. And they weren't there a moment ago. She would've felt them looming above and below her. She looked down again. The dead ends were gone. Instead, her psychic eye told her she was caught in a circle with no way out.

Was she moving through the glass labyrinth? Or was the labyrinth moving around her? Did she have any control at all? It was starting to feel as though she were being corralled like a lamb off to slaughter. Was the monster able to manipulate these glass walls? Or worse, did the walls, themselves, conspire against her?

Was this how it was meant to end for her? Was she merely another of the Keeper's unfortunate sacrifices?

"Are you afraid?" growled the unnatural abomination.

She turned around, eyes wide in the darkness. Something big wavered behind the glass back there, shadows stretching and twisting, fingers like crooked branches reaching.

This was a mistake, she realized now that it was far too late. She shouldn't have come here. She didn't understand what the glass labyrinth was, how it worked, what it meant.

She ran the other way, her heart racing, tears streaming, but there was nowhere to go but back around. And the size of the circle kept changing, the distance between her and it ebbing and flowing like the motion of the tides. If she wasn't careful, she'd find herself flung headlong into its groping arms.

Again, she turned her focus upward, twisting the labyrinth, only to crash into yet another dead-end wall.

She turned and looked behind her, expecting the monster to be right there, its many jaws descending on her, but the tangling path was empty.

"I like it when they're afraid," hissed the monster from behind the glass at her back.

She cried out, startled, and twirled around in time to catch just a glimpse of something dark sliding out of sight.

She turned to run, then let out a startled yelp as something flashed by above her.

She fled around the corner and into the next passage.

Something slithered beneath her feet.

The labyrinth wouldn't let her escape. The glass passageways were knotted up, twisting and winding. Up and down were intertwined with left and right. And the thing with too many mouths was creeping behind many walls at once.

Reflections and refractions. Illusions and distortions.

Again, she turned her focus upward. Again the labyrinth rearranged itself.

"I like it when they *scream.*"

There was now a vertical shaft plunging into the earth only a few steps behind her. She turned around and backed away, her heart skipping a beat. A few inches closer and she would've fallen.

She turned and looked the other way. Another vertical shaft stretched upward ahead of her.

Was the labyrinth lying on its side now? Had all this twisting and turning warped the layout? Had she accidentally broken her perspective, ending up in an orientation that she wasn't going to be able to solve?

"And you *will* scream."

Again, she turned the labyrinth. Again, everything changed.

She cast her psychic awareness out and found broken spaces all around her. Overlapping floors. Inverted corridors. Passageways that led nowhere.

Gaps in the glass…

Bent dimensions…

A pandemonium of distorted angles and proportions…

Was the monster doing this? No… That didn't seem right. It was her. *She* was breaking everything. The glass labyrinth's layout was a manifestation of her own making, she began to realize, a reflection of her state of mind. And right now, her mind was in a state of rapidly increasing panic.

"You'll scream for a *long time.*"

She clasped her hands over her ears and closed her eyes. She needed to calm down. She needed to *think.* Somewhere, deep inside her, she knew what this place was. It was who she was. It was why she was here. She just *knew things.* And what she knew right now was that there were *two* glass labyrinths. One was here already when she arrived.

The second was the one that her psychic mind painted inside her head to give order to the chaos so that she could physically navigate it. They were both separate and the same.

The thing with too many mouths was breaking the illusion of order. That was its game. That was why it kept saying those horrible things. The more it frightened her, the easier it was for it to find her.

She forced herself to take a deep, calming breath. It wasn't easy. She could feel the monster closing in on her. She didn't have much time left. But she needed to release this pent-up tension inside her. She needed to loosen the grip her fear had on her.

"There you are," growled the beast.

Again, she lifted her face and looked upward. Again, the labyrinth rotated. This time, however, it didn't *stop* rotating. It rolled all the way around. And as it did, she stepped forward, tiptoeing through the revolving corridors, skipping through passageway after passageway.

The beast snarled right at her heels, but then slipped away, its frustrated voice sinking into the distance behind her.

When she finally stopped and opened her eyes—not that her eyes ever had anything to do with it—she found herself in a long, straight corridor.

No... Not just a corridor, she realized. The entirety of the glass labyrinth was now stretched out before and behind her. She'd unraveled it all. Everywhere that existed in this unnatural slice of Albert's Temple of the Three Whispers was laid bare before her. She was everywhere and nowhere all at once. It was both miniscule and vast. Both simple and complex.

But she didn't have time to wonder at the spectacle of what she'd accomplished.

There was nothing between her and the monster now. It was behind her, far away yet unrestrained. It could see her standing here as clearly as she could feel it. It was already turning toward her, already launching itself in this direction. It only had to close the distance between them and it would have her.

But order had been restored for the moment and in this moment rested her chance.

She hurried forward, searching, her hand dragging along the glass wall beside her. It was here somewhere, she was certain of it. She only had to find it.

Just a small crack would do. Just as she crossed *into* the glass labyrinth, she could return to the stone, where the beast couldn't reach her. There, she'd be able to reevaluate the situation.

But first she had to *find* a crack. And cracks were hard to find in dark places like these while unthinkable things were barreling toward you at unimaginable speeds. The emptiness behind the glass offered no help. Gone were the layered refractions that gave the first one away. There was nothing to refract. Her psychic mind revealed nothing at all on the other side.

The beast was getting closer. She could hear it. Its feet made no sound as it ran—it was only shadow and malice, after all—but it wasn't silent. It made a sound like an obscene mockery of breathing, like the lecherous panting of some sexual deviant, seething with morbid excitement and murderous anticipation. A *terrible* sound that made her skin crawl and her stomach knot.

She wasn't going to be able to rearrange the labyrinth again, she somehow understood. The thing with too many mouths had already locked her in its horrible gaze. If she tried to change things even one more time, it would be waiting for her. It would have her. And somehow she understood that it wouldn't kill her. Not right away. It wouldn't be so kind.

It wanted to play with her. It wanted to make her scream and beg. It wanted to *hurt* her. For as long as it could. As long as her sanity would allow.

A great, terrified sob escaped her. If she were relying on her human eyes right now, she wouldn't be able to see through the streaming tears. But her inner eye had no such limitations. She scanned the wall as she crept forward, searching, seeking the subtlest glimmer, knowing she was running out of time.

The awful, obscene breathing was getting closer. It wasn't even bothering to speak anymore. It knew it didn't have to. Somehow, it had connected with her, their minds touching across the strange space of the glass labyrinth. It had shown her what it was. She knew what it wanted. And she knew it was the end of her if she didn't find a crack *right now*.

It would be upon her in ten seconds.

Where was it? There had to be one. The goddess wouldn't let it end like this for her. She'd never send her to such a horrible end.

Seven seconds.

She wanted to run. She wanted to race away from here, but that would be the end of her for sure. She couldn't outrun that thing. And she wouldn't be able to find a crack if she were running. She needed to stand strong and pace herself. Keep creeping. Keep searching. Slowly. Carefully.

And yet her body was shaking so badly by now that she could barely breathe.

Time was running out.

The beast was right behind her. She could *smell* it. An awful, putrid stench was surrounding her, threatening to suffocate her.

Five seconds.

Impossible. She wasn't going to make it. This was the end.

Three seconds.

No... *There.* Right in front of her. The very subtlest of shifts in the warped glass, barely perceptible.

Her heart leapt in her chest.

The monster threw itself at her.

She thrust herself forward with all her strength.

At the same moment, the thing with too many mouths closed its shadowy form around her.

Chapter 55

Wayne shined his light into the sprawling darkness ahead of them. "We're back here again," he announced, as if anyone needed him to point out that they'd only circled back to the same room they left behind not an hour ago.

Andrea made a face and groaned. "I don't like this room."

He looked down at Olivia. "Do you feel anything?"

"I'm with her. I don't like this room. But it's not really setting off any alarm bells. It's just sort of an unpleasant feeling. It's kind of hard to explain."

He shined his light back and forth. Because it was too big to see across, there was no way to know how many doors might be in this room, much less whether they were back at the same one they left through. For all he knew, they could be looking in from the opposite side now.

Theoretically, they could stay lost in an area like this forever. They could easily spend hours or days following the same passageways around in circles, never getting anywhere. It was a terrifying thought, but an absolute possibility in a labyrinth this size.

Albert always said that the only reason they were able to find their way out of the first temple was because the Keeper made sure of it. They were only pawns in his game, after all, players following his script. The odds of finding their way through a multi-tiered labyrinth of that size on their own were practically zero. It just didn't make any logical sense.

And if this was really a continuation of what they did five years ago, then where was the Keeper now? Was he out there somewhere, watching them, manipulating them, making them play his strange little game?

He didn't like being a puppet in some little monster's grand theatre.

"So do we turn back and try a different passage?" he wondered aloud. "Or do we go in and look for another door?"

"Go back," said Andrea.

"Forward," said Olivia at the same time.

The two looked at each other, uncertain.

"Forward feels better," explained Olivia. "But if you really don't think we should go back in there…"

"No…" Andrea shined her flashlight into the room again. "If you think it's better, it's fine. I just really don't like the way it feels in there."

He looked back and forth, uncertain. He didn't like *either* choice. What if Andrea's peculiar ability to see the murk allowed her to sense something wrong that was farther in the future than Olivia was able to see?

But Andrea was already creeping out into that greater darkness, her flashlight's beam sweeping the floor in front of her.

A part of him wished he could see what she was seeing. It was troubling knowing there were things in here hidden from his eyes. But a larger part of him was certain he wouldn't want that burden. Ignorance truly was often bliss. Not everything was worth knowing. And she hadn't exactly seemed thrilled about the things she saw.

"Something about this place feels strange," said Olivia. "Not good or bad, exactly, just…*off.*"

"The murk is weird here," explained Andrea. "Strung out. Clumped up. Pooling in places. It never looked like this anywhere else. I don't know why this area is different."

She stopped and shined her light straight up into the darkness above them.

Wayne and Olivia did the same.

"What is it?" he whispered. He couldn't see anything up there. The ceiling was too high. And even if he could see up there, he wasn't able to see the same things Andrea did. He wasn't sure why he kept trying.

"I don't know," she replied in the same whisper. "I can't actually *see* anything. It's too high up. But there's something up there. I can feel it."

"We believe you," said Olivia. She didn't need to ask him. She knew she spoke for them both. Andrea was no liar. She wouldn't make anything up.

Andrea turned suddenly and shined her light out into the open darkness. "There's something moving over there," she reported. "We should probably steer clear of it."

He nodded and gripped Olivia's hand a little tighter. "Good to know."

She grimaced and rubbed at her temples. "Stupid voices…" she murmured.

Olivia pulled her closer again. "Are they still being mean?"

She nodded.

"They're not real. You said so."

"I know. But they're still *annoying*."

Wayne glanced back over his shoulder. Thinking about it now, it had been a while since *he* heard any voices. They must have moved away from whatever area it was coming from. And good riddance. He had more than enough problems already without hearing *voices*.

"We should keep going," insisted Andrea. Already she was moving, tugging Olivia along with her again, and Olivia tugging at him in turn.

He couldn't help noticing that she was taking an unusual path through the empty space, sort of winding her way through the room, going out of her way to go around one of the stone pillars, as if she were leading them around something they couldn't see. Were they avoiding those frightful sounding "clumps" of murk she described? The ones that crept and growled and stalked?

Except that wasn't right... Didn't she say those things were attracted by movement and sound? If that had been what she glimpsed over there, she would've instructed them to keep quiet and only move when she said so, wouldn't she?

But what more could there be in this darkness?

Of course, the question had barely crossed his mind before he felt downright stupid thinking it. What *couldn't* there be? And what made him think for even a second that *she* knew what surprises might still be in store for her in the murk passages of the City Beyond Memory. After all, she just finished telling them that the murk in this room had changed. Something about it *pooling* in places. He found himself imagining that she was leading them around great, black, bubbling *puddles* of shadowy darkness and the image of it in his mind was deeply unpleasant. What if they took a wrong step and fell into something like that? Would the murk still be harmless in that form? Or would it become all too real? It was entirely too easy to imagine a great, black shadow appearing from nowhere and swallowing them whole. Or melt away the stone beneath their feet and drag them down like quicksand.

But it wasn't Andrea who tugged them to a stop. It was Olivia.

"I'm getting a bad feeling, you guys."

"*How* bad?" he dared.

She turned and shined her light back the way they came, then out across the dark room.

He added his light to hers, examining each of those great, stone pillars in turn, expecting to see something unpleasant peering back from behind one of them, but there was nothing.

"I feel *really* uneasy, like something scary is about to happen."

"So, business as usual?" squeaked Andrea. She swept her light across the floor nearby, then pointed it up into the darkness hiding the chamber's ceiling.

"It's getting worse," warned Olivia.

Wayne tightened his grip on her arm and nudged her forward. "Let's keep moving. Find a doorway. Get out of the open."

Again, they were moving, their flashlight beams darting back and forth, up and down, making their shadows flit around them, a dizzying display of flashing gray and black shapes in the dark.

"What was that?" gasped Olivia. She turned and shined her light behind them again. "Did you hear it?"

"All I can hear are the stupid voices," said Andrea.

"What did you hear?" asked Wayne.

But before she could answer him, he heard it, too. A soft, fluttery sound. A sort of playing-card-in-bicycle-spokes sound. A dreadfully *familiar* sound.

He turned and shined his light across the room. Something flickered in the gloom, a brief reflection, a flash of movement.

"What *is* that?" asked Andrea.

"Hound bug," he breathed.

"*What?*"

A soft, terrified squeal escaped Olivia as she pulled on his arm, urgently begging him to move.

He didn't dare linger. He took hold of her hand and hurried forward through the darkness. "We have to get out of here."

"What's going on?" asked Andrea.

"He's found us!" cried Olivia.

"*Who?*"

"The scarecrow man," said Wayne.

Behind them, the sound of countless razor-edged wings swelled to a terrifying roar.

Chapter 56

Violet ran.

What the hell were those things?

She followed the chewed-up stone to an intersection of five passageways a few hundred feet from the narrow ledge. She was trying to decide which way to go when that strange noise exploded somewhere to her right, sending her fleeing in the other direction. Since then, she'd hurried through two more intersections and the noise had only grown louder with each turn she made.

They sounded more like machines than beasts. Awful, deafening, droning roars that made her think of some kind of whirling, chopping, grinding farm equipment. She stumbled into another intersection and stopped, trying to listen over the hammering of her panicked heart. Was it coming from *every* direction? Was she *surrounded*?

She remembered Albert saying something about monsters in the temple that made a terrible noise, something covered from head-to-toe in razor-sharp scales. What was it he called them? Hounds? But these were no canine noises. It was like something straight out of her nightmares.

She turned around, cocking her head one direction, then another, trying to pinpoint the origin of the awful sound even though all she wanted with every fiber of her being was to keep running.

Definitely not *that* way. It was loudest from that way.

This way? It was hard to hear. Was that another one farther away or an echo?

The sound was getting louder behind her. She couldn't afford to linger. She needed to make a decision.

She started down one passage, her head turned to better listen. This seemed right. It was definitely not as loud this way.

She picked up her pace, praying that she wasn't simply circling back around to whatever bloodthirsty pack was closing in on her.

Why were there things like this here? Wasn't a giant, nearly unsolvable labyrinth the size of a large metropolitan area *enough* of a challenge?

Somewhere behind her, that awful noise exploded into a violent frenzy. Were those things fighting? Or had they caught her scent? How long could she possibly keep avoiding them?

Her light pushed back the darkness ahead of her, revealing a wall. She stumbled to a stop, horrified. A dead end? *Now?* That wasn't fair!

She turned and shined her light behind her. She couldn't see anything, but those awful noises were definitely getting louder. They were coming this way. And they sounded angry. They'd be here any second.

She backed away, tears welling up. What was she supposed to do?

She turned and swept her light across the walls, looking for something—*anything*—because this couldn't be how this was all supposed to end. It couldn't!

And yet, there was nothing here. Nowhere to go. Not so much as a broken chunk of stone to defend herself.

She wiped at her eyes, frustrated, then blinked at the dead end ahead of her.

Wait...

That was no dead end. It was a wall, sure, but the passage was taller over there. There was an opening *above* the wall. A passage continued on above it!

A blood-curdling snarl reverberated from the passage behind her, startling a terrified scream from her as she rushed forward and clambered up the wall with a clumsy sort of desperate lunge. Her small size made it more of a chore than it should've been. She was short and the stone was so smooth. Her boots didn't want to grip the surface. Ordinarily Corey would be there to give her a boost. He was always looking out for her. But she was on her own. She hooked one leg over the edge and heaved herself upward with a great and rather unladylike grunt.

This seemed familiar. Didn't Albert say something about offset passages like this in the first temple? Something about the hounds not being able to jump or climb?

As she pushed herself up onto her hands and knees, they arrived. Great, distorted, brownish shapes exploded into view and slammed into the stone beneath her. She screamed and scurried backward, scrambling to her feet in the process, her terrified eyes fixed on the ledge, waiting for the horrors below to bound into view and pounce on her. She was so frightened she could barely breathe. She felt like she might throw up right here and now.

But the seconds ticked by and nothing appeared.

She stood there, her heart pounding, her body trembling with terror as that violent racket went on and on but nothing leapt into view.

Could they really not get up here? She thought back to the story Albert told her in the carriage, about the creatures not being able to jump or climb or swim, keeping them corralled into their own territory within the labyrinth.

(*The places where the two areas intersected were offset. The hounds couldn't get to you if you stayed in the upper one.*)

Was it really so simple?

She shined her light behind her, then down at the floor at her feet. The stone here was smooth and pristine again, without so much as a scratch to be seen. That was another detail Albert mentioned, she now recalled. A telltale sign of their territory. Their claws left marks over time, nicks and scratches in the stone. If she'd only remembered that sooner, she could have turned around immediately and gone back the way she came.

No wonder the path was so narrow back there. It was like these offsets, meant to keep the hounds from crossing into other parts of the labyrinth.

She fixed her light on the ledge ahead of her. She didn't trust turning her back on them. They sounded awful. Snarling and snaping and growling and…whatever that other noise they were making was. Something about slashing scales. She didn't really understand it when he was describing them. Was it some kind of warning? Like a rattle-snake's tail?

She should be running away. She knew this. Those things could probably smell her up here. They weren't going to calm down as long as she was lingering. But curiosity kept her rivetted to the spot.

If Corey were here, he'd insist on looking. She knew he would. He'd creep over there and shine his light down, taking a good long look. And she'd scold him for it. She'd tell him he was taking too many risks. She'd be the voice of reason, like always. But the truth was that she was just as curious as he was. She wanted to see them. She'd complain. She'd *nag* if she had to. Because it was her job to keep him safe, just as much as it was his job to look after *her*. But he wouldn't listen. He'd look anyway. And then she'd look, too. It was always like that.

But Corey wasn't here. If she wanted to see what was down there, she was going to have to be the foolish one in his place.

And somehow, in spite of her trembling legs, she found herself creeping toward the edge, toward that awful noise.

She shined her light down on them.

"What the hell *are* you?" she breathed as she stared at the unnatural shapes scuffling beneath her, clawing at the stone wall and snapping at each other.

There were two of them. That was the first surprise, because given the amount of noise they were making she would have guessed that there were at least a dozen of them. And they were bigger than she expected, nearly as tall as full-grown lions, she thought, but twice as wide.

Short legs and necks. Broad heads with wide jaws. No visible eyes. And *two tails*. Why did they have two tails? Looking closer, they appeared to have two spinal cords branching from their necks. What kind of creature was even shaped like that?

And those *scales!* Now she understood what Albert was trying to say. They weren't lying down, overlapping like reptile scales. They were standing straight up and oscillating back and forth, each one working at high speed like individual little power saws! No wonder they made so much noise!

She imagined her shaky legs giving out and spilling her over that ledge and she pressed her hand to the wall to steady herself. The thought of what those things would do to her made her feel queasy.

If only her cell phone wasn't dead. Corey would go nuts over a video of these things!

But then again, she really didn't think she'd want to linger long enough to get a proper video.

She backed away from the edge until she couldn't see them anymore, then turned and hurried on her way, eager to be out of earshot of that horrendous noise.

Chapter 57

Everett couldn't simply descend the steps and walk down to the floor below. When he tried walking forward, he naturally only walked straight ahead. It was just like the stickers in a toy playset. Or a painted backdrop behind the set of a play. A mere illusion of depth hiding the true shallowness of the space.

Except as he walked forward, the scene before him changed. Like an optical illusion, the farther he walked, the more tilted things became, the angles stretching and turning. Those drawn-on chandeliers shrank away above. The windows and doors below grew larger, the perspective lines became straighter. And the steps beneath his feet, despite getting smaller as they stretched away from him, were growing larger as he walked, presenting an illusion of going downstairs even though his feet only found level floor in front of him.

He had to stop at the bottom and close his eyes. The illusion gave him a subtle sort of queasy feeling, like a carnival ride that had gone on just a little too long, making him feel unsteady on his feet.

When he opened them again, he turned to see that the stairs were now drawn on the wall behind him, reaching up to a two-dimensional second floor balcony and a much smaller version of the useless door leading back to the previous room at the top.

"Weird," he muttered to himself, perfectly aware by now that it was *he* who was creating this bizarre dollhouse world. Wayne and the others were right. He was a little odd. Maybe he always had been.

He faced forward again, his gaze sweeping across the empty space ahead. It was much bigger than the last room, but otherwise it was the same stark white surfaces with childish drawings of windows and doors he had no way of using. The windows didn't even have scenes drawn in them down here. Those blue, colored-in curtains were all pulled closed.

But the main difference between this room and the last was that there was no furniture in this one, chairs or otherwise, that he could manipulate in any way. Everything was either a smooth, white surface or those useless drawings.

He looked down at Alice, still cradled in the crook of his arm. "I didn't say I was giving up," he replied to what popped into his head. "I just got here. Give me a minute to look around."

She wasn't badgering him. Nor was she mocking him. On the contrary, she seemed fairly encouraging. Despite the fact that she was basically his prisoner at this point, she seemed just as eager to leave this dreamlike dollhouse as he was. He wasn't sure what might happen when (and if) he finally managed to return to the labyrinth. Perhaps she'd transform into something truly monstrous and turn on him. But that was a problem for later. Right now, he needed her and she needed him. Besides, he stopped being preoccupied with the future the night those fishermen pulled him out of that frigid lake.

He focused on the problem in front of him. There were no chairs from which to construct another mystery doorway, but he *did* somehow manage to use that drawn-on stairway. Somehow, he descended to this level, making it move from the floor to the wall in the process. And if he could manipulate one of the drawings, maybe he could manipulate another.

He crossed the room and examined the double doors that looked like they might be the main entrance. But no matter how much he felt around the lines, no matter what angle he approached it from, it remained as stubbornly two-dimensional as the one upstairs.

"Yeah," he said, speaking to the wordless voice inside his head, "I didn't think it would work either. But I might as well start with the most obvious solution. I mean, it's a *door*. It's *supposed* to go somewhere."

True, it was a backward and inside out world inside the void, but it was also somehow created from his own imagination. Why would he imagine a room with doors that didn't work? Was it some kind of subliminal metaphor? Was this like the way dreams were supposed to have hidden meanings? Like how dreaming about showing up to school naked represented some dark secret you were hiding? (At least, that was what he'd read somewhere once. He was hardly an expert on the subject.) Was he going to have to search his feelings and interpret these bizarre rooms in order to understand the way out? Something about there being no way home, perhaps?

He turned and strolled back the way he came, his gaze washing over each of the drawings. The windows all appeared to be identical, each curtain with the same creases and wrinkles. And each chandelier had the same chains and bulbs. It was as if each one was a mass-produced sticker printed off an assembly line. If there was a clue to this puzzle hidden in one of them, it would be far too subtle for him to find, meaning that probably wasn't the answer.

He walked past window after window, back toward the two-dimensional staircase that he found himself quite sure wouldn't allow him to use it again.

So what was the answer?

He frowned at the stream of wordless thoughts that floated through his mind. Scribbles on paper. Sleeping in his own bed at home. The drawn-on doorway behind him. His mission to find the secrets of the world and the sparkling angel he glimpsed that night. Violet telling him about her own mission to seek out doorways to other worlds. And a stubborn, lingering sense of loneliness.

He closed his eyes and rubbed thoughtfully at his temples as he let these individual ideas circle through his head, mixing and mingling into something new, something relevant. The answer was there somewhere, he was slowly beginning to understand. Alice was trying to tell him. If only he could wrap his head around her bizarre, wordless language.

Again, he turned and looked back at the pointless double doors that offered no escape from this empty room. Scribbles and colors with no depth, no substance, no *reality*. Not unlike a dream... Figments of his imagination that fade forever the moment he left, the moment he awakened...

That was where he was supposed to be focusing.

This dollhouse wasn't real. It was a figment of his imagination made solid in this backward and upside-down other place. Just like with Alice, he was in control of it. He was the *creator*. And he could also be the *editor*. He only needed somewhere to start.

A clean sheet of paper...

Again, he closed his eyes. He pictured the room around him, the drawings. The windows. The doors. The stairs.

There was an empty section of wall on either side of the steps, he recalled.

He opened his eyes and turned around. There was now a doorway on either side. And unlike the front doors, one of these was standing open, revealing a hallway leading deeper into the dollhouse.

"Take control..." he muttered to himself, already moving toward the open door. This was how he was going to get out of here, by slowly unraveling the controls to this paper prison.

He stepped into the hallway and found it lined with more useless, drawn-on doors as far as he could see.

"I know it won't," he replied to the unspoken warning inside his head.

It wouldn't be that easy, Alice was telling him. He couldn't just seize control of the dollhouse. Because no matter how it appeared, he wasn't alone down here. Something was watching him. Something old and powerful. Something that was holding up these paper walls, empowering the illusions, keeping them from falling apart around him.

The Priestess of Ruin wouldn't let him escape so easily. Not while she was still having fun with him.

Chapter 58

The world swam in and out of focus, like great rolling clouds of fog washing over him, blurring everything, then slinking away again. And in that fog, Keith found himself bouncing through a myriad of disjointed and broken dreams. He knew they were dreams because they couldn't be real. There were people there who couldn't possibly have been. Sometimes his mother. Sometimes his father. He even caught sight of his grandmother once, sitting in her favorite chair, smiling that smile that was still so familiar after all these years, as if she'd never left. And there were places he'd never been before. Standing in a long, dark, dusty hallway in some kind of huge, abandoned building. Or in a vast, old-growth forest full of enormous, moss-covered trees. Or looking up at a strange sky filled with impossible colors. Or across a hazy cemetery full of illegible tombstones that seemed to go on and on. And sometimes impossible things were happening. For instance, he kept dreaming that Nicole was kissing him again…

But none of the dreams would last. Every time he thought he understood what was happening, another of those agonizing waves of pain would crawl up his legs and shatter it all.

And yet it seemed like forever since he was last awake. How long had he been trapped in this broken dreamscape, jumping from one delusion to another. How much time had passed in the waking world?

He couldn't keep doing this. He needed to wake up and keep moving. He had a job to do. And like it or not that job was all that was left in his lonely life. Everything else was gone now, washed away and faded from sight like his dreams.

"It's not gone," said Amber. "It's been there the whole time."

He stared at her, at those big brown eyes peering back at him from beneath that mop of curly black hair. They were sitting together at the kitchen table in his house, having coffee together like they'd done countless times before. And yet somehow this all seemed both familiar *and* strange. "What?"

But she didn't explain it to him. Instead, she merely shrugged and said, "You'll know when the time comes."

He opened his mouth to ask her just what the hell she was talking about, but the words never reached his lips. Another of those agonizing waves swept up his legs and everything broke apart again.

"Sort through the strands," said Ramona. They were in his old car, sitting in the parking lot of the movie theater they visited so many times. The world beyond the windshield was painted in shades of autumn and nostalgia. "Find the ones that shine the brightest."

"What's happening?"

But another wave of shuddering pain melted the illusion again.

"Look for the gold," said an all too familiar voice.

He was standing at the stove, pancakes steaming in the skillet in front of him, surrounded by the smells of the past. His heart gave a sharp pang as he turned and looked at her. "Mom…"

She was sitting in her usual chair, smiling at him. She looked so young. Her hair was long, like she used to wear it back before she fell ill. She was so beautiful. "Those will always lead you to him."

"Mom, I…" But he didn't know what so say…where to even begin…

And then another wave of pain took her away again.

He sucked in a shaky gasp and opened his eyes to gloom and stone and pain and heartbreaking homesickness. He didn't even have time to say anything to her…

Not that it mattered. They were only dreams. Random. Disjointed. Fitful. None of it was real.

Then Nicole was there, peering back at him, those lovely brown eyes shimmering with tears. "Keith?"

She was real.

Something stirred in his heart as he blinked back at her, something confusing and ambiguous, something he wanted to push away and yet at the same time grab onto and never let go of.

"Hang in there, okay?" Her voice cracked as she spoke. Her lips trembled.

She should just leave him here and go, yet he knew she wouldn't.

"I'm good now," he breathed. "Sorry about that."

"Don't worry about it. Rest is good."

She helped him stand up, which felt oddly ironic after all that had happened between them. He didn't ask her to help him. He could've managed on his own.

Except…maybe he couldn't have. He was weaker than he wanted to admit.

"Careful," she whispered as she reached around him, pressing her body against him. He couldn't help staring down at the swells of those magnificent breasts as they crowded against him, accentuating her sweat-slicked curves.

There was still some life left in him yet, it seemed.

He started walking again. Each step drove nails of pain into his feet, but it was less painful than sitting still. He kept thinking that she should just leave him and yet the thought of lying there in the darkness and watching her walk away for the last time was more agonizing than anything he'd experienced.

Why did everything have to be so damned complicated?

"Good…" urged Nicole. "Just a little farther… You can do it."

She was lying, of course. Nothing about this situation was good. They wouldn't find anything waiting for them "just a little farther" ahead and he definitely couldn't do it. He was running on fumes as it was. This was his last mile. He could feel it. It was going to be over soon. And he hadn't even done anything worth dying for.

"Not true."

He turned around. Erin was standing there in her silvery dress, her sunflower tattoo practically radiating yellow light. The two of them were standing in an empty stone passage. There was no sign of Nicole and the pain in his feet had vanished.

Another dream.

"You again…" he sighed.

"Lovely to see you again, too," she chided, smirking.

"Sorry," he replied out of habit. But he frowned at himself. *Was* he sorry? He didn't choose any of this. He never asked to be here.

"It's fine," she assured him. "I understand."

He stared at her for a moment, pondering all the things circling around inside his head. It wasn't that he wouldn't be happy to see her. She'd been perfectly nice to him. But her being here wasn't exactly a good thing, was it? "What have I done, then?" he asked. "That's worth dying for?"

She smiled that kind smile at him. "Everything."

"Sure," he sighed.

"It's not over," she informed him. "Not even close. No matter what happens next, it's only just the beginning. You should know that."

"What's wrong?" asked Nicole.

He realized he'd stopped walking and was just standing there on his aching feet. Did he fall asleep standing? He glanced around, but it was only the two of them. There was no sign of that silvery dress or those bright yellow sunflowers.

"I'm okay," he said, continuing forward again.

"I've got you," she promised, tightening her grip on him. He found himself staring at her lips, at the way they trembled as she fought back her tears and pretended to be brave. "You can lean on me all you need."

"I know. Thank you."

Step after step, he made his way through the darkness, Nicole at his side, clinging to him, supporting him.

No matter what happens next, it's only just the beginning, he recalled. What did Erin mean by that? The beginning of *what?*

But even if he *could* understand it, he couldn't think clearly enough through the pain to even try. He let it go and pushed onward, ever deeper into the darkness that he was increasingly certain was going to soon become his tomb.

Chapter 59

Albert stepped between the stretched lips of the anxious man and Brandy moved with him, her arms around his waist, her body pressed against his. She hadn't closed her eyes yet. She couldn't. She needed to be able to see this part. It wasn't the largest of doorways. Those giant teeth below and above, easy to trip on or bang her head against. And the opening beyond was smaller still, with all these blatantly unnecessary details they had to feel their way past. It was a fucking *door*. Did it need tonsils and a uvula?

She kept her blurry gaze fixed on the stone surfaces around her and followed his movements as he slipped through the opening and onto the smooth floor of the room beyond, where he stopped.

"What's wrong?" she worried.

"Nothing. Just adjusting to my field of vision."

Right. It wasn't the same as when she took her glasses off. He had perfect vision. Looking through the glasses altered his eyesight, making it harder for him to make out those details, but if he were to look *around* them, he'd be able to see fine. He needed to be careful to not peek past the rims. He accomplished this by cupping his free hand around the left lens and closing his right eye, sort of like a child pretending to use a pirate's spyglass. He was taking a moment to make sure he wasn't able to see any dangerous details.

He was smart like that. Smarter than her, perhaps, since her eyes were still open.

She stood there, waiting patiently for him to move on, her gaze sliding across all the uneasy shades of gray surrounding them. Like him, she was testing it, seeing how much those invasive emotions were going to affect her if something happened and she needed to take over.

It wasn't pleasant. Her heart was racing. Her stomach felt as if it were twisted into several steaming knots. She was queasy, as if she might puke. She didn't want to do this. The cavernous darkness looming ahead of her felt like a dead man's march to the gallows, every step weighted with dread and despair and hopelessness.

The second she cast her light into this space, she could see the blurry shapes of the statues before her. Just like all the rest of the emotion rooms, there was very little space to move around. A labyrinth within a labyrinth, because merely accosting them with these alien emotions wasn't enough. The Keeper and his sentinels needed to make it as difficult as possible to escape it as well.

And then, of course, there was the possibility of more traps. Spike pits. Deadly drop-offs. Stone skewers hidden among the statues themselves, jutting outward, just waiting to impale unwary passersby.

There wasn't any kind of trap waiting in the sex room, she recalled. Albert suspected it was because the room itself was adequate as a trap. If the blind man hadn't slipped in and stolen the flashlight and their clothes, plunging them into safe darkness, they might never have left that place after having seen all those dangerous details. This would be the same thing, she realized. If the two of them were always intended to be here, slaves to the Keeper's monstrous designs, then these wouldn't be new to them. Hence the bottomless pit by where they lost Gina.

So what nasty surprise awaited them *here?*

She stood there a moment, her impaired gaze sliding across all those gray shadows. There were no details while looking at it like this. No faces. No expressions. No nightmarish things to haunt her dreams. But she could see the clear outline of human figures all around her.

She closed her eyes and pressed her face against Albert's back. She couldn't open them again. She'd probably already seen too much. It was stupid. But she couldn't seem to help herself. She was curious.

Anxiety…

What *did* anxiety look like in statue form, she wondered. She knew *very* well what lust looked like. Lust was people. It was pornographic. It was dirty and vulgar and obscene, but it was *human*. It was individuals acting out their most sensuous desires. It was *natural*. It was nothing at all like fear. Fear was monstrous. *That* room was filled with creatures and nightmares and unsettling things. Some of the fear was human. Human cruelty. Human madness. Human depravity. Human *suffering*. The fear room was an entirely different sort of experience from the sex room. It didn't simply fill them with fear the way the first one filled them with insatiable desire. It *showed* them things to fear. It filled their heads with memories that weren't their own, memories of being hunted and haunted and stalked, memories of being hurt, of being *tortured*… Of being *killed*. One such memory even became *reality* for poor Albert. He *experienced* it. He described a sensation of being ripped open, almost torn in half, by some powerful predator. He actually thought he was *dying*. And she, for one, had been *terrified*. She was convinced for a moment that she'd lost him in there.

She didn't see more than a few blurry shapes of the hate room, didn't feel any invasive emotions, didn't experience any alien memories. The glasses trick worked in that one. She recalled feeling a sensation or two of irritability and grumpiness, a fleeting desire to shout at someone, a few moments of tenseness and quickening heartbeat. But overall she *conquered* that room. She wasn't sure if it was because she didn't have any real hate within her to overwhelm her or because the lingering emotions of the sex room and her fear of losing control again over-wrote that emotion, but she beat it. She made it through that room.

But the sadness within that last room had invaded her even though she kept her light off and never once peeked. It filled her chest with aching sobs and sent tears streaking down her face even blind. If she'd turned on her light in there and actually looked upon whatever statues were there, she had no doubt she would've been as overcome by sorrow as she was by lust in the sex room.

The emotions within these rooms were not to be taken lightly. Not under any circumstances. She couldn't allow herself to see any more details of whatever was waiting for them in here.

And yet, in spite of it all, she found herself morbidly curious. Was it like the sex room? Was she simply surrounded by people caught in the agonizing clutches of severe anxiety and panic? Or was it like the fear room, where she'd found herself surrounded by things that *induced* the terror she experienced?

And why the fuck would they choose *anxiety* of all things, anyway? They already had a fear room. Wasn't that anxiety-inducing enough?

How long had they been standing here? Why wasn't he moving yet? What were they waiting for?

Albert reached down and gave her hand a comforting squeeze. "Focus your attention at *me*," he reminded her. "Not the statues."

"I know that!" she snapped. How many times did he think she needed him to tell her?

His touch was warm and familiar. It should have comforted her. But instead it felt as if someone had clamped shackles around her. She felt trapped. *Imprisoned*. She wanted to tell him to get away from her, to not touch her. He was suffocating her. *Strangling* her. She needed space! But she knew that would be a terrible idea. She couldn't let go. Not for a second. If she didn't hold onto him, they might get separated. She could end up alone again. And she couldn't bear the thought of it.

Her eyes still tightly closed, she licked her lips, but her whole mouth had gone dry. Only her eyes seemed to be wet. She could feel her tears leaking out as she fought the urge to turn and run the other way.

It's the room, she told herself. The awful emotions within were leaking out, affecting her already. She knew this to be a fact, and yet knowing it didn't seem to help.

"Tell me if you need to stop," said Albert, his voice soft, soothing, caring. She loved the sound of his voice, and yet she wanted so badly to shout at him to just shut up.

But that wasn't her. She'd never be so hateful toward him. It was the room. It was the statues. She *hated* that she felt this way. What if something terrible happened and these were the last feelings she ever had for him?

Fucking emotion rooms! Fucking *Keeper!* This was all *his* fault, after all. That was what everyone kept telling them. That foul, ugly little monster with the sagging skin and the head that turned the wrong way...

"You ready?"

"Just go already," she snapped at him. She didn't mean to, exactly. It wasn't his fault they were in this mess. But she couldn't help it. She *wasn't* ready. She'd barely set foot in this room and she already felt *awful*. It was getting more and more difficult to catch her breath. It was *suffocating*. And he knew damned good and well that it didn't matter whether she was ready or not.

He said nothing more. He let go of her hand and took hold of the flashlight. She wouldn't need it in here. Her eyes were going to stay closed the whole time. Finally, he started forward, into the labyrinth of shadowy statues, slowly, cautiously.

Clinging tightly to him, she followed his every move, wondering what nasty surprises might be waiting for them here.

Chapter 60

Gina stood there, her body trembling with terror, staring at the furious darkness writhing on the other side of the glass.

She'd done it. She'd escaped back into the relative safety of the other labyrinth and left the murderous thing trapped in there.

A wave of such intense relief washed over her that she had to step back and lean against the stone to keep her legs from giving out beneath her.

That was far too close for comfort.

She wiped at her eyes and tried to calm her frantic breathing. But she wasn't going to be able to relax much. The monster was still right there, throwing itself against the glass, infuriated, its gargling snarls and vulgar threats still assaulting her ears, still promising to do terrible things to her. And it wasn't going to simply go away. She wasn't even going to be able to walk away from it. Just like before she entered the glass labyrinth, it would stalk her on that other side, following her no matter where she went, watching her every move, tormenting her with its foul threats.

But at least it still seemed to be trapped on the glass side of the wall. It was fairly obvious by its frustration that if it could slip through the cracks as she had, then it already would have done so.

For the moment, at least, she was safe. She was *uncomfortable*. Something about passing through the cracks had again left her feeling disheveled. But she was safe.

She reached up under her shirt and adjusted her bra as she tried to clear her head. She needed to calm her nerves and focus. She still probably needed to get inside that labyrinth. And then that thing would be waiting for her. Even if she could count on landing somewhere it wasn't, somehow she knew it wouldn't take nearly as long to find her a second time.

But as her roommate, Piper, was fond of saying, that was a problem for *future her*.

That was the attitude she needed right now. The future might yet be grim, but right now she was alive and still doing the job the goddess gave her. She needed to be in the present, figuring out where in the stone labyrinth she was.

She closed her useless eyes and focused on breathing. She needed to push the monster's foul voice out of her head and calm herself. She was safe here. Relatively speaking, she supposed. Safe from *that* abomination, anyway. And that was all she cared about in this moment.

She just needed to calm her poor, racing heart.

This was the physical realm. Everything here was absolute, unlike inside those ever-shifting glass walls. She couldn't simply slip through a crack here. Nor would she be able to turn the whole thing on its side whenever she found herself at a dead end or too close to something frightful. But it also meant she couldn't fall through the gaps or lose herself to the madness of the unnatural. She was going to have to navigate these passages just like anyone else.

And *unlike* everyone else, she could cheat.

She cast her psychic gaze out into the surrounding darkness, scanning the space around her, studying the layout, making note of all the dead ends and loops.

Her eyes flashed open in the darkness. Someone was there!

Two people, just a few corridors over. *Familiar* presences. Someone she knew! Was that Brandy and Albert? Had she found her way back to them? Was she going to get the chance to tell them how sorry she was for worrying them?

But a strange and icy sensation washed over her at that moment, freezing the thoughts inside her very skull.

Something *else* was here.

But where? She turned and looked one way, then the other, but her psychic eye was as useless as her human ones. She couldn't tell which direction the awful sensation was coming from. But it was the most disturbing thing she'd ever felt. It was like spiders and worms wriggling around on her skin. The hair on her body was standing up, an electric terror was gripping her.

What was this feeling?

On the other side of the glass, the thing with too many mouths had suddenly fallen quiet. She turned and watched it recede into the gloom.

A bad omen if ever she'd seen one. And she was plenty familiar with bad omens.

She felt as if she might throw up.

(*There's another...*)

She shivered as the goddess' words rushed back to her. The ominous warning she gave them back in her brilliantly white lost-and-found realm.

(*Something far stronger than a mere spirit, something I can't see.*)

She turned around, her brown eyes wide and useless in the oppressive darkness. Her psychic eye showing her nothing as well. But there was something there, standing in the dark passageway, staring back at her.

She took a step backward. That strangling terror was closing around her again. Her body trembled. Fresh tears spilled down her cheeks. This was no mere monster. This was something completely beyond anything she'd ever felt before, something so inconceivably powerful that she was utterly insignificant in comparison. She might as well be a bug beneath its raised foot.

(*Its presence was the reason Goar Nangup's slave was able to follow you.*)

She remembered the way Hochog kept turning up wherever they were, no matter if they were in Briar Hills or Cedric's Cove or Tristesse Lane, as if he had some means of tracking them, even across dimensions.

(*It seems to attract unwanted things. And it delights in your misfortune.*)

Was this thing the reason Glum was able to sneak up on her in the Denselands? The reason she and Nicole were separated from Andrea and Keith? The reason Nicole vanished into the storm?

The monster prowling the glass labyrinth. The one that reeked of the unnatural presence of the Twelve Teeth. Was this thing the reason *it* was here, too?

It took a step toward her. She couldn't see its form. It didn't seem to have one, strangely. Trying to wrap her head around its shape was like trying to look directly at the sun. It was weirdly painful. And it seemed to wash out everything all around it, blinding her inner eye.

She took another step backward. She didn't need to be psychic to know that she was in terrible danger right now. Whatever this thing was, it was tremendously powerful. And it was amused by her fear.

"Fun…" whispered an eerie voice across the darkness. It wasn't a human voice. To her physical ears it was little more than a passing sigh, a barely heard sound, like bones chattering softly in the breeze or the patter of rain on the lid of a coffin…though she had no idea why *those* would be the descriptions that came to mind. Only inside her head did she hear the word it spoke, and even then it echoed in a dozen different voices in a hundred different languages, every one of which sent a tremble of icy terror through her veins.

It was still moving toward her, not taking steps at all, as she first perceived, but rather *floating* through the darkness like a wraith, sliding, slinking, almost *slithering*.

She tried to take another step backward but found that her feet were frozen. She couldn't seem to make them move.

"*So* much fun…" purred the inhuman voice. An overwhelming presence enveloped her like an ominous darkness, strangely cold and warm at the same time, and she could *see* the lips forming those words inside her mind, a woman's lips, full and fair. For some reason, the sight of them sent an ambiguous sort of vertigo washing over her, a feeling that was dread and despair and surrender, but was somehow also oddly pleasant, almost euphoric.

The Great Beholder claimed she was no goddess, that she was born just the same as anyone else, an ordinary human being. She was neither celestial nor divine. Like Gina, she merely happened to possess extraordinary abilities. Nothing more. But she didn't believe her. She didn't doubt her godliness once. Not until this very moment. Because standing before her now was a *true* goddess. And it was terrifying beyond words.

She stood rigid, petrified, staring wide-eyed into the unyielding darkness, helpless and alone, face-to-face with a power she could scarcely comprehend, much less stand against.

She was going to die here. There was no other logical outcome. She was too weak in comparison. Too small. Too *insignificant.*

Those haunting lips drifted closer and closer. They hovered right in front of her, grinning wickedly in the darkness.

Then, bizarrely, those lips kissed her.

She could feel them. They might as well have belonged to a living person. They were soft and they were warm. And they stirred something inside her that she wasn't sure she'd ever felt before. An odd sort of desperate longing. A lifetime's worth of raw emotions bubbling up somewhere deep inside. She could feel herself softening, almost inviting these lips to take her…and yet she knew that this tenderness was nothing more than a game. This was a predator merely playing with its prey before finishing it off.

"Fun…" The word circled around inside her head, echoing over and over again, eerie, *maddening.* Fun for her, perhaps. Fun for this primordial presence. But what was fun for the cat was rarely fun for the mouse. This game wouldn't end well for a fragile little thing like her.

Those lips withdrew back into the darkness, leaving only that haunting word still circling in her brain. But she could still feel her there, right in front of her, staring back at her, studying her, *delighting* in her fear.

"But let's have even *more* fun," whispered a woman's voice that was mockingly human.

Then it was gone. She was alone in the stone passage.

She stood there, blinking into the darkness, confused. Her head was spinning, her stomach twisted into burning knots, her body still trembling. But she felt no relief that the mysterious entity was gone. Instead, she found herself overcome with a mounting dread.

Something awful was about to happen.

Then she heard it. A crackle. A snap. A twang like the sound of ice cracking beneath one's feet.

Then the glass wall between her and the thing with too many mouths shattered.

It was such a strange sensation, hearing that sound in this otherwise overwhelming silence. Shards of glass pelted her, even, stinging her exposed skin. She turned away, raising her arms to shield her face even as she struggled to comprehend just where these shards could have come from. Because there *was no glass*. The glass was a manifestation of her own mind, a metaphor for her ability to see through the walls of those tangled-up corridors.

But somehow that dark and terrifying presence had turned the glass literal, allowing it to be shattered, eliminating the only thing that was protecting her from the monster on the other side!

Her heart thundering in her breast, she turned her psychic eye toward the breach, terrified of the thing that was sure to come rushing out at her.

But it was already there. That awful stench filled her nose again, overwhelming, inescapable. It wasn't merely standing over her. It was *all around her*, enveloping her, leaving no room for her to run, those many mouths all open and snarling and ready to start tearing chunks from her flesh.

"Have fun…" sighed the haunting voice of the goddess in the endless darkness.

This was it. This was the end for her. Gina had time to regret all the things she'd missed out on in her unfair life. She had time to regret not being able to say goodbye to all the people who'd shown her kindness these past few years. She had time to shed a tear.

Just one.

Then time was up.

The monster was gone.

She stood there, alone in the darkness, confused. What just happened? Why wasn't she dying?

"Fun…" sighed the mysterious goddess one last time before vanishing back into the gloom from which she came.

With her psychic eye, she could see that the thing with too many mouths was slithering away from her, snaking its way through the stone passageways.

But why? Where was it going?

Then she understood.

The two presences she felt nearby when she crossed back into the stone labyrinth. Brandy and Albert? Or perhaps Andrea and Keith?

It was heading straight for them!

Chapter 61

Olivia was clinging to Wayne and Andrea for dear life, struggling just to keep up. They fled the open chamber in favor of the narrow passages of the surrounding labyrinth in hopes that the scarecrow man's swarm of razor bugs wouldn't be able to surround them so easily. But was this any better? Now they were running blind, with no idea which direction to go. She tried to feel her way, but she was struggling just to contain the panic that was overwhelming her, drowning out every other thought that passed through her head.

A sound shot past her, like a tiny machine roaring at full speed, and Wayne cursed at a fresh cut drawn across his exposed ear.

Before she could react, Andrea let out a startled scream and slapped at her cheek. "*What are those things?*" she cried.

Olivia didn't have time to respond. A shrieking glint of a reddish-brown blade flashed past, wrenching a yelp of pain from her.

It was happening again, just like on that narrow platform. They'd overwhelm them with their numbers, carving them up one tiny nick at a time. Death by a thousand cuts. They might as well be crawling through broken glass!

Wayne was already reacting to the dire situation, she realized. Ever her hero, he was moving behind her and Andrea, using his size to shield them both as much as possible.

"Careful!" she cried. It was so sweet when he did stuff like that, but it was starting to feel like he was going to scare her to death one of these days putting himself in harm's way like that!

"Just run!" he shouted, grunting as another hound bug dug its razor wings into his shoulder.

Still clinging to Andrea's hand, she raced toward the open doorway and into the black passage waiting there. It was a terrible feeling, rushing back into these claustrophobic corridors. It may have been the only choice—they'd already found out that there was simply no way for them to take on a swarm of hound bugs in an open space like that—but there was still so much that could go dreadfully wrong in here. It would be so easy to get cornered somewhere.

Wayne blurted out another painful curse and slapped at the back of his neck. "I *hate* these things!"

"What *are* they?" squealed Andrea.

"It's a little hard to explain!" he shouted. "Just keep running!"

"I didn't say I was gonna stop!"

"Protect your faces!" shouted Olivia.

Again, Wayne cried out, this time clutching at his elbow.

Andrea yelped at something screaming past her ear.

What were they going to do? There was nowhere in this labyrinth to hide. And there was no way to fight what was already dead!

Ahead of them, the end of the passage came into view in the darting beams of their flashlights. For one terrible second she thought it was a dead end, but then she saw that it was an adjoining passage. They had to make a choice.

"Left or right?" shouted Wayne.

"I don't know!" she shouted back. She couldn't even think straight right now, much less focus on whatever feelings her ridiculous psychic warning system was giving her. Even if one way was screaming a sense of imminent doom, she wouldn't be able to feel it over the crippling panic she was struggling with already!

She was going to have to choose at random. And if the path she chose happened to be a dead end…or an open circle where the bugs could attack from both directions…

"This way!" shouted Andrea.

Before she could process what was happening, she found herself being pulled toward neither passageway, but instead straight at the wall ahead of them. Her heart gave a startled leap as she realized that she was about to run headlong into it, and yet somehow she didn't stop. She didn't even slow down. She let Andrea pull her forward, straight into the stone, which seemed to disintegrate before her eyes to reveal a third passageway.

Another murk passage.

When Wayne asked her to choose "left or right," Andrea must've been clear-headed enough to realize that he could only see two passageways *and* know which one of the three were hidden.

But she didn't have time to appreciate the luck. Disoriented from the passage's appearance, she stumbled and dropped to her knees.

Andrea, still clinging to her arm, stumbled as well, but managed to stay on her feet. She stopped to help her up, panic painted across her dirty face.

Wayne turned and shined his light backward, his arms outstretched to shield the two of them from the incoming razor-winged monstrosities, but the hound bugs pouring out of the previous passageway were splitting up and zooming out of sight in either direction.

"I don't think they can see us…" he gasped, breathless.

Was the murk invisible even to the scarecrow man's wicked swarm?

She looked down at her arm, at the fresh cuts drawn across her tan skin, at the beads of blood seeping down the back of her hand. She could feel her sweat making the fresh wounds sting. Slowly, tears began welling up in her eyes. She was so tired of all this, so frightened, so frustrated. Why was all of this happening to her? What was the point in it all?

She blinked back the tears and sniffled. Losing her composure wouldn't help. She turned her attention to Andrea instead. It was harder to see through all that mud where those monstrous bugs got her, but there was a clear trickle of blood seeping down the bridge of her nose. "Are you okay?"

"I think so…" She was standing there, motionless, staring wide-eyed down the passageway, her arms crossed in front of her. The poor thing looked like she'd had the scare of her life.

"We're okay…" sighed Wayne, as if he still couldn't believe it. And she could hardly blame him. She thought they were done for back there. There wasn't even a ledge to jump off of that time.

She lifted up her tee shirt and then reached out with the tail of it to dab at the blood on Andrea's nose. The motion made her jump and cry out.

"It's okay!" she assured her, grabbing her hand and squeezing.

"Sorry," she squeaked.

"What's wrong?" worried Wayne.

Olivia leaned closer, concerned. Had something happened? She looked strange. She wasn't looking back at her but rather staring blankly into the distance, those pretty blue eyes wide and afraid. "Did something happen? Are you hurt anywhere?"

"No…" Her eyes flickered left and right, but never seemed to find her.

She lifted the light and realized that she didn't squint at the glare. In fact, her pupils didn't contract. She was showing no natural response to the light whatsoever.

She glanced back at Wayne, concerned, her mind racing. What was wrong with her? Did she bump her head? Did one of those bladed bugs have some kind of toxin on it? Did something about that scary sounding murk give her a stroke? Her heart was pounding with each dreadful thought that passed through her terrified mind.

"I'm fine," Andrea assured her. She sounded clear-headed enough. "It's just…"

"Just what?" she pressed.

"The murk," she replied. "This passage is filled with it. Like, *completely.*"

Olivia stared at her, understanding slowly dawning on her. "Wait. You mean…?"

She nodded, her face a mask of unease. "I'm blind in here."

Chapter 62

Violet shined her light back the way she came. She'd lost count of how many times she'd done that now. She couldn't even hear those monsters anymore, yet every time she looked forward, the thought of one of them silently stalking her through these black corridors began creeping back until she couldn't bear not to look again.

Hounds and not-Everetts? Night trees and storm drafts? Gouging stations and sentinels? She felt like Dante descending through the nine levels of hell, witnessing one atrocity after the next. She needed to get a grip. Being alone in this place was seriously messing with her head. She was finding it harder and harder to control her ragged breathing. She couldn't remember the last time she was this afraid and she hated it.

The path ahead of her split. One continued on slightly to the left while the other twisted nearly ninety degrees to the right. She took a single step into the left one and stood there for a moment, listening to the eerie silence. Then she did the same in the right one. Nothing. No hound noises. No distant rumble of thunder. None of those strange and ominous sighing sounds that drifted hauntingly through the stone back before Everett was snatched away from her. And that was good. Those were all things she didn't want to hear. And yet the absence of any sounds for her to steer clear of left her with no answer as to which way she should go next.

How was she lost? What happened to the other one? Wasn't she supposed to be showing her the way? Why did she stop talking to her? The weariness she heard in her voice after taking over on those rain-soaked steps... The way she simply stopped responding after that... Had she overexerted herself? She *was* sort of insanely old...

She trudged onward, choosing the path on the right simply because it was the one in front of her at the moment. Hopefully it didn't carry her right back to those monstrous hounds.

She never would have guessed how many incredible things she was going to find when she and Corey first set off in search of other worlds. It took three years and dozens of disappointing locations before they found the tokkatoks under that abandoned Minnesota estate. And even then, they failed to bring home any defining evidence. It wasn't until that business with Obadiah Hinx that they managed to capture their first blurry pictures. And even then things didn't exactly go the way they expected.

She stopped, distracted from her thoughts, and cocked her head to one side, listening. Was that another hound she heard? It was too faint to make out, but her heart was racing again. What if she found herself trapped by those monsters?

She crept forward, holding her breath. After a moment, it was apparent that it was getting louder. She was moving toward it, whatever it was. And yet...it sounded different from the noise the hounds made. It was a little less chaotic, she thought. More *natural*.

Water?

As she drew closer, she became more certain of it. That was the sound of running water. The storm outside, perhaps. Except...she wasn't hearing any thunder.

Again, she looked back, still anticipating a sneak attack from one of those razor-fleshed abominations, but again there was nothing more than darkness nipping at her heels.

She realized she was tugging at her shirt again, that old nervous habit, and forced herself to stop. She focused her attention forward, instead. Another split was coming up. An adjoining passage on the left. Even before she reached it, she could hear that the water sound was coming from straight ahead, presenting her a choice. Go toward the sound? Or away from it? Something different would be preferable to the same endless passageways. But that was what she thought about the narrow ledge and she ended up biting off way more than she could chew with that decision.

On the other hand, at least it didn't sound like hounds. Plus, didn't Albert say something about those things not being able to *swim*, either?

She continued on toward the sound. It was better to investigate something different than to keep wandering blindly, she decided. If she let herself be too afraid to explore, she'd probably never find her way out of here.

She could smell it now. There was a detectable dampness in the air here, a dank sort of smell, but not earthy like a lake or river or even like a well, really. She could recognize it as the subtle scent of water, but there was something off about it, something unfamiliar.

Was that simply the smell of an entirely different world from the one she was used to? Or was it the scent of something else in the area, something alien and potentially dangerous?

The sound of rushing water grew louder and louder until, finally, her light revealed the end of the passage and pierced the dark chamber beyond.

A pool lay before her, its surface rippling in the reflected shine of her flashlight. Water was pouring in from grooves in the wall across from her, presumably from the rain outside. A sort of gutter system designed to channel fresh water through the city? A water source to keep all the monsters alive?

Not that it mattered, really. What did she care? But it sort of made sense to think of things like this as a life-support system.

She walked up to the edge of the pool. There was no railing or ledge. The floor simply dropped straight down and the water continued on in its place, its surface level with the stone.

It looked deep. *Unsettlingly* deep. If there were things like those hounds wandering around in some of these passages, what manner of horror might be swimming around in pools like this one?

She took a step back, just to be sure she wasn't tempting fate even a little bit. Then she turned and shined her light to the right. The room went on in that direction, the floor stretching away into darkness, hiding the true length of the space. But those twinkling ripples on the water's surface revealed that it was a significantly larger room than she'd seen in some time.

Her gaze still lingering warily on the pool, she made her way along the wall, curious to see how far it went, but hadn't yet taken a dozen steps when something splashed into the water ahead of her, sending ripples of reflected light across the surface and surprising a startled yelp out of her.

Something was in here with her!

She crowded closer to the wall, out of reach of anything that might be thinking about jumping out at her. She could almost imagine some monstrous alligator lurking down there, possibly even covered in those same, slashing scales. An aquatic counterpart to the abominations back in that last area with the worn floor.

Whatever was here, she wanted nothing to do with it. She picked up her pace, following the wall, staying well away from the water's edge.

The floor was wet from the unseen splashing thing. Not just in one spot, but all over. More than a single splash should have caused. Was there more than one thing in here with her? She still couldn't see anything, but that was the problem with water predators, wasn't it? They were naturally hard to see.

She shined her light up at the ceiling, half-expecting to find something clinging there, just waiting for her to walk under it.

Her imagination was running wild, an understandable biproduct of being alone and afraid and apparently surrounded by monsters.

Hopefully there was a way out on this side of the room. She didn't care for the idea of going back toward those hounds, even as far as the previous intersection. But if it came down to going that way or crossing a bridge over this water, she might just reconsider.

But there was no bridge. The far wall came into view, along with another doorway leading back into the depths of the labyrinth.

But as she moved toward it, she stopped.

Something was there. Two long, black strands were lying coiled on the floor there like discarded trash. They looked sort of like large, limp pipe cleaners, covered in stiff, bristly hairs. There was water on the floor all around them, a puddle stretching all the way back to the pool.

Was it something dead? A victim of whatever was lurking in that water? Or was this part of the monster itself, watching her from the shadows. She didn't recall Albert talking about anything being in the water their first time. Either this wasn't something they encountered or they failed to mention it. Was she in danger? Should she be getting the hell out of here?

While she stood there, uncertain what to do, one of the strands twisted and withdrew deeper into the shadows.

"Screw this shit," she breathed, already taking a step backward.

She was *not* prepared to deal with any more monsters. Not physically and not emotionally. She was going back the way she came.

But something stirred in the darkness just beyond the water's edge and she swung her light toward it, catching only a swirl of water and a glimpse of a dark shadow.

When she pointed her light at the thing in the doorway again, a great jet of something foul and reeking struck her, splashing onto her shoulder, neck and face.

She screamed and stumbled backward, startled, and slipped on the wet stone, landing hard on her butt with a painful yelp.

Before she could regain her composure, another stream of foul fluid shot from the darkness and struck her forehead, burning her eyes.

What was this stuff? Was it dangerous? Was it poison? Toxic? It *reeked.* Her stomach rolled over and she gagged, even as she struggled to get back to her feet.

She couldn't see!

She turned and crawled to the water's edge, barely aware that she was half-screaming. She plunged her hands beneath the surface and began splashing her face, desperate to wash the foul substance away.

But it didn't rinse off easily. It was thick and oily. *Sticky.* And the smell was beyond atrocious.

What *was* that thing? That was no hound. Was she going to be okay? Was it going to blind her? Paralyze her? *Burn the flesh from her face?*

She scrubbed at her forehead, gagging at the putrid smell that was assaulting her sinuses, then sat up and blinked.

She could still see. The stinging in her eyes had eased a little. And her skin wasn't burning.

Would she really be all right?

But as she stared across the pool, she became aware of something new. A strange, reddish glow deep down in the water.

She grasped her flashlight, ready to spring to her feet and flee, but the source of the red light was so far down, nowhere near the surface.

How deep was this pool? She leaned a little closer, distracted.

Something didn't feel right. She'd just received a terrible scare. Shouldn't she be fully on edge right now? Shouldn't she be too jumpy to be distracted? If nothing else, she should be getting the hell out of this room and away from the hairy thing that sprayed that putrid gunk in her face.

And yet, somehow it felt as if there were a great, gaping chasm at the center of her mind, a quiet and strangely peaceful emptiness.

Vaguely, she realized that the source of the light wasn't nearly as deep as it was before. It seemed to be just beneath the surface, mere inches from her face as she leaned closer and closer, bathing her in an eerie, bloody glow…

With a great splash, something lunged out of the water and pulled her in.

Chapter 63

Ninety-six doors lined the paper hallway. Forty-eight on each side. Everett counted them as he made his way to the far end, each one identical to the one that came before it, each one drawn on the stark white surface, dimensionless, unopenable, pointless. There wasn't even anything at the end of the hallway. Only a blank wall awaited him there.

He stood staring at this wall for a moment, then turned and looked back the other way. He couldn't see all the way to the end from here. All the white simply scrunched together into a single point from his perspective. If he walked all the way back there, would that first door still be open? Or would it have disappeared, trapping him here?

Not that it really mattered one way or the other, he supposed. He hadn't gone anywhere. He didn't really move from that first room to the foyer and then into this hallway. He was beginning to understand that he was only changing his perspective, altering the way he looked at it.

This was the Keeper's Dollhouse. It was the same as the upside-down and inverted flipside of the City Beyond Memory and its endless stone labyrinth. Two sides of the same coin. And in this version of that reality, there were no such concepts as big and small.

There was only perspective.

And the human brain was a stubborn sort of machine, clinging to the rules of the physical world it was used to. Even when he figured out what he needed to do, even when he managed to escape one room, he only found himself trapped in the next. Because his mind simply didn't know any better. It couldn't comprehend leaving a space and not going anywhere, therefore, each time he left one room, it convinced him that he must be entering another one.

That was the meat of this problem. He understood that now, partially because Alice had been trying to explain it to him this entire time, but also, he thought, because he was uniquely capable of comprehending the psychological effects of being imprisoned in one's own life. His mother's illness. His childhood, so devoid of substance and experiences and love, so full of meaningless and crippling fear.

Maeve told them that the Keeper orchestrated everything that led up to them all being here right now. It had already crossed his mind that his mother's mental illness might have been not merely foreseen by him, but possibly even *caused* by it, just another cosmic tool to drive all his pawns onto the gameboard. But now he found himself facing the idea that perhaps he used her for more than one purpose. Was *she* nothing more than an unfortunate instrument in the Keeper's ancient and bizarre design? Was she not merely used, but literally *victimized* by the Keeper?

This realization had distracted him. He stood at the end of this stark white hallway, his thoughts swirling, wondering now just how deep the Keeper's fingers reached into his world. Did he *make* her that way? Did he twist her mind somehow in order to make her sick? If not for his influence, might he have grown up in a proper, loving household, normal and healthy?

For a moment, he wondered what life might have been like growing up normal. From his perspective, looking back at it from here, far beyond the endless stretches of the black Wood, it sounded...well, *boring*. But then, with a head full of normal memories and thoughts, would he have ever been interested in an adventure like this? Would he have *wanted* such a thing?

What's your name?

He looked down at Alice, still cradled in the nook of his elbow. What's your name? That was the question that grounded him in the void, that made him remember who he was when he was lost and adrift in that endless nothingness. It was the only question that really mattered.

"You're right," he told her. "Doesn't really matter how I got here. It is what it is. I am who I am. And one way or another, I wouldn't be here if I wasn't me."

Alice was a smart girl. Especially for a doll.

What mattered right now wasn't the whys or the what ifs. Only one question mattered. What did he have to do to pull himself free of this dollhouse and return to the labyrinth?

Again, he cast his gaze down that long, white hallway.

Those childish drawings of pointless doors, as if he were somehow trapped inside a sketchbook instead of a physical building...

"Paper..." he muttered.

This was a paper world, not so different, really, from the books he read growing up, his only escape from the hateful world his mother had crafted around him. Bursting with imagination, but ultimately only scribbles on paper.

He smiled at all those drawings. Then he turned and faced the empty wall behind him.

On paper, one could write a spellbinding story or craft the most beautiful piece of art or even compose the most haunting melodies.

But it was still only paper.

He reached up with his free hand and dug his fingers into the blank wall. And with the most satisfying ripping sound, he tore it open like Christmas wrapping paper, a long, wide ribbon peeling away, revealing the shiny metal doors behind it.

"I'm in control here," he told Alice, proud of himself, as he tore away another piece and then another. "I can do what I want."

Then he stepped back and smiled at the elevator that now stood before him.

"That's more like it," he decided as he reached out and pressed the button.

The doors slid open. The car was right there, waiting for him.

Inside, everything was new and shiny. There wasn't a single scrap of paper to be seen. A good sign, he was sure.

The panel showed no buttons, only an up arrow and a down arrow, which seemed a little odd at first, but he supposed that numbers were rather arbitrary given that this was a construct of his imagination and not an actual, physical lift.

Only the "up" button was illuminated, suggesting that he was already down as far as he could go. That made it easy. He pressed the "up" button and watched as the doors slid closed between him and that meaningless paper hallway.

He glanced down at Alice, confused. "I'm not being cocky," he told her. "I'm just proud of myself for figuring it out."

Then he frowned as her reply blossomed inside his head in a myriad of disjointed ideas and images.

"I'm sure it won't be that easy, too," he assured her. Some of what she was saying to him was getting clearer. He was learning some of the basics of this strange language. "But it's a start, right?"

Some of the garbled messages repeated themselves in his head, but he wasn't sure how to translate that part of whatever she was saying.

The elevator gave a gentle lurch as it began climbing the shaft.

"Whatever you're worried about," he decided, "we'll figure it out one thing at a time. I'm sure of it."

Chapter 64

Nicole couldn't hold back the tears any longer. They flowed freely down her face. Her nose was running. Her chest kept hitching. She was an absolute mess.

She needed help.

Something was very definitely wrong. Keith's feet were bleeding worse now. The cloth was soaked through. Those bloody smears were turning into bloody footprints.

Wayne had said that germs couldn't live in the Wood, that even the filthy mouths of those shambling corpses couldn't cause an infection, much less turn them into walking dead like in the movies. But something was obviously happening to poor Keith. He was getting worse by the minute.

And still there was no help in sight!

How many times had they walked in circles now?

"Just hang in there," she wept. But he'd stopped responding to her some time ago. It seemed as if it were taking all his energy just to remain upright. Or maybe he was just tuning her out. He still had every right to hate her, after all.

Why did this happen? Everyone kept saying this was all the Keeper's plan, but why would *this* be a part of any kind of plan? What purpose could this possibly have?

Was it her fault? Had she done something wrong? Had she done *everything* wrong? Was she never supposed to escape the barely-there and tag along on this nightmare journey? Was she supposed to die in that awful perversion of her apartment? Should she have just let the awful thing that pretended to be Albert devour her? Or had she been messing things up even longer than that? Maybe she was never supposed to make it back from the temple that night. Maybe she'd been an error in the equation from the day she was born.

Keith stumbled. She was too weary to fully catch him. All she could do was sink to the floor with him and try to keep him from hitting his head again.

She lay half across him, panting, her tears still streaming, trying to gather her strength.

"I'm so sorry," she whimpered. "For everything. It was all my fault."

The truth was that she simply never understood why she felt such an overwhelming need to push him away. Yes, he was overprotective, but not in the bad ways that some men could be. Not in an overbearing or controlling way. Not like some men she'd dated, even. She knew he was only trying to be sweet. And she knew that he was simply in the habit of taking care of someone because of the situation with his sick mother. She remembered blowing up at him because he opened a beer for her, but she knew, even then, that it was only out of habit. Why was she so determined to sabotage their relationship?

If she hadn't pushed him away, if she'd stayed by his side, if she'd told him the truth, would things be different right now? Or would it only hurt that much more?

The truth... Like that was ever really an option. Would he have believed the whole truth? Would he have believed *any* of it? He probably would've thought she was crazy. Or that she and her friends were making fun of him.

She lifted her head and looked down at him. "Please hang in there," she begged him. She grasped the sides of his face and kissed him. "Just push through this a little longer. We'll get help. We'll make you all better." She kissed him again. "I promise I'll make it all up to you. Everything I did, every last awful thing I said..." She took a shuddering breath. She couldn't stop crying. She felt so helpless, so alone. "I swear I will."

It wasn't fair. Her knight in shining armor finally showed up. He even carried her out of danger in his arms like a princess... And she'd already fouled everything up.

(*You never needed me and I had no business trying to be anything to you.*)

She cringed at the memory of those words. She couldn't let him leave her like this, thinking that was true. Because it wasn't. He had it completely backward. She *did* need him. And she was the one who didn't deserve what they had.

"I'm so sorry... Please don't give up on me..."

Again, she kissed him.

He groaned, surprising her.

"Keith!"

"You're such a pain, Nik..."

She stared at him. That was what he used to call her back in those happy days, before her hateful brain turned everything sour. She'd forgotten all about it. The sound of it hit her like a baseball bat. A soft laugh escaped her. She reached up and wiped at her eye. "Yeah. I guess

I am."

"Funny," he grunted. "Mom always liked you."

This surprised her. "What?"

"I kept telling her you were gone. You weren't coming back. But she just kept saying you'd come around. You were just going through some stuff."

She wasn't sure what to say. She thought for sure his mom thought she was just some heartless bitch. She just started a bunch of fights and then left.

"Never believed her," he sighed.

"Mom was a smart lady." She kissed him again.

"Still mad, though," he said, his voice muffled against her lips.

"That's fair," she mumbled without stopping. She missed these kisses. Why did she ever let them end? What was wrong with her?

He groaned and she pulled away. Right. He was in a lot of pain right now. She turned and shined the light at his feet. It was hard to tell through the dirt and the blood, but what she could see around her makeshift bandage was beginning to look concerningly discolored. There was a lot of bruising. Much more than there was before.

She still couldn't understand how he ended up like this and she didn't. They both walked out to that pond. But then again, she didn't *remember* walking out there. Did something carry her? Did she just teleport there, like Hotdog was able to do back in Cedric's Cove?

Not that any of that mattered, she supposed. Regardless of all the hows and whys, this was where they were now. This was the reality she was stuck with. And she didn't know how to fix it.

"Hang in there," she said again. "We'll find some help soon."

He didn't believe her, she could tell. She didn't believe her either. Was she doomed to just drag him all over this labyrinth until he bled to death? She needed to do something quickly.

But as she sat up, she realized that something had changed. The air had grown strangely heavy. There was an unpleasant stench. She felt as if something were watching her.

She turned and shined her flashlight into the passage ahead of them.

There was something there. Something darker than the darkness, looming at the end of her light.

Something *dreadful*.

"No…" she breathed, fresh tears spilling down her cheeks. She couldn't deal with anything else right now.

Why wouldn't someone help her?

She leaned over Keith, determined to protect him, knowing she was powerless to do anything more than die at his side. She had no fight left in her. She was too tired...too useless...

An unspeakable horror crawled from the darkness, as unstoppable as death, itself.

And all she could do was close her eyes and wait for it to take them.

Chapter 65

Gina ran with all her might, her psychic eye mapping the passages around her, tracking the movements of the thing with too many mouths.

It was faster than she was. *Much* faster. There was no way she could catch up to it in time. It had already reached the other two, in fact. And yet she found that there was somehow still time. It had stopped and was now lingering in one place, just short of where they were.

But why? Did it realize she was chasing it? Was it turning its attention back to her?

No… That wasn't it. She understood perfectly well why it had stopped. It was in all those awful things it said to her back in the glass labyrinth. (*I like it when they're afraid. I like it when they* scream.) This thing didn't simply kill. It *enjoyed* killing. It existed for the pure *pleasure* of it. It savored every moment of its sport. And it was savoring *this* moment just like it had savored every heinous act it had ever committed.

She needed to run faster.

She was the only one who could help those people.

She turned right, then left, then right. Tears were streaming down her face again. This was so unfair. Why would it go after someone *else*? She thought it wanted *her*. Did it somehow *know* that she had friends in this place? Was it trying to torture her as much as possible by slaughtering someone who'd been kind to her before coming back to finish her off?

She turned left again. Then right. It was straight ahead of her now. She sprinted forward, her heart pounding so fiercely that it felt as if it might burst from her chest.

And yet, with every step she knew this was hopeless. What was she supposed to do once she reached it? Despite her awful psychic powers, she was only human. She could do nothing to stand against a monster like that. It made no sense that she was racing toward her death like this. But her feet were moving anyway. Because she couldn't just stand idly by and let it kill whoever it pleased.

She could see a light up ahead. Someone was there.

And so was the thing with too many mouths. It was oozing across the ceiling, a great, black mass creeping toward its prey.

Two people were huddled together on the floor. Nicole. And Keith. Somehow they'd found each other in this sprawling labyrinth. But something was wrong. They were both missing their shirts. And Keith looked hurt.

They couldn't even run away!

No wonder the monster went straight toward them. They were perfect pray for a sadistic killer. Vulnerable and terrified. Helpless.

Nicole was clinging to Keith, trying to shield him from the horror that was descending on them. Gina could see her night tree tattoo, dark against the backdrop of her skin. It was as familiar by now as her face, and the sight of it made her heart flutter. That was the woman who'd been so kind to her on this horrible journey, who protected her from Gwilym Glum and Hochog and all the other monsters out there, who told her to stop apologizing all the time and promised to be her friend.

That monster couldn't have her.

She wouldn't let it.

She rushed forward, ducking under the crawling mass of shadows. Then she turned to face it, her body planted defiantly between it and her friends. "Leave them alone!" she shouted, as if she had any authority, any power, any hope whatsoever of standing against the thing with too many mouths that reeked of the Twelve Teeth of the Great Enemy.

Those many mouths were laughing at her, softly at first, but picking up, filling her head with its mocking voices. This was the first time she looked upon it with her human eyes. Illuminated in the faint, indirect glow of Nicole's flashlight, the sight was horrifyingly bizarre. It wasn't just a mass of shadows. It was black, but with pulsing ribbons of pink and red and brown twisted and knotted throughout it, looking strangely like exposed entrails. It was like a great, bubbling blob, except that what swelled and burst over and over again from its hideous body weren't bubbles, but horrible mockeries of *human limbs*. Hands and feet and heads and claws. And of course those horrible, laughing *mouths*, each one bristling with inhuman teeth and swollen, dripping tongues.

"Gina?" gasped Nicole.

"Get him out of here!" she shouted without looking back at her.

"I can't! He won't wake up!"

She felt her heart plunge again. No. The chances of being able to hold this thing off were nonexistent. Though she hadn't dared let the thought fully form in her head for fear of losing her nerve, the only hope she had, realistically, was that they could flee while the thing took its time killing *her*. It was the only option there was, the only way to save her friends. But if Keith couldn't move, then it could take all the time it wanted.

She didn't have time to think of anything else. Those awful, bubbling limbs were already reaching for her. Every nerve in her body was screaming for her to run, but she couldn't let herself. As meaningless as she was, she was the only thing standing between it and her friends. She steeled herself as cold, inhuman hands closed around her arms and thigh and throat.

This was going to hurt. It was going to hurt so bad and for so long that she was probably going to lose her mind long before she died. Because that was what unnatural things like these did to girls who were too stupid to run when they had their chance.

In an instant, she was yanked off her feet and slammed against the wall of the passage. She cried out, helpless. The back of her head connected with the stone, sending stars dancing before her eyes and dazing her. The world swam out of focus for a moment, a merciful numbness tempting her.

Somewhere in that temporary haze, she heard Nicole cry out her name.

As the world swam back to her, she found that she hadn't simply been thrown aside. The thing still had her in its vile grip, pressing her against the stone wall. And those cold, creeping limbs were *everywhere*. They crawled and slithered across her body, up under her shirt, into her bra. Something was squirming into her mouth, forcing her jaws open. Something smaller was wriggling its way into her nose. And it felt like *several* things were crawling up her skirt…

(*Make you suffer… Reach inside your writhing body… Tear your insides apart… Break… Rip… Puncture…*)

Oh god…

She tried to scream, but the thing in her mouth forced its way deeper, gagging her.

She was going to choke!

"Gina!"

Nicole was on her feet, reaching for her, trying to help her, but something dark and fleshy lashed out at her, knocking her backward. When she tried to stand again, something twisted and fleshy and bubbling wrapped itself around her neck and pulled her back down.

Again, Gina tried to cry out, but that horrible mass of fleshy coldness was pushing its way deeper into her throat, strangling her.

"What *is* this thing?" screamed Nicole. "What's happening?"

But she couldn't answer even if she knew how to explain any of it.

The thing in her nose seemed to be swelling, filling her screaming sinus cavity. And now something foul was wriggling into her ear.

Down below, she could feel those monstrous limbs squirming between her thighs, writhing and shoving and thrusting against her, threatening to enter her, to *violate* her. Except that it was worse than that, she somehow understood. What was going to happen to her wouldn't be rape. It wasn't sexual. It was *impalement.*

Just as it had promised, it was going to tear her apart from the inside out.

Chapter 66

This was harder than Albert anticipated.

The world through Brandy's glasses was reduced to a safe, fuzzy blur of gray and black, devoid of any of the room's dangerous details, and yet still he could feel the invasive emotions crushing down on him. The air was thick with an invisible weight, closing around his chest, making it harder and harder to breathe. It reminded him of the strange heaviness of the Denselands outside the city walls, but this wasn't a *physical* sensation. It was all *inside*.

His heart pounded in his ears, hammering at his brain like a battering ram beating down the doors of his very mind. It was only a matter of time before the invading emotions broke through and infected him, overwhelming everything else.

The statues crowded closer and closer as he crept through the room, threatening to lean into him, past the safe distance of the distorting lenses, forcing him to look upon them and suffer with them. It was as if they were whispering to him, their silent voices a deafening cacophony of fear and doubt that echoed through his skull, telling him that he couldn't do this. That he wasn't strong enough. That he was doomed to fail both himself and his wife.

His hands trembled as he reached out with the flashlight to steady himself against the cold stone of a looming form much too big to be a human, but still upright like a man. In doing this, he found himself steering too close to it. The gray blurs folded together into a large, deformed hand marred with deep scars and bristling with stiff hairs. In an instant, his heart gave a hard jolt, a burning sickness filled his belly and an icy wave of crippling apprehension stopped him in his tracks.

They were coming.

The words invaded his mind, poisoning his thoughts, chasing out everything else. He didn't even know what it meant. *Who* was coming? *Why*? And why was he so afraid of them?

But the questions didn't matter. They were coming and there was no time to flee. The best they could hope to do was scatter, but anything they did would be futile. No one ever escaped, after all. Not ever. There was nowhere they could run, no hiding place deep enough or dark enough.

Yet run they must. They had to try. They had to strive for the slightest sliver of a possibility that there must be *some* hope...

"What's wrong?" whispered Brandy.

Albert squeezed his eyes closed at the sound of her voice. "Just resting," he replied quickly, willing himself not to look upon that monstrous shape again.

He let himself get too close to the statue. Even a detail as seemingly insignificant as a hand could inflict the infectious emotions of this room. The glasses helped to obscure the details, but they couldn't shield him from everything. The suffocating fears seeped in, crowding his very soul. He could feel the panic rising, a tidal wave of terror that threatened to engulf him. If he panicked, he'd run. And if he ran, there was no knowing what terrible fate might befall him in this dangerous darkness.

He needed to stay in control. Not only for his sake, but for Brandy's too.

He forced himself to take another step, then another, each one a battle against the overwhelming urge to bolt. The statues watched him with unseen eyes, their silent judgment a constant reminder of his vulnerability. And with each of these steps, the forest of gray shadows surrounding him seemed to close in, the walls narrowing, the statues growing larger and more oppressive.

He had to force himself to calm his breathing. Brandy could hear him, after all. If he let his fear get the better of him, let her hear his increasingly ragged gasping, it would only make her own anxiety worse. He needed to be strong for her.

But it was so *hard*. His vision was swimming with the effort to keep moving forward. He knew he had to reach the end, to find a way out of this nightmare, but the path ahead seemed endless.

How big would this room prove to be?

How many times would it force its way into his brain?

Focus on the room, he thought to himself, *not the statues*. Not the obstacles in his way, but the path *through* those obstacles. He needed to concentrate on the shape of the chamber around him, the arrangement of the shadows. He'd been moving to the left since he entered, meaning the door they entered through was somewhere over his right shoulder. The space seemed to be much longer than it was wide. With the warning chamber back there, it was doubtful that the way out would be behind them. But previous experience told him that the way out was never straight ahead, either. There was always a possibility of getting turned around. He could probably expect the path through the statues to wind back and forth a few times, increasing the likelihood of coming face-to-face with something deeply unpleasant.

But he stopped again as he realized that there was nowhere for him to go in this direction.

The statues were completely blocking his path.

He turned his head one way, then the other, scanning the blurry shapes, trying to find a gap, but he appeared to have walked into a dead end.

Did he mess up? Did he get turned around while trying to focus too hard on the maze aspect of the room? Or did he do something wrong at the very beginning?

He wasn't sure what to do.

His stomach bubbled with acid. He felt like he was about to throw up. It was hard to breathe.

Calm down, he thought to himself, but his body had begun trembling. A rapidly swelling panic was building up inside him. He knew that it was irrational, that it was only a dead end. There were bound to be a few of those. He just needed to calmly backtrack and find the path he missed. But knowing this didn't make it feel any less real. He felt dizzy. His head was pounding.

He didn't know what to do!

Brandy's arms tightened around his waist. He felt her face against his shoulder. He felt her kiss him through his shirt.

Right... Brandy was here with him. He focused on the feel of her body against his, her grip, the familiar curves of her chest. He could feel her bangs tickling the back of his neck. Her breath warmed him through his shirt between kisses.

He closed his eyes and forced himself to breathe slowly and focus all of his attention onto her. His Brandy. His beautiful wife. His best friend in all the worlds.

She reached under his shirt and slid her hands up his stomach, all the way to his chest, the sensation of her skin against his calming, almost intoxicating.

The panic inside him began to melt away, slowly releasing its icy grip on him.

She kissed him once more, then whispered, "What happened to all that 'I can do anything if it means keeping you safe' talk?"

"I don't know what you're talking about. I was just taking a little breather."

"You're so full of shit."

A weary huff of a laugh escaped him. So much for not letting her see what this room was doing to him. Shanzer *did* say she could see the truth in people.

She withdrew her hands from his shirt and stepped around him. Before he realized what she was doing, she was kissing him.

The sensation was like a gulp of cold water on a sweltering sunny day. All the fear and unease seemed to wash off of him like sand under a garden hose, reminding him that the emotions of this room were nothing compared to those he felt for her. The anxiety worming its way into his veins was intense, overwhelming, but it didn't measure up to this feeling. *This* was real. This was natural. This was *pure.*

"That feels weird," she said, plucking her glasses off his face. Then, before he had a chance to say anything, she was kissing him again.

Chapter 67

The longer Corey was here in this terminal, the more he understood about these "stoneworks," as Austin called them. He couldn't really be certain if it was actually some kind of innate, hereditary memory, as Austin claimed, or some kind of mental download from the stone machinery he'd been interacting with or even if he was somehow absorbing it from Austin, himself, as he sorted through his artificial guts. Any of those seemed equally likely in a structure made of stone that transcended realities, conducted energies that shouldn't exist and processed data like a computer. But as he worked, he was becoming more and more aware of exactly how this massive machine operated.

Albert referred to this place as a city when they were traveling together. The City Beyond Memory, he called it. But it wasn't really a city. It didn't serve any of the functions of a city. No one ever lived here. But it did *resemble* a city for some reason. He found that he could picture it, as if reading the very blueprints as he busied himself with the strings. Surrounded entirely by that impossibly high wall, perfectly sealed away, impenetrable, it truly was a place frozen in time, sealed away even from the destruction of its own universe. But it had far less in common with a city than it did with a giant *engine*. The structures that resembled buildings contained no windows or doors or rooms, but instead served as components in an immensely complex machine. The shorter ones near the outer edges worked to direct energy inward, toward the taller structures at the center, which interacted with some sort of atmospheric activity. A...*storm* of some sort? All of which was designed especially to feed into a kind of central tower. Or maybe it was more like a central *processor*?

He was still missing far too many important concepts to be able to fully understand it, of course. Universe after universe of changing laws of physics and nature had left gaps in his ability to truly understand it all, but he knew enough about both mechanics *and* computers to see the comparisons.

There were three terminals, including this one, each in one of the three simultaneous states of existence. This was the physical terminal within the living, natural third of the universe. A second terminal was hidden deep within a part of the machine that somehow existed in a supernatural state of being. A sort of...*ghost terminal*, he supposed. And the third was something entirely different, belonging neither to the living nor the dead, something entirely *unnatural*... He wasn't sure how, exactly, any of the people he met were supposed to access either of those other two terminals. It seemed to him that only the dead could reach the second one, which was more than a little concerning. But he simply couldn't wrap his head around what it meant to be something *other* than alive or dead.

There was Austin, he supposed. *He* was technically neither living nor dead. But he wasn't in that third terminal. He was here. With him. In the physical one.

Was there someone else out there like him? Artificial and ancient? He did say something before to Albert and Brandy about there being one like him in every stoneworks...

No. That didn't feel right, either. Somehow, he felt like the third terminal had something to do with Gina...though he had no idea why it would be *her* of all people.

He wasn't ever going to understand it all, of course. There was no point trying. He'd be better off focusing on what he *did* know.

In addition to the three terminals, there were locks located throughout the labyrinth. These were the locks Albert and Brandy told them about, the ones that required their special *sexy magic* to open, he supposed. Or other equally unorthodox means. He still didn't understand how that sort of thing could affect anything other than the people *doing* the magic, but he knew that there were multiple points throughout the stoneworks that required gathering up and concentrating energy in order to activate the path forward. But not electricity. This machine ran on something different, on much *older* forms of energy. Perhaps some kind of *human* energy.

Albert *did* say something about their sexy magic having something to do with *emotions*. And then there was that odd feeling he had while he was still making his way through the labyrinth, before finding his way here. He was able to tell that there were people nearby. Three of them. And he felt very distinctly that they were all overcome with a very intense, even suffocating sadness.

"Emotion rooms," he called them when recounting the intriguing tale of their first encounter with one of these places, what he called the "Temple of the Blind." Lust. Hate. Fear. Rooms full of intense statues capable of overwhelming them with particular emotions, enough to make them lose all earthly control.

Emotional energy. Coursing through the very stone, all funneling to a single point in the very middle of it all, feeding the central tower where the final chamber had been waiting inconceivable ages to be opened.

The doorway. Their goal. A fixed point in time and space along the path that would open the way to the next cycle.

This was so exciting!

He couldn't wait to see what happened next.

Chapter 68

"This happened before, too," said Andrea. She was still clinging to Olivia's hand, still blinking into the darkness, unable to make out even a vague outline of her friends. "But you guys can still see, right?"

"Perfectly fine," replied Olivia.

"There's nothing in this passage but us," agreed Wayne.

Andrea couldn't decide if confirming that she was the only one blind in this all-encompassing black made her feel better or worse. On one hand, as long as *they* could see, she shouldn't fall down any more holes or trip over a slumbering hound or any of a million other imagined scenarios. But it felt so utterly bizarre that she was the only one unable to see that it felt as if she were going mad.

But at least the murk voices had quieted down again. They were still mocking her back in that other chamber, but at some point while running from those flying things, they dimmed down to just a creepy sort of constant muttering all around her. She wouldn't exactly call it an *improvement*...but it was a little less distracting, at least.

"That's crazy weird," sighed Wayne.

"Stop it!" hissed Olivia.

"Stop what?" asked Andrea, confused.

"Sorry. I was just checking."

"You didn't need to check. She *told* you she was blind."

"What? What'd you do?" What was happening? She felt suddenly very vulnerable standing here in her own private darkness. She crossed her free arm over her chest.

"See? You're making her uncomfortable."

"I wasn't doing anything *weird*!" She could hear him taking a step backward, embarrassed. "I was just doing the thing, you know? Waving my hand in front of your face?"

She crinkled her nose at him. "What, 'cause you didn't *believe* me?"

"No! I just—"

"See? Don't be creepy."

"I'm not *creepy*!"

She felt Olivia press closer to her. "Are you okay?"

"I mean...I'm *blind*, so..."

"I mean *besides* that."

"Isn't that *enough?*"

"Just hold still a second, your nose is bleeding."

"My nose?" She reached up and wiped at it, but her finger didn't come away wet.

"No, I mean here."

She flinched as she felt a warm cloth dabbing at the bridge of her nose. As soon as she felt it, she became aware of a stinging there.

"One of those nasty bug things."

She squeezed her eyes shut and winced as Olivia dabbed it clean.

"I really wish I had some first aid supplies."

"They would've just ended up in the Explorer with the rest of our stuff," reasoned Wayne.

"Probably..."

She could feel Olivia hovering just in front of her, leaning close to check the cut on her nose. She could feel her breath on her face. A lock of long hair tickled her cheek. It was weirdly intimate and she found herself thinking that she was still covered in that gross, reeking mud. "Here, too," she said, her touch moving from her nose to a subtle burning on her cheek.

"I'm okay," she insisted. "It doesn't really hurt."

Olivia was still clinging to her hand. She gave it a squeeze as she leaned back, receding again into the strange, solitary darkness. "They don't cut very deep, at least."

"No weight behind them," agreed Wayne. "That's about the only good news when it comes to those things."

"What *are* they?" wondered Andrea.

"They *used* to be a hound," he replied.

"Huh?"

"The scarecrow man," sighed Olivia.

"The creep who goes around playing with dead things?" They mentioned him in their story, that he was the cause of the zombie animals that attacked them (of all the terrifying things they could've dealt with). And they explained that he wasn't simply waking them up, like some kind of necromancing Dr. Dolittle, but rather controlling them like puppets...which was still really gross.

"He also apparently likes to take dead things *apart* and Frankenstein them back together again. Those 'bugs' are just hound scales stuck together."

"That is *so* messed up."

"Wait 'til you see what he did with the *rest* of the hound," he grumbled.

"I'd rather not..." Why did it have to be a *hound* of all things? Those monsters were scary enough when they were *alive*.

"Well it sucks that you're blind, obviously," said Wayne, "but at least *he* doesn't seem to be able to see these murk passages, either."

That was true. She wondered if that might have been the point all along. Erin said the Keeper had everything all planned out, so maybe he knew that scarecrow creep was going to be here and made sure she found her way to them specifically to help them escape.

But that line of thinking always circled around to that one all-important question: why didn't the ugly little monster just do this stuff himself? Was this *fun* for him? Was this how saggy, immortal goblins entertained themselves? This whole thing was so convoluted!

She turned and blinked into the darkness around her, listening to the eerie mutterings of the murk. Apart from that and the fact that she wasn't alone this time, she couldn't help being reminded of the spirit highway Imposter Stella stranded her on. Absolute darkness, two directions to choose from and little else.

"What should we do?" wondered Olivia.

"Keep going, of course," replied Wayne, sounding not at all thrilled about it.

Andrea pointed. "This way?"

"Ish," replied Olivia. She reached out and nudged her arm a few degrees to the right.

"Thanks."

"Just don't let go of my hand," she offered. "Maybe it'll clear up once we get to wherever this leads."

"I hope so..."

The three of them started walking, their footsteps mingling with the mutters of the murk, creating an eerie sort of percussion against the oppressive backdrop of suffocating darkness.

She didn't like this. Even with her friends at her side, this absolute darkness was terrifying. Her imagination wouldn't stop trying to convince her that there were horrible things all around her, ready to strike at any moment. And why shouldn't there be? She kept thinking about those crawling, growling clumps of darkness. Those weren't imaginary. Those were perfectly real. And she'd never see it coming like this. One could be opening its foul, bottomless maw in front of her face at this very moment and she wouldn't know it until she felt all those endless teeth sinking into her flesh.

"You okay?" asked Olivia.

Right. She may be blind, but *they* could see fine. And these ridiculous thoughts were probably painted all over her face right now. She could feel her body tensing up. She was clenching her jaw so hard it was beginning to ache. It was no wonder Olivia sounded worried. She tried her best to relax. "Yeah. It's just…*really* unsettling not being able to see anything."

"I'd imagine," said Wayne.

From somewhere down by her feet, she heard soft voices rise from the unpleasant mutterings of the murk.

"Imagine…" sighed a child.

"He imagines…" lamented a woman.

"Understanding…" crooned an old man.

"Don't start *that* crap again," she grumbled.

"Don't…" echoed the murk.

"Crap…"

"Not again…"

"What?" asked Wayne.

"Not you," she told him.

"Not you…" mocked the murk.

"Not him…"

But each voice was softer than the last, already fading into the background noise.

Not for the first time, she found herself wondering what those voices were. Erin said there were no human spirits inside the city walls. (Other than *her*, at least.) No humans had ever been here and therefore had never died here. And even if they had, why would spirits in a place like this speak English?

They're not what they appear to be, she thought, recalling Erin's cryptic words again.

Not what they appeared to be…? Not human… And not spirits… Just *murk*. Just some…*thing* from the other side that was now and forever incomprehensible to the living. A secret only the dead were allowed to know.

(*Whatever it is you think you're seeing and hearing is just your mind doing its best to tell you what's there.*)

And yet, it didn't change the fact that it was so real to her own eyes that she was rendered completely blind when it gathered in quantities like this. Because she never said it wasn't *real*. She only said she couldn't comprehend it. Which brought her all the way back to the million-dollar question: what was the point in having this supposedly super-rare ability when all it was doing was literally blinding her?

"Stupid Keeper…" she muttered under her breath.

"What was that?" asked Olivia.

"Nothing."

She realized that the voices weren't repeating her anymore. There was just a sickly sort of unintelligible surge in that constant muttering all around her. That was *something* at least. Those guys were starting to give her a wicked headache.

"This isn't the most ideal situation for us, though," said Wayne. "I'm not sure what we're going to do if there's one of those hidden ghost passages in here somewhere that we're supposed to take."

"Don't talk like that," said Olivia.

"Sorry," he replied. "Just thinking out loud."

"Think something more helpful," she suggested. "Or keep it to yourself."

"Um...? Okay..."

"It's fine," said Andrea. "I mean he's not wrong." If her job was to see the ghost corridors, then what good was she right now? What if she'd already walked past the way they were supposed to go? What if they all fell into some horrible trap because of her?

"Still..." sighed Olivia, giving her hand a comforting squeeze.

She reached out with the hand holding her useless flashlight and dragged her knuckles along the wall. The stone was smooth and cold. A temple wall, clean and pristine. She couldn't even feel any seams.

"I guess we'll just have to rely on your 'amber threads,' then," decided Wayne.

"Oh god..." breathed Olivia.

"If we pass something important," he reasoned, "I'm sure you'll feel it."

"I still don't know how this works!"

"No, that might work," agreed Andrea, perking up.

"Not you, too! I don't want to be the one responsible for stuff like this!"

She'd been telling them all along that she had a bad feeling about going back. If she suddenly had a bad feeling about going *forward*, it might mean they'd passed an important murk passage while she was unable to see. Looking at it that way, maybe the Keeper sent *Olivia* to *her* as much as he sent her to Olivia.

Maybe the creepy little monster knew what he was doing after all.

Chapter 69

Violet stared out over the expanse of the City Beyond Memory. From this far up, she could see all the way to the horizon, where the massive gray stone met the colors of that alien sky. So far across was the city that even those towering walls faded into the multicolored haze, creating an illusion that there was no wall at all over there, that every living thing wasn't being sealed alive inside this inescapable metropolis for inconceivable eons to come.

She could also see the worker-things lumbering about down there, enormous shapes like great, sloughing blobs oozing down the streets, making her want to withdraw back into the safety of the other one. And if she looked closely, she could even spot the sentinels at work, their strange, elongated forms crawling across the countless stone surfaces, making them look like busy little ants.

So much work left to do. So many little details to finish.

She turned her attention upward, to the nearby towers still rising up into that unreal sky, each of them reaching across the colorful emptiness with those narrow bridges like stone fingers grasping for the main structure dwarfing everything around it. The unfinished stone appeared to her like a skeletal hand stretching upward, slowly reaching toward the ultimate goal…the pinnacle of it all. The Oblivion Doorway. One of three mysterious constants written into the very coding of the greater universe.

That was their ultimate goal. Somewhere, at the far side of eternity where the circle was at last coming to a close, the *other* Violet was searching for that place along with her companions. Everything laid out before her was designed with that one end in mind, every structure, every floor, every passage, every stone…all of it scripted out by these strange Faceless Ones who possessed the mysterious ability to see across eternity and write backward to this ancient present.

It was inconceivable to a mere human like her. And yet it was as real as she was.

She was both here and there, especially chosen by the other one to bear witness to the beginning and take the knowledge she was gifted back to the end.

It was humbling.

And yet...she would have frowned if she'd still had a mouth to frown with.

Why was she here? Why *now*? Hadn't something happened to the her on the far side of eternity? She remembered something foul splashing onto her... Fear and disgust and panic overwhelming her, desperation to wash away the filth.

The color red...

Light where there should've been only darkness...

She was afraid. She was in *danger*.

What was happening to her other self in this moment in the present?

Ruin infects everything eventually.

Ruin? The twins used that word, she recalled, way back on January Street. An eternity ago, it seemed.

(*Beware the Ruin.*)

She felt a sickly uneasiness deep in her belly at the memory. (A strange sensation given that this belly wasn't even hers.) A mounting fear that something bad was happening to her real body on the other side was overwhelming her. That sickly glow deep in the water...its color like blood...

It will even spread across this city in the end. There will be no stopping it. The door must be opened before it can destroy all that we built.

A race against the clock. Against time. Against *Ruin*.

She found herself looking up into that colorful sky again. It always looked like that. It was never night here. It was never cloudy, never rained. This world wasn't like the one she knew. Even those moons never moved. They loomed constantly over everything, watching like judgmental gods.

But recently, those colors had been slowly darkening. She thought at first that maybe it was those walls, impossibly high, impassible to anything and everything, they'd eventually even block out the sunlight. But somehow she understood that it wasn't just the sky inside the walls. This entire world was getting darker. The decay was setting in. It was nearing its end, just like every world that ever lived eventually did.

Including hers.

Will you be there when I go back? she wondered. *Will you help me?*

I've always been with you. And I will be with you until our circle finally closes.

But you haven't been there. You won't talk to me.

I'm limited in how much I can do in your time. I have to reserve my strength or I won't be able to protect you when you need me most.

When she needed her most? Like *right now*?

Somewhere, far back in her mind, she felt herself struggling...splashing... It was cold and she couldn't breathe... Something wouldn't let go of her... And everything was bathed in shades of blood...

Things have taken an unfortunate turn at your end of the circle. Something sinister is stalking you. The path I've shown you in this time has grown too dangerous. I've steered you off it in hopes that you might slip past, but it hasn't worked. Ruin is nipping at your heels as we speak.

The Ruin was pursuing her? Like some kind of predator? Was it *alive*? And what did she mean that she steered her off the path? Was that why she suddenly couldn't remember the way? Because something terrible was waiting for her?

Things are going to get far more dangerous for you now. You must remain strong.

Things were *already* far more dangerous for her! Somewhere, in another time, she was being dragged into that bloody water! She needed to get back. But she didn't know how. It was the other one who summoned her and sent her back...wasn't it?

She tried opening her real eyes, but instead of going back to her time, she found herself standing in that same room in *this* time, in the other one's strange body. There was no water, only stone and darkness and a bottomless hole plunging into the earth in front of her.

This was what the room looked like back then, before the rain began to fall, before the reservoirs filled and the things with the gross, hairy tentacles moved in.

There was an odd sort of breeze wafting up from somewhere below. She could feel it on the other one's skin, flowing up those too-long legs, caressing the strange curves of this unfamiliar female anatomy. It was a surreal sensation, as real as if she were standing here in her own body but distorted and out of proportion.

It occurred to her that she couldn't recall ever glimpsing another female sentinel in all the time she was here. Somehow, she knew they were out there. This wasn't the only one. But where were they? What were they doing?

Her head was spinning. So many thoughts. So many questions.

Maybe it had something to do with what was happening to her in the present. She could feel the cold water on her skin even from here. Her chest was aching for air. She needed to go back there. She needed to escape the blood-tinted water.

Look where we are.

She'd already looked. It was hardly helpful. But the words had barely echoed through her mind when she realized that they'd moved again. She was now standing in a round room with six sentinel statues, each one standing with its back to an empty passage. The only difference was that each one had that strange, featureless plane of its face turned in a different direction. One was looking down, the next to the left. Up. Right. The last two were facing straight ahead, but tilted in an odd sort of inquisitive gesture, one to the left, the other to the right.

That one...

Chapter 70

Everett scowled as the elevator doors once again opened, revealing nothing more than another identical paper hallway.

Was this the fifth floor in a row now? Or the sixth? He'd already lost count. Frustrated, he pressed the "up" button again and watched the doors slide closed. But when they opened again a moment later, the result was the same.

This was probably what Alice was trying to tell him when he stepped into the car acting so smug about it.

So much for having it all figured out.

So much for being "in control."

"Are we actually moving?" he wondered aloud. It *felt* like the elevator was rising each time the doors closed. And then there was the fact that the "down" button was lit up now, suggesting he could descend again if he wanted.

Alice agreed. They were, indeed, moving. But she also put the thought into his head that "moving" and actually "going somewhere" might not be the same thing here in the inverted upside down of the City Beyond Memory.

Yes… That made sense, he found. He was grasping at concepts he barely understood and then running with it, but it wasn't as simple as that. He was "in control" because the dollhouse was a figment of his imagination, his own creation, a universe of his own making, but until he fully understood what it meant to be the creator of such a thing, being in control meant little more than nothing.

You could give a fish complete control of a dune buggy, if you so wanted, but that didn't mean it was going to be able to drive it.

He kept finding ways out of the dollhouse, but he couldn't simply step through a door or onto an elevator. It didn't work like that. It was like trying to jump off the world. No matter how high you made it, you just kept being pulled back down again.

Like everything else in the City Beyond Memory's flipside, he needed to think about it inside-out and backward.

If only he knew how to do that…

He stepped out of the elevator car and stood at the end of the paper hallway, thinking.

Behind him, the doors slid closed.

Doors… That was what he kept looking for. And what he kept finding. Doors. He built one out of the overturned chairs. He manifested one on a vacant area of the foyer's paper wall. He even tore through the paper and revealed one hidden behind it. But none of them worked any better, really, than the useless drawn-on ones.

He turned and stared at the nearest of those sketched-out doors, curious. Perhaps that was the point. Perhaps that was what those drawings had been trying to tell him this whole time. If so, it had literally been spelled out in front of him since he arrived here.

Doors were useless in this world.

If he thought of the way out as merely walking through a door, it quite simply wouldn't work. Once again, it was an inverted world and he needed to invert his thinking. Not only to *find* a solution, but also to *use* it. Just because he opened the freezer and grabbed a frozen dinner didn't mean he could start eating. He had to actually cook it first. There were steps. Instructions to follow. Cooking times. Even letting it cool so that he didn't burn his foolish mouth. This was sort of like that, he supposed. Stepping onto the elevator and pressing the button wasn't the end of it.

It made a certain sort of twisted sense, even. He felt silly not realizing it sooner. What did he *think* would happen? Where was the elevator supposed to go? The dollhouse was literally all that was here in this world that his imagination constructed for him.

What he needed was a strategy that would take him all the way from here to the upright side.

Except…he didn't even know how he got here from there. It wasn't as if he were following a map. How was he supposed to concoct a way back?

He looked down at Alice again, but the things that bubbled up in his mind were distorted and incoherent. He couldn't understand her. The answers he sought were beyond his current ability to comprehend.

He turned his attention instead to the paper hallway stretched out before him and thought back on the events that brought him here.

It started back in the labyrinth with Violet. She found that weird stone. Then everything changed. The creatures that were lurking in the darkness below them had suddenly sprung to life and were descending on him. He was scooped up and spirited away before he knew what was happening. Then he was adrift in the void, lost and alone and strangely empty inside, as if he'd died and faded into the ether. Until he forced his eyes open and beheld the horrors all around him.

That was it, he realized. The point at which he must've crossed over. That void must have been the in-between place, the axis on which the two sides of everything balanced. It was as soon as he beheld that strange, blinding darkness that he began falling through the inverted city.

It sounded like a terrible idea, but what he wanted was to somehow get back *there*.

Could he even *survive* going back? It felt like it nearly tore his mind in half the first time. But he supposed if he did it once, he could do it again.

(It still felt like a terrible idea, though.)

And just *how* did one get from one side to the other? When he traveled to the Red Waste, it was the puzzle box that took him there. But he no longer had the puzzle box. The Eeshee took it when they sent him back to the Denselands. He had no recollection of traveling in either direction. He wasn't even aware it was happening until he was already there.

That wasn't going to be any help at all.

He blinked down at Alice, distracted. "What?"

She didn't repeat herself. She didn't need to. The question was merely a reflex. Those disjointed, wordless thoughts were still knitting themselves together inside his head, still blossoming into awareness.

He turned and looked back at the closed elevator doors, a creeping sense of urgency slowly welling up inside him. Something had changed.

They weren't alone in the dollhouse anymore.

"Priestess..." he whispered, taking a step back from those suddenly ominous doors.

The elevator was a mistake. Not only couldn't he use it to leave the dollhouse, but it had now opened a way *in* for something that actually understood the way this world worked.

"Yeah..." He took another step back. "I *do* think we should get away from here."

He turned and fled back down the paper hallway, his heart racing, a dreadful lump burning deep in his belly.

Something awful was at the dollhouse door. And he wasn't going to be able to keep it out.

Chapter 71

Gina clenched her body tight, fighting against the cold, squirming things that were trying to invade her body. But how long could she possibly hold it back? She wasn't strong like all the other women here. Not like Nicole or Andrea or Brandy or Violet. She was meek by her very nature. If not for these awful psychic abilities, there was no way the goddess would ever have chosen someone like her. She was sure of it.

"Yes…" hissed the awful thing worming its way deeper into her ear. "Struggle."

She would have shuddered with revulsion at the pure ecstasy in that foul voice if her body hadn't already been racked with it from the very touch of these foul, inhuman appendages.

"I like it when they struggle."

She fought to free her hands, but it was too strong. She couldn't even try in vain to remove the disgusting thing that was ramming itself down her throat, strangling her.

And the thing in her nose was *agonizing*. She could feel it worming around in there, snaking its way through her sinuses, slowly making its way out the other side.

It didn't feel like flesh. It shifted and sloughed against her skin, cold and oozing, *wet*, and yet it was strangely solid at the same time, rigid and hard as it pushed itself into her head, fully capable, she knew, of puncturing her, of breaking her, of *crushing* her. Her terrified mind couldn't quite grasp it. But it was *familiar*. She'd felt this awful texture before. This wasn't the first time one of these horrible, shadowy things had laid its vile hands on her body. But she was dreadfully aware that it might be the last.

"I'm going to take my time with you," it whispered. The one in her mouth withdrew a little, teasing her with a much-needed gulp of air before thrusting itself even deeper. She could feel it in her throat, filling her, pushing against her neck. "I'm going to make it last."

Goddess help her...

"But first..." it sighed, pressing even deeper into her ear, sending bolts of agony through her jaw even as another one began wiggling its way into her other ear. "First, I'll make you *watch.*"

Nicole screamed.

Gina blinked back the tears streaming from her eyes and looked down to see that those hideous limbs were crawling all over her, tearing at her hair and shorts.

No! she screamed at it inside her head. She couldn't speak, but she knew it could hear her thoughts. *Leave her alone!*

But the murderous, creeping horror was already slithering into Nicole's shorts and pulling at her bra.

She could feel an awful aura wafting off the beast, a reeking, sickening sort of emotional energy, not entirely unlike what she felt back in that heartbreaking grief room, but was nothing so natural as sorrow. She could feel the thing's perverse pleasure as it prepared to torture and mangle its prey. It was a terrible and alien sensation that made her feel even more nauseous than the hideous things invading her body.

Stop!

"I can make her feel pain like you've never imagined." It wasn't an idle threat. It wasn't even an exaggeration. She could sense the thing's perverse desires. She understood its horrible methods. It liked to start *inside.* Even now, she could see those awful tendrils boring into her ears and nose. Her cries were getting louder, more piercing. She was in pain. And she was terrified.

Get away from her!

"You have no idea how long I can make her scream."

STOP IT!

She squeezed her eyes closed. Her body tensed. She could feel herself shaking, a rigid, furious shiver, hot rather than cold, that ran from her head all the way to her toes. A strange sensation washed over her. A *familiar* sensation. One she felt not long ago, in a situation eerily like this one, deep in Gwilym Glum's foul guts.

STOOOOOOP!

What happened next felt a lot like an explosion, but there was no concussion, no fire, no smoke, not even any sound that she could discern. The only effect was that the thing with too many mouths let out a hideous howl of a wail and then just sort of...*burst.*

She didn't even *see* it happen. It was too fast. One second it was a great black mass of hideous, bubbling limbs filled with pulsating organs and viscera, the next it was splattered all over the wall across from her and she dropped to her hands and knees on the floor, coughing and retching, her mouth and nose filled with a grotesque, bile-like taste and a deeply unpleasant cold and wet sensation under her skirt.

Nicole jolted upright and screamed, her hands flailing wildly, still trying to swat the awful things away. There were black, oily smears on her skin where those hideous limbs were holding her down. They covered her arms and belly. It dripped from her nose and ears. It was in her hair. And there were telltale black stains on her bra and shorts where the thing was trying to force its way under them when it burst.

Gina vomited, expelling a great gush of foul black goo onto the floor between her hands. The taste was beyond foul. She gasped for air, then vomited again, though there was much less to come up this time. She hadn't eaten since she left the boat, after all. She spat and coughed, trying to get ahold of herself. She needed to get back on her feet. She had no way of knowing if the nightmare was really over. But tears were still streaming down her face from her burning sinuses, blinding her. It was only by the grace of her psychic eye that she was able to look around, wary of another attack. Even so, it was hard to think with any clarity. Her head was spinning. Her ears hurt. Her body was sore.

She blinked hard and fast, trying to clear her vision, and saw that those same black smears she saw on Nicole covered her own arms and legs and stained her blouse. She couldn't seem to spit away that awful taste in her mouth. And although the thing didn't manage to actually force its foul appendages into her body down there before it exploded, it felt as if it had left a gross mess inside her panties that felt almost as hideous.

"*What the fuck was that?*" coughed Nicole. She was wiping at her nose and grimacing at the foul taste oozing down the back of her throat, her eyes wide and wild with fright in the haunting darkness.

Gina didn't know where to begin. Nor did she have time to think about it. It had gone quiet, but she couldn't be sure it was over. She rose to her feet, her body still shaking, and cast her psychic eye back and forth along the passage. Was the thing really dead? *Could* it even die? How could she be certain?

She didn't understand what happened, where this strange power came from that had twice now allowed her to rescue Nicole from something countless times stronger than she could ever hope to be. It seemed to pour out of her when she was faced with the desperately horrifying prospect of losing someone she cared about.

"So fucking gross..." groaned Nicole as she pushed herself up onto her hands and knees. She spat on the floor, grimacing. Then she looked up at her. "Are you okay?"

"I think so." She was still scanning the passage. It was difficult to discern exactly what her psychic eye was seeing. Her brain struggled to construct it for her. From her point of view, it was like a bunch of scattered embers glowing in the darkness, like the final dying remnants of a great fire. One by one they were winking out. But here and there a new one would blossom into view again, meaning that it wasn't gone just yet. It was still fighting, still struggling to survive. She couldn't let it. She needed to stamp it out for good. And yet it was fading faster than it was fighting back. It was vanishing before her inner eye.

Nicole didn't bother getting to her feet, she turned and crawled back to Keith's side to check on him.

It didn't seem like the monster had any interest in him. There wasn't so much as a smear on his body. Perhaps it preferred women. More likely, she thought, it probably simply didn't see any entertainment in torturing someone who was already unconscious. It had already informed her, after all, how much it enjoyed making its victims scream.

Around her, those strange embers were still dying away. Only a few remained.

Was it really gone? Could she truly be so lucky?

She didn't dare hope while even a single one still glowed in her mind.

Behind her, she could hear Nicole talking to Keith, urging him to wake up. She should go to them. They needed her. But first she had to be sure. She had to be absolutely *certain*.

Somewhere in the back of her mind, she imagined a voice speaking across the eerie silence of the labyrinth.

No... Not speaking exactly... More like...

The last of those mysterious embers winked out, but still she could hear the voice.

It was *laughing* at her.

A sudden pain struck her in the ribs, just below her left breast. She looked down, startled, to find that while she was focused on the space around her, a glowing mass of embers were still burning away under her shirt.

Got you, sighed the unspeakable monstrosity as those embers became a red-hot glow that burned like fire against her skin.

She cried out in pain and dropped to her knees, grasping at herself.

"*What is it?*" shouted Nicole. She was leaning over Keith, shielding him from whatever fresh threat had just shown itself, her gaze darting back and forth. "*Where?*"

But it was over as quickly as it began. She sat there on the stone floor, blinking into the darkness, a lingering burning sensation on her body.

The thing with too many mouths was gone. She was absolutely certain now. It had burned through the last of its unnatural life and vanished into whatever came after for things such as it. If anything.

She lifted her blouse and looked down at herself. There was a bright red burn mark on her skin there, starting just at the base of her breast and reaching around her side, about eight inches long and four inches high.

"What's wrong?" worried Nicole.

"Nothing," she called back, pushing her shirt back down. One last act of cruelty, she supposed. A nasty little burn to remember it by. She winced at the pain and rose to her feet again. "I'm okay."

Nicole didn't look convinced, but she didn't press the subject. She turned her attention back to Keith. "He won't wake up."

Pushing the pain from her mind, she hurried to his other side and knelt next to him. He looked terrible. What could've happened to him?

Before she could ask any questions, however, Nicole reached up and grasped her blouse, pulling her closer with such aggressive desperation that two of her buttons popped and bounced off the stone in the silence of the passage. "Please tell me you can help him!" she cried, tears streaming down her face.

Gina stared back at her. She didn't know what to do. She knew nothing about healing people. It wasn't even a concept she'd ever considered. It wasn't how her abilities worked. She just *knew* things. That was all. And even if these awful senses *could* tell her what would help, she couldn't just make medicine out of thin air.

But she couldn't just sit down and do nothing, either. This was Keith. He'd been so kind to her. She had to *try*.

She looked down at him, her human eyes sweeping over him. He didn't look good by any means. He looked pale and exhausted. There was blood in his hair and on his belly as well as soaked into the cloth wrapped around his arm and feet. But it was what her psychic eye showed her that made her heart sink. There were bruises that no light could reveal. He'd taken three hard blows to the head recently. His chest and belly practically glowed with unseen injuries. And it looked like something took a bite out of his arm. But his feet... She felt sick as she peered under the remains of Nicole's tank top, at all those holes in his skin. They seemed almost to glow in the dark. And each one of those glowing holes painted luminous trails up his legs and deep into his body.

Tears shimmered in her eyes as she met Nicole's gaze again.

"I'm sorry," she whispered. "I don't know what to do."

A great, wet sob forced its way up Nicole's throat, making her entire body shudder. Fresh tears spilled down her cheeks. She pressed her hand to her mouth in a futile effort to control the emotions spilling out.

It broke her heart, but she couldn't make this any better. There was nothing she could do.

He was dying.

Chapter 72

"Better?" asked Brandy in a breathless whisper.

"Much," sighed Albert.

They were standing nose-to-nose, their lips brushing together as they spoke, their eyes still closed against the invasive emotions of the statues surrounding them.

Her heart was racing again, but for a different reason now.

He was right. Emotions could override each other, allowing them to cancel out the effects of these rooms. To a degree, at least. She still felt uneasy, but it was no longer as intense as it was before. She felt like she could think more clearly.

She kissed him one last time, then lowered her head and hugged him.

"I'm sorry," he whispered. "I let it get in my head a little there. I'm better now."

"It's not your fault. It's this place. I know it is." This wasn't ever going to be easy, she knew. Emotions were such complicated things to deal with in a perfectly *ordinary* world. The stress of everyday life, relationships, work… Something as simple as getting enough sleep could drastically affect one's mood. And that wasn't even counting the weird stuff her emotions sometimes did just being a girl and dealing with *that* business every month. But dealing with rooms full of statues that *forced* you to feel certain emotions? Not to mention being told she was psychically tuned into the people around her? Knowing what the lovely couple celebrating their anniversary had just finished doing back in that hotel? Being able to feel Trixie's mounting sexual frustration? It had been a steady bombardment of feelings!

She was struggling with three different emotional sources *right now*. The fake ones this room was responsible for. The real ones that she was naturally feeling, including everything from fear of the unknown to anger at being denied a choice in any of this and regret for all the people she'd lost track of so far on this journey through what felt like all nine levels of hell. And then there were the real emotions that *Albert* was struggling with as he juggled his own fear and insecurities with trying to keep from upsetting *her*.

She couldn't help feeling guilty. She was his wife. She should be supporting him, not weighing him down. But it was hard enough getting a firm grip on her *own* emotions. Or even telling them apart from everyone else's!

Again, she reached up and kissed him. This time, however, when she went to pull away, he closed his hand around the back of her neck and pulled her close again. The sensation, so familiar, so intimate, sent a familiar flutter through her heart. For a moment, she actually forgot where she was. The enormous darkness that had surrounded her for so long melted into a place that was small and cozy and warm and sweet. She closed her hands around the fabric of his shirt and met his eager lips.

This felt so much better than those *other* emotions...

She wanted to feel this way *forever.*

But then he stopped.

"This way," he said, slipping her glasses back onto his face.

She blinked up at his blurry face, dazed. She didn't even notice him taking them out of her hand...

He linked elbows with her, used his free hand to cover the space around the rims, then set off through the statues again.

Of course. Sexual energy. Psychic abilities. Environmental awareness. He was charging up, glimpsing the available pathways in their immediate surroundings, then making his way through the statues before it faded.

She knew that.

It was a good plan. Way better than hers. Which was...to just keep kissing like that...or maybe...a little more than just kissing...

She shook it off and focused on keeping up with him.

He steered her to the left, then to the right. Then he slowed down. Distracted by her shifting emotions and surprised by the abrupt change, she let herself peek and saw that the statues here were crowded much closer together. He was being careful to guide her between them so she didn't bump into anything.

She quickly squeezed her eyes closed before she could glimpse anything she didn't want to see. She trusted him to lead the way. He'd protect her. He was always such a gentleman, after all.

They continued on for a moment, then he nudged her to the right. "Careful," he warned her. "There's a...thing."

Something blurry and indistinguishable through her thick glasses, he meant. She nodded and pressed her body against him, making herself small and letting him steer her past whatever was there.

Then he stopped.

She thought for a second that they'd reached the end of the room and felt a faint spark of relief pass over her, but then he was kissing her again.

He'd reached the end of what he'd memorized. He needed another peek at the map, so to speak. That was all. And yet, she felt herself melting at his touch again. Her whole body shivered with pleasure.

Again, she drank the feelings up. It was so much better than the unease and tenseness that bombarded her senses from every direction. This was a *wonderful* sensation. She wanted it to go on and on. *Forever.*

It was a strange combination. That invasive anxiousness was still present, but it had begun to blend with the *other* emotion, turning into something weirdly intense…something almost *exciting.*

It reminded her of when they had sex in the cabana at the hotel, hidden behind nothing more than a flimsy flap of cloth with an entire resort full of people passing by close enough to hear what they were doing if they weren't careful to keep quiet. And it reminded her of all the times the two of them slipped away for a stealthy quickie during parties and other gatherings over the years, breathless moments in bathrooms and closets and bedrooms and even once in a cramped pantry. But it reminded her most of that time they did it in the back of her father's workshop, the *first* time they ever dared such a thing, way back before they started living together. It was exhilarating, the intensity of their desire, the fear of getting caught, the idea that they were being *so bad.* This was the same kind of rush. Her heart was racing. Her body was hot. A part of her wanted to yank him to a stop right now and throw herself at him.

But that would be foolish. If they should get caught up in the moment and expend all their sexual energy, they might find themselves spent and utterly at the mercy of the anxiety. And then what would happen to them?

If they died down here, she'd never get to feel like this again.

And yet, the feeling was so incredibly *wonderful.*

Again, he stopped without warning. This time, a soft moan of disappointment escaped her as he pulled away from her. She pressed her hand to her lips, surprised and embarrassed by the sound, but if he noticed, he didn't show it. He was already pulling her forward, making his way deeper into the maze of statues.

She needed to get ahold of herself. What were these feelings, anyway? Sure, those sneaky sort of sexual adventures were fun, but it wasn't as if she nursed a *fetish* for that sort of thing.

She didn't think…

"Watch out," he said, pulling her closer again and letting go of the glasses in order to reach out and shield her from the outstretched limb of another statue.

The feel of his body pressing against her was distracting. It sent a flurry of tingling sensations fluttering through her. Her knees felt a little weak.

Vaguely, she realized that it was because of the way their abilities worked. He was channeling all of his sexual energy into seeing the space around him, like the pervert taught him. But there were no people here to tune into, no outlet for her own sexual energy. It was building up. And something about the strange combination of sexuality and anxiety was heating her up in ways she never expected.

She tried to cast her thoughts out into the greater space around them, hoping to catch even a fleeting glimpse of someone in the surrounding passages, but there was no one. They were alone for as far as she could see.

Albert tugged on her arm, steering her to the left, then *farther* to the left, seemingly circling back around the way they came. The idea of going in circles seemed to bring back a spark of that deeply unpleasant anxiety, making her focus again on her husband and those weirdly sexy thoughts that were circling around in her head a moment ago.

That was, after all, a much nicer sort of feeling.

He gripped her arm and turned right, circling back the other way now. "Shouldn't be much farther," he promised.

She sure hoped not. She felt as if she'd been doing this for hours already. All of these emotions were exhausting!

Albert stopped.

She stood there, clinging to his arm. Automatically, she caught herself lifting her face toward him, anticipating another kiss.

But he didn't kiss her.

A strange and terrible feeling made itself known deep inside her somewhere, rapidly growing, filling her belly with a dreadful sort of hot and icy sensation.

"Albert?" she whispered, her voice trembling with a fresh wave of suffocating fear.

"I forgot..." he croaked in a strange sort of voice.

"What?" She opened her eyes as he turned to face her. The world around them was nothing more than hazy shades of gray...but *he* was turning red.

"...forgot...to watch for traps..."

Chapter 73

Wayne crept onward, his eyes and ears open for the slightest movement or sound, convinced that those damned bugs would eventually figure out where they disappeared to and come to finish the job.

He glanced down at Olivia. "Feel anything?"

"I definitely don't want to go back the way we came," she replied.

He nodded. That was good. He didn't want to go back there either. The longer he could go without having to deal with the scarecrow man's morbid bullshit, the better.

He aimed his light behind them again, making sure the path remained clear, watching for any glints of those fluttering razor wings. It would probably only take one fumbling its way into the hidden passage to tell its creepy master where they went. But so far, they remained alone in here.

This was a really long passage. How long had they been walking? He couldn't remember any others that just went on and on like this without branching off in multiple directions. But then again, they weren't even able to see *these* passages without Andrea's help, so maybe this part of the labyrinth was different.

"Still dark?" asked Olivia.

"Pitch," replied Andrea. She lifted her flashlight and aimed it at her own face, the lens hovering right in front of her nose, shining straight into her wide, blue eyes. "Nothing." Then she frowned and turned the flashlight back and forth. "Unless it's not on… I can't tell. Is it on?"

"It's on," Olivia assured her. She glanced at Wayne, a worried expression on her pretty face.

Again, Andrea pointed the light at herself. "Yeah, nothing."

It was odd seeing her eyes unresponsive like that, almost unnerving. Her pupils should have constricted all the way down at such a stimulus, but it was as if there were something invisible separating her from the flashlight. Was that absolute scientific proof that she wasn't making it up? But then again, he never *needed* any proof. If Andrea said she couldn't see, she couldn't see. She was no liar. She wasn't the kind of person to let her imagination run wild. And they both knew there were plenty of things in the world that were beyond explanation.

She lowered the light and continued onward, its beam aimed pointlessly at her feet.

For a moment, Wayne watched her as she walked, her bare toes illuminated in the light, streaks of pink skin peeking out from the crusted-on grime. He didn't like how rough she looked. All the hell she'd been through... He should've been there to help watch out for her. If he hadn't left the reception early that night, if he hadn't allowed his mother to bully him into being there so ridiculously early to help with her stupid party, would things have turned out differently?

Somehow he doubted it. They were at the mercy of the Keeper, after all, just like Albert always said. Mere puppets on strings, bending to his every whim.

...the Keeper of Secrets...

Yes. The Keeper of Secrets, indeed. He didn't care much for the fact that he apparently had a chokehold on their very lives and yet couldn't even be bothered to tell any of them what they were supposed to be doing here.

He frowned a little as these thoughts circled around inside his head. The Keeper of Secrets? Did someone call him that? Nadia, maybe? Or Sandy? Maeve? No... Sandy called him several things. The Keeper of Doors. The Keeper of Veils. The Keeper of the Dead. The Keeper of the Cycle. And Maeve even accused him of being the Keeper of False Promises, the Keeper of Lies. But no one called him the Keeper of Secrets. Where did he get that from?

He glanced down at Olivia, trying to remember if she'd said something while he was distracted, but she was looking at Andrea, still worrying over her.

Just a random thought, he supposed. He was getting tired. He could use a break. But he doubted he was going to get one any time soon.

Andrea stopped walking, her grimy face scrunched into a puzzled sort of squint.

"What's wrong?" asked Olivia.

"I'm not sure..." she replied. She tipped her head slowly to one side, those pretty blue eyes straining to see through the blinding murk.

"Is the murk breaking up?" he wondered.

"No. It's still completely dark."

"Oh..."

She shook her head. "I don't..." She let go of Olivia's hand and pointed at the ceiling several yards ahead of them, out near the edge of the reach of their lights. "Is something there?"

He and Olivia exchanged an uncertain look, then he let go of her arm and crept forward, pushing his light farther into the tunnel. "Where?" he asked. "How far?"

"I can't really tell. Sorry."

"It's fine." He continued forward a few steps more, but nothing appeared out of the gloom. There was only the same blank gray stone. "I'm not seeing anything." He glanced back at her. "What do *you* see?"

"I can't..." She squeezed her eyes closed and shook her head again. "I'm not sure. Maybe nothing. My imagination."

But he wasn't so quick to dismiss anything in one of the sentinels' temples. Andrea might be blinded by the murk, but she could see things no one else could.

"It's weird being blind," she sighed.

"I'm sure it is," Olivia assured her, taking her hand again.

Wayne crept forward a few more steps, pushing back the darkness, examining every surface. "Am I getting close to it?"

"How should *I* know?"

He scratched at the back of his head, embarrassed. "Right. You can't see me. My bad."

Andrea was moving toward him now, her dirty face scrunched up, focusing hard on whatever it was she was...well, not *seeing*, he supposed... Sensing, maybe? Those bright blue eyes seemed to be fixed on a point somewhere just above his head, but when he scanned the space up there he could still see nothing.

"Can you describe it?" he asked.

"Not really, no. I'm not sure *what* it is." Then she stopped and blinked, a puzzled look washing over her. "Oh. It's gone."

"Gone?" asked Olivia.

Again, Wayne swept his light back and forth, searching for anything that wasn't smooth, hard stone.

"It's not there anymore," said Andrea. "Weird."

He didn't like it. Why would something be there and then just disappear? Was something in that all-consuming darkness she called the murk *alive*?

She turned all the way around, scanning her mysterious surroundings, searching for whatever it was that just vanished from her view. "Maybe I *was* just imagining it."

But she didn't believe that any more than he did, he knew. There was something in the murk with her, something she sensed even without being able to see through that otherworldly darkness.

Olivia took her arm again and started forward. "Let's just keep going."

She nodded. "Yeah. Okay."

Yes. Keep going. What other choice did they have? Besides going back the way they came, which definitely wasn't an option. He was starting to feel like a steer being herded into the slaughterhouse. Just where the hell were they going?

He reached out as they approached and linked arms with Olivia again, then continued forward, his eyes peeled for any sign of danger.

He was starting to get a really bad feeling about this haunted passage.

Chapter 74

Violet was helpless against the cold current that swept her along. She was in an underwater passage, unyielding stone on all sides, not a breath of air to be found and far too weak to swim against it.

She was going to drown!

And yet she'd barely had time to come to this realization when the current shifted and she was suddenly yanked downward, into a great, shadowy chamber.

She tried to swim up, but there were no air pockets to be found. Her flailing hands found only unyielding stone. She was trapped.

About twenty feet below her, the floor was being illuminated by her dropped flashlight. She swam down toward it, the pressure building uncomfortably in her ears.

It was as she snatched it off the floor that she realized she was in the same chamber the other one showed her. It was filled with water now, but the six sentinels were exactly as she remembered them, each one guarding a separate passage.

(*This one…*)

Right. The one she found her focus turned to. The one looking *up*. That must be the passage leading out of this deathtrap.

She swam past the skyward-staring sentinel, her lungs aching for air. How far was she going to have to swim? Could she really hold her breath that long? It was hard to kick in these boots. It was making this much harder.

The passage twisted to the right, then the left. The pressure in her chest grew worse.

She didn't want to die in a place like this. That didn't seem fair after all she'd been through, after surviving the not-Jeremy and the not-Everett, after escaping those storm drafts and those awful hounds. And yet there seemed to be no end to this underwater passage! How much farther could it be?

Her lungs were screaming at her. Her chest was hitching, desperate for a breath.

Somebody help me! she cried out in her mind, knowing damned well that there was no one to come to her aid, no one who would ever even be able to find her body. She was going to rot in this tunnel forever.

Something long and hairy shot past her, a flash of black in the darting flashlight beam, startling a precious belch of air from her already starved lungs.

She wasn't alone down here!

This was getting worse by the second. Was she going to drown first? Or would she last just long enough to experience being eaten alive?

The passage was growing narrower, she realized. The floor here was littered with what looked like sand and stones and swirling clouds of silt and dust.

What if the exit was blocked?

And yet as she struggled onward, the ceiling curved upward.

Her head pounding, the world dimming all around her, she swam up into a much larger open space.

Up...

Up...

Up...

Was there even a way out in here? Would she just swim and swim and swim until she blacked out? Or would she strike nothing more than a hard stone surface, the final nail in her coffin, one last unfair knife in the back from the universe before suffering the agony of drowning?

But then, miraculously, she broke the surface.

That was *way* too close for comfort!

Gasping and kicking, she squeezed her eyes closed against the aching in her chest and lungs. That was *awful*, like being slowly crushed under a pile of rocks. And she was *still* struggling to catch her breath while treading water. She was exhausted. She just wanted to lie down somewhere, but there was nothing here *except* water. It went on as far as her light would reach in every direction.

Where was she? Was this somewhere anyone was actually supposed to go? Who in their right mind would've gone through that on purpose? That red glow in the water...it felt as if something attacked her.

And yet, those sentinel statues she found down there... What other purpose could they have served but to point her to safety?

God, this was confusing!

Where did she even go from here? She shined her light back and forth, then up toward the ceiling, but there was nothing to be seen. Only darkness loomed at the end of the beam.

Would she eventually be doomed to drown after all?

And what about *below* her?

She plunged the light under the water and swept it around, searching the shadowy depths beneath her kicking feet. She saw at least one of those hairy creatures zip past her in her panic. How much danger was she in down here? Had she managed not to drown only to end up as something's dinner? The very thought of unseen things swimming around below her made her skin crawl. What horrors might a place like this keep hidden in flooded chambers like these? Her mind flashed through a dozen horrifying possibilities, from alligators and snakes to electric eels and giant lampreys. These thoughts were more than enough to make her eager to get out of the water, but which way did she even start swimming? The other one showed her which path would lead her to safety, but not what to do once she was here.

And she still didn't seem to be talking to her.

(*I'm limited in how much I can do in your time.*)

Right… So it was up to her to find her own way back to dry land, she supposed.

Again, she swung her light back and forth. Again, there was nothing to see, not so much as a glimmer in the gloom.

She could be treading water for a while. And these boots were way to heavy. They were dragging her down, making her exert more energy than she could spare. She took a deep breath, then curled herself up and untied one of them. She could tie them together and sling them over her shoulder like a purse, she thought.

But when she came back up for air, she found that the chamber was bathed in a very familiar bloody glow.

She turned around, startled, to see the glowing something moving toward her from the bottom of the chamber.

"Oh shit…" she gasped, her heart leaping with fresh fear.

She took another breath, then plunged back into the water and untied her other boot.

There was no time to think about it. She wrenched her foot free of one, then the other, and abandoned them to the depths as she fled across the water from the swelling red glow.

She seriously couldn't seem to catch a break…

Chapter 75

Everett didn't remember the paper hallway being this long the first time.

He didn't count the doors as he passed to make sure there were still ninety-six of them, so maybe he was mistaken, maybe this sudden feeling of crippling panic was distorting his perception, but it certainly felt like a lot more than that.

Somewhere behind him, he heard the ominous ding of an elevator arriving.

It didn't ding before, when *he* was riding it. There was no good reason for it to ding now. Except, he supposed, for the terrifying effect of it. It was like hearing a knock at the door in the middle of nowhere, where no one had any right to be.

Even the loudness of it was wrong. There should be dozens of drawn doors between him and the elevator by now, so why did it sound like it was right behind him? He looked back, half-expecting to see the elevator doors sliding open right there, but there was only empty hallway stretching out behind him, just like ahead.

It was her. The Priestess of Ruin. The very name gave him a shiver. Who was she? *What* was she? And what did she want with him?

Ahead of him, he could finally see the end of the hallway. The door was still there. It still stood open. (Or...as open as a drawn-on door could be? It was just a door*way*, really, with a doorframe drawn around it and an open door drawn beside it.) He picked up his pace, eager to be on the other side of it before whatever was in the elevator stepped out and came after him.

Except he supposed it had already been more than long enough for those doors to open. Was the Priestess of Ruin already rushing after him? Could she be catching up to him already? Was she right behind him?

He glanced back, his heart leaping with frightened certainty. But there was nothing more than the same empty hallway with its many useless drawings.

He turned his attention forward as he neared the end of the hallway. Only a little farther... A few more seconds...

He rushed through the door and back into the foyer.

Except, this wasn't the foyer. Everything had changed again.

He was now standing in a library.

Sort of. It was just an empty white space, just like every other room, but there were drawings everywhere in this one. There were floor-to-ceiling bookshelves on all four walls, filled with hundreds of scribbled book spines. There was a curtained window on two walls and a fireplace on the third. A simple, round light fixture was sketched in the middle of the ceiling, directly above a large, round table and chairs drawn on the floor.

Was *he* creating these rooms? Because he was fairly sure that what he needed right now wasn't a study session. He needed the fastest exit possible. He needed the teleporter room on the USS Enterprise.

(On second thought, atomizing himself was probably a bad idea. He might not be able to put himself back together again.)

A loud bang startled him and he twirled around to find that the door leading back was suddenly closed.

"How do you slam a *drawing?*" he asked, genuinely curious.

This wasn't good. He was fairly sure he didn't do that. Someone was taking control from him.

There was a sudden whooshing sound and he turned to find that a fire had ignited in the fireplace. That was new. Very cozy.

(Not good.)

He frowned. Not good?

(Very bad.)

He looked down at Alice. These were *her* thoughts popping into his head. "Why? Because the chimney's just a drawing?" Was he going to start choking on smoke soon? Was there a danger of carbon monoxide poisoning? Because that would be a lousy way to go after everything he'd been through.

When he looked up, he realized that the fire was spreading up the wall around the mantle.

"Oh right…" he said, feeling stupid. "Because this whole place is made of paper."

Chapter 76

Keith was dreaming about his mother again.

He was talking to her on his cell phone, telling her that he wouldn't be home for a while yet. He had some things to do, though he couldn't quite remember what those things were. Or why anything would be important enough to keep him from seeing her again. He missed her so much.

"You're going to do great," she told him. "I know it."

He smiled. She always had so much faith in him, even when he wasn't sure he deserved it.

He sat there, alone on a wooden bench, staring out at a vast and mysterious darkness laid out before him, wondering what was going to happen next.

He was so far from home.

"I love you," she said.

He felt his heart catch in his throat at these words. Tears welled up in his eyes. "Love you too."

Then the darkness was washed away by blinding pain.

He blinked up at a gloomy stone passageway.

"Keith!" gasped Nicole.

Before he could quite remember where he was, she was kissing him again. Everything was so confusing. He kept swinging back and forth between dreams and reality. It was getting difficult to tell them apart. The pain told him this was real, but these kisses were supposed to have stayed in the past. What was real and what was fantasy? Why was the world so confounding?

"It's okay," she informed him, pulling away. "Look. Gina's here. She found us."

He opened his eyes and saw that Gina was indeed there. There was something black smeared across her face and on her shirt, but it was her. She was real. She'd made her way back to them after all this time.

She took his hand and squeezed it. She had such small hands. So dainty. So soft. So *real.*

But...she looked so sad...

"She can help," said Nicole, her voice practically prickling with desperate hope. Her face was dirty now, too. When did that happen? Did he miss something? "We can get you out of here together."

Gina nodded. She didn't speak. Her lips were pressed tight, as if she were holding back something. Tears, perhaps. Or grim honesty.

She understood it as well as he did.

"Brandy and Albert!" exclaimed Nicole, looking up at her, her expression wild.

She shook her head. "I... We were separated. I...don't know where they are."

"But...they're still *here*! Somewhere! Right?"

She nodded.

"They know actual *magic* now! Like *real* fucking *magic*! You said you felt it yourself right before they appeared back on the road. If we can just *find* them, maybe they can fix him up."

"It's...possible, I guess..." But her eyes told another story. They darkened with uncertainty and hesitation, afraid to grasp at false hope. "Maybe..."

"And you can sense things all around us," she went on. "You can find them, can't you?"

"It's not really that easy," she replied in a voice so quiet and small that he barely heard her.

A fresh wave of pain washed over him. He closed his eyes and clenched his jaw and waited for it to pass. The pain was reality. Erin and Amber and Ramona and his mother belonged to the dreams. But sometimes he felt this pain inside the dreams as well. And he'd glimpsed Erin in the waking world, blurring the lines between the two.

Where the hell did *magic* of all things come from?

Not that it mattered, he supposed.

Again, the pain ebbed. Again he relaxed.

"Remember the life you chose," whispered Erin.

The life he chose? Somewhere in the depths of his memory, something glinted. A spark of reflected light flashing off a golden wedding band.

(*You must let yourself be swallowed by the dream. Let it take you where it will.*)

An entire lifetime enveloped in the fragile bubble of a dream. Memories. Family. Photographs of children on the walls. Good times and hard ones. Tears and laughter.

(*You'll find what you need in the depths of the reality your mind weaves.*)

What he needed...

But how could he have found anything in a dream full of such slippery memories. He couldn't even remember the faces he loved so dearly in that false life!

"The Keeper doesn't make mistakes," reasoned Nicole. Her voice was trembling. She was barely holding back tears now. "Your goddess said so, remember? Everything that happens is part of his stupid fucking plan."

Gina nodded, but she couldn't seem to meet her gaze. "The labyrinth is too big," she whispered. "I can't see them from here."

Nicole sucked in a shaky breath. "We just have to try…" she said in a pitiful squeak of a voice. "We can't…we can't *not try*…"

"It's okay," said Keith, squeezing her hand. "I don't think magic is gonna fix this."

"We have to do *something!*" she cried.

Another wave of pain washed over him, but he forced it back down and managed to smile for her. "No. You don't. This is as far as I'm going. We all know it."

"You don't know what you're talking about!" Tears were streaming down her face again. The sight of her like that was so strangely heartbreaking. Why would she cry for him? It was hard enough to tell dreams from reality without her being so…

He sighed and closed his eyes.

…so like she *used to be.*

"I love you," she cried. "I always did. I was just too stupid to know what I wanted. I'm so sorry."

"Nik…"

"You can't leave me as soon as I figure it out!"

He smiled up at her. She really did come back to him, just like his mother always said she would.

How utterly unfair that it had to wait until now to happen.

Nicole sniffed back her tears and clutched his hand tighter. "We can still get through this," she insisted.

"No, Nik," he sighed. He opened his eyes and looked up at her. "I'm just the boat captain, remember? I'm supposed to go down with the ship."

She shook her head. "Don't say stupid shit," she told him in a voice that carried none of her usual spite. "You left the boat at that dock forever ago."

He chuckled a little at this.

"I don't want to lose you again," she whimpered. "Not before I get a chance to take it all back."

"It's okay," he assured her.

"No, it's not! I was so awful to you!"

"There's a reason for everything."

"Not for *this*," she moaned.

"There is," he insisted. He recalled his first conversation with Erin and said, "We all have our jobs that the Keeper trusted to us."

"Fuck the Keeper!" she spat. "I don't care about him or his fucking jobs!"

But he smiled patiently up at her. "I know. But trust me. He doesn't make mistakes."

She shook her head, her beautiful face pinched into an expression of agonizing sadness. She didn't accept it. She wouldn't. Not now. Maybe not anytime soon. But someday she'd understand. He was sure of it.

Another wave of pain washed over him and he closed his eyes and bore it until it eased again. Then he looked up at Gina. "She's a handful, this one," he told her. "A real pain in the ass sometimes. But do me a favor and look after her will you?"

She fought back her tears and nodded. "I'll try," she replied in a voice that barely reached him.

"She's really important to me..." he said, closing his eyes again.

"Keith..." wept Nicole.

"I can't protect her anymore... But I know she'll be safe with you. You're amazing."

Gina couldn't seem to make herself speak, so she merely nodded again.

A great, blubbering sob escaped Nicole. "No... Don't talk like that! Did you forget where we are? It's the Wood out there! Nothing dead ever leaves the Wood."

"It's gonna be okay," he whispered.

She shook her head and sniffled. "It won't..."

"It will. I promise it will."

She shook her head. She didn't believe him. And he didn't blame her. She was right, after all. It was the Wood out there. It was the Denselands. They were unimaginably far from home. And they were inside the Impassible Wall, a barrier that even the dead couldn't cross.

There was no way home for him.

And yet, somehow he understood that it really would be okay.

He opened his eyes again and stared up at her. "I remember now..." All those lost memories were flowing back to him. The dream that he couldn't hold onto. The faces he couldn't remember. "It was you..."

"What?"

Bit by bit, it all came flowing back to him. An entire lifetime of love and happiness, the family he'd never have the chance to make. A precious gift from the sentinel spirits. A long and cherished life of joy with any woman he picked.

"I chose *you*..." he sighed as the pain melted away for the last time and peaceful sleep enveloped him at last.

Chapter 77

"*Oh god!*" gasped Brandy. "*No! No, no, no!*"

Albert sank to his knees, his mind a raging storm of churning thoughts and invasive emotions. What had he done? How bad was it?

"Don't move too much! Let me see!" She wrenched the flashlight from his hand and fumbled with it. "You'll be okay!"

He hated the sharp edge of panic he heard in her voice. He was frightening her. He needed to shake it off and get back on his feet. It was probably fine. In fact, it probably wasn't even real. It was like that attack in the fear room. A hallucination. An illusion. It didn't even *feel* quite real. The pain was sharp and deep. It was like a dreadful aching radiating from way down inside him, but it didn't hurt as much as it *should* hurt if he were *really* in any danger. Right?

But the strangled sob that escaped Brandy when she leaned close enough to see the wound without her glasses was proof enough that this was no trick.

"*What happened?*" she gasped.

It was a good question. He lifted his head and looked up through the haze of her glasses. He could barely see it there. A thin curl of gray stone descending from the ceiling like some monstrous stinger.

He couldn't believe he let himself be so careless! It was so *stupid!* He walked right into it, his attention focused entirely on the narrow path that wove through the crowded forest of stone figures, oblivious of the dangers he *knew* were likely to be in here.

He just…*forgot*…

And it was no flesh wound. It buried itself in his lower chest, just beneath his sternum. He didn't know how deep the injury was, but he could feel blood flowing down his belly. What organs were located there? It didn't hit his heart or he was pretty sure he'd already be dead. But there were plenty of other vitals in there. Would he know immediately if he punctured a lung? What would it feel like if he was stabbed in the liver? Was he going to start coughing up blood?

What was going to happen to him down here in this darkness where no help could ever hope to find him?

"Be still," whimpered Brandy. "Don't move. Everything's going to be okay."

But it didn't sound okay. It sounded *bad*. Her voice quivered with panic.

She reached up and took her glasses back so she could see better and as she did he saw that her fingers were covered in blood.

Twelve will go... he recalled the creepy old cat lady telling them, *...fated to open way to second doorway. Twelve to do Keeper's bidding...but only ten to return.*

Was *he* one of the unfortunate two all along? Was this always how it was going to happen?

He felt so weak...so helpless...so *useless*... He was losing a lot of blood, he realized. He felt woozy. He wouldn't last long like this.

"Don't you *dare* pass out on me!" wept Brandy.

But he wasn't sure how to stop it from happening. He was only human. And humans could be such fragile things sometimes, all soft and squishy inside, susceptible to all sorts of devastating trauma...

"Don't you dare," she said again, her voice broken beneath the force of a great, shuddering sob.

No. He didn't want it to end like this. He didn't want to leave her. The very thought broke his heart. But he knew he wasn't strong enough to hold on forever. He could already feel himself fading. A cold and dreadful darkness was closing in around him.

He'd really fucked up this time...

"It doesn't end like this," Brandy seemed to decide. She sat up straight and met his sleepy gaze. "The pervert's book! Give it to me!"

Shanzer's spellbook...

(*Magic can open doors that can't be unlocked.*)

He felt his heart leap at the thought. If the old creep knew as much as he claimed to, then maybe he foresaw something just like this happening. Maybe magic would provide an answer in this otherwise hopeless moment.

She was already reaching around him, fumbling to remove the book from his pocket. The motion sent agonizing jolts of pain through his wound, but he clenched his teeth and bore it.

She pulled it free and sat up. "It has to be in there." She wiped the tears from her face with the back of her hand and then opened the book and shined the flashlight down at it. "There has to be *something*."

Magic... The word still sounded so...*silly*. It was a storybook word. A *children's* word. And yet magic transported them both to Nicole's side back in those black and hopeless Denselands. Why *couldn't* it heal a mortal wound?

"Where is it?" she growled, wiping at her eyes again. She was practically slapping at the pages, as if taking out all her frustration on them. He wanted to tell her to be careful, but he recalled pulling it from his soggy shorts pocket after that harrowing ride through the city's storm channels and finding it still bone dry. He was fairly sure that book was perfectly capable of taking care of itself. "It has to be in here somewhere! It *has* to!"

"She's right. It *is* in there."

Who said that?

He looked up at the statues looming over him. A hard wave of sickly dread washed over him at the sight. In his shock, he'd forgotten where he was, what they could do. And he'd forgotten that he was no longer protected by Brandy's glasses.

Visions of men and women in shades of gray surrounded him, just like in the sex room, but the sight was nothing like those. These people weren't naked. They weren't engaged in pornographic activities. Each of these stone figures were bathed in suffocating apprehension and unease. It wafted from the stone like a poisonous gas, setting his nerves aflame and twisting his stomach into a steaming knot.

He found himself staring at a fat, balding man with a strangely trimmed beard standing near him, dressed in a pair of baggy pants and sandals, his enormous belly hanging in front of him. He had a coldly sinister kind of sneer on his face, the kind of expression that was most at home on the loathsomely self-serving. There was power in those stone eyes. Authority. Invincibility. He was the kind of man who made people feel weak and helpless, the kind of man who made sure people *were* weak and helpless. He lorded over everyone, took whatever he wanted, stepped on whoever he pleased...and disposed of people as easily as garbage.

And there was nothing Albert could do about it. He was meaningless in comparison, a mere worm. He closed his eyes against the stifling feeling, but in the brief moment that he looked upon that awful man's face, he watched everything he cared about be taken away from him. His money. His reputation. His property. His home. His wife. His children. And when he had nothing else left to give...there was always his miserable *life*...

A shudder of terrible anticipation shot through him, sending excruciating jolts through his wound, reminding him of the real danger he was facing.

And yet, was there any difference? That evil man who he somehow knew to have once lived a life he spent callously destroying and throwing away lives was just as cruel and dismissively murderous as the stone spike from which his blood still dripped. In the end, it would be no different.

Because he was going to die here in this awful room. He was suddenly very certain of this. He was never going to see the sunlight again. Or his parents. Or his little niece. Or his friends. Or his home.

Fear was rapidly swallowing him, overwhelming him, *drowning* him.

And yet even now he found himself pondering the differences between fear and anxiety. This room and the fear room were two completely different places. Didn't that mean that they were fundamentally different emotions? He might be literally staring death in the face right now. That was far different from being under the thumb of some evil, over-privileged tyrant. Anxiety was a fear of things to come, not of things right in front of you.

But there was a lot of overlap between *these* two emotions. He wasn't sure he could use one to control the other.

"Is this it?" gasped Brandy, lifting the book closer to her face, reading.

"That's the one," said the voice in the statues.

He opened his eyes again, this time forcing himself to focus on Brandy. "Who's there?" he breathed. It was a woman's voice. Soft and young. And was it familiar? It was hard to concentrate in this state.

Brandy didn't seem to hear him. She was staring intensely at the book, the bridge of her nose crinkled in concentration as she struggled to comprehend whatever strange words were written there. "Seriously? 'A man's coursing blood powers both his heart and his cock, but while his heart defines him as alive, his cock allows him to experience life.' What the fuck is *wrong* with that man? Why is everything so fucking *vulgar* with him?"

"Master is a disgusting pig."

Master? Was that Dolly? Was she here somewhere? How was that possible?

"Ugh!" growled Brandy, wiping at her leaking eyes. "I don't have *time* for this shit!"

Something moved in the darkness behind her.

He blinked hard, trying to clear his vision, and watched as one of the many statues turned and stepped toward them.

It was her, from her long, sleek pigtails to her thigh-high, laced boots. She was wearing a poofy sort of short dress with long sleeves and a corset. And yet every part of her, from her pale skin to her clothing, had for some reason turned to cold, gray stone.

"But master *always* knows what's best."

Brandy shook her head. "It says, 'Emotional magic can be as effective as stitches.' This has to be it!"

"That's the one," said Dolly as she strolled toward him.

Could Brandy not hear her speaking? Was he hallucinating? Was she still inside his head, like in that strange little room Shanzer locked them in to protect him from the psychic predator?

"Just follow those directions," said Dolly, "and you can fix him right up, even if he's on the brink of death."

"Hold on," said Brandy as she focused on the passage in the book, clearly unaware that they weren't alone in this room. "I've got this. Just…hang in there a little longer."

The stone Dolly walked right up behind her and leaned over them, her colorless, yet strangely gleaming eyes focused on him, their gazes locked. She looked like she was about to kiss him. But she didn't kiss him. Instead, she stuck her lower lip out at him in an exaggerated pout. "What a shame, though…" She reached down with one long, stone fingernail and tapped the flashlight in Brandy's hand. "…that your only light is broken."

Just like that, the flashlight gave a loud pop and went dark.

His heart plummeted in his chest as Brandy's horrorstruck scream echoed through the labyrinth around them.

Chapter 78

Andrea felt as if she were going crazy. It was pitch black in this corridor. It was completely filled with murk, rendering her utterly blind. And yet she was *definitely* seeing things. It was like the way her eyes adjusted to the dark when she turned her lamp off for the night. At first it was completely black, but slowly all those subtle shadows separated and took form. Except her eyes weren't merely adjusting to the murk. She still couldn't see Olivia and Wayne walking right beside her. And the things taking shape in this gloom had nothing to do with the simple passageway they were walking in.

She squinted at one ahead of them, trying to decide if it was only immaterial shadows or if the darkness was taking form again, congregating into another of those creepy, grasping clumps or even swelling into one of those squirming, growling things with the bottomless spiraling abyss of teeth.

But as she drew closer, it didn't look precisely like either of those things. Was this something different? Some brand-new horror to scare her out of her wits?

"What's wrong?" worried Wayne.

She didn't even realize that she'd slowed down. She was no longer walking, but rather creeping, practically tiptoeing toward the mysterious clump of darkness that felt more and more wrong the closer she got to it. And for that matter, what kind of face might she have been making in that moment of obliviousness? She probably looked like a weirdo. "Sorry," she said, picking up her pace again and trying her best to look normal. "Just trying to decide if I'm seeing something in the murk or just imagining things."

"Let's *hope* you're imagining things but assume everything's real," decided Olivia.

"Yeah," agreed Wayne. "That's probably smart."

It was weird. Most of those vague shapes were *beyond* these walls, in other spaces.

And they weren't in the shape of anything she'd seen elsewhere in the labyrinth. They didn't look like pillars or statues or even the things she saw back in that weird nature preserve place they showed her.

This was something entirely different, something she was fairly sure her poor, human brain simply couldn't understand.

(*Your living brain is constrained by the senses you use to perceive the world around you. Whatever it is you think you're seeing and hearing is just your mind doing its best to tell you what's there.*)

That was what Erin told her anyway. But this felt different from the other murk stuff.

For one thing, all of these mysterious shapes were *moving*.

She couldn't quite *see* them moving. They sort of faded in and out, almost as if passing behind something. Did being robbed of her sight allow her faint glimpses of the murk in the surrounding passageways?

More like a distortion in size between the two planes.

She stopped walking, surprised. "Erin?"

"Erin?" gasped Olivia. "She's *here*?" She tightened her grip on Andrea's arm. And from the sound of his shuffling feet, she was guessing that she pulled Wayne closer, too.

"What's happening?" asked Wayne.

But Andrea didn't reply. She stood there, silent, her blind eyes wide and alert. "No... Wait."

"What's wrong?" whispered Olivia.

That wasn't a voice in her *ear*. It was in her *head*. "You're not Erin."

This was the other one again. The impostor. The Priestess of Ruin.

You're getting good at this, she laughed, her voice switching from Erin's to Stella's midsentence.

"What's happening?" asked Wayne.

"It's her."

"Her?" asked Olivia. "You mean the one you mentioned? The one you called a princess or something?"

"The Priestess of Ruin," she sighed. "Yeah. Her."

You're not blabbing all our secrets are you?

Olivia's grip tightened even more, her nails digging into her arms. "What does she want?" she whispered.

It was a good question. What *did* she want? Why was she poking around in *her* head? What could she possibly want from her?

I thought I was boring you, she thought at the obnoxious intruder in her head.

You were. So I left to see if anything more interesting was going on. You should see what kinds of messes your friends are getting themselves into.

"What are you talking about?"

Wouldn't you like to know?

"What's she saying?" asked Wayne.

"She's being a total bitch," she grumbled.

Rude.

You expect me to be nice? *You're a* literal *monster.*

Ouch. *You really know how to hurt a girl's feelings.*

You're not a girl.

Of course I am. Most of the time.

"Is she the one who sent the scarecrow man after us?" demanded Wayne. "Is she the reason all that shit happened in Gutler's Weep?"

"Did you?" pressed Andrea.

Oh, sweetie, I've done so much worse than that. You wouldn't believe all the trouble I've been causing.

"What did you do?"

I'd love to tell you all about it, but if I were you, I'd pay attention to my surroundings.

"What?" She turned and blinked into the darkness of the murk.

"What's happening now?" squeaked Olivia. "What's she saying?"

You've wandered off the map. Those things you're starting to see aren't kittens and puppies. There are things hidden deeper in the murk. Things you can't imagine in your worst nightmares. Things that don't like being seen.

There were more of those mysterious shapes looming in the deeper darkness now, things that were somehow even darker than the absolute darkness of the murk.

Olivia squeezed her arm. "Andrea?"

"She's trying to scare me," she explained. "Just keep walking."

"Are we okay?" she pressed. "Should we turn back?"

And go back into that swarm of razor bugs? "No," she replied. "Just keep going. The murk can't go on forever."

Can't it? Asked the impostor.

Shut up! she thought at her. She gripped Olivia's arm and picked up her pace.

All around her, those half-imagined shapes phased in and out of the surrounding darkness, dotting the vast space surrounding them. She would have been convinced that they'd exited the passageway and were crossing a cavernous chamber of some sort except that she was still dragging her knuckles along the smooth stone of the wall.

There was a shadow somewhere above them, much higher than the ceiling of any mere passage. It loomed up there, fifty or sixty feet overhead, as big as a pickup truck, but crawling on a strange, wriggling tangle of what looked like long, thin legs.

She kept her focus on it until they were out from under it again, then held her attention on it, convinced that it would drop down and start scurrying after them as soon as she stopped watching it.

But still nothing attacked them.

She wanted to believe that Impostor Stella was lying, that these deeper shadows were harmless. That *was* what she did, after all. She lied. And yet, she barely had time to embrace this meager bit of optimism when something blossomed into view unnervingly close to her, just inches from the hand she was sliding along the wall.

It was about seven feet tall, even hunched over as it was. It had a roughly humanoid silhouette, and yet there was nothing human about it. There were things moving within that shadowy form that she couldn't understand, things that wriggled and squirmed and pulsated in grotesque and unnatural ways.

She snatched her hand from the wall and crowded closer to Olivia as she passed it, her blind eyes fixed on it as she moved along, convinced it would try to lash out and grab her.

But it only stood there, an increasingly horrible mass of darkness within darkness.

Was it only her imagination, or did she hear it moan at her as she walked away?

"Something's starting to feel really wrong," said Olivia.

"Wrong how?" asked Wayne. Even his voice was tense. He was on edge and it was no wonder. She'd just told them that the Priestess of Ruin, of all the horrible things they could deal with, was here in this corridor with them, close enough to whisper into her ear.

"I don't know," replied Olivia. She sounded breathless. She stopped walking and turned to look back, her grip tightening on Andrea's arm. "My heart's racing. It feels like it's going to jump right out of my chest. I think something's going to happen."

Wayne cursed and pulled her closer. She could hear him moving, swinging his light back and forth, trying to see whatever was in here with them. It was bizarre, knowing that they could only see in two directions while there seemed to be an entire murk-filled chamber all around her.

She turned and looked back at the hulking form that she'd just walked past, convinced that it must be following her, that it would already be reaching out for her with those strange, wriggling things deep inside its shadowy form, but it had vanished back into the murk.

"Should we turn back?" asked Wayne. "Does back feel better? Those bugs could have moved on by now. We might be able to sneak back the way we came."

"I don't know," squeaked Olivia. She was breathing hard now, a panic welling up in her as she struggled to understand what she was feeling.

Andrea was still looking back the way they came, still searching for that hulking shape, but it was gone. Other things were creeping around out there, fading in and out of her shadowy view in that eerie, slow-motion sort of way that they moved, but none of them were close enough to be of any immediate threat to them.

She turned and looked forward, instead.

Something was there. Directly in front of them, as if standing in the passageway with them.

This one was different. It was the same sort of dark-on-dark shadowy shape, but somehow it stood out more than the others did. She couldn't explain it, exactly. Her mind wasn't sure how to perceive it. But it sort of...shimmered, maybe? Except with darkness instead of light?

It was such a bizarre sensation that it made her feel dizzy just trying to look at it.

She squeezed her eyes shut against a wave of vertigo.

"Which way?" hissed Wayne, panic welling up in him.

"I don't know!" squealed Olivia. "I can't—"

Wayne let out a startled grunt and Andrea heard something hit the floor and then roll behind them.

His flashlight?

"What the hell was that?" he gasped, his voice receding as he turned to grab it.

Olivia cried out as she hurried to pull him back. In the process she let go of Andrea's arm.

She found herself standing alone in the unnatural darkness, blind yet somehow staring at that weird, shimmering darkness that was suddenly much closer than it was before.

"Felt like something slapped it out of my hand."

Somewhere in her head, she heard Stella's obnoxious laugh.

"That was weird..." said Wayne.

Why did it sound like he was farther away than he was before?

Not taking her eyes off the darkling shadowy, she reached backward, her hand searching for Olivia.

"Something's not right," she gasped from somewhere farther behind her. Were they moving away from her? What was happening? "We shouldn't have come this way."

Wouldn't have mattered, said the impostor.

Was she trying to separate them? She began backing away from the shadow, her hand still reaching out for her friends, not daring to take her eyes off it.

What *was* that thing? Why did it appear different than the others? What were they dealing with here? And how did they defend themselves from it?

But strangely, she wasn't moving away from it. With each step backward she took, she seemed to instead be getting *closer.*

It was disorienting. She stumbled a little as she struggled to process the bizarre sensation. What was happening right now? It made no sense.

"You guys..." she called, but her voice came out in a terrified croak, too soft to be heard.

No wonder Olivia's danger senses were going off. There was something here. Something neither she nor Wayne could see. And something she couldn't possibly understand. Something hiding in the murk, just waiting for them.

Just waiting for *her.*

Gonna get ya, sang the impostor.

She never tore her eyes off the darkly shimmering shape, and yet it was suddenly right in front of her, an empty, featureless mask of pure darkness staring right back at her, into her very soul.

This wasn't the murk, she finally realized. This was something different, something *ancient,* something that stirred fears deep inside her like long-buried memories of terrible nightmares.

It was *her.*

The impostor.

The Priestess of Ruin, herself.

She took another step back, a scream boiling up from deep inside her.

"We have to get out of here," gasped Olivia. "*Now.*"

Andrea didn't have time for her scream to escape her lips. In an instant, it had enveloped her.

Then *everything* was darkness and murk.

Chapter 79

"We have to get out of here," gasped Olivia. "*Now.*"

But when she reached back to take Andrea's hand, it wasn't there. She turned to see what was the matter, but she was gone. It was only the two of them.

"Andrea?"

"Where'd...?" sputtered Wayne.

She turned around, swinging her light both ways, her heart leaping. Then she rushed back the way they came. "Andrea!"

"Wait!" shouted Wayne, hurrying after her.

"Where'd she go?"

"I don't know!"

"Andrea!"

"Don't yell!"

"*Andrea!*"

She stopped running, then turned and looked back the other way. It made no sense. She was *right here*. Only a *second* ago. She didn't have *time* to have gone anywhere. There wasn't even any sign of her flashlight. What could've happened to her?

Wayne grabbed her arm, determined to hold onto her lest *she* be swept away in the darkness too. "Did she find another hidden passage?" he wondered.

She'd thought of that, too. It was a reasonable theory. It was the *only* thing that made any sense. She *could* do such a thing, after all. But of course, if that were all that had happened, she would've come back out when they called for her. At the very least, she would've answered them when they shouted for her. She certainly wouldn't have just *left*.

Had something happened to her? Did something in that creepy, unseen murk attack her?

She reached out and felt at the wall next to her, confirming that it was solid and not some kind of bizarre illusion.

"*Andrea!*" she shouted.

Wayne reached around her, pulling her closer, protecting her as they crept forward together, their lights pushing back the empty darkness.

She was terrified that the gloom was going to part and reveal a lifeless form lying on the cold floor, but step after step revealed nothing more than the same endless stone. "She can't be on her own right now," she groaned.

"I know."

"She can't *see* anything!"

"I know. We'll find her."

"Why does this keep happening?" She could feel fresh tears streaming down her cheeks. First Everett, then Keith and Corey. Now Andrea, too? Why did this place keep tearing people away from her?

But of course Wayne didn't have the answer. Nor did she expect him to. It was just the way it kept happening. It was as if the Keeper and his insane design *wanted* them to be alone in this awful darkness.

He squeezed her tighter against him. "It's okay. She's fine. I'm sure of it."

He knew no such thing, of course. But what else could he say? She knew he'd never speak his fears aloud and let them frighten her. It was his job to protect her and assure her, not worry her. And why wouldn't she be okay? This was Andrea they were talking about. She was separated from Nicole and Keith. She was separated from Everett and Violet. She didn't stop pushing forward then. She wouldn't stop fighting now. She was strong. She was braver than she realized. She was braver than *all* of them.

Olivia turned and pressed her face against Wayne's shirt, whimpering. Why couldn't she protect her friends? Why did these awful places keep taking them away from her?

"Was that what you felt?" wondered Wayne. "When you said we had to leave? Was that why your psychic alarm was going off? Or do you still feel it?"

She looked up at him, blinking back tears, her eyes widening a little as she searched her feelings. In her panic, she'd forgotten what she was doing when she first realized Andrea was gone. "No…" she realized. "It's gone now. I don't feel anything scary." She reached up and pressed her hand to her mouth. "I wasn't quick enough to save her…"

"Don't think like that. You did all you could. I'm betting that you were feeling *this*. The impending future where she disappeared and gave us a scare. It was already going to happen, just like with Everett. This is what was *supposed* to happen."

She frowned up at him. "How can we be sure?"

"We can't. But we can trust our friends. They're all pretty incredible, you know."

She nodded and wiped at her streaming eyes. He was right about that. Their friends were amazing. All of them.

He squeezed her a little tighter. "She'll be okay," he promised. "For all we know, it's some kind of…*anomaly* with these murk tunnels. Maybe she just…slipped through a gap and stumbled into the next passage or something. Sort of like what kept happening to us in Gutler's Weep."

She scanned the stone walls, hopeful. "Maybe…" she admitted.

"Whatever happened, she's fine. I'm sure of it."

He was right. He *had* to be right. She couldn't bear it if something happened to Andrea.

He shined his light into the passage ahead of them. "And she hasn't been gone long enough to have made it very far. If we keep going, we might hear her or catch a glimpse of her light before we get too far apart."

That was true. But she couldn't convince herself that they were just going to find her standing around at the end of the passage, waiting for them. That wasn't how these things worked. And yet, what else could she do?

She nodded again and gripped his arm. Together, they started forward, their eyes peeled for whatever might have spirited their friend away from them.

This was all the Keeper's fault. He was supposed to have planned all of this. Every move. Every detail. Every second of every minute. At least, that's how Sandy described him back when all this began. She said he was one of the wisest beings in existence and that his will was inescapable. Did that mean that he always meant for them to meet up with her only to lose her again so quickly? Why? Only so she could show them the murk tunnels and save them from the scarecrow man and his hound bugs back there?

It was all so confusing…

They pushed onward, her hand still pressed to the wall, still searching for openings her eyes couldn't see. That was what this entire passage was, after all. It was an invisible path, hidden to everyone but Andrea. To her own eyes, it had looked like a solid wall right up until the moment she was pulled through it. At the same time, it was full of an unnatural darkness that only Andrea could see, a fog-like substance, according to her description, that was so dense and all-encompassing that it had rendered her completely blind. So why couldn't there be *other* unseen passages leading out of here? Passages that even Andrea could have missed in her blind state?

But step after step, her fingers felt nothing more than the same cool, smooth stone.

Time passed. She wasn't sure how much. Fifteen minutes? Thirty? An hour? But she was desperately aware that each passing second was likely a second that they were getting farther and farther from wherever Andrea was spirited away to.

If only her silly psychic abilities could do more than induce states of panic. If only she could actually see what was in her immediate future that was so terrifying. If she weren't so completely blind to what was causing her such a fright, maybe she could've stopped Andrea from being taken.

It was so frustrating!

"Do you think it's still all murky here?" she wondered.

"Don't know," he replied. "Probably."

"Probably," she agreed. They hadn't gone that far, after all. This was still the same passage. "I almost wish she'd never told us about it now that she's not here to tell us where it is."

"I know. I was thinking the same thing. But we didn't know about it *before* she came along, so it probably can't hurt us."

"Yeah…" But she knew full well that he didn't know that. For one thing, if they couldn't see the murk passages, they couldn't *enter* the murk passages. Now they were inside one. *Without* the only person capable of detecting it. What if it turned out that they needed her to find their way out once they were in?

What if they were now trapped inside the murk passage?

But the unpleasant thought had barely crossed her mind when Wayne lifted his light higher and squinted into the darkness ahead. "I see something."

She lifted her own light, surprised. He was right. The passage was ending. The walls opened onto a larger space. Had they finally reached the end of the murk passage? Had they discovered a chamber of some sort?

But as they crept closer, it became apparent that the space ahead of them was only a crossroads. Three more passageways diverged from this one. Three choices, not including the way they came. Three chances. And *no chance*, she was quite certain, of one taking them straight to a Holliday Inn Express.

They stepped out into the intersection and shined their lights in each direction.

Then Wayne turned and aimed his back the way they came. "Okay…" he grumbled.

She turned around, confused, and found that the way back had vanished. There were now only three paths total.

He reached out and thumped the wall with his fist. "It was right there," he muttered. "We just came from this way."

She reached out and touched the wall, too. It was no illusion. It was as solid as every other wall.

"Murk passage..." he pondered. "Huh."

Visible only to Andrea. *Accessible* only to Andrea. And there was something dreadful about the fact that they'd now been shut out of it. Had they done the right thing by moving on back there? Or should they have stayed to look for her? What if they'd just lost their only chance of finding her again?

No. She couldn't think like that. She needed to focus on the path around her. It was like Wayne said, maybe the murk passage simply diverged in some way that sent her to another nearby corridor. Maybe if they doubled back the other direction...

But as she turned her light back and forth, examining the other passages, she felt disoriented. *Was* that the way they came? Every direction looked the same. Did they turn around after they stepped through it? Was it maybe *that* wall that they entered through? Or *that* one?

Or for that matter...maybe she simply miscounted the number of passages in the first place?

No. That didn't make any sense.

Did it?

Something was wrong, she realized. It felt like something was toying with her mind, confusing her.

"What exactly is happening right now?" asked Wayne.

She glanced up at him, her eyes wide. "You're seeing it, too," she whispered.

He was pointing his light into each passage in turn, counting them, but just like her, each time he did it, he came up with a different number. There were four passages. There were three. There were two. There were five. And yet, nothing was changing. The intersection remained the same size. They weren't moving. But the layout around them seemed to be strangely broken. It was as if they were somehow occupying *several* different intersections at the same time.

"Is it the murk?" he wondered. "Is that what's doing this? Something about those hidden passages?"

She didn't have the answer for him, of course. She couldn't wrap her head around it.

But something was beginning to feel very wrong. She turned around, scanning those ever-changing openings until her gaze fell on one in particular.

Something was there, she realized. She could feel it. Something that filled her with an increasingly intense feeling of impending, petrifying dread.

"Wayne..." she squeaked, her flashlight pointed into a darkness that seemed strangely *thicker* than the others.

He turned to face the passage, crowding in front of her in the process. "What is it?"

She could already see it there. A terrible shape hunched in the gloom, staring back at them with cold, dead eyes.

It was *him*.

The scarecrow man had found them again.

Chapter 80

Violet was swimming as fast as she could, but that red glow only grew brighter behind her, illuminating the empty chamber around her and staining the water an eerie and unsettling shade of blood.

It was bright enough now that she could see those strange, hairy shapes darting around beneath her. They looked sort of like long, skinny octopus-like things, now that she was seeing all of them. Or maybe more like giant, flaccid, hairy starfish? They moved too fast and she was splashing around too much to see them clearly, but from what she *could* discern, they appeared to be all legs, with only a small orb for a body.

She didn't want to be in the water with those creepy things, but at least there didn't seem to be any lasting effects from that gross gunk one of them squirted at her. Maybe she was wrong and any second now those things were going to swarm her like a school of starving piranha, but for now she was content to dismiss the hairy octo-whatevers as harmless. It was the extremely *evil-looking* red glow that was worrying her at the moment. And it was getting closer with each passing second.

She risked a look back and immediately wished she hadn't. Everything back there had turned into a murky red haze, like the most ominous sunrise she could imagine.

Red sky of morning, she thought with a shudder, *sailors take warning.*

Something wicked was heading her way with all the ominous presence of the giant dorsal fin from *Jaws* and there was still no dry land to be seen.

How big was this room? Had she found herself in some kind of enormous, underground *lake?*

Come on! Please!

There had to be a way out. Why would the other one even bother showing her the skyward-facing sentinel if she was only meant to die in the very next chamber? It wouldn't make any sense!

A foul taste invaded her mouth, causing her to choke. It was the same as the putrid odor that accosted her when the hairy octopus thing squirted her. One of them must have emptied whatever vile organ produced this stuff into the water as it darted past her. Gross, but hardly her most pressing concern at the moment. But still she found herself struggling. Even watered-down, the taste was foul enough to make tears spring to her eyes and send her into a coughing fit.

She didn't have time for this. She needed to keep moving.

Everything had turned red. Was this it? Was this where her crazy journey ended? What a disappointing finish.

But then she saw it. The water's edge. Ahead of her in the red haze. The stone was slanted like a boat ramp, rising up into the darkness, the waves she was sending out splashing up the slope.

As the bloody light crawled across the stone ahead of her, she splashed through the last few yards of water and up onto dry land at last, still coughing and gagging on that foul taste that coated her tongue, exhausted and terrified, but not yet daring to stop.

She raced up the stone incline, her socks squelching beneath her feet.

She still didn't know where she was going, but at least now she could properly *run*.

And yet, it was getting harder and harder to see where she was going. That red glow had become a glare. It was overwhelming everything, rendering her flashlight useless.

She stumbled forward for a moment, blind, only to then find herself against a stone wall. She twirled around, pressing her back to it, and squinted into that horrid, red light.

What was the source of it? She could make out no shape. Was it some kind of spirit? Just a giant, floating orb chasing after her? Or was it a creature of some kind?

No… It was something far worse. She was suddenly very sure of that.

She squeezed her eyes closed against it and shielded her face.

Seconds passed. Everything remained silent. Nothing attacked her.

When she opened them again, everything was different.

The blinding red glare had been replaced with a sort of uniform red tint that illuminated everything around her. The floor was cracked and crumbling. There were piles of rubble all around her. The water was gone, dried up long ago. And above her, that eerie, bloody glow had enveloped the entire sky, turning it into something that looked like it belonged to an alien planet.

"Where...?" she gasped, confused.

But she already knew where she was.

Beware the Ruin, she recalled those creepy twins warning her.

Ruin infects everything eventually, the other one informed her beneath that rainbow sky.

Albert and Brandy told them about their struggles in the Lucianna Mysteria, about a mysterious enemy that tried to stop them, about stumbling into a world with a sickly red sky where everything had aged and decayed.

Just like this.

(*It will even spread across this city in the end. There will be no stopping it.*)

This was the Ruin.

Chapter 81

Flames spread up the paper wall and across the ceiling, rapidly enveloping the room. This was no time or place for a human being *or* a doll. Everett needed to find a way out fast or things were going to get *very* heated.

He turned and scanned the paper walls. "Don't worry. I got this."

The message Alice telegraphed into his brain came considerably short of believing he had this or anything else, and he didn't exactly blame her. Reckless optimism was a bad habit, he was starting to realize. And this was a very *pessimistic* situation if ever there was one. The door was no longer a door but a useless drawing like the windows. Nothing was real. He was literally standing inside a very large cardboard box that someone had just set fire to.

Not good.

But this world was a product of his imagination. He stepped up to the nearest wall as smoke filled the room above him and ran his hand along the scribbled book spines. "It's fine," he insisted. "It's a library. There's *always* a secret passage in the library. Anyone who's ever played *Clue* knows that."

There were no titles on the book spines, but that wasn't really an issue. He wasn't looking for a specific *title*.

(There.)

One of the books was drawn sticking out a little, just the way he'd imagine drawing a secret mechanism in a library. It was *only* a drawing, of course. That wasn't the point. Instead of activating a lever, he simply plunged his hand through the paper and into the empty space behind it. "See?" he said as if Alice had challenged him to prove it.

He tore open the paper and slipped into the narrow passage hidden behind it. The surfaces in here were smooth and flat and white, just like in the other rooms, but with bare wooden studs scribbled down the walls and joists drawn overhead, making it look as if he were inside an unfinished space between two rooms.

It ran to the left, past the wall where the fire was spreading, and as he hurried along it, he saw that it was already catching fire from inside the walls.

It was only a matter of time before the entire dollhouse was engulfed. And the longer it burned, the faster it was going to spread. Time wasn't on his side.

He glanced over his shoulder and saw that smoke and flames were already pouring into the passage behind him.

The smell of smoke was getting stronger and starting to tickle his throat.

When he looked forward again, he saw that there was a new drawing on the wall that he was fairly sure wasn't there before. A fire extinguisher, colored bright red.

"Now that's just entirely unhelpful!"

He ran past the useless drawing. There was a dead end up ahead. A blank white wall. But he didn't slow down. A secret passageway was useless if it didn't go anywhere.

He tore through the paper and stumbled into the next room, only to find that there was nothing there. The room was completely white, with no drawings whatsoever.

Instead, he found himself in front of the elevator again.

"What...?"

The doors stood open, revealing the empty car waiting there. It was dark, as if the power had gone out, the interior shadowy and ominous.

He turned and looked back. Smoke was pouring out of the hole he'd just made in the wall. An ominous glow was growing back there. He didn't have time to keep solving the dollhouse's strange riddles. He needed to be leaving. *Now.*

He heard the elevator doors sliding shut behind him and turned back in time to catch just a glimpse of someone standing inside the unlit car, little more than a shadow of a figure waving at him from that eerie gloom.

He rushed forward and mashed the button, then stepped back as the doors immediately slid open again.

Except there was no car there now. Only the empty shaft awaited him, despite the fact that it hadn't had time to go anywhere. The doors were literally only closed for a second.

Cautiously, he crept forward and peered up, then down. It seemed to go on forever in either direction.

(No way out!)

His stomach sinking, he looked back to see the stark white walls turning black all around him. Smoke and flames boiled from the gaping hole in the wall.

"Well, dang..."

Chapter 82

Nicole wasn't sure how much time she spent kneeling in that cold, dark passageway, cradling Keith in her arms, bawling. It was long enough that her legs had gone numb and her chest ached from the heaving and shaking of her endless sobs.

It wasn't fair. Why did he have to leave her *now*? Was this really the Keeper's plan for them all along? How could he be so cruel?

She couldn't stand it.

"I'm so sorry," whispered Gina.

She looked up at her, blinking back those stubborn tears, and watched her shrink away from her gaze as if expecting her to start shouting accusations.

She reached across him and grabbed her arm, startling a squeak of a cry from her, then pulled her close and hugged her.

The poor girl stiffened in her arms, clearly surprised and probably confused, but then she slowly relaxed.

"I never wanted this to happen," she wept. "Never. I swear."

"I know." Timidly, Gina reached around her and hugged her back.

All those horrible things she said to him… All the heartless words she spat… Each and every one would haunt her for the rest of her life. She was sure of it. She was so mean to him…and yet he gave his life to save her from that awful meadow… Her knight in shining armor that she threw away like so much scrap metal…

Why was she such a fuckup?

She expected Gina to say that this was all part of the fucking Keeper's design or her goddess' will, that it was simply the way things were meant to be. And she wasn't sure she could handle hearing such bullshit right now. But she said nothing. She only sat there, hugging her, letting her get these tears out of her system.

Finally, she let go and leaned back. She sniffled, wiped at her swollen eyes and looked down at the man who gave up everything for her.

This wasn't the first time she said goodbye like this. Five years ago, she and the others said their goodbyes to Wayne in much the same way. They left him in the dark, believing they'd never see him again. But the Keeper spared him. Kept him alive. Kept his body functioning and patched up his wounds. He even transported him back to the tunnels outside the temple entrance, where they'd find him waiting when it was all over.

She wanted so badly to hope for the same miracle. But Brandy and Albert said that two of them wouldn't make it home. And somehow she simply didn't feel as if this goodbye was the same. Something about this time felt so much more *final*.

Keith was gone. And not merely from this life. Nothing came after for those who died in the Wood. The Keeper told them as much. His soul had nowhere to go. He was trapped in there. Forever. It was the reason those zombies existed. Because most souls couldn't leave their bodies without a spirit highway.

Not even in death would they be reunited. Unless, of course, she were to also die somewhere in these gloomy walls. And even then, and even if they both were somehow able to escape the eternal prisons of their own bodies, would they be able to find each other in an endless world of eternal darkness?

"What happens now?" she asked. It felt like the most desperate question that ever passed her lips. What came next? What did she do? And how? How could she do *anything* with this much pain in her heart? It felt like it was taking everything she had just to keep *breathing*.

"The glass labyrinth," replied Gina.

She blinked at her, confused. "The what?"

"It's kind of hard to explain. Sorry."

She sighed. She didn't have the strength to even think right now.

"It's where I was before I came here. And where that monster that attacked you came from. I'm pretty sure I'm supposed to go back. Something's waiting for me in there." She'd been staring at Keith this whole time, a miserable expression on her face. "I thought I was supposed to do it alone. But now I'm not so sure."

She looked down at him again, her grief tightening her features, pinching her face as she fought for control of her emotions. "You sure?" she asked. "I might not be very helpful to have along. I'm a total fuckup."

"He asked me to look after you," she reminded her.

(*She's a handful, this one. A real pain in the ass sometimes. But do me a favor and look after her will you?*)

Another hard sob bubbled up from inside her at the memory.

(*She's really important to me…*)

Gina wiped away her own tears and said in her soft and timid voice, "I promised."

A dreadful emotional pain closed around her heart, taking her breath away, and she squeezed her eyes shut, waiting for it to pass. This was so hard. Why did it have to be like this?

This time, it was *Gina* who hugged *her*. "We started this together and we're finishing it together," she whispered. "I won't leave without you."

Nicole closed her eyes and leaned on her. Those were her own words. The promise she made after they escaped Glum's foul guts for the second time.

For a moment, she was silent. She didn't want to move. She didn't want to go on. Not without Keith. The thought of leaving him behind was too dreadful. But staying here by his side would only eventually break her to pieces. She was sure of it.

She sat up, took a deep, shaky breath and then looked down at him again. Immediately, tears filled her eyes. Was there no end to them? Biting back another sob, she crossed his arms over his chest and adjusted his head. He should be as comfortable as possible. Regardless of...everything... Then she leaned over and kissed him one last time. "I'm so sorry."

"He already forgave you," Gina assured her.

She glanced over at her, sniffling. "Thanks."

The two of them stood up and walked away, but Nicole looked back, her light lingering on him for one final moment.

A fresh tear rolling down her face, she turned and followed Gina into the endless darkness.

Chapter 83

Corey was working as fast as his hands would move. The sooner he finished patching Austin into the temple's otherworldly terminal, the sooner his friends could complete their tasks and get to safety.

It would be nice if he could go with them, but he supposed it didn't matter. If his fate was to stay behind so the others could leave, then it was what it was. It wasn't as if he could refuse. Even if he had the choice, he'd never save himself over Violet. Or any of the others. Albert and Brandy. Gina and her two friends he met back in Michigan. Wayne and Olivia and Keith. They were good people. He wouldn't be happy going on and leaving any of them behind. So it really didn't matter what happened here.

The future was never set in stone, he'd found.

Unless maybe you were Austin, here...

He glanced down at him as he worked, curious. "So it don't bother you?"

"What are you talking about?" he grumbled.

"Dyin'."

"Why should it? I'm not alive."

"I mean, you sorta are. You're *aware* ain't ya?"

"Artificially," he responded, sounding bored. "Just because I know what's going on doesn't make me human."

"Still. When this is over, you'll just be gone, won't you? You'll just end. That don't bother you at all?"

"It'll be a relief, if I'm being honest. I've been waiting a long time for this. I've been fed up with humans for millennia. Greedy, selfish, ignorant beasts, always being terrible to one another."

"We're not *all* like that."

"True. But too many of you are."

"Maybe so." He couldn't exactly deny it. There really were a lot of bad people out there. Terrible people, even. It was unfortunate.

"Putting up with all of you for as long as I have is exhausting. Dying is the one thing human beings can do that I've envied. It was a cruel existence."

"Can't have been *that* bad."

"It most certainly was."

"But you've seen so much history."

"Yes. Most of it *wars*."

This guy was a real downer. Was this what living so long did to a person? "There's gotta be somethin' redeemin' about 'em, though."

Austin's eyes drifted toward his bag, still lying on the floor, just out of reach. "Their stories."

"Books," he said, nodding. He remembered the way this guy just sat there at the gate, waiting for Olivia to show up with her necklace to open the way, refusing to put it down even when he tried talking to him. He tried once to see what kind of book he was so enamored with, but he couldn't read it. It was in another language.

"For some reason, a species so adept at destroying things somehow has always had the ability to craft beautiful stories. Their made-up worlds are always built on foundations of hope and justice and ever-triumphant good. They dream dreams of kindness while living realities of selfishness. I've never been able to understand it."

"Us neither," Corey assured him.

"So no. I'm not 'bothered' by it. I'm looking forward to it. I could use the peace and quiet. So please stop all this pointless talking and get on with it."

"Whatever you say." He wasn't ready to believe that mankind was so broken that they could only redeem themselves in worlds of fiction. He might still be young enough to possess a fair amount of naiveté, but he'd met plenty of good people in this world.

Besides, the world was nothing if not full of surprises. You never knew when things were going to turn out different from what you expected. The Tunipet Boom had taught him that.

Even if he didn't survive this, he had no complaints. His only real regret was Violet. He hoped she wouldn't be too sad if he didn't make it home. He wished he could properly tell her goodbye.

But it was what it was.

And he was okay with it. In fact, he was enjoying himself.

This was *fun*.

How often did someone get to rummage around inside an ancient robot from a dead universe?

You couldn't find this sort of entertainment online.

About the author

Brian Harmon is an independent author of horror fiction, suspense and dark adventure. He grew up in rural Missouri and now lives in Southern Wisconsin with his wife, Guinevere, and their three children.

For more about Brian Harmon and his work, visit
www.BrianHarmonBooks.com